*He didn't look dangerous,
not at first glance.*

Still, a girl can never be too careful on a blind date, and that's why I'd insisted Mr. Sand meet me in a popular steakhouse nestled in a casino dead center on the Las Vegas strip. It was, I thought, the most public of all places.

Yet now, watching the way shadows from the muted lighting sought out the unhealthy hollows beneath his eyes and cheeks, and the way he toyed with his blue cheese and endive appetizer, I decided the most ominous thing about Mr. Sand was a deeply embedded sense of self-control, and the only thing I was in danger of dying of was boredom.

Of course, that was before I really knew him. . . .

And before my death the very next day.

Books by Vicki Pettersson

THE SCENT OF SHADOWS
The First Sign of the Zodiac

THE TASTE OF NIGHT
The Second Sign of the Zodiac

THE
SCENT OF SHADOWS

THE FIRST SIGN OF THE ZODIAC

VICKI
PETTERSSON

An Imprint of HarperCollins*Publishers*

EOS

An Imprint of HarperCollins*Publishers*
10 East 53rd Street
New York, New York 10022-5299

Copyright © 2007 by Vicki Pettersson
Author photo by Derik Klein
ISBN: 978-0-06-089891-5
ISBN-10: 0-06-089891-7
www.eosbooks.com

First Eos paperback printing: March 2007
First Avon Books special printing: October 2006

HarperCollins® and Eos® are trademarks of HarperCollins Publishers.

Printed in the U.S.A.

10 9 8 7 6

To Roger.
Everyone has a reason.
You're mine.

Acknowledgments

Props go out to Ellen Daniel for being my first, and for a long time, sole reader. Also to Kris Reekie and Linda Grimes for trusted help, and the membership at large in what was my virtual classroom for many years, CompuServe's Books and Writers Forum. Suzanne Frank fielded every newbie question I could throw her way, but more importantly, joined me in search of the perfect mojito. I have to thank my Folies girls for allowing me to read between numbers, putting up with me on a bad writing day, and providing inspiration. That means you, Kris Perchetti. Finally, heartfelt thanks go out to Miriam Kriss for saving me from the slush pile, and to Diana Gill, who pushed me harder, and made me better, than I thought possible. Oh, and to Gary Sassenberg, who started it all.

1

He didn't look dangerous, not at first glance. Still, a girl can never be too careful on a blind date, and that's why I'd insisted Mr. Sand meet me in a popular steakhouse nestled in a casino dead center on the Las Vegas Strip. It was, I'd thought, the most public of all public places. Yet now, watching the way shadows from the muted lighting sought out the unhealthy hollows beneath his eyes and cheeks, and the way he toyed with his blue cheese and endive appetizer, I decided the most ominous thing about Mr. Sand was a deeply embedded issue with self-control, and the only thing I was in danger of dying from was boredom. Of course, that was before I really knew him. And before my death the very next day.

At the time I had no way of knowing Mr. Sand's true intentions, not like now. Besides, who knew homicidal maniacs came wrapped in horse-faced packages with little to no fashion sense? Beyond that, he was so skinny his Adam's apple bobbed like a buoy above the opening of his pressed shirt, while knobby bones protruded at both knuckles and wrists. Ichabod Crane in a poorly fitted suit. Not exactly intimidating.

Looks aside, the next mark against him was his first name.

"Ajax?" I repeated as our soups arrived, not quite sure I'd heard right.

He nodded, lifting his spoon, though I noted he didn't actually use it. "Ajax."

"Like the cleaner?"

His smile was tight. "Like the Greek warrior."

I mean, really.

Cursing my sister for setting me up on yet another blind date—and myself for letting her—I nevertheless tried to plant my feet firmly on the bright side of things. At least this one could walk without dragging his knuckles on the ground. And even if the woman in me had recoiled at first sight, the photographer in me had something to do.

I tried to picture Ajax in a bank, as he'd already told me how the world's financial industry would fall flat on its ass without him, but I couldn't quite imagine him languishing behind a desk. There was too much movement, too much latent energy in those snaking limbs for that. His fingers twined and untwined, his bony elbows rose to rest on the table only to drop a second later, and his eyes darted around the dining room, taking in everything but never fully settling. I'd like to still those relentless limbs with my camera, I decided. Take time to study those shifting eyes. See just who Mr. Sand became when seen in two dimensions instead of three.

He looked at me like he knew what I was thinking.

And it was that look, those eyes, that sent up the first red flag. I don't mean the color, a blue so light it was nearly transparent, but more the way they tried to own me. I licked my lips, and his eyes dropped to watch my tongue dart out. I ran a hand through my bobbed hair, and felt him following the movement so that my fingers fisted there. I exhaled deeply, forcing myself to relax, and for some reason that made him smile.

I was jumpy, I confess, but I recognized that hungry look.

I'd seen it once before, long before I'd ever started dating. I'd hoped never to see it again.

"So, what do you do for a living?" Ajax asked, finally breaking the silence. "I mean, you don't just live off Daddy's money, do you?" This was followed by a shallow "just joking" guffaw, one belied by how carefully he continued to watch me.

I ran my fingers over the stem of my wineglass, wondering just how long it would take Ajax to notice that mine weren't the hands of a debutante, but those of a fighter. "I take photographs."

"Like weddings or models or something?"

"Like people. Shapes. Shadows. Usually night shots using natural lighting and gritty settings. Reality."

"So . . ." he said, drawing the word out, "you don't make money at it?"

"Not yet."

He looked at me like I should apologize. He probably was a fucking banker after all.

"Sounds like a waste of time," he said, then turned away from my stare.

His little jab stung more than it should have. Normally I don't care what people think, but lately, looking at the world through a refracted lens, viewing the worth of places and people and objects in terms of light and shadow, black and white, wasn't as satisfying as it used to be. Restless, I had recently begun taking more self-portraits than anything else; zeroing in on singular things like my knuckles, constantly red and callused from nylon punching bags, or my eyes—right or left, rarely both—which were tawny and earth-colored during the day, but blackened like a clouded lake in the dark, or when I was extremely angry.

Instead of looking for enemies in the faces of strangers, I'd begun turning the camera on myself, and I didn't need Freud or even Dr. Phil to tell me I was searching for something. Question was, would I like what I eventually found?

"Banking, on the other hand," I began sweetly, once the

server had delivered our entrées, "sounds absolutely captivating. Please don't skip one fascinating little detail."

Ajax's mouth creased even thinner than his hairline. "God, I should have known by looking that you're nothing like your sister."

I didn't really consider it an insult, but I was sure my eyes had gone black as tar. "And how, exactly, do you know what my sister's like?"

"I read her profile in *Playboy*," he said nastily, and shoved some saffron potatoes into his mouth.

In turn, I settled my own fork on the side of my plate. So that was it.

Though similar in build, Olivia and I had taken vastly different approaches to both our sexuality and our lives. The issue Ajax was referring to had come out three months earlier, and while I didn't approve of Olivia's overt approach to sexuality, I understood the reason behind it. Ironically enough, it stemmed from the same origin as my own.

Good ol' Ajax here had probably also read the recent article about the Archer family empire in *Fortunes and Fates* magazine:

"Lacking the acute business sense of her gaming magnate father, Xavier, and the brilliant social acumen of her glamorous sister, Olivia . . . and, indeed, any notably positive attributes whatsoever, Ms. Joanna Archer seems to have eschewed her public duty as one of the richest heiresses on the planet for a life of frivolity and self-interest."

Self-interest I could understand, but frivolous? Like writing scathing gossip columns about other people's lives was brain surgery?

So it seemed my sister hadn't given Ajax my phone number. In all probability, Olivia didn't know him at all. Apparently he'd been counting on someone who looked and acted like a Playmate, and hoping that perhaps my reported self-interest, along with my inheritance, could be funneled his way. That he'd have a chance with the token black sheep of the Archer dynasty.

Wrong, Ajax, I thought, picking up my wineglass. On all accounts.

"Look," he said, spreading his hands before him as though discussing stock options. "I just came to Vegas for a good time. I thought I'd look you up since we seem to have some of the same interests . . ."

A.k.a. my money.

". . . and see if you wouldn't mind showing me around. That's all. Why can't we just have some fun?" When I only continued to stare, he dropped his bony elbows on the table with a force that shook the plates, and abandoned all pretext of civility. "Or, fine. Why don't you pretend that you have a sense of humor?"

"I could," I said, nodding slowly, "but then I'd have been laughing from the moment you walked in the door." See? My sense of humor was as broad as anyone else's.

"Bitch."

I drew back at the venom in his voice, surprised my words had cut so deeply, so quickly. Then again, a fuse that short had probably been lit long before I came along. "What's wrong, Ajax? Things not going according to plan? Let me guess. Here you are in Vegas on some sort of pilgrimage, to forget for one weekend exactly how disappointing your life has turned out, and now mean, spoiled Joanna Archer is screwing it all up. Is that about right?"

I have this ability—I like to think of it as a gift, really—to see clean through to people's sore spots. I hone in on a bruised psyche and press. Not nice, I know, but then Olivia was the Miss Congeniality in our family.

Ajax's reptilian features had rearranged themselves as I spoke, and he now looked like a glowering python. "Thanks for the psychoanalysis, babe," he spat, "but all I really wanted from this weekend were a couple of easy lays."

This, I assumed, was where I was supposed to throw my wine in his face. I didn't, though. I liked Chateau Le Pin, and took a long, considering sip of the vintage '82 I'd made him buy. "And what? Your mother wasn't available?"

Ajax's head jerked like I'd struck him, and suddenly a different man sat there. It was like the still picture I'd imagined before, a person comfortable in his skin. A warrior living up to his name. Surprisingly, I was the first to blink.

"You like to argue," he said, and it wasn't a question. "You like to fight."

He was right, I did. But suddenly I wasn't exactly sure what I was up against.

"Insult my mother again," he said in a ragged whisper, "and you'll find yourself in a fight for your life."

And just like that a bolt of lightning seared over the gilded room, arching across the beveled ceiling to snap like fangs between us. The air was a live wire, crackling so the lights, wall sconces—even the candles—flickered as if flinching, and an invisible force funneled around us, sucking all the energy in the room toward our table and leaving me breathless. There, in the eye of that storm, I watched the flimsy skin layering Ajax's bones melt away, altering his face into a slab of bone, teeth, and cavernously slanting eyes. His smooth skull grinned at me across the table, eyes aflame, while a banshee's howl sprung from the gaping mouth.

I was half out of my seat before I caught myself, before I blinked . . . and the bony, aging banker returned, staring at me benignly. Nobody else in the room had moved. Nobody screamed. Classical music pulsed softly from artfully hidden speakers, and the steady thrum of conversation and clinking utensils blanketed the unnatural howl still rebounding in my mind. The table wasn't marked or singed, and the vanilla taper winked softly between us.

Ajax chuckled, his voice rumbling like thunder in his thin chest.

I stared at him, but it was as if an invisible curtain had risen between us, and I sensed nothing of his thoughts. No bruised ego, no unveiled sore spots to push. My little intuitive gift, it seemed, had abandoned me completely. I did know one thing, though. The bumbling tourist act was just that—an act. The man who sat before me was cruel, possibly insane, and most assuredly dangerous.

"What's wrong, Joanna dear? Seeing things? Something, maybe, that reminds you of a sweltering summer night? Shadows lunging at you from the desert floor, perhaps?"

A tremor inched its way up my spine, and for the first time in a long while I was at a loss for what to do. I was a frozen hare beneath that gaze, and Ajax simply waited, like a skilled predator.

I could call the maitre d' or security, I thought. Have Ajax eighty-sixed from the restaurant and casino, never allowed to return again. Though I wasn't sure what reason I'd give. That I was having a bad time on this date? That the man before me had just flashed me with his freakin' skeleton? That a monster lurked beneath his flaccid, aging exterior?

Or that he knew something about me no one had a right to know?

"I told them it was you, you know," he said, picking at his dry-aged Black Angus. "They didn't believe me, they said it was too obvious, but I knew. I could scent you the moment you walked in the door."

I forced myself to focus on that. "Scent me?"

"Yes. You smell like the desert sage in full bloom after a summer storm." He wrinkled his nose before turning haughty again. "But you don't even know that, do you? You haven't been told who you are, or a single thing about your lineage. In fact, I'd say you're about as helpless as an abandoned babe without a tit to suck."

He laughed, and leaned in even farther, closing the short distance between us. I battled the urge to run from the room like a screaming child, and sat my ground. As he'd said, I *was* a fighter.

"Now, I'm going to give you something else to psychoanalyze, Joanna Archer. It'll probably be one of the most important things you ever learn, so pay careful attention." He licked his lips, eyes steady on mine. "Pheromones. Do you know what they are?"

Thrown by the change of topic, I nonetheless forced a nonchalant shrug. "A chemical. A scent animals give off to attract others of the same species. So?"

"Not only the same species. Different species as well. Opposites. Enemies." He let the last word linger on his tongue, slipping the syllables out the same way a priest would slip the sacrament in. I stared at those thin lips, wondering where he was going with this, where I fit in, and how I'd made an enemy out of a man I'd never met. Could he really be that sensitive about his mother?

"See, Joanna, you have an extra component to your biological mix. It's weak, true, not yet fully developed, but it's there. Like a rose not yet grown from bud to bloom. Or . . ." Here he paused to draw in a deep breath, then exhaled slowly as if he found it sweet, ". . . like the invisible note of fear a fox leaves behind as it flees a chase."

My pulse points began to trip, hot and fast. Anorexic demon or not, he did *not* want to get me started on hunting and being hunted. I'd nearly a lifetime of experience of being one or the other, and there was a chip on my shoulder about it the size of a small state.

"See, I'm like the hound, anxious to get on with the chase, and with a nose so precise I could drive you to the end of the earth." He smiled serenely. "Guess what that makes you?"

"The hound master?"

The humor fell from his face again, and thunder rumbled along the walls. This time I was prepared, though, and didn't flinch. Ajax opened his mouth to say something, but changed his mind. Instead, he took a slow sip from his glass of wine, swirling it languidly in its crystal bowl. I watched, transfixed by a single bloodred drop studding his pale bottom lip. The lips moved.

"Lesson number one. Know thy enemy."

And he blew outward. Blended with the lacy texture of aged Bordeaux was a scent so fetid it brought bile to my throat. It was toxic decay, a concentration of acidity and rot rising so sharply the fumes burned the lining from my nose. I coughed, covering my lower face, but kept my eyes on his while trying to process what my nose was telling me. It was Ajax. He was somehow emitting, or spewing, his essence onto my senses. And my nose, never this sensitive before, told me he was dead inside. Decomposing, even as we sat there.

"Now you'll know me forever . . . both where I go and where I've been." He smiled again, and his grin was as rancid and spoiled as his fermented breath. "Even the mere thought of me will conjure my scent in your mind."

I forced myself to swallow back the last of the bile.

"It'll be a link between us," he continued, winking obscenely. "My gift to you."

"I don't know what you're talking about," I said, palm still cupped over my mouth, and I didn't, but I could suddenly smell him everywhere. Why hadn't I been able to moments before? And how could everyone else consume food in a place that reeked of death and decay?

"You don't know, do you? And that's going to make it all the more precious when I kill you." His fingers twined, untwined. "I just love to kill the innocent."

Slowly, I lowered my hand from my face. I'd been called a number of things in my adult life, but *innocent* had never been one of them. Neither, for that matter, had *passive*. Folding my arms across my chest, I let my fingers curl into fists. "And how, exactly, do you intend on doing that?"

"With my right hand," he said, pleased I'd asked. "And the serrated poker beneath my jacket."

He lifted one side of his coat, and my breath lodged somewhere between my throat and chest cavity. Sure enough, a multihooked blade as long and thin as a fencer's sword glinted in the candlelight, winking at me. He lowered the lapel. All around us hushed chatter continued, an incongruous contrast to the stillness that had slowed every cell of my body. I lifted my eyes, and this time I didn't have to blink.

The monster was there. Even if I was the only one who could see him.

"Now get up," he said, "and slowly walk to the door."

"Fuck you."

No way was I going to let this crackerjack near my back . . . even if every instinct in my body was crying out for me to bolt, and quick. I might be able to outrun him; he certainly didn't *look* fast, but then he hadn't looked psychotic either.

"Get up," he repeated, louder, "or I will kill every person in this dining room, starting with the woman behind me."

My eyes flicked to the woman in question, a petite blonde with hair piled fashionably atop her head to reveal a creamy white nape. Her back was to us, her head momentarily tilted back in a soundless laugh. With that thin barbed blade, Ajax could rend the tendons from her neck before she'd even caught her next breath.

Her companion, a handsome man with sparkling eyes, caught me looking and smiled. I looked away. It was the smile of a person untouched by violence, a look I'd never worn in my adult life. I doubted my dinner partner ever had either.

"I don't care," I lied, returning Ajax's stare.

He laughed as if we were also enjoying a pleasant evening in each other's company. "Of course you do. See, that's why you're the good guy and I'm the bad guy." The humor dropped from his face, along with his voice. "Now get your ass out of that chair."

I remained seated.

The smooth white bones beneath his cheeks flashed. Then there was the slight rustle of fabric, the unmistakable chink of a weapon being unsheathed beneath the table, and Ajax's shoulder rotated in a motion that would end in a killing blow. My stomach clenched but still I didn't move. He growled, and it was an expectant, warning sound.

"Wait!" I said as his muscles tensed. He stared back at me with those soulless eyes, and I knew he'd have done it.

He'd have killed that woman without blinking, and the man across from her would never smile again.

"See?" Ajax said quietly. "I told you you're one of the good guys."

I didn't answer, just pushed away from the table and rose, my eyes never leaving his. But then I did something even I couldn't have anticipated. I picked up my wineglass, swirled, and put it to my lips.

Perhaps it was the intensity of the moment, or maybe Ajax's lesson in odorous acuity really had hit home, but the flavors I inhaled from that glass were the most complex, the most vibrant, and the richest I'd ever tasted. I could scent the clay of the plateau vineyard in France where the fruit had been harvested, and somehow I knew the grapes had been picked on a windless, rainy day. The juice had been aged in French oak, and the winemaker had regularly tested the barrel with a steel ladle, his artist's palate telling him when, exactly, to go to bottle. Inhaling all these things—things I had no right to sense or see—they became a part of me, their knowledge burrowing into my bones.

I drank deeply, almost ecstatically, like the saints you see on the ceilings of cathedrals, martyrs looking expectantly toward heaven in their final, lingering moments on earth. All the while Ajax watched me with those glassy death-eyes, like he could tell exactly what I was doing and feeling and tasting. I lowered the glass, then blew in his direction.

He froze, alarm furrowing his brow. I don't know what he scented of me just then, but it wasn't the fear he so clearly expected. Still, he regained his composure quickly and jerked his head toward the exit. Unwilling to let go of the wine that still held so much life and passion and vitality in it, I turned with it still in my hand. Then, fingering the stem like a nun with her favorite rosary beads, I slowly made my way out the door.

The Valhalla Hotel and Casino was like any other jewel in the crown of a corporate gaming giant. It boasted live entertainment, fine dining, and slavish customer service to those wagering amid the garish lights of clanging machines and crowded pits. It clung doggedly to its Viking theme; as long, that was, as it didn't interfere with the more important one: making it easy for people to give away their money. The fact that my father owned Valhalla changed none of this.

It did, however, mean that I was recognized, deferred to, and often approached by those who worked there, and that's what I was hoping for as I reached the restaurant's foyer and stepped out onto the main casino floor. Perhaps somebody would become suspicious at the possessive grip Ajax had on my left arm. Or maybe I could somehow signal security via the Eye in the Sky, an in-house surveillance system so advanced it could catch even the most nimble-fingered gambler switching dice. It wasn't advanced enough, however, to stop a barbed poker from sawing through my spine, so while I held onto the hope for help, my gut told me I was on my own.

"Parking garage," Ajax ordered, standing so close I could feel his body heat radiating through his jacket. I followed his instructions, as anxious to get him away from the other guests as I was to ensure that all my vitals remained intact.

We wove around glassy-eyed tourists and dodged cocktail waitresses dressed as Valkyries delivering drinks to both the fallen, and not yet fallen, heroes of the replicate Great Hall. All the while Ajax kept close, his stewed breath a constant reminder of the evil lurking beneath the ill-fitting dinner jacket.

The crowd thinned as we passed the tower elevators, and when we turned into a corridor leading to the convention area, I felt him relax, which was good. I wanted him relaxed. And I wanted him confident. Add a little distraction, which I'd have to improvise, and by God, I might just get out of this alive.

"What did you mean earlier?" I asked, hoping my voice

revealed only frightened curiosity. "You told 'them' you knew it was me?"

"We've been hunting you a long time, Joanna. You wouldn't believe the manpower or the means we've employed in trying to locate and unmask your identity."

"What identity? And who are 'we'?" I asked, catching our reflection as we passed a gilded mirror. We looked like any other couple out for a night in Vegas; in a rush, a little strained perhaps, but positively determined to have fun. I was wearing black pants, a matching cowl-necked sweater, and heels. My wrap and bag were slung over my right arm, and I held my half-full wineglass in my left. It wasn't exactly combat clothing, but I could move well enough if—oh, say—a *serrated poker* were being held at my back.

Ajax shot a condescending look my way. "Does it matter?"

I didn't suppose so. I moved on to something that did. "And how did you find me?"

"Let's put it this way: you bear a striking resemblance to another of our enemies." And he chuckled, clearly intent on being vague.

As we rounded another corner, my steps only a fraction ahead of his, I noted pockets of people lounging along the perimeter of the wide carpeted hallway, some reading papers and sipping tiny cups of espresso, others conversing quietly in groups of threes and fours. Most, I saw, wore badges, stragglers from whatever that day's convention was. Unfortunately, none of them looked like they could stop the bus, much less a maniac with a blade.

"Turn here," Ajax said, indicating the marble alcove housing the garage elevators. He placed his right hand, his killing hand, on my shoulder, ensuring that I did so.

I know it may not have seemed like it, but this was what I wanted. I'd trained in contact combat for so long that such openings were glaring and instinctive. This was my chance, and I'd get only one.

Yanking my shoulder easily from beneath his grasp, I half

turned, half stumbled, and pointed my wineglass at him. Slurring my words, I yelled, "Pervert! Don't ever touch me again!"

Papers were lowered, eyes raised, heads turned. Visitors to Vegas were always ready for a show, and public domestic disputes were a popular spectator sport. I played up my Jerry Springer moment for all it was worth.

"By the way, I lied when I said your brain stick wasn't that small!" Sloshing what remained of my wine on Ajax's suit, I met his murderous look with a contemptuous one of my own. Then I reeled away, slammed into the corner of the wall, tripped, and sprawled inelegantly across the marble floor.

Everything happened fast after that. An elevator door chimed. Ajax growled. A woman screamed. And I rose to my knees, the stem of my shattered wineglass clenched firmly in my fist. Grabbing me by the shoulder again, Ajax whirled me around, and as he did, I buried the crystal shard deep into his neck.

His growl scuttled off into a strangled gurgle, and his eyes went round with shock and pain. He still had the wherewithal to lift his blade, the bastard, but my training and fury had taken over, and I slammed the heel of my palm into his nose, driving it with the force of a woman who knew how to put her hips and shoulders into a blow. He'd have a fuck-all time of breathing now.

I took out his left knee with my heel and he cried out again, crumpling to the ground like a marionette's abandoned toy. Only a top-notch surgeon would help him walk again. I wanted to do more, and I had a clear shot at his kidney. Remembering the joyous smile of the woman he'd threatened to kill, I reared back pitilessly and aimed the strongest part of my body into the center of his being. I kicked—

And missed. Something, someone, slammed into me and I backpedaled madly, but couldn't regain my balance in three-inch heels. I would have crashed into the steel doors behind me except the elevator had opened, and instead I was wheeled into the mouth of the car, along with my new attacker. I grunted as the wall broke my fall, knocking the breath from my body.

Ajax was struggling on the floor against two men in black suits, fighting to reach me, his killing hand stretched toward me. His smell was strong in my nose—sooty hatred and soured defeat—and his pain and his fury were top notes, burning off hot and fast. Then the elevator doors shut. I was free of the abominable Ajax, but trapped inside a steel box with, beneath, and against a new and unfathomable threat.

Very few things are certain in this world, even fewer when the adrenaline and heat of a combat situation are still on the rise. As the elevator ascended, here's what was certain. The person pinning me against the wall was male. He outweighed me by at least fifty pounds. And as soon as I got an opening, he was going to lose his left nut. The man crowded in close, as if he knew it too.

We jockeyed for position, me trying to gain enough space and distance to land a forceful blow, him defensive, but doing nothing to launch an assault of his own. I didn't care. I wanted out; out of his grip, out of this box. Out of this whole nightmare. Gradually, though, his voice penetrated the fog of anger and fear that kept me swinging.

"Stop fighting! It's okay. You're safe . . ." He gasped this, struggling to shield his family jewels. "C'mon, Jo-Jo! I'm not going to hurt you!"

Jo-Jo. Only one person on this earth had ever called me that. I looked up, shocked, into a face I hadn't laid eyes on in almost a decade. And froze.

Is it possible for a heart to plummet and swell at the same time? Because I swear that's what mine did. I sagged against the wall, and the body I'd trained to be so capable and strong was suddenly shaky and faint.

I spent a moment more cursing my traitorous, overactive,

estrogen-ridden, double-X-chromosome-carrying hormones. Then I turned and soaked in the sight of my first lover.

His features were more angular and defined than I remembered, though his expression was one I was intimately familiar with—intent gentleness. He had a scar just below his hairline, which must have required stitches, and I wondered briefly how it'd gotten there. Dark hair curled over the collar of his shirt, not too long to keep him from looking respectable, but long enough that he could be a chameleon if he chose. I'd always loved those wild curls, and my fingertips twitched as I looked at them.

He was taller than the boy I'd last seen; wider too, but the hips locking me in the corner of that elevator car were still slim as daggers beneath tight black jeans, and his scent was the same heady mixture of spice and soap and musky heat that had always held me captive.

Like Pavlov's dog, I damned near started to salivate.

"Hello, Ben," I said, resisting the impulse to reach out and smooth an errant lock from his forehead. It was a pretty anticlimactic greeting after so many years. I swallowed self-consciously, aware his eyes had yet to leave my face. He was studying me, I knew, in the same way I'd studied him, and I managed a shaky smile and tried for something with a bit more flash. "That's a hard . . . badge you've got there."

He pulled away quickly, shifting so his chest was no longer touching mine, and I was instantly sorry I'd said anything at all. Staring down at the badge like he'd forgotten it was there, Ben shook his head as the elevator dutifully rang the fifth floor. The doors opened to the parking garage, and it was suddenly, oppressively, quiet.

"Christ, Jo," Ben said, breaking the silence. "Are you okay?"

In the years since he'd last asked me that question, I'd become an expert at taking care of myself . . . and Ben had become a cop. One didn't need a psychologist to tell you neither result was surprising. I'd been on my back in the

ICU that first time, and he'd been sobbing, his adolescent face contorted with tears and guilt. But I knew Ben better than most, or had at one time, so I also knew regardless of what had happened to me—to him, and to us—a cop was what he was always meant to be.

Opening my arms in a courageous gesture that said "see for yourself," I discovered I couldn't stop them from shaking, and crossed them quickly over my chest. Still, I was obviously unharmed.

"God, when I saw that knife . . ." He lowered his forehead to the wall, shut his eyes, and let out a breath so deep he could have been holding it for years. He recovered himself almost immediately, though, straightening to his full seventy-four-inch height. "If I'd known the guy was armed I would have told my team to move sooner."

"That would have been helpful," I said jokingly, but I was suddenly reeling. *You have your own team? How old were you when you made sergeant? What the hell are you doing here?*

Do you still smile in your sleep?

"We've been tracking that guy for months," Ben was saying. "He's wanted for assault, battery, attempted rape, and God knows what else. He also cheats at craps—"

"The bastard."

"—so we had to do this right. It had to go down smooth, but when I saw you in that restaurant—" He broke off and looked at me like it would have killed him to lose me all over again.

Suddenly the eight years, seven months, three weeks, five days, fifteen hours, and fistful of minutes since I'd last seen him dissolved into ether, meaningless dust. I realized the powerful, strong, and capable woman I'd proudly become would give anything to have Ben Traina look at me like that again. Pitiful, isn't it? But true.

Then the sermon began. "Are you insane? What the hell are you thinking going out with a guy like that? You, of all people, should know better."

My eyes narrowed. Two years older than me, and he'd always thought he had the right to lecture. "Well, I always could pick 'em."

He only colored slightly at that, not the bright-cheeked blush I remembered. Good for him, I thought. All grown up, and even more overbearing.

"I see your cutting wit hasn't dulled any."

"Sharpened it just this morning," I said. *It used to be what you loved about me most.*

He stared at me for a long moment, then shook his head and laughed. The low, rich sound touched me in all the right places.

"Come on," he said, punching the elevator button that led back to the lower levels. "We have some serious talking to do."

We returned to a hallway clogged with the shouts of police and medical personnel. Ajax was cuffed in spite of his injuries, and though he was looking the other way, his head immediately swiveled when I exited the elevator. Strange, but I didn't have to wonder at that.

I could smell him too.

In salute to this shared intimacy, I blew him a victorious kiss. Ignoring the suddenly snarling and furious criminal writhing on the floor, Ben led me away, pushing through the voyeuristic and morbidly curious onlookers. Being of a practical nature, and somewhat of a voyeur myself, I took the opportunity to check out his ass. I sighed. Still fabulous.

And with that the foremost thought in my mind, I followed the first and only man I'd ever loved back into the chaos of Valhalla.

2

I'd never been able to hide anything from Benjamin Traina. We met when I was in fifth grade and he in seventh, when our bodies had held more similarities than not. We had a common passion for kickball and tag, and an equally strong hatred for a bully named Charles Tracy, whom we mercilessly dubbed Upchuck, and made unrelenting gagging noises whenever we passed him in the halls. Though our friendship was instant, born of youthful energy and the childish faith that things and people could be divided into two groups—right or wrong, good or bad, black or white—romance didn't bloom until four years later. An accidental meeting at the movie theaters found our hormone-crazed bodies—now very different, thank you—locked in a clinch even the onscreen stars couldn't match. Only later did Ben admit the meeting hadn't been exactly accidental.

There's something about seeing an adult you knew in childhood that makes them marginally vulnerable to you, and vice versa. There's also something comforting in thinking that if they made it this far, relatively unscathed, then maybe you didn't turn out half bad either. So I settled across from this man I both knew and didn't, and felt both vulnerable and comforted . . . and was surprised to realize I minded neither.

"How's your father?" Ben began once we'd been left alone in my father's cavernous conference room, located on the fifteenth floor of the Valhalla hotel. There was a table the size of a small airplane between us, and our coffee cups were reflected back on the deep, polished mahogany.

"Great," I replied, lifting my cup. "Or so I hear. I never see him."

"Do you want me to call him? See if he can come down?"

I jerked my head. I'd stopped needing my father long ago, and Ben knew that. "He's probably at home counting all his money. I'd hate to interrupt."

My family was nouveau riche, and my father's story had probably launched a thousand capital ventures in gaming and resort management, the majority of which failed. In the most capitalist city of the most capitalist nation in the world, Xavier Archer remained an icon of unparalleled and, seemingly, unquenchable ambition. His rise had been meteoric: his competitors found him cagey, his investors brilliant, and the rest of the world knew him only as driven.

No offense to my paternal grandmother, whom I'd never met, but he was also a nasty and cruel son of a bitch.

Ben inclined his head, and I could tell he was as proud of my independence as I was of his accomplishments. Both had been hard won. "And what about you? You sit at home counting your millions as well?"

"Nah," I said, shaking my head. "Just counting the same million over and over again."

"When you're not going out with hardened criminals, you mean."

"That's merely a hobby."

He smiled, eyes shining, but pushed the tape recorder on and recited his name, badge number, and the date and location of this interview. Then he turned his attention back to me. "We should get this over with."

"All right." And I told him everything. I said I had a rule about never saying no when someone asked me out, though I didn't say why, and he didn't ask. There'd have been no reason to mention it at all, except it explained what I was doing with Ajax in the first place. For some reason it was important to me that Ben know it had been the date that was blind, not me.

I spoke about the serrated poker, what it looked like, and I alluded to the woman in the restaurant, before moving on to the part about the pheromones and how Ajax had said he knew I was the "one." That was the only point where Ben looked at me strangely, and I shrugged, unable to explain it myself.

The rest of the time he simply took notes, glancing up intermittently, cop face firmly fixed as if we'd only just met. This was fascinating—I felt like an audience member at an old Siegfried and Roy show, one who couldn't believe what they were seeing, and didn't dare blink lest the stars disappear altogether.

An hour and a half later Ben turned off the recorder and leaned back in his chair. "That's good, Jo. We should have enough here to put Ajax away for a while."

I toyed with the buttons on my chair that controlled the room's media center. "Doesn't mean you will."

"No," he said, not looking at me. "It doesn't."

We both knew the system had loopholes. Sometimes, I thought, the bad guys just disappeared. We were silent for a time. I nervously sipped my cold coffee.

"You have a good eye for detail," Ben said, glancing up. "Probably comes from your martial art training, huh?"

"It's not an art." Krav Maga was martial, no doubt, but in eight years of training I'd never once considered it an art. It was violent and dirty street fighting. Ten years earlier my instructor—now a friend, Asaf—had immigrated to the Nevada desert and brought with him the discipline, the system, and the knowledge of Krav Maga from the Holy Land. His first student, I had soaked up his instruction like a desert rose watered after a scorching summer drought.

We trained for life-threatening situations—knives, guns, multiple attackers—driving ourselves to fight on in the face of fatigue. We trained, as he told me that first day, for the possible, the eventual, and with the conviction that survival depended on breakneck reflexes and split-second reactions.

"No human predator is going to pull his punch just because you're a girl," Asaf told me in that wonderful clipped cadence of his. Of course, this was something I already knew. My *possible*, my *eventual*, had already happened.

When Ben saw I was going to say nothing more, he rose, shoved his hands in his pockets and stared down at me. Mr. Authority. "I should put surveillance on you. If there are others out there, like Ajax said, then we—"

"Don't even think about it."

"Exactly." He sighed, and ran a hand over the back of his neck. "Sure you won't even consider it?"

"I won't be stalked."

"Followed, not stalked," Ben corrected, somewhat irritably. "They're police officers."

"I won't be followed, then."

"Even if I'm doing the following?"

I stood too. "Even then."

He shook his head. "Mule."

" 'Know thyself,' " I quoted, wanting to see if he'd take the bait.

" 'Knowledge is power,' " he answered, an even more tired cliché than my own.

One side of my mouth lifted. " 'All our knowledge merely helps us to die a more painful death—' "

" '—than the animals that know nothing,' " he capped, shaking his head. " 'And a little knowledge is a dangerous thing.' "

We both smiled. We'd collected quotes as teens, dueled with them, and it'd become our own language, not unlike the silly, secret ones of very young children. It was another love we'd once shared; the English language, and the way the masters could turn a phrase, and the world on its ear, in only a few words.

"How's your wife?" I blurted, then cursed silently, feeling myself color. I didn't really know this Ben Traina. And we no longer belonged to one another. "Sorry. You don't have to answer that."

"No, it's all right," he said and, amazingly, slowly, smiled. "But you'd have to ask her new husband."

I blushed even more. Ben cleared his throat and picked up a crystal paperweight, flipping it in his palm. "Saw the article on your family."

I studied him for judgment or sarcasm but found none. I licked my lips slowly and watched him watching me. *Interesting.* "So you read how I'm a slacker with no ambition and few abilities or admirable goals?"

He scoffed as he put down the paperweight, then skirted the table between us to take me by the hand, and led me to the window that overlooked the glittering Las Vegas Strip. His palm was warm and dry, and my own looked dwarfed inside of it. Even as a boy he'd had great hands. "They should have interviewed me. I have my own theory about the 'prodigal daughter of the Archer dynasty.'"

That quote stung. I withdrew my hand and turned on him. "Why? Because you know me so well?"

"I think I do."

I folded my arms over my chest. "I can't wait to hear this."

"Okay." Ben mimicked my pose, leaning on the glass wall, looking as though he were reclining against the night. "First, it's your birthday. Twenty-five years old. Happy Birthday."

He remembered. I glanced down at my watch so he couldn't see the sudden moisture in my eyes. "You're about twenty-four hours early, actually, but thank you."

"You're welcome. Second, you're not aimless, merely restless. You battle between a fleeting need for security and a constant one for complete freedom. You can't lie about who you are, and therefore you can't feign interest in your father's business, or imitate your sister's social grace, regardless of how successful they are."

He paused, brows raised, and I motioned for him to continue. In a quieter voice he added, "You think too much, and you're haunted by things you can't change. You have a strong sense of right and wrong, with little tolerance for the in-between, and zero patience for deception."

"Anything else?" I said, a bit tightly.

"Just one. You're a photographer, but not as a means of commerce or even as a form of communicating with the world. The lens is actually a barrier shielding you from the rest of us. It's a way of distancing yourself from your subjects so you can study them. Or hunt them."

"That's a bunch of crap!"

Ben grinned. "You're also quick-tempered."

Hunt them, I thought, shaking my head, annoyed. It was the same wording I'd heard earlier that evening. *We've been hunting you for a long time*, Ajax had said. He'd been trying to scare me, of course, but now Ben was saying it as if *I* were the predator, like some sort of skulking vampire, on the lookout for O-positive. "You're reading too much into it."

"You've been out every night this week."

"Wait," I said, holding up my hand, but otherwise going very still. "You've been watching me?"

"You're using yourself as bait, aren't you?" he persisted, ignoring the question. "That's why you go out alone, at night, in the most dangerous parts of town."

I clenched my teeth together, hard. "I go out at night because it's quiet, and because light and shadow are a photographer's main tools."

"You seem to be more in the shadows than the light."

"So what?" I tried not to sound defensive, but it was hard.

"So, why?" he said. "Why spend your days training like

you're going into battle, and your nights on the streets seeking it?"

I know that's what it looked like from afar, from the outside looking in, which was the only way Ben could possibly see it, but it was more than that. Not that I was going to explain it now. "Maybe I'm just dedicated to my craft," I said, lifting my chin.

"You haven't been taking your camera."

I whirled away from him, turning as much from the understanding his face held as from the shame that my secret—what I thought was a secret—had been so easily found out. I rubbed my arms, trying to erase the chills that had shot along them. A part of me was thrilled; he'd kept up on me, hadn't forgotten me, still cared. Another part was furious. How could I have not seen him? Part of the point of these nocturnal excursions was to look for men—a man—who were looking for me.

"Joanna?"

"I can't believe you've been following me." My voice cracked. I cleared my throat, but it felt scratchy and dry, like all my words would stick to its walls.

At least he had the grace to sound apologetic. "It was an accident the first time. I was on a stakeout and I just saw you. I trailed you to make sure you'd be safe, but it didn't take long to realize you weren't trying to be safe." His voice loomed closer, just behind me. "Why, Jo-Jo?"

"I've just been feeling . . . restless lately," I finally said, which was the truth, if only half of it. Most of the time I felt like I was being bitten by a thousand fire ants buried deep beneath my skin. Or like someone was stoking a fire in my soul. "I feel like something's going to happen, but I won't know what it is until it's too late."

Ben put his hands on my shoulders, which I wouldn't have tolerated from anyone else, and turned me so I was facing him. "You're looking for him, aren't you? Tempting him. Testing him."

I clenched my teeth so hard my jaw ached. It had been

such a good cover too. Confirmed slacker. Lazy little rich girl. Token black sheep of the Archer dynasty, the one others could point to and say, "See? All the money in the world *can't* buy you happiness."

The writer of the *Fortunes and Fates* article hadn't caught on. Neither had Ajax or any man I'd dated before him. Not even my family, or Asaf—who knew only that I slept badly—were aware of what I did, or why. Nobody had seen that it was all just a cover. Until now.

I shook my head. "I'm just taking pictures."

"And if you happen to find *him* locked between the crosshairs of your lens?" Ben asked, watching me again with his cop eyes.

I didn't have to ask whom he meant. I met his gaze as I'd met Ajax's, unblinking. And just to see who this new Ben Traina was, I said, "I kill him."

His answer was immediate. "Good. Any other long-term goals?"

That jerked a laugh from me. I was surprised my throat had even let it escape. More surprised at Ben for laughing with me. Where was the lecture? Where was the warning that should've followed? The PSA about the long arm of the law? Then again, I didn't really need it. Despite my words, my actions were all defensive. But I think the real reason we both let it slide was because the "him" we were referring to was the one who'd ultimately driven us apart.

"Long-term goals?" I repeated, before shaking my head. "Just survival, Traina. I'm just trying to survive."

Which wasn't entirely true. I already had the survival thing down pat.

Ben turned back to the glass wall and looked out with a sigh over the city we both patrolled. I joined him, pressing my forehead against the cool glass, and let the lights below blur into a blinding stream of nothingness. We call it camera shake in photography; when the camera moves and the shutter is open long enough to cause an overall blur. The effect was mostly undesirable, except for times like this.

Together we looked out at this strange city where the play of shadow and light was more pronounced than in any other until finally he said, "There has to be more to life than survival."

There hadn't been for me, I conceded, not for a long while. But with Ben standing close, knowing about my past and not flinching, I began to think there might be. I raised my eyes to find him gazing at me. Not just gazing, but seeing.

How long had it been since I'd been truly seen?

And the look on his face was so soft and clear it was practically translucent. Probably, I thought, a good reflection of my own. Just then, I would have loved to frame that face with my camera lens. Capture that moment, and him, forever. *God, what a beautiful man.*

I froze suddenly. "Please don't tell me I said that aloud."

Ben straightened, grinning wickedly. "You did. You said I was beautiful."

Embarrassed, I turned away, but his hand, wide and firm and warm, grasped my shoulder. He turned me toward him again and held all of me there; body, eyes, and mind.

"If I'm beautiful," he said, thumbs tickling against the inside of my elbows, "then you're the most stunning woman I've ever seen."

I ducked my head automatically, though my pulse points hummed. "My sister's stunning," I said, "I'm strong."

"You're stunning and strong," he murmured, and moved in closer.

I lifted my head and leaned into him. It felt natural, and my pulse throbbed. "Go on."

His lips quirked up at one side as he drew me against him. "You're stunning and strong, Joanna Archer, and you're about to be kissed."

And I knew exactly what he would taste like. Ambrosia. The breaking of a fast. Water, pure, clean, and spring-clear after a ten-year drought. All the relevant clichés applied.

How masochistic, I thought, sighing as his mouth molded

to mine. Instantly back in love with a man I'd spent a decade trying to get over. Anyone have a dull razor blade? Cat-o'-nine-tails? Old, rusty nails?

Yet this was also a first. The first taste of a man whose lips and arms and body touched the expected places in unexpected ways. The first hint of underlying passion, like touching a battery to the tip of my tongue, that metallic zap of pure power just aching to course over into me. The glory of a man whose flesh and cellular structure spoke to my own but, biology and chemistry and pheromones aside, one who just felt fucking great wrapped around me.

"Jo-Jo?" Ben finally said, breaking away.

"Hmm?" I still hadn't opened my eyes. It'd been so long. Why hadn't I known I needed this, wanted it—had been missing it—for so damned long?

"You're groping a senior officer."

I smiled against his shirt and moved my hand. "Gonna put it in your statement?"

"Gonna ask you for a date." He pressed a kiss to the crown of my head. "You never say no, right?"

I pulled back and peered into his face. "I object to the implication. I say no to some things."

"Gonna say no to me?"

"No."

He smiled, lifted a hand to my face and caressed it, his touch impossibly gentle. I wasn't used to being handled gently. In truth, I wasn't used to being handled at all. Certainly not by a man who could be both as hard as granite and as soft as a feather. So much new to discover here, I thought, lifting my head to kiss the hollow of his neck.

"Your cheek is bruised," he murmured, voice hoarse.

I leaned into him, offering up that cheek for feathery kisses and pointed attentions. All wit and sarcasm and guarded inhibitions fled—in Ben's embrace I wasn't an heir to the Archer family empire, as so many others saw me, or a wounded warrior bent on vengeance, as Ben had claimed with such certainty. I also wasn't a woman fighting for normalcy—fighting, but losing—which in fact was how I saw myself. I was just a woman. So often that was all a woman wanted to be.

"I didn't think you'd ever want to see me again," he murmured. His heart cracked through that voice.

Startled, I stared up at this man, so unflinching and honest and *whole*, and saw—for the briefest moment—the boy who hadn't had the strength or experience to be any of those things.

"I didn't either," I admitted.

"But you'll go on a date with me?"

I nodded.

"Tomorrow night?" he asked urgently, as if to make up for lost time.

I nodded again.

"So, what's changed?"

I shrugged. "Now I have seen you."

And that was it. Life sometimes flips on you like that. One minute you're looking at your reflection in the water, not entirely sure you like what you see, and the next minute you're upside down, submerged in a world where even familiar things look new. I put a hand to Ben's cheek just as he'd done to mine and softly said good-bye. It was a fragile and new beginning between us, and like a new parent cradling life, we were both being gentle with it.

But I smiled as I left Valhalla. Of all the qualities Ben had attributed to me earlier, he'd forgotten flexibility. I'd grown up as well, and had learned to adapt to the situation and to the moment because I'd had to. That's how I could rebound from being attacked to being kissed in the same night. If I hadn't possessed the ability to roll with the punches, I might as well have died facedown on the scorching desert floor.

Exactly as I'd been left to do over a decade ago.

But here, on the eve of my twenty-fifth birthday, I decided

I was ready to look at my world anew. Perhaps Ben was right, I thought, his kiss still fresh upon my lips. Survival was all well and good, as was the elusive search for normalcy. But maybe neither was enough anymore.

3

It was midnight as I made my way home, exactly twenty-four hours before my next birthday, and the nightly bacchanal that was Las Vegas was in full swing, a strange cross-culture of midwestern hedonism and foreign bafflement. The Strip was a neon necklace strung from one end of the valley to the other, like gaudy costume jewelry dressing up the desert night, and despite the sharp November air, every street, walkway, and aerial tram was packed with tourists. Their gazes were wide-eyed and expectant, like they expected someone to drop money in their lap at any given moment.

I bundled into my wrap, then my car, and gassed it past Bellagio and Caesar's before hurtling over the wash that flooded the Imperial Palace's parking garage every monsoon season. Lowering my window halfway, I allowed the cool air to bite at my cheeks and ruffle my hair. Even if my mind hadn't been buzzing with thoughts of Ben, or images of Ajax writhing on the floor—and then, again, more thoughts of Ben—I'd have been wide-awake. Vegas came alive at night, and so did I.

I'd often thought how boring it'd be to grow up in a

place where everyone was the same . . . until I realized that everyone really was, essentially, the same. They watched the same television shows, ate at McDonald's, had their coffee at Starbucks, and hopped the same airplanes to return to whatever state or country they thought made them different. While they were here, however, no matter what color, shape, or accent they sported, they wanted identical things. To be entertained. To get lucky. And to be allowed to dream, just for a while, that anything was possible. Despite its checkered past and dubious press, Vegas spoke to people of hope. And hope, as they say, makes fools of us all.

I left all that frantic hope behind me and turned onto an asphalt-slung back road only the cops, locals, and well-tipped cabbies knew about. Within five minutes I was coasting along Charleston Boulevard, the glitter of the Strip replaced by littered alleys and underpasses, where the unlucky huddled in wary groups rather than optimistic ones. These were the people tired of playing the fool, and the dichotomy between these two faces of Vegas was not lost on me.

That was how I first spotted the homeless man pawing through a steel trash bin, his tattered duster whipping violently around his calves . . . on a wind-free night. He glanced up as my headlights arched over his graffiti-tagged domain, a giant rat reclining on two legs, beady eyes following my vehicle until the possibility of danger had passed.

Two minutes later, as I turned onto an unpaved shortcut, another vagrant appeared—dressed similarly, no less— and half scuttled, half walked toward my racing vehicle, gazing right at me through the window as I passed. I trailed him in the rearview mirror, wondering at the way he followed my path into the middle of the road and just stood in the dust, watching as I sped away.

I didn't see the figure in front of me until it was too late. Tires squealed, the windshield cracked with a sonic boom, and a body careened over my roof, thumping and wheeling overhead before disappearing into the inky night. Tumble-weeds scraped my doors like fingernails, rocks battered the tires and underside of my car, and I spun twice, carving dizzying whorls into the dry desert bed before miraculously coming to a rest without flipping.

The pitch of night—complete on this barren desert side street—couldn't mask the smell of burning rubber, or the ragged sound of my breath breaking in sharp spurts from my lungs. It took a moment to get oriented again, but when I did I found myself facing the direction I'd come. In the background were the circus lights of the Strip.

In the foreground was a man crumpled on the desert floor.

I began to shake. Then, before shock could set in, I began to move. Grabbing my cell phone, I pushed from the car, the screech of door against bramble arching in the air like a lonely cry for help. My headlights illuminated the person I'd hit, but it seemed to take me forever to run on jellied limbs and slide to a crouch beside him.

I don't know how I recognized him, perhaps it was the long coat, but even before I reached the crumpled figure I knew I'd find that beggar. The one I'd already seen. Twice.

Multiple smells hit me at once. Pungent body odor, the man surely hadn't washed for weeks; vomit, sour and smelling of the bottle; and something greasy, whether his hair or clothes or the dinner he might have unearthed from that trash bin, I didn't know. There was another scent too, one I couldn't name. I knew only that it was him, and I tried to ignore the voice in my mind telling me there was no way he should be here. That it was impossible. That I'd left him miles back in the dark.

His face was turned away from the beam of my headlights, and a wiry beard kept me from seeing if a pulse beat in his neck, but his limp limbs were turned in impossible angles and gruesome directions. It didn't look like an ambulance would be necessary. Shaking, I touched his skin for a pulse. I had just killed a human being.

His head rocked, eyes opened wide, and he screeched in my face. I fell backward, gasping, and quickly scrambled out of reach. His cry hadn't been one of pain. It even sounded joyous, like he'd made some sort of discovery. It sounded, in fact, like he'd cried, "Eureka!"

He hollered again, this time drawing out the syllables, and I couldn't tell whether he was laughing or crying, but that twisted, mutilated body began to shake. "Eu—re–kaaaa!"

I reached for the cell phone I'd dropped, but was stopped by the man's voice; throaty, strong, and surprisingly authoritative. "Don't touch that phone!"

"I—I'm just going to call an ambulance."

"Don't need no ambulance."

I pushed the emergency button. "You need a doctor."

He just looked at me and grinned, still sprawled on the gravel like some beat-up and forgotten doll. I waited for a dial tone, the emergency operator, for anything that would connect me to someone who could help, but the phone had gone dead. It must have broken when I'd dropped it.

I looked at the vagrant and knew I couldn't move him, but I couldn't leave him there either. I'd never leave someone else helpless and vulnerable, alone in the desert. "I'm going to drive my car over, and we'll find a way to get you in, okay?"

"No, no. I'm a quick healer," he said, and just like that the leg beneath him straightened with an audibly sickening pop. "See?"

I didn't. I thought I might vomit, but I didn't see. "Let me get my car anyway."

Ignoring his protests, I jogged back to the car and slipped into the seat. Then I pulled alongside the man, who was now, amazingly, sitting up, and—careful not to bean him in the head—pushed open the passenger door to view him through the other side.

"Told you I heal quickly," he said, waving at me with a hand that was broken just above the wrist. The torque of the movement was nauseating, but not as much as the way he suddenly jerked the arm upward, snapping it back in place. We both stared at the arm, poised midair. Then he gave me a little finger wave, grinning. "Bet you can't do that."

I opened my mouth but nothing came out. The wrist, obviously healed and fully functioning, appeared as good as new. That's when I realized the dusty ground, the man, and even my car, were as dry as they'd been before the accident. There were no body fluids or blood; no urine released as battered muscles convulsed then went lax with injury. I glanced from the wrist into clear eyes that watched me intently, corners crinkled in a knowing smile.

"Uh . . ."

Stepping from the car, I watched from over the hood as he slowly straightened. He was still bent at the waist, but he'd been stooped like that back beneath the underpass and appeared otherwise fine. Which brought me back to my original question. How had he gotten here?

"How—How . . ." It was about as much as I could manage, and I had to settle for the truncated version. "How?"

"I told you. Quick healer. Like you." And he began to walk away.

I put my hand to my cheek, where he'd pointed. It was the one Ben had touched, the one that had been bruised and tender. I frowned. The soreness was gone.

"Sir, come back." I rushed to catch up. "What's your name?"

He doubled over instantly and began to laugh; maniacal, breathless spasms rocking his body back and forth while tears streamed over his grimy cheeks. I looked around to see what was so funny, and came pretty quickly to the conclusion it was me. His laughter broke off into wracking coughs, and he bent over, hacking away. I pounded on his back, trying to help.

"You ever read comic books?" he asked, straightening suddenly, all signs of ill health vanishing with the movement.

I wiped my hand on my pants. "You mean like Donald Duck?"

"I mean like Superman, Wonder Woman . . . Elektra." He said this last word with all the panache of a seasoned lounge act, fingers splayed in the air with theatrical introduction.

"No." This whole conversation was getting stranger by the moment. I took a step back, muttering to myself, "What do I look like? An adolescent boy with cystic acne and bondage fantasies?"

"Not fantasies," he said, overhearing me. "History. Research. The truth multiplied by the collective consciousness equals fact stranger than fiction." He began chuckling again.

"Sorry?"

"I'm a superhero!" he announced, raising his arms like a competitor in Mr. Olympia. "Hero to the superheroes. Command leader of Zodiac troop 175, division of anti-evil, La-as Vegas!"

After what I considered an amazingly brief period, I closed my gaping mouth. I even formed words. "I really think you should get in the car, sir. I'll pay for an exam."

"You're sweet," he announced to the desert, grabbing my arm. "So sweet. So good. One of the good guys. Like me."

Yeah, I thought. Just like you. "Ah, look. At least let me take you to the shelter. They'll give you food. You'll have a place to stay for the night."

"Day is night and night is day in this, your city, your home," he said, pointing back toward the neon lights. "Vampires, if they existed, would love it here. Cats too." He craned his neck at me pointedly. "It's a great place for all nocturnal hunters."

"What did you say?"

"I said hunters. Like you. Like me too, because I found you." He jumped, performing a dusty heel click. "Eureka!"

Now, getting run over by my Jaguar XK8 coupe could hardly qualify as a discovery, but I wasn't going to argue the point with someone obviously suffering severe mental trauma. Then again, I thought, studying his lopsided grin, maybe I hadn't hit him hard enough. "Let me take you to the hospital. You really need help."

"Aren't you kind?" he said, tearing up, grasping my arm again. "Aren't you special? I can just *smell* the uniqueness on you."

I jerked away and stumbled as Ajax's short lesson on pheromones flashed through my mind. I was suddenly very aware I was standing in the middle of the desert with a complete—and, apparently, completely mad—stranger. "Look, mister, I don't know what you're talking about. There's nothing special about me. Got it? You just need help."

"You don't think you're special? How sad. So sad." He shook his head, and really did seem dispirited by the thought. "But you are. You have special skills. Warriors' skills. That's why you're being watched."

"By whom?" I asked, though I already knew of two people. Ajax. And Ben.

"Power is knowledge, and knowledge is power. Know thyself. All our knowledge merely helps us to die a more painful death than the animals that know nothing . . ."

I'd have sworn on my life Ben and I had been alone in my father's office, but we spoke the final words together. ". . . and a little knowledge is a dangerous thing."

We both stared, the cold, dry night sharpening between us. He was no longer bumbling about. And I was no longer feeling kind. "Where did you hear that?"

He tilted his head at my threatening tone. "You must develop your skills. Realize your potential. Your power, indeed, lies in your knowledge, but right now you know nothing."

I decided then I'd had my share of nutcases for one night. I turned my back and began to walk away. "You don't know me, old man."

His next words halted me cold. "You're Joanna Archer, sister to Olivia, daughter to Xavier and Zoe. You have a birthday tomorrow, midnight, an auspicious one . . ." He waited until I'd turned back. "Auspicious, that is, if you live long enough to see it."

And I was on him before I knew it, the lapels of his tattered jacket twisted in my fists, my face thrust in his despite the stench and craziness that lived there. "Who are you?"

He placed his hands over mine, and I felt the strength in them and was surprised by it. You couldn't tell by looking at him, and that was something I should have remembered. You could never tell who a person really was just by looking.

"Your second life cycle ends today. Tonight, Joanna." He lifted my hands from his lapels, gently, and returned them to my sides. "I've come to warn you."

I shook my head, and wrapped my arms around my body, but kept my eyes on him as I backed away. "You talk in riddles, old man."

"Ah, but you're a straight shooter, aren't you? An Archer, you are." He made a motion like shooting an arrow into the night, and tilted his head, considering me. "Not just a hunter, though. A target too. The hunter becomes the hunted."

The wind suddenly picked up, shifting so a breeze blew my hair across my cheeks, setting the hem of the man's trench coat fluttering around his ankles. He lifted his nose, and his nostrils drew wide, then narrowed again. "Smell that? They know you're here. But don't worry. They know I'm here too."

"I don't smell anything," I said, and I had no idea what he was talking about.

He tilted his head in that crazy way he had. "Because you haven't been taught to recognize their kind. Close your eyes and think of once living things decaying in the ground. A pet rabbit buried then unearthed after a week. Fungus rotting on overripe fruit. Hot sulfur rising from a hole in the earth to taint the wind. Now try again."

I turned my face into the wind just to humor him, and immediately caught a whiff of something that reminded me of sulfur. Possibly tin. A rusty can.

With the flesh of a long-dead animal sweating inside.

"Christ." It smelled like Ajax, and I turned my head away sharply, only to find the bum regarding me solemnly. The look sent chills through my spine and into the soles of my feet. Someone this crazy shouldn't look so sane. I pivoted to leave. Fuck this guy. He could just stay here with his riddles and delusions and rotting scents.

His voice rose, carried to me on the filthy breeze. "You were walking through the desert when you were sixteen years old, leaving your boyfriend's house in the early morning hours, smelling of passion and love and hope, the same scent that clings to you tonight, in fact."

My heart was beating so hard I wouldn't have been surprised if it leapt from my chest into my hands. How did a homeless man who jumped in front of cars and smelled like a sewer know anything about my personal scent? How did he know about me? I turned to find him closer than I expected. So close I had to hold my breath.

"You were attacked by a solitary man who seemed to be everywhere at once," he continued, dark eye boring into mine. "You were raped, strangled, and left for dead. You awoke with a broken memory beneath the scorching midday sun, and no idea of who you really were. Your memory gradually returned, but you never fully recovered your burgeoning sixth sense. You mended your broken body and turned it into a machine, a weapon, a warrior's tool. Good thing too. You'll need it now."

"How do you know all this?" God, but I hated how small my voice sounded.

"I told you. I have my talents. You have others."

"You mean, like a superhero?" If that's what he thought, he obviously had the wrong girl; my life was a fucking soap opera, not a comic book.

The man pursed his lips and looked up as if reading the

stars like a map. They were powerful pinpricks this far out in the desert, brilliant and spearing sharply from the sky in the clear night. "I can't help you now, Joanna. It's too early by a moon's rise. I just came to warn you. If you survive, I'll be in touch."

Then he began trudging off in that halting gait, heading for the void of empty desert space. But he paused a moment later, and for the first time his body language was uncertain. "Joanna?"

I stared back at him and shivered.

"Make sure you survive."

Funny, but *that* was the sanest thing I'd heard all day.

Sanity had been a relatively elusive state since my rape almost a decade earlier. The strange desert interlude with a man who had no business knowing about me brought back just how hard I'd fought since then for even a modicum of normality . . . though I suppose the novelty of being threatened with a serrated poker might have had something to do with it as well. Either way, both strangers had talked openly about things that had gone unspoken in my family for years, chatting as easily about my patchwork past as if they were asking me to pass the salt . . .

What's wrong, Joanna? Seeing things that remind you of a sweltering summer night?

You were attacked by a solitary man who seemed to be everywhere at once.

You were beaten, strangled, and left for dead.

It was true, I had been. But as a rule—one meant to keep that hard-won sanity in check—it wasn't the truth I generally chose to concentrate on.

After the attack, after I'd healed about as much as a person can heal from such a thing, and after I'd spent nine months in hiding, I did eventually finish high school. I wasn't going to let myself be trapped, or further victimized by a man who'd already taken so much from me. My anger and fear were replaced by determination and the belief that just because someone tried to make you into a victim didn't mean that's what you had to be.

So I did normal things. I went to college, and majored in photography and art. I pushed my mind just as I pushed my body, stretching myself socially before I had a chance to freeze or petrify, and turn into something hard and brittle and dead before my time.

And I forgot, or told myself I forgot, about the child.

It also became important for me to escape Xavier's gilded cage, that architectural behemoth so falsely resplendent on the outside, but with the moldy invaders of sorrow and blame that'd moved in after my attack. So I lived in a dorm, I had a roommate who kept a record of the men she slept with on a wall calendar. I joined a sorority—okay, only for about a minute, but still—and I pushed myself to date, making sure my gut reaction, that first impulse to withdraw and automatically say no, was kept in check. That's when I made my rule: never say no. Of course, I sometimes cursed myself and the rigidity of that rule—I'd lost count of how many groping hands I'd had to wrest away—but fending off drunken frat boys was a cakewalk after what I'd been through.

And I'd been extremely careful not to wall myself off, which was why Ben's comments about hiding behind my camera had touched such a nerve. Okay, so I stalked the city streets when I should have been home preparing a meal for a husband and two-point-five brats. Big deal. But I'd found, in the shadows of this city—my glittering town of dollar buffets and neon dreams—a lack of judgment about such things as what was normal. When I took my camera to the streets, nobody cared about my past or my name. When I tiptoed through the shadows of ugly alleyways, looking into faces that stared fearlessly and openly back at me, I could stop striving and pretending to be whole. And I could just *be whole*.

But now some bum who thought he was a comic book hero was telling me someone was going to try and attack me again. Worse, there were reasons, despite the man's incoherent rambling, to believe what he said. One, I already had been attacked. *Pretty good sign.* Two, our conversation had smacked of more than obscure riddles and hidden meanings. It'd mirrored Ajax's, if not exactly, then in word choice and content. They both claimed to know me from my scent. They both declared I was special in some way. They each said I was still being watched.

Thirdly, other than my name, family, and past, that scruffy, stinking vagrant had spoken of details nobody knew, some of which I'd purposely forgotten myself. The clincher was, he knew the words I used to describe myself, words that defined who I'd become, filling the holes left in my psyche by a young girl's inability to defend herself.

Weapon. Warrior. Hunter.

Because despite all my hard work to become a whole woman, and a relatively open one, I was still keenly aware that he—the attacker—had never been found. He never saw the inside of a cage . . . at least not for what he'd done to me. And he was still out there. I felt it in my ancient fractures. I heard his voice every time dusk set along the Strip.

But I had a place here; in this world, this city, these streets. I'd made it for myself through grit and determination, and I wasn't going to give it up now just because an anorectic psycho and some deranged bum had knocked haphazardly into my life.

No, I swore, speeding home on the neon-slicked streets. Not me. Not without a knock-down, drag-out, fuck-you fight.

4

The first thing I do every morning is make coffee, put on sunscreen, and take my birth control . . . the goal, of course, to be alert and protected at all times. Today I added a couple of aspirins to my caffeine cocktail, showered away the stiffness from last night's train wreck of a date, and readied myself for a last minute meeting with the infamous Xavier Archer. His secretary had called just after eight to say he wished to meet with my sister and me, and though she asked my availability, I knew it wasn't a request.

I agreed to the afternoon appointment, then searched my closet for something Xavier might find appropriate, knowing, in truth, he didn't think it appropriate to be seen with me at all. I was a gross embarrassment to him, for things I both could and could not control, and it was laughable to even try appeasing him, though long ago I had tried. By now it was just about keeping up appearances and playing the game.

As one might imagine for a gambling maverick, my father was big on games.

Comfort won out over making a good impression, and I

settled on a fitted T-shirt with three-quarter sleeves, stretch jeans, and my favorite leather boots—I'd already had them resoled twice—all in black. Throwing on a scarf and pea-coat, I then drove the five miles from my modest tract home to my father's custom-built compound. You couldn't miss it. It took up an entire city block on the far west end of town. I was admitted by a guard with sideburns, large jowls, and a bodybuilder's physique—Elvis on steroids—and moments later pulled into the circular drive of a home more suited to the Côte d'Azur than the Las Vegas valley. On the way in I met up with Olivia.

Physically, my sister and I were opposites in all ways that counted. I sported a straight, uncomplicated chin-length bob, while she seemed to walk around in a perpetual shampoo commercial. My face, though unlined and fine-boned, was rarely made up, while Olivia regularly held court at the Chanel counter. Today she was also dressed in Prada pink—obscenely cheerful for the month of November—and flanked by her favorite accessory, her best friend, Cher. I sighed as I looked at the two of them standing together beneath the dome of the marble portico. They were like pastry figurines atop a wedding cake; just looking at them gave me a sugar high.

I lifted my hand to shield my eyes as I approached. "I think I just burned my retinas."

"Ha ha," Olivia said to me before turning to Cher, dimples flashing. "Joanna thinks being caustic makes her appear intelligent, not to mention morally superior to those of us with a Neiman's card."

Damn, that was a good one for a woman who'd once worn bunny ears and a fluffy tail.

"You know, it could just be the sun, Joanna, dear." Taking in my black-on-black ensemble, Cher snapped her gum loudly, also pink. "Olivia tells me you only come out at night."

"Only if there's a full moon," I replied, trying not to let it bother me that Olivia would speak of me to Cher at all. She and I had a long-standing enmity, born on the day we met, half a dozen years earlier. She was a southern version of Olivia, a sharp-tongued shrew in the guise of a belle, with a manipulative nature that would make Scarlett herself blush. She didn't take herself too seriously, which I rather thought a good thing, but she didn't take anything else seriously either, and that I just found irresponsible. She also had the ear of the woman I considered my best friend.

"Well, that explains your color, darlin'." Cher pressed a cool, bejeweled finger to my skin. When she lifted it, the color didn't change. She repeated the test on herself with more satisfying results.

"Touch me again and you'll lose your finger."

She lifted that finger to her lips and blew me a kiss.

I barely contained a snarl. "Flirting won't work on me, Cher. I don't have a penis."

"Are you sure?" She smiled, lashes opening and closing like butterfly wings, and before I could answer, turned away. "I'll be waiting for you in the drawing room, Livvy-girl. Don't forget, we have a date for high tea at four."

"It's a fucking family room," I muttered, watching until she disappeared from sight. I turned to find Olivia regarding me with sad eyes. "What?"

"Why do you have to take shots at her?" *At us*, said her expression.

"Easy target."

"She's my best friend."

"I know." The words settled uneasily between us. Finally, I cleared my throat. "Come on, let's get this Daddy Dearest moment over with. I wouldn't want you to miss high tea."

"You could come with us," she said as we entered the wraparound hallway leading to the office wing.

And maybe after that I could stick burning pokers beneath my fingernails. "I don't think so."

"What about tonight?" she persisted. "Want to come over?"

"What's wrong? Malibu Ken already have a date?"

"No, but my sister is having a birthday. I thought we might have a party, just the two of us."

The need in her voice both softened and hurt me. It *had* been a long time since we'd done anything together, just for fun. Then, remembering the way she'd stared, I also wondered how much of our alone time was reported back to Cher. *I love you, Olivia, but . . .* "I already have plans."

And I was desperate to tell her about them, about Ben. I just couldn't with Cher's face and voice so fresh in my mind.

Olivia's lower lip popped out. "But aren't you curious to know what I got you?"

"Does it involve the color pink, or a grossly overvalued designer initial stamped on it?"

"No. It doesn't involve crosses or holy water either. You're perfectly safe."

"Ha ha."

But Olivia linked her arm in mine as we continued walking, making it hard to cross my arms over my chest, and utterly defeating my snarl. Damn it, she was like PMS kryptonite. She instinctively knew how to sap a bad mood of all its energy.

"Stubborn," she muttered, singsonging it, as if to herself. "Too stubborn to admit any weakness—"

"Don't start this again."

"And too in love with life to just shut down completely."

In love with life? I raised a brow. "Olivia, I sleep all day—when I'm not training—and wander the dirtiest, grittiest morasses of this city's butt crack at night."

She only smiled. "You volunteer at the soup kitchen once a week. You take portraits of the homeless to raise awareness, and as a tribute, marking that they're here. You let them know that you, at least, see them. And you've helped dozens of teen runaways return home, and if they couldn't do that, found them a new one."

I stopped dead. "How do you know all that?"

She shot me that secretive smile over her shoulder and

kept walking. I had to rush to catch up. "Because I don't just chair the events that cater to the rich who feel better about themselves for eating a five-hundred-dollar dinner that they can write off at the end of the year. I talk to the people who talk to the people you help. Those who pay for plates might call me Ms. Archer, but those who are given a free meal call you 'friend.' "

"I'm going to puke now," I said, embarrassed . . . and secretly pleased.

"Mind the carpet."

But by this time we were making our way across a room of marble, one markedly different from that of any other in the house. The floors were bare, the three windows un-adorned, and its core was shaped like something called a "stupa." That, Xavier had once explained, was a mound the old Tibetan lamas built to house the remains of great meditation masters when they died.

Now, I don't know what a Tibetan stupa was supposed to look like, but other than the white marble adorning every surface, ceiling included, this looked just like the inside of a crypt.

Xavier had jazzed it up a bit, of course. There was a glass case in the center of the room, spotlit from above, holding the first full English translation of a thirteen-hundred-year-old manuscript—*The Tibetan Book of the Dead*. Nice and cheery. There was also a dais at one end of the room, large enough for a throne, which was what Xavier eventually planned on put-ting there. Right now there was just a large gold-framed oil painting, featuring snowcapped mountains hovering over gently sloping grassland, and wildflowers combed over by gentle winds while mountain yaks grazed between them.

Now, leading up to the dais things got a little less pasto-ral and a little more interesting. A phalanx of vertical prayer wheels sat aligned like wooden soldiers, though I'd never seen anyone spinning them and I didn't know what they were for. What did an overbearing, self-centered, ego-tistical gaming mogul pray for anyway?

But none of this was as weirdly perplexing as the masks. Xavier claimed they came from a Sherpa village, high up in the Himalayas, and while there was no reason to doubt him, I had no idea what connection Xavier Archer thought he had with the Himalayans. He was from the Bronx. Exotic in its own way, but slightly different.

The first mask was made of copper, an elongated devil's face that leered at us as we entered the room. That one never failed to make me shiver. Halfway into the room some round-faced god of corroded burlwood blew visitors a wispy kiss through pursed lips. Yet another god attended the office door, this one wearing a pointed crown, crimson mouth open in a silent painted scream. If these weren't enough to ward off all ill intent, the security camera staring from the corner with its cycloptic red eye would certainly finish the job.

A buzzer sounded next to the door. "Come in, ladies." Then a clicking sound as the oak doors unlocked.

Xavier's office was more in line with what you might expect from a gaming mogul. Gone were the spiritual hoohahs and totems. This room was all dark wood, oversized furniture, and chocolate walls. The coffered ceiling soared with smoked mirrors and crown molding, and hand-painted cabinetry held an impressive collection of dusty hardbound books, spines uncracked. The man himself was no less grand and imposing.

Xavier Archer has the sort of presence that rocks lesser humans back on their heels. He often waves his hand through the air like some European monarch, indicating that his subjects should sit. He did this with us, his daughters, and the only sign that this appointment was different from an acquisition merger or a meeting on quarterly earnings was his refusal to look up from the notes he was scribbling at his desk.

We sat in a pair of uncomfortable mahogany chairs. He'd changed little in the months since I'd last seen him; still built like a field ox beneath his custom Armani. His jaw was squarely defined, and he had one bushy brow that arched singularly across his forehead, which I knew he was sensitive about but refused to change. If you didn't know any better you could mistake him for an aging linebacker. But everyone knew better. Xavier Archer made sure of that.

"Hello, Daddy," my sister said when he finally looked up.

"Hello, Olivia darling." A smile flashed as he set down his pen, then disappeared as he glanced at me. "Joanna."

"Xavier," I replied. He stared at me with his muddy eyes. I focused on his brow.

Clearing his throat, he leaned back in his chair. "You girls are probably wondering why I summoned you today."

"Not at all."

"First, Olivia," he said, ignoring me. "I heard about your attempt to garner a position at Valhalla. How many times have I told you? I don't want any daughter of mine working. What would people think?"

"What do they think now?" I muttered. They both pretended not to hear.

"I expect you to grow up, get married, have kids, get divorced, and live happily ever after." He drummed his index fingers together. They looked like two sausages fighting. "Understand?"

"Yes, Daddy," Olivia said softly.

"What if she wants a job?" He looked at me and blinked, as if wondering why I was there. "What if she wants a job?" I repeated, louder.

"You mean like taking people's pictures for free?" Xavier had never hidden his derision for what he considered my "wasteful" hobby. He scoffed. "I don't think so."

I couldn't help myself—the defenses that automatically sprung up when I was around Xavier surrounded my sister as well. "I'm just saying maybe it's not enough to expect her to be mere decoration for you or some future husband to wear upon his arm."

Olivia put a hand on my arm. "Jo—"

"Olivia has a job. She's my daughter."

Yeah, and the benefits are lousy. I held my tongue, though, because Olivia was looking pained beside me.

"Now. If that's all cleared up?" Which meant, in his mind, it was, but I made a mental note to speak with Olivia about it later. "I heard there was a ruckus at Valhalla last night, Joanna. Care to explain?"

A ruckus? Is that what he called being attacked by a madman wielding a serrated poker? I smiled tightly. "Sure. I'll explain. I saved a few dozen of your precious high rollers from being hacked to pieces by a homicidal maniac. A good thing too. It would have been hell on the carpet."

"Don't be facetious."

"I wouldn't dream of it."

We glared at one another over the polished glasstop desk, each daring the other to say another word. We'd been this route before, and more than once. Xavier thought my sarcasm and sharp tongue were unbecoming, and that I should be more like Olivia; demure when his associates' eyes lingered too long on her figure, sweet when an insult about her intelligence was flung over her head. Quiet even if she disagreed with anything he said.

I thought these expectations were asinine at the very least, bordering on deranged, so naturally I saved a great deal of my pent-up sarcasm for him.

Olivia gently cleared her throat beside me, causing me to break my stare.

"I understand the police had to be called in?" Of course that *would* be his greatest concern. Image, I thought, must be maintained at all times.

"The police were already there. They'd been tracking the guy for months." I didn't mention my reunion with Ben.

"Because he's killed before?"

"And he cheats at craps."

His eyes narrowed dangerously at that. "Perhaps you should be more selective about whom you date in the future."

Yeah, I'd kinda figured that one out for myself.

"You had something to tell us, Xavier?" I said, loving the way his teeth ground together when I used his first name.

"I do. Something of grave importance." He looked at us expectantly, almost pleasantly. Odd, I thought, if speaking of something truly grave. "It affects you, Joanna, more than Olivia."

Also odd that he would concern himself with me at all.

"I am not your real father."

My breath left me in a rush. "Thank God."

Olivia squeaked next to me.

"Excuse me?"

I cleared my throat. "I said, how odd."

"Yes, I know it must come as a shock. I only recently found out myself." He waved, indicating an open envelope on the corner of his desk. I picked it up, studied the type on the front, noted the lack of a return address or, indeed, any identifying mark, then removed the single sheet of paper enclosed within. Sure as shit, it said I wasn't his daughter. It wasn't signed.

"Got more proof than this?" I asked, waving the paper in his direction.

"I think there's proof enough." And he wasn't talking about the letter, which meant he wanted it to be true.

I leaned back and let the note fall to the floor.

"But, Daddy—"

"Don't worry, Olivia, dear. I had tests done this week. You and I share the same blood."

I wanted to say she hadn't looked terribly worried, nor did she appear all that relieved now, but Olivia was wringing her hands and suddenly speaking fast. "But—But we're really sisters, right?" I looked at her. "Even if only . . . half sisters?"

Bless her. Sweet, sensitive Olivia. She was better than the rest of us put together. I put a hand on her arm, to let her know it didn't matter either way.

"You share the same mother, yes."

"She has a name," I snapped, and his head jerked, reminding me again of a bull. "Zoe."

In the nine years since she'd disappeared, without a note or a trace, Xavier had never, to my knowledge, spoken of my mother. I imagined it would be the same with me. Ten years from now, or ten minutes, he'd have blotted my existence from his memory. I too would be a ghost, wandering the hallways of this house; another name not to be spoken by the servants, though I doubted my memory would haunt anyone.

"I know her name." He pushed away from his desk and stood. His standard power stance. "Olivia, if you'll excuse us now, I have some things to discuss with Joanna alone."

She didn't move, but bit her lower lip uncertainly and glanced again at me. I patted her hand again. Xavier's face reddened, his nostrils widened, and that solitary brow lifted high. I waited for the snort and hoof stomp. "Olivia!"

"Yes, Daddy." She rose.

I shot her a reassuring smile. "I'll talk to you later."

The door shut with a soft click behind her. It sounded like the report of a gunshot in the ensuing silence.

"So who is he?" I said without preamble. There was no need for pretense now.

"Who is whom?" he said, flipping open the humidor next to his desk.

"The man who fathered me," I said. "My real father?"

He waited until his Cohiba was cut and lit, and puffed twice before his eyes found mine. "I neither know nor care."

No, he wouldn't. He never had. "So you've done it, then. Finally washed your hands of me. Gotten rid of the great embarrassment of the Archer family dynasty."

"Don't be dramatic, Joanna. And, remember, this was your mother's doing, not mine."

"But you must be so relieved," I continued, honeyed sarcasm dripping from my voice. "No more pretense. No more stilted introductions, or uncomfortable silences at Thanksgiving. Why, you never even have to see me again."

"That's right," he said, and in spite of myself I flinched, immediately hating myself for it. "Your inheritance is disavowed, obviously. I had the papers changed yesterday. I won't support another man's child. Olivia will receive everything." He looked at me, the smoke rising between us, beautifully symbolic. "You are not my daughter."

"But Xavier." I stood too, and leaned forward on his desk, passing through the smoke. "How will it look?"

He'd already thought of that. "As far as the world is concerned you will remain my daughter. Estranged, but still mine. Understand?"

Just another possession, I thought, carelessly cast aside.

"You'll keep your house, your car, and a small monthly allowance since my daughter seems to care for you, but the family business, the homes and investments, they all belong to Olivia, and rightfully so."

"And the name?" I said, my voice going dead soft. "Do I get to keep the name?"

He hesitated. "It was your mother's too."

"One she obviously cherished."

He stiffened. "You may leave now."

I almost laughed at that. I had left long ago. He'd just never noticed.

"Oh, and Joanna?" His voice stopped my hand on the doorknob, and I turned. He was already seated again, angling a stream of smoke upward. He spoke from the corner of his mouth. "Stay out of Valhalla. If I hear of one more incident compromising the reputation of my property, I'll throw you out myself."

I used the only weapon I had left. "No wonder she left you."

He picked up his pen and began writing again, never looking up. "She left you too."

Well, that was the crux of it, wasn't it? My mother *had* left me. Sure, she'd left Xavier and Olivia too, but they hadn't been recovering from a life-threatening attack. They hadn't felt it as yet one more in a string of devastating losses. They hadn't needed her like I had.

But there was no point rehashing all that now, I told myself. My mother had walked away from her family—simple as that—and like the rest of my joyful past—not—it was behind me. So as I left Xavier's office I imagined stomping down on the memories that voicing my mother's name had evoked, grinding them back down with the heel of my boot into the mental grave where all my old pains rested. I was no longer that fragile-minded teen with a damaged body and a weary soul. I didn't need or want my mother in my life anymore.

I'd just reached the foyer and was shooting imaginary bullets at Xavier's giant portrait when I heard the snuffling. It was a faintly strangled sound, and as easily recognizable as the beating of my heart. I found Olivia standing at the large leaded windows overlooking the side lawns, her body in silhouette, her curves and curls and color mocking the severe lines of the cold glass panes. Her arms were wrapped around her core like she was holding herself together . . . and had been, I thought, for a long while. My heart dipped at the fragile, if stunning, picture she made, and I descended quickly into the sunken living room. I knew she heard me; her head tilted, but she didn't turn.

"Hey," I said softly, laying a hand on her shoulder. "Where's the One Name Wonder?"

"Outside," Olivia sniffled, and I knew it was bad when she didn't insist I call Cher by her proper name. "Waiting in the car."

"You're going to be late for high tea," I said, turning her toward me and wrapping my arms around her. All the latent maternal instincts I'd never wanted scuttled forward whenever I saw my sister with tears in her eyes. Sure, I teased her about things we both knew didn't matter, but if anything truly touched her heart, my hackles went up like a she-wolf protecting her cub.

"Are you sure we can't get together tonight?" she asked,

looking down into my eyes with her own imploring ones. We were usually the same height, but she was teetering on four-inch Manolos. "I really want to spend some time with you."

"I have a date," I said quietly, and watched her face fall. "With Ben."

She clasped her hands together with a surprised cry of delight, and her teary eyes suddenly shone with something more. "Oh, Joanna!"

"Don't make too much of it," I said, but even I was having a hard time keeping the excitement from my voice. "It's just a date."

"But it's Ben. Benjamin Traina," she sighed heavily, and crossed her hands over her heart. "I always knew you two were meant for one another. Oh, you have to tell me everything!"

"I will," I promised. "Tomorrow."

"Tonight," she insisted, squeezing me.

"Olivia . . ." I tried to make my voice firm, but her excitement was contagious. Besides, she was the only one who knew, who could know, what this meant to me. "All right. I'll stop by your place around eleven-thirty or so. We should be finished by then."

"I'll give you your gift then too, though it can't compete with Ben Traina!"

What could? I thought, pulling from her grasp. I smoothed her hair from her face and smiled. "You should go clean up. You'll be a mess for tea time."

She nodded but didn't move. "Are you okay?"

I shrugged. "I'm used to it." And then, because I knew she needed to believe it, I forced a bright smile. "Really. I'm fine."

Another nod, then she squeezed my hand before we both turned toward the door. We couldn't talk in Xavier's house. Nothing happened within these walls that he didn't somehow find out about. Yet Olivia surprised me. As we exited the foyer into a bright winter day and I turned in the opposite direction of Cher's waiting Corvette, Olivia grasped my forearm, her grip unusually strong.

"You're the only family I truly have left," she said, looking me hard in the eye. "Without you, I'd probably believe all the things they say."

I didn't have to ask who she meant. People who wrote magazine articles about her but never dreamed of conversing with her. People who looked her in the chest rather than the eye. People who forgot there was a person beneath all the beauty and gloss, and, yes, that included Xavier.

"Olivia Archer," I said, taking her hands in mine, "you *are* all the things they say, and more. You're beautiful, kind, intelligent, and strong. You're true and you're loyal, and even though you possess a baffling penchant for mud baths"—she choked out a strangled laugh at that—"you are also my sister. Beneath the high sheen of your society face lies a solid core of strength, and a spirit stronger than I'll ever possess. Touch that in your mind when you begin to forget, okay?"

She nodded, teary, and I let her go before we both started blubbering on Xavier's palatial steps. I wouldn't give him the pleasure. Still, halfway down the steps I turned. "And Olivia?"

She paused, and I raised my voice so it would carry to her, Cher, and whatever listening devices might be lying in the shrubbery. "Blood sister or not, I'll never, ever leave you."

And I wouldn't. She was all I had left now too.

5

Ben Traina forgot nothing. The Italian restaurant was the same place he'd taken me on our first date, years earlier, in a borrowed pickup truck and a suit that didn't quite fit. This time his clothes did fit—a snug pair of jeans that made me look twice, and a worn leather jacket that called for a third glance—and the vehicle was his own, though still a four-wheel drive and still souped to the nines. The restaurant had hardly changed at all.

Taverna Deliziosa was an intimate Italian-American hole-in-the-wall that lived up to its name. The dual scents of Italian sausage and fresh bread greeted us at the door, and Sinatra wafted from invisible speakers. The dining area was simply one large room with heavy velvet curtains to soften the corners, and photos of Italian sports and movie stars adorning the crumbling brick walls. A mahogany bar lined the opposite side of the room, its mirror reflecting us back on ourselves, and its edges adorned with greenery, grapes, and old Chianti bottles. Individual tables sported red-and-white checkered cloths, and were topped with atmospheric gold hurricane lamps that did little to brighten the room.

There were a fistful of couples dining tonight, and a Mormon family with an absolute brood of children had taken up the long trestle in the corner. Only one man was alone, his back to us as he sat hunched at the bar. I studied his face through the bartender's mirror but saw nothing to alarm me. A retiree probably; older, graying, and harmless looking enough, but I still maneuvered so my back was to the wall and the scope of the entire room available to me. If Ben noticed, he didn't let on.

"The waiter knows you by name," I said after a bottle of Panna and a bread basket had been placed in front of us.

Ben shrugged out of his jacket. He was wearing a short-sleeved, collared shirt, and it moved nicely with his body. I looked up, trying to focus on his words, but his lips were equally distracting. "They keep cop hours and it's on the way home."

He said nothing about it being the setting for our first date, so neither did I.

"Seems I'm a little overdressed, though," I said, motioning down. I'd worn slacks in concession to the blade sheaths fastened at my boot and lower back, but had chosen a bright coral top to stand out against the contrasting black, its neck draping nearly to my navel. A short battle with double-sided tape had ensured it concealed all the right spots, while a matching purse easily concealed my aluminum *kubotan*, only six inches long. I could have the blunt steel barrel in my hand in one quick move. I might be paranoid, but I was *fashionably* paranoid.

"That's all right," Ben said, leaning his elbows on the table. "I'm enjoying looking at you again, Jo-Jo."

I blushed, such a novel reaction for me that I was forced to look away.

We'd seen each other just once after the attack. I'd just been discharged from the hospital, and it was a long enough period for the bruises to have faded from my skin but short enough that neither of us had yet become the people we were today. I didn't talk much back then—didn't see or think or taste or feel much either—and I'd been too afraid to call him or to meet, knowing that the sweetness of the moment—being pierced beneath that concerned gaze as he remembered how I'd felt beneath him—was the same thing that would make it bitter.

I was right. I hadn't been able to clear that bitterness from my throat long enough to reach for words, and didn't know what to say even if I had. *Do you still love me? Why won't you touch me? Please stop looking at me that way.* So after moments turned into minutes, the silence prolonged, the younger Ben had run out of words as well. He looked, then walked, away. And I was left feeling more alone than ever.

"Jo?"

"Sorry." I shook my head, realizing both he and the waiter were now looking at me.

"I asked if you'd like some wine with dinner." He laughed, a little self-consciously. I must have been staring at him forever. "I don't know what you drink anymore."

"Wine would be great," I said, forcing a smile, but I had to wonder if we should really try to start this again.

Once upon a time—and it was a long time ago now—we could've married, and continued on together. Or we might have just as easily drifted; a simple slipping away of two people who'd grown up and apart. Either way it would have been a choice unmarred by tragedy.

Instead, the unnatural death of hope lingered between us, a love murdered as surely as I was meant to be. So the question was, in this world, in my current reality, was that something that could be overcome? Because I was frightened by the long dormant emotions stirring inside me. It felt like I was on the verge of something risky and steep. An emotional precipice I could either leap from into a headlong tumble or pull back from and wisely head for safety. For a full decade now I'd chosen only safety.

"You're thinking too hard, Jo," Ben said, with a smile that made my world tremble.

I leaned back casually, just reclining, I thought. Calm as an earthquake. "How can you tell?"

"Your eyes go black," he said, peering into them. "Nervous?"

"Petrified," I said, surprising us both with my honesty. He laughed, and I was startled at the way it boomed out of him at first, then settled into a rumbling chuckle. Were you supposed to forget your first lover's laugh?

"Don't worry, I don't bite," he said, leaning forward again. "I wouldn't dare."

My gaze dropped to his lips. Too bad.

I searched for a subject that wouldn't stir my hormones or remind us of the past or, God forbid, make my heart start that perilous tumble, finally settling on a part of his life that had nothing to do with me. "Do you still write?"

He nodded. "I've graduated from poetry, though. I'm into mysteries now, whodunits. Nothing published yet, but I'm still trying."

"I'm glad. Your poetry was wonderful."

He shrugged, a self-conscious rolling of the shoulders that gave away just how much it still meant. "It keeps my mind agile, anyway. I like creating the worlds, the characters, the situations."

"And solving the mysteries?" I asked, and he nodded, popping a piece of bread in his mouth. "Is that why you like being a cop?"

He stopped chewing, looking thoughtful for a moment. "I'm not sure I do like being a cop." And even he looked surprised at the admission.

"Then why do it?"

"I have to. It's a compulsion. A calling."

"An obsession?" I asked warily.

He looked at me. "Yes."

I hesitated. This was fragile territory again. "Because of what happened to me?"

He blinked, but his expression didn't change. I guess he figured if I could speak about it so openly, he could as well.

"And because I can't just live a comfortable life on the sidelines while horrible things happen to people who can't protect themselves."

I just stared at him, determined to say nothing until he answered my question.

He shrugged again, but there was a tremor, a visible fury, beneath the movement this time. "What do you want me to say, Jo? Yes, what happened to you, to us, marked me. It changed the way I viewed the world. How could it not?"

I found I couldn't meet his eye. "But how can you let it still affect you?"

Ben circled the question like a tiger, coming at me from another direction. "What about your career, then? The photographer who captures the truth but remains safely on the other side of the lens. Nobody and nothing touches you, is that right?"

I folded my arms over my chest. That wasn't right at all. My photography was good *and* relevant. Granted, Xavier's criticism about not making money at it was *almost* true, but my photos had been heralded for their clear and unflinching look at Vegas's most forgotten streets. When I snapped a photo, I leeched the neon from the scene, and what remained was even more startling for its stark simplicity. People lived on these streets. Teens were corralled into prostitution on these corners. There was a great deal more lost out there every day than in all the glittering casinos combined. I wanted people to recognize and think about that.

"We all become who we need to in order to survive," I said stiffly.

"And who have you become, Joanna? A warrior? Some superwoman bent on vengeance who needs no one and nothing?"

Strange choice of words, I thought, pursing my lips. "Criticizing?"

"Simply asking." But we both knew there was nothing simple about it.

"I was changed too, Ben," I said, taking up the offense.

"When someone holds out their hand to me I don't grab it readily. I'm always on the lookout for the fist behind their back." My eyes automatically traveled to the lone man sitting at the bar.

"Most women don't think that way."

"Yeah, and I envy those women. I even remember, vaguely, what it was to be one of them." I leaned back in my chair and blew out a long breath, aware that I sounded way too bitter to be just twenty-five. "But more than envy them, Ben, I fear for them. I especially fear for the ones who will become like me."

We used our waiter's return with the food and the wine as an excuse not to talk, but when we were alone again, Ben said, "There's no one like you, Jo."

I rammed my fork into my pasta. "Don't try and sweet-talk me now. You've pissed me off."

He smiled and I wished he wouldn't. I felt myself toeing that precipice again. *Tumble, tumble, tumble.* It made me want to push him away and run from the room, screaming. It made me want to draw him near and into my bed, sighing. I had more practice with the former, so I pushed.

"The knowledge of violence is my playmate, Ben," I said, twirling angel hair around my fork. "I bed down with it in the evening and wake with it again in the morning. That's never going to change."

"I know about violence, Jo. Seeing what I see every day on the job . . ." He shook his head, poured wine into our glasses, and took a sip, his eyes growing dark. "It's enough to make me want to head out onto the streets with you instead."

I drew back. "But that's—" *Not what I'm doing*, I wanted to say.

"Wrong?" he finished for me, mistaking my puzzlement for disagreement. "Why? How's it different from the way you scour the streets? Searching. Stalking."

"I take photos. I just look. I've never . . . touched someone," I lied. I had. Once. But to be fair, he'd touched me first.

"You think I shouldn't feel this way because of my badge." It was a statement, not a question.

His defensiveness intrigued me, even as it gave me pause. "That badge gives you access, power over other people." Maybe I was oversensitive to the power one person chose to wield over others just because he could, but this seemed pretty straightforward to me.

But Ben was already shaking his head, breaking a piece of bread apart in his hand, dipping it in the oil. "What this badge gives me is a second pair of eyes. Good thing too, because if I had to filter every foul rotted thing I see in this city through my own eyes I'd go mad. But this way it's bearable. It won't climb into me."

Then what was that look? I wanted to ask him. What was that flicker I saw skirting his gaze, adding a hard glint to his narrowed eyes?

It occurred to me then that this was just as much of a blind date as the one with Ajax. I didn't know who Ben really was. I knew the boy he used to be—the one tormented by his father, disappointed by his mother—but where had the past ten years taken him? What had he been doing? Why did he get divorced? And when did he get the tribal tattoo I'd seen branding his left shoulder when he reached for the bread?

Why, after all this time, had he asked me out?

"Has it ever, Ben?" I said, thinking his answer might tell me a little about all those things. "Gotten into you, I mean?"

He didn't reply for a while, staring into the flame of our hurricane lamp as he chose his words carefully. "There was this call last week, the third time a unit was sent to this guy's house in a month. Typical asshole wife-beater . . . except this time he'd decided to beat on their two-year-old son. So the boys show up, he greets them with open arms, throws the door open, calls them by name. 'Hey, Harry! Hey, Patrick! How ya doin'?' "

Ben shook his head in disgust, gesturing with his fork. "Invites them right in because he knows his wife isn't going to say shit. Meanwhile, the only thing holding that boy's left leg together was his unbroken flesh. The hammer was right there on the coffee table."

"Oh my God."

"Yeah," Ben said, still shaking his head. "And that prick is standing there with this shit-eating grin because we know he did it, he knows we know, and there's not a damn thing we can do about it.

"So the boy gets taken to the hospital, patched up—though everyone knows it's like putting a Band-Aid over a bullet wound—and sent home with that bitch who won't lift a hand or say a word to save him."

"Ben," I said softly, knowing he wasn't really talking about that woman, but another. "That's not fair."

He looked at me for a moment, then his expression cleared and he shook his head on a sigh. "No, maybe not. But it's not fair having to watch this man go free either, hoping next time he'll make a mistake. That there'll be a witness around who isn't too scared or young to speak up against him. And that's what really gets me. Sometimes, all I want is to be that witness."

I nodded, because I could see what he was saying, easily. What was a little bit of patty cake with some bastard's face when he'd just sent his kid to the E.R.? It wasn't the same, Ben was right about that. Child abuse and wanting a little payback weren't even in the same universe.

But it still made me take a second look at the man across from me. Where was the boy who'd seen everything in terms of black and white? When had he become comfortable with that particular shade of gray? Granted, most people never even had to entertain these sort of moral questions. His job planted him firmly in that muddled area, and who was to say I wouldn't feel the same? That I too would need, as he called it, a second pair of eyes?

Who's to say, I thought uncomfortably, my mind veering to Ajax and the way I'd gone for the jugular—literally—when defending myself against him, *that I didn't already?*

There was silence again, and when the scraping of our forks across the plates became the loudest thing in the room, I began to fear we'd reached an impasse, that this was where it would end between us—the idea of violence between us—the same as it had all those years ago.

"How's Olivia these days?"

Back to neutral territory, I thought, not knowing whether that made me want to laugh or cry. "Great," I managed, over the lump that'd grown in my throat. "She's an engineer at a space sciences laboratory. She devises innovative new ways to enhance sexual performance in a weightless environment."

"Remind me not to fly NASA."

I had to smile at that. Ben was one of the few guys who had never fallen under Olivia's spell, and believe me, he was in a definite minority. Then again, Ben Traina had only ever had eyes for me.

"She's still beautiful and flighty and trusting," I said, aware of those eyes on me now. I thought about that for a moment. "You're one of the few people who never put her down, you know that? I always loved that about you."

He looked surprised. "Why would I? She's as beautiful inside as she is out. Tough in her own way too."

"Yeah, but nobody else seems to realize that."

"Maybe it's because she doesn't let them." At my raised brow, he said, "Hey, you're the one who said we all become who we need to be in order to survive."

True. I nodded, though it made me wonder again. Who had he become?

"Anyway," he said, laughing self-consciously, like he knew what I was thinking, "I don't want to talk about Olivia tonight. Go back to what you always loved about me."

That surprised another laugh out of me. "Narcissist."

"Damn right."

I decided to risk a little. "I can't tell you everything," I said, leaning forward. "I'd need all night and we don't have time."

His lids went heavy, eyes growing soft. There was the Ben I knew. "Then tell me one thing."

I didn't even have to think. "I loved the way you never tried to change me. I loved how you never compared me with my sister. I loved your honesty."

"That's three things," he said, and linked a hand with mine. His palms were wide and smooth and warm, and the heat from them flowed up my limb, flooding my body. I could have orgasmed right there, just from his touch, and I wondered if he was feeling as light-headed as I.

"Three of my favorites," I agreed, squeezing lightly, licking my lips, tasting wine—and hope—as warmth flooded me again.

"I suppose I'll have to ask you out again to hear the rest," he murmured, tossing me a knowing look.

I toyed with my pasta, letting out a slow steadied breath. "Your books," I finally said, "how do they end? The murderer is caught? The villain punished? Justice is served?"

"That's the standard M.O. for mysteries."

"And they all live happily ever after?"

He thought about that for a moment, then nodded. "Those who are still living at the end of the book, I guess. Yeah."

Sadly, that sounded more like fantasy than mystery to me, but I didn't want to tell Ben that. I swallowed hard before glancing back up. "So. How's this story going to end?"

"The guy gets the girl, of course." And he shot me that dizzying grin. I returned it without hesitation, and just like that all thought of control dropped away. The room and all the people—single guy at the bar included—folded in upon themselves and disappeared. I bit my lip, he licked his, and we leapt together.

Three hours and two bottles of wine later we emerged from Taverna Deliziosa as though from a cocoon, sated with food and wine, but further intoxicated by long looks, meaning-filled laughter, and the touch of fingertips across flickering stretches of candlelight.

Outside, we fell on each other like ravenous wolves.

The crisp air bit into our skins but dissipated like steam upon contact with the heat streaking from Ben's body into mine. He kissed me, first pressing me against the building, the stark contrast between the cold brick behind me and his heated grip making me gasp and grind further against him. Next we were leaning against a low cinder-block wall, me straddling his straightened legs as his left hand snaked up my bare back to knot in my hair, pulling lightly. His right hand found access into my scooped blouse, and he fondled me there, echoing his caress with his tongue, mouth firm and rich on mine, tasting of un-checked lust and Italian grapes. Finally, we found our-selves reclining in the cab of his truck, his lips working my nipples through the silk of my blouse, teeth teasing, while his hands cupped me both above and below. I moaned and felt the echo slide down my body into his until it hummed through the erection pressed against my thigh.

Each time we moved I had no memory of doing so, and each time I allowed it, submitting to the desire I saw fir-ing his dark eyes, and answering the breathless demands he whispered against my flushed skin. Only the sharp look and disgruntled muttering of the man who'd been drinking alone at the bar reminded us we were still a part of the world at large . . . and necking like teens in a park-ing lot.

Ben pulled away and leaned his forehead against mine, his breath coming in short, jagged gasps. Far off, to the east of the valley, a bolt of lightning scissored across the sky, followed by a low growl of thunder. I closed my eyes as if warding away the storm and smiled into his mouth. "Move your hand one inch higher, Traina, and you're go-ing to have to arrest yourself."

His laughter was choked, hot on my cheek, and spoke

more of his passion than words ever could. It was a shock to find our passion could just start up again, like a match set to kindling, sparking thick in the throat, flaring in our loins, and burning the years that had gathered in between to ashes.

Not only that, but in the time we'd been outside I'd utterly forgotten my surroundings. I'd neglected to peer into the shadows, or look behind me, or hold onto even a tenuous awareness of my surroundings. I'd forgotten to sniff at the air for something foul or putrid, or about demonic faces leering at me in candlelight, or even that I'd been warned to survive the night.

What can I say? There was only Ben, his skin scenting the air, his touch turning the storm-ridden November evening into a humid, tropical night. Years of training melted away under the heat of his flesh. If I had an Achilles' heel, I thought, Ben was it.

"Come home with me, Jo-Jo," he whispered.

I moaned against his throat. Oh, how I wanted to. In his home, in his arms, in his bed, finishing what we'd started here. It was where I wanted to be. And where I belonged.

"I can't," I said, then repeated it to myself. I couldn't just let myself pretend the last ten years had never happened. I wouldn't lose sight of the woman I'd become. That was the woman I needed to be.

"Too soon?" he asked, then sighed—regretful, frustrated, understanding—at my answering nod. "Better than too late, I suppose."

"I'm meeting Olivia in . . ." God, was it already eleven? "Half an hour. We have some things we need to discuss."

He didn't ask what, and I didn't offer. Instead he leaned back and peered into my face, arms still linked around my waist. "And I suppose making plans with her was a way to keep you from spending the night with me?"

"Don't be arrogant," I said. "Yes."

He smiled, looking satisfied as a milk-fed cat, and lifted

a hand to graze my cheek. "Are you always so practical, Ms. Archer?"

"Hmm." I kissed his throat, my tongue a tickling trail just below his earlobe. Barely suppressing a shudder, he ran his fingertips up my spine, letting them linger and play along the lines of my bare shoulders and neck. Or I thought it was his fingertips. Pulling away, I reached up and touched cool, slim metal, brought it back in my hand and peered at it in the dim light. "What is this?"

But I knew before I'd even finished the question. The slender silver chain, a double-stranded braid, was simple and inexpensive, and had been given to me by Ben on my fifteenth birthday. But I hadn't seen it since shortly after that. I thought it'd been lost in the desert.

"You left it at my house," he said, his voice softer, more hoarse. "On that last night."

Our last night, I corrected silently as he reached out and gently plucked it from my fingertips. I bent my head and he draped it around my neck, fastening it there. Closing that circle. I let out a deep breath, felt tension I didn't even know I was carrying drain from my body just as the first raindrop fell to my skin.

I fingered the chain, already warming around my neck. "Thank you."

He bowed closer, bending to me so we were forehead-to-forehead in the thickening rain. Each other's umbrella. "Sure you won't come with me?"

I shook my head, rolling it softly along his, because I knew if I opened my mouth the answer would be yes.

"So practical," Ben whispered, dropping a kiss on my cheek. "What if, for once, you didn't worry about consequences? What if you just did what you wanted?"

I pulled away to look at him, my eyes traveling down to his lips, then back up again. "I just did."

"Do it again."

So I did. I leaned forward, took his face in my hands,

and the sky above us exploded with light. We pressed against each other, body and bone, and he lifted me so my legs were wrapped at his waist, fused at his hips, anchoring me against him. I nearly didn't make it to Olivia's at all.

6

"Come."

The word, the last Ben said to me before we parted ways, hummed through my mind as I drove to Olivia's, like a bee addicted to the pollen of the same sweet flower, refusing to settle and be silent. *Come.*

I was holding the card he'd pressed into my palm before I drove away . . . and before I returned for one last kiss and drove away again. He'd printed his home address on the back of it, with a message saying he'd leave the door open for me. Just in case. I almost put the card in my purse before deciding against it. It was very schoolgirlish of me, but I wanted it close and instead tucked it into the hollow of my back as I headed into Olivia's building.

Unlike me, Olivia lived in the center of town, buying a condo in a chic residential high-rise that came with its own valet, dry-cleaning service, and a twenty-four-hour concierge. Though it wasn't my style, I had to admit the place was stunning, and convenient for those who wished easy access to the six mile stretch of neon playground a mere block away. Gleaming plate-glass windows bowed high into the sky, reflecting the polished wood interior in its shimmering sheets. Discreet lighting dotted the complex's foyer in artful little niches, and the design was duplicated in Olivia's apartment nine floors above.

I stepped from the elevator and was poised to knock when the door flew open to reveal my sister, clad in bright coral sweats, an even brighter smile lighting her expectant face. There were some things only a sister could understand. A giggle escaped me, surprising us both, and that was all the encouragement she needed. She squealed, her high-pitched voice shattering the sound barrier, and wheeled me inside before the dogs came running.

"You look fabulous, brilliant, stunning!" she rattled in quick succession, before pressing a finger to my swollen lips. "And you've been kissing! Tell me, tell me, tell me!"

"Can I get a drink first?"

"Martinis are already prepped," she said, and disappeared with a skip into the adjoining kitchen. "I'll bring them to the living room."

I grinned at this sign of her excitement and headed into the core of the apartment.

The kitchen, where Olivia could be heard happily singing to herself, lay to the left. The bedroom was tucked around a slip of an alcove off to the right. I crossed the penthouse foyer, stepped down into the sunken Italian-marbled living room, and found myself facing a sheer wall of glass revealing the un-real estate of the Las Vegas Strip. It was a block so densely lit it could be seen from the stars. Tossing my coat over an overstuffed armchair, I positioned myself in front of the window to wait.

I felt framed, a statue displayed on a very high shelf, out of reach, and almost eye level with storm clouds so thick they reflected the city's lights back on itself. Strange. The effect was one of condensed power, like electricity boxed between concrete and cloud, the light in between magnified to manic proportion. As the storm's muffled rumble signaled its approach from the west, I turned my back on the wild city and relaxed in the bright and feminine luxury of Olivia's home.

Olivia—again, unlike me—had surrounded herself with things. Beautiful, numerous things. There was a collection of fine crystal on a floor-to-ceiling sweep of built-in shelves. She had a preference for Scandinavian designs; the clean lines of Orrefors mixing with the bright, whimsical creations of Kosta Boda. Next to that was a marble fireplace, unlit and unused except as a holding place for some of the trees and plants that seemed to sprout from nearly every corner and niche in the room. I rubbed the leaf of a wildly trailing spider plant, wondering how she did it. The things absolutely thrived under her care.

Instead of a sofa, she'd placed an oversized daybed with high scrolled sides in the middle of the room, piling it high with bright chenille pillows. A large tray inlaid with mother-of-pearl and onyx sat in the middle of the bed and was used in place of a coffee table. Candles burned everywhere— colored ones, scented ones, tea lights and tapers—and a television unit, rarely used, was tucked inconspicuously off to the side.

Despite this colliding mishmash of color and items, Olivia's home managed to feel airy and alive. She even had a cat skulking around here somewhere, full of attitude and ever waiting to trip a person up.

I lifted a copy of the latest computer journal from the tray, and noted it was already thumbed through, dog-eared, and marked in places. The first time our father—*her* father—had caught Olivia reading a scientific journal, we were all clustered around the breakfast table, pretending to be a normal, well-adjusted family. I'd known for a while she'd been reading *Popular Science* and *Computers Today*, and was teasing her about it, calling her a technogeek and, on my more caustic days, Bill Gates's wet dream.

"What the hell do you think you're doing?" Xavier had said, staring from her to the magazine that had fallen from her hand.

Startled by his sudden appearance, she nonetheless recovered, and lifted the periodical between two well-manicured fingers to use as a lipstick blotter. Watching from over the rim of my coffee cup, I'd been surprised to see that instead of angering Xavier, this seemed to pacify him. Olivia avoided looking at me for the rest of the morning. And I never teased her about her reading habits again.

I tossed the magazine back down and nestled myself among pillows the color of buttercream and scotch. There, I removed my weapons, placing my purse with the *kubotan* on the tray in front of me, along with the fixed-blade at my back. I left the short blade where it was; sheathed and secured in my boot. I felt too naked if bereft of all my weapons.

Olivia, carrying two oversized martinis, raised a brow at the knife settled between her vanilla candles and knickknacks, but there was no widening eyes or surprise. She was as used to my weapons as I was to her scholarly journals.

"Vodka martini, straight up, two olives stuffed with Roquefort," she said, winking. "Just in case you haven't already had an orgasm today."

"Be still my heart," I said, taking one of the glasses. She settled across from me and folded her legs beneath her.

"Happy Birthday!" she said, raising her drink in a toast. "Here's to you always being older than me!"

"Thanks. I think."

"And," she said slyly, "here's to Ben Traina bringing your hormones back into whack."

I lowered my glass. "My hormones weren't out of whack."

"Yes, they were."

"No, they weren't."

"Yes, they were."

I scowled. She smiled sweetly. "So, is he everything you remember? Different? The same?"

How could I tell her? What words could explain how the

edges of the boy had been whittled down into such a finely sculpted man? Sure, there were some sharp edges too—and I was determined to be careful of them—but how to tell her about the new passion ignited between us? That he made Michelangelo's *David* look practically wilted? There was just no comparison between my girlish feelings for Ben and the thoughts I entertained now. Perhaps Olivia was right and he *had* brought my hormones back into whack.

"He's more, Olivia. So much more." And I left it at that.

Despite this inability to articulate my thoughts, Olivia was satisfied. Her eyes went dreamy and she sighed into the bowl of her martini. Reaching down, she absentmindedly stroked the cat that had appeared from nowhere—what was its name again?—and said, "You're finally going to get laid."

I choked on my cheesy olive. "Excuse me, but how do you know I haven't been?"

"Because you're always too tense," she said, shaking her arms. I think she was illustrating how to relax. "You treat sex like a combat sport, like that 'dog maga' stuff you practice."

"It's 'Krav Maga,'" I bristled, "and I do not."

"You do," she insisted. "You treat it like it's a battle to be won. You wear your femininity like a badge, and you're daring someone to make you flash it."

"That's ridiculous," I said, pretending not to wonder at that. "Besides, none of my lovers have ever complained."

"Because they're probably afraid your viselike vagina would squeeze off their manhood. Like those credit card machines that suck up the card and won't give it back." And she laughed gaily, waving off my outraged cry. "Besides, we're not talking about lovers, we're talking about *love*, and you haven't allowed yourself to go there since Ben."

My mouth snapped shut. True. Even I'd thought those emotions had dried up like a shallow lake bed beneath the desert sun.

"Like you're an expert," I muttered.

"Darling, *I* fall in love on a daily basis," she said, waving a hand around her. "I love that tree and this drink and Luna here." Ah, that was the name of the beast twining about my legs. I reached down and scratched Luna behind her ears. Her throat rumbled. Outside, lightning flashed. "I love you," Olivia continued, "and I love Ben for loving you too."

I must have looked surprised at that. My hand stilled on Luna's back.

"You know he does," she said.

"Maybe he does," I nodded cautiously, stroking the cat again, "and maybe I know it, but how do you?"

Olivia leaned forward. "Because how could anyone know the real Joanna Archer and not love her?"

I smiled at her sincerity but looked away. It wasn't that the sentiment wasn't appreciated, but her rhetorical question brought to mind that afternoon's confrontation with Xavier.

Olivia, sensing that, quickly changed the subject. "Don't you want to open your present?"

I nodded, but didn't reach for the package in the corner of the coffee tray. "I need to ask your help with something first."

"Want me to take Ben for a little ride? Break him in for you?"

"I think I can handle that on my own," I replied dryly.

"Too bad," she said, demurely sipping her martini.

"I want to find out who my real father is," I said. "I think Xavier knows, but he's keeping it from me."

"Why would he?"

"Knowing him, it's probably just a power trip, something he can use to keep me under his thumb." I frowned and tapped my finger against my glass. "But I was thinking about it this afternoon. What if he knows where the guy lives? What if Zoe mentioned it to him at some point?"

"What if," Olivia finished for me, "she returned to this man when she left Xavier?"

I smiled at her use of his name. "So you'll help me?"

She looked at me like I had the mental capacity of a two-year-old, which was unsettling. "I've already begun." She rose and jerked her head, indicating I should follow. I did, leaving my present, my martini, and Luna on the couch behind me.

Mother Nature was apparently determined to make the city of light look like a dimly flickering bulb. The glass wall extending through the bedroom normally offered up a 180-degree view of the valley's surrounding mountain ranges. Tonight, though, the oddly low cloud cover kept us from seeing even two feet beyond the glass. Lightning slashed at the sky, and as thunder rumbled directly overhead, I shuddered, thankful we were safely inside.

I turned my attention to the computer console, and sure enough, the machine was already on, bathing the corner of the room in an unflattering greenish hue. Circling to the other side, I saw the screen dancing with lipstick tubes and bottles of fingernail polish. I'd have wondered where Olivia found such a thing, but knew she'd probably designed it herself. Then I watched as she positioned herself in front of the monitor, placed acrylic against the ergonomic keyboard, and became the Olivia Archer most people never imagined.

Her fingers flew, following paths that could as easily access data from government sites as blow through a game of FreeCell. She'd gotten her first fake ID this way, and as a teen I'd had her pull up my psych evaluations as well.

Joanna Archer is suffering severe physical and mental trauma due to the attack and subsequent sexual assault she endured six months ago. Well, duh.

Olivia hummed absently, her eyes fixed on the screen, brows pulled down despite repeated botox injections, and glossed mouth pursed in pretty concentration.

She had discovered computers around the same time I had escaped into Krav Maga. Our mother had left no indication that she would ever be returning, and our father had so thoroughly removed himself that neither of us even thought of turning to him, and I was emotionally unavailable, which left Olivia to fight her demons alone.

I've always felt guilty at how I shut her out in those early days, but this—a skill few possessed—was the good that had come from it, as strange and unexpected as a lotus blooming in a trash heap. She'd developed an identity outside of her physical body, one completely at odds with the way others thought of her. She may have had a body manufactured in Sin City, but she had a mind to rival the finest graduates of MIT.

In short, she was an unnaturally talented, self-taught computer genius.

With an underground website catering to hackers and their faceless clients, her business generated a far greater income than her generous monthly allowance from Xavier. There were bulletin boards on everything from the technology needed to take care of outstanding parking tickets to assistance establishing offshore bank accounts, and help in funneling untraceable money into those accounts. Her screen name? The Archer, of course.

Because Xavier had discouraged Olivia's interest in anything beyond basic cosmetic application, she'd developed the habit of working at night, an M.O. that served her exceedingly well. To the outside world it appeared she slept all morning, spent her days shopping or lunching with the ladies, and partied all night. But most of the time she could be found here, and this, I'd realized, was Olivia's warrior side. The part of her that flipped the bird at Xavier and everyone else.

"See," she was saying, pointing at a graphic flashing at the top right corner of the screen, "there are multiple levels to break through in order to access your birth records. Shouldn't take more than an hour. We'll see if Mom covered her tracks as well as she thinks she has."

I nodded like I understood, but was distracted by the tool bar at the bottom of the screen. Another screen was currently in use. "What's that?"

Her gaze followed my own, and I thought I saw her body jolt. The screen had my name on it. Mine and another.

"Nothing." A quick dance of fingers and it vanished.

"Olivia," I said, slowly enunciating each syllable of her name. "What was that? You're not trying to find that . . . that child, are you?"

"No!" she said, too fast, and crossed her arms. It was more a protective move than a defiant one. I stared at her, hard. Olivia might be queen of the computer, but I knew body language.

"Don't play affronted bimbo with me." I jabbed a finger at the screen. "What're you up to?"

Her cell phone rang just then, the theme from *Pretty in Pink* saving her from reply. I raised one brow, indicating we'd pick this conversation up later. Some things, and some people, were best kept in the past. She quickly turned her back to me and flipped the phone open. "Hello?"

I turned my attention back to the screen, letting thoughts of unwanted children fade from my mind. Slowly, the computer was working through the records at Sunrise Hospital. I studied it, toying absently with the chain at my neck as I watched the dates and files flash in front of my eyes, and wondered how Zoe had fooled everybody so thoroughly about my parentage for so long? And why?

Had she cheated on Xavier, and didn't want to risk losing him, or his money? But then, why just up and leave sixteen years later? And why, at least, had she never told me? She knew there was no love lost between he and I.

"But it's almost midnight," I heard Olivia say in her best bubblehead voice. This was followed by a sigh that said the person on the phone already knew this and didn't care. "Look, it's just not a good time, Butch."

She rolled her eyes when she saw my expression, and I shook my head. Butch? She was dating someone named Butch? "My sister's over and we're just having—"

I heard the timbre of a masculine voice arguing his point, but the boom of thunder drowned out the words. I picked up

Luna, whose tail had gone bottle-brushed at the accompanying flash of light, and tried to stroke her fur back down into something resembling feline. Outside, rain began to pour in sheets over the glass walls.

"Yes, I know it's raining," Olivia was saying. "No, you can't stay until the storm passes. You can pick up your things, but then you have to go. 'Bye."

She threw the phone across the room and it landed on a pink sea of down comforter and frilly pillows. Then she stalked over to her closet and pulled out handcuffs. And a whip. I stared, openmouthed.

"Don't ask," she muttered, adding a studded dildo to the loot. "I thought it would be fun. That was before the condom broke. I panicked at the thought of wading around in his gene pool, you'll see, and threw him out without giving back his toys. He's come to collect."

"Must have found a new playmate." She gave me a sharp look, and I grinned. "No pun intended."

"Fine with me. He was too obsessive for my tastes anyway. He wanted to lick me in the weirdest places. And he could spend hours smelling me. Not to mention he had more hair than a woolly mammoth."

"Aren't those extinct?"

"So we believed," she said, and threw some sort of belt—I didn't want to know what it looped around—into a pile that was growing at an alarming rate.

"Don't worry," I said, picking up a tube of lipstick with a penis-shaped wand. "If he gets overly amorous, I've got your back."

"Not necessary," she said, yanking the tube from my hands. I picked up Luna instead. "He looks like a Hell's Angel, but he's relatively harmless."

I saw what she meant when she opened her door to a six and a half foot ape dressed entirely in leather a minute later. I actually thought he looked rather like a large bulldog, complete with sunken eyes and hanging jowls, and she was right—he was hairy. I could see where Olivia might balk at banging chromosomes with a physiological mutant.

"Jo, this is Butch."

"Yes, it is," I muttered, giving the giant a hesitant nod.

Luna apparently experienced a similar reaction. She took one look at Butch and sprung from my arms like an Olympic platform diver. "Ouch, shit!"

The bundle of fur wheeled across the marble floor, scrambling for purchase with a click-clack of sharpened nails, and disappeared into the bedroom. As I watched, the stinging marks on my arm became angry pink ribbons, then filled with bright red blood, promising scarring.

"Shit," I said again.

"Are you all right?" Olivia rushed over, leaving Butch in the foyer.

"He never did like me," Butch mumbled, shutting the door behind him.

"She," Olivia corrected as Butch joined us in the living room. "She never liked you. And maybe she would have if you hadn't stepped on her tail. Twice."

Butch just shrugged. Big bad bulldog.

"You two stay here," she said, catching my eye. That meant she didn't want him following her into the bedroom. "I'll just get your things and find Jo something to wash off with."

She disappeared, leaving me with Leather Man. He was practically wearing the whole cow—when he started moving toward me I almost expected him to moo.

"Want me to take a look?" He held out his hand. I hesitated, without reason, though I generally didn't need one. I didn't know Butch, but there was some sort of unease or smothered energy that I didn't like. The drop-point knife was still sitting on the coffee table, close enough to see, but far enough away to be as useful as a butter knife. Still, I had the folded blade in my boot, and was confident enough to hold out my arm for his inspection, testing us both. If there was something off about

Butch, I didn't want him around Olivia, and better I find out about it than she.

He took my wrist gently, gazing at the scratch almost clinically, a concerned enough expression on his fleshy face. I relaxed a fraction. Then he raised my arm and inhaled deeply of the wound, nostrils flaring. That's when I saw.

The pads of his fingertips were curiously smooth, almost shiny with luminescence, and unlined. Without prints. I forced my arm not to tense beneath his touch and quickly returned my eyes to his face.

The lightning flashed outside, firing the room and slashing across his features to illuminate chiseled bone and hollow eyes; a skeleton's bony sneer with teeth shaped like daggers. His hold tightened a fraction, just the fingertips, those too-smooth pads, but it was enough to make me still and wait for an opening to reclaim my arm.

As thunder rolled across the sky, Butch smiled lopsidedly. "Do you know what time it is?"

I didn't look at my watch. "Yeah. It's time for you to let go of my hand."

His fingers tightened over mine, and given one moment more I'd have broken them, but he dropped my arm suddenly and walked away. Tensed, braced for a fight, this unbalanced me. He just drifted away like he'd never sniffed at my skin in an intimate way or held a look of naked hunger in those hollow eyes. Retrieving my long blade from the coffee table, I tucked it in the waistband of my pants, then grabbed the *kubotan* from my purse, concealing it in my pocket. And I followed him into her bedroom.

"I think that's everything," Olivia was saying. Her back to us both, she was bent over a mound of stilettos and boots emptied from her shoe closet. She continued talking, her voice a breathy staccato thrumming in the air, but I don't think either Butch or I heard a word. There was something else going on, like the dark undercurrent stirring beneath a placid lake just before the monster struck. I inched toward Olivia, my back to the wall. Butch, strangely enough, kept his gaze on the bedside clock. It was one minute to midnight.

"Olivia," I said in my quietest, deadliest voice. "Get behind me."

Two pairs of eyes looked at me, but only one seemed surprised. Butch merely looked amused. I moved to my sister's side.

"How about that. Ajax was right." He shook his head wonderingly. "It was you all along. Hidden in plain sight. Xavier's daughter, no less."

Whatever the hell that meant. "I'm not Xavier's daughter."

He laughed. "Then whoever hid you knew what they were doing."

"Excuse me? What's going on here? Am I missing something?"

"I thought it was her," Butch said, jerking his head at Olivia. "It was the closest I could come to scenting you, but once I was in her . . ." He shook his head in a sorrowful gesture. "I thought I was going anosmic."

Then he slid a smoothly curving scimitar from behind the nape of his neck. I had to give it to these guys—whoever they were, they had unique weapons.

"Whoa!" Olivia's breath escaped her in a whoosh. I don't think I was breathing at all. "I've heard of unsafe sex, but this is ridiculous!"

"It was you we were after," he said, ignoring her. "You I detected on your sister's skin, your signature scent all along. But what I can't understand," he continued, looking at the bedside clock, tapping the flat edge of the blade against his palm like he was waiting, "is how you recognized me. You don't fully come into your sixth sense for another . . . thirty seconds."

Midnight. Like that homeless freak had said. *Make sure you survive.*

"Signature scent?" I mimicked, my eyes also on the clock. "Kinda girly, don't you think?"

"Well, I'm a right softie at heart." He flashed those dagger teeth. "Tell me, Joanna, been smelling things lately? Interesting things? Foul things on the wind?"

I swallowed hard. "What, Ajax tell you that too?"

"Common knowledge. You're turning twenty-five, right? That's when the metamorphosis begins."

"Excuse me," Olivia said, "but do you two know each other?"

Butch smiled and took a step forward. "Not as well as we're about to."

"That's enough, Butch. One more step and this stiletto's going up your ass." We all looked down at Olivia's hand. I frowned, recognizing the ebony pump as one of her favorites. The same thought must have occurred to her. She dropped the shoe and picked up another. "*This* stiletto's going up your ass."

I sighed. Bless her for trying.

Butch returned his eyes to me. "Get ready, innocent. Your first real breath will also be your last."

I only had a vague notion of what he was talking about, based on snippets from a very unreal last twenty-four hours, but I knew a real threat when I heard one.

Ten, nine, eight . . . the seconds inched by, midnight looming. Outside, thunder cracked like a whip overhead, and the sheet of pattering rain deteriorated into a full-force onslaught of sleet and hail. Wind whistled, rattling at the walls, and the building began to shake in palsied tremors. Some of Olivia's knickknacks tinkled, others shattered, and then the core of the building began to rock on its braces. An explosion sounded as we crossed into midnight.

"Olivia, get back!" I had to yell as the tempest blew through the bedroom. It was like being at the top of a tornado's funnel, poised to be sucked inside. Then the glass wall began to splinter, a sound like fingernails raking a chalkboard, sending spasms up my spine. I resisted the impulse to cover my ears, and went for the blade at my back instead. Butch tensed and raised his scimitar. A bolt of lightning arrowed the sky as Olivia screamed behind me, and there was a flicker of movement from the corner of my eye.

And then I saw nothing.

Molten licorice, smoking iron, and bright flames filled my mouth. I was singed, burning from the inside out, and my teeth felt like they were being collectively yanked from my jaw. I knew somewhere in my mind I'd been hit, and my fallen knife now lay uselessly on the floor, but that knowledge was the only lingering connection between brain and body. The synapses controlling movement had been severed by the bolt, much like how the muscles continue to twitch in a decapitated chicken's body. I couldn't tell if I was still standing or had fallen. In the whiplash of that storm, I totally lost myself.

Once, in my early teens, I'd ventured into the high desert during a flash flood, driven by a youthful sense of adventure and an even greater sense of invulnerability. A stray dog had been my unlikely companion that night, and as it galloped unevenly across the rocky terrain, I saw it struck by lightning. Its golden fur disintegrated instantly into ash, and smoke streamed from its body like a signal for help. When I reached the fallen animal's side, its eyes were wide saucers, unblinking, and the heat emanating from that blistering body warded me off. This was how I felt now; sightless, terrified, and smoldering. And just before all my senses were lost, I felt an acute pain sear through my left shoulder.

Then there was nothing. No pain, no light, not even darkness. I couldn't tell if my eyes were open or closed, and my body felt like I was suspended in water; numb, floating, and impervious from all sides. I knew I was in trouble, if not already dead, but I was unable to react, and had no idea how long I remained in this state.

It felt like forever.

It felt like a nanosecond.

Then the lingering tendrils of Olivia's scream were back in my head, and a smell so putrid it clogged every cell of my body had me lifting my hand to my mouth to keep from vomiting. Realizing what I was doing, amazed that I *could* move, I lowered my hand again and, still sightless, located the edge of my boot. I flipped open the folded blade and threw it into the heart of that rotting stench.

The air exploded, and crashed over me in waves, like maggot-ridden garbage spilling from a bag, and the scream that accompanied it was inhuman. I fell to my knees, indescribably weak, and allowed my head to fall into my hands.

When I lifted it again, the world had miraculously righted itself and the bedroom was eerily silent. The strange indoor storm had abated. The glass wall was whole and unmarked.

And there was a dead man on the floor in front of me.

7

"Jo? Are you okay?"

I lifted my head. Olivia was huddled in a corner, cradling Luna, the cat's head tucked protectively beneath her arm. I nodded, and turned back to where Butch lay sprawled at my feet like a giant toad.

"What happened?" My voice rasped like it'd been cut to ribbons by a tiny razor.

"Y-You did what you had to do, Jo," Olivia said, misinterpreting my question. "He came at you with that big knife and I thought for sure he'd kill you. But you didn't back up. You didn't run. You didn't even waver. I couldn't believe it."

I glanced at the clock next to her and did a double take. It was 12:01. I couldn't believe it either. Only a minute had passed since the onset of that tempest? "What about the storm?"

Olivia looked momentarily confused, and glanced uncertainly from me to the window, where a patter of raindrops stroked the glass. "It stopped, I guess. I hadn't noticed."

Hadn't noticed? Hadn't noticed an electrical bolt had damn near sliced her sister in two? Hadn't smelled my flesh burning?

"Help me up." I held up my hand and she reached for it, but Luna whirled in her arms, hissed, and swiped at me.

"Fuck you," I said to the feline, and pushed myself to my feet. I was a bit wobbly, but alive.

"That's no way to talk to someone who just helped save your life!" Olivia scolded before burying her face in Luna's furry nape. "Is it, my precious pookie?" Her voice came out muffled. "My pookster? You love Auntie Jo so much you risked one of your nine lives to save her."

"What do you mean?"

Olivia didn't answer at first. Then she turned her face toward mine, cradling the cat to her cheek. "Look at his eyes."

My legs were shaky, but they held as I crossed to Butch's body. I nudged him with the toe of my boot, and he rolled like a sausage to his back. He would have been staring sightlessly at the ceiling . . . if there hadn't been four long scores across each eye. The lids had been shredded with scalpel-like accuracy, slim incisions but deep, lacerating each eyeball.

"I think I'm going to be sick."

Olivia joined me next to the body. "You'd be dead if Luna hadn't leapt when she did."

But why would a cat attack a human? A man, no less, whom it was obviously afraid of? I turned to ask Olivia this just in time to see her eyes go wide with shock. The heroic feline was unceremoniously dumped on the bed. "Jo! You're injured!"

I looked down and saw the blood seeping through the left shoulder of my blouse. Part of me was surprised I hadn't felt the injury before. Another part knew it was a bad sign I hadn't. "It's okay," I told her, knowing it wasn't. "It doesn't hurt."

"Lie down. Let me get something to staunch the wound, and we'll call an ambulance."

I was in no shape to argue. Perhaps it was only psycho-somatic, but I *was* feeling a bit dizzy all of a sudden. Luna hissed as I plopped down among the pillows, then leapt from the bed, over the corpse, and streaked away. I closed my eyes.

I must have drifted off because when I came to again Olivia was seated next to me, pressing a clean towel to my wound. I winced as fresh pain coursed through me, and was about to tell her she shouldn't have used the good towels when the first tear fell.

"Hey," I said, reaching up to wipe it away. "Hey, it's okay. I'm going to be fine."

"I know," she said. Her face crumpled anyway. "I just keep seeing that monster—he really looked like a monster!—and he wouldn't stop staring at you." She shook her head side to side, as if to dislodge the memory. "I thought for sure I was going to lose you. Again."

I tried to make my smile reassuring. "Well, you didn't lose me, and you won't ever lose me. It's just a little scratch. See? The bleeding has already stopped."

She sniffled. "I guess."

We sat in silence, Olivia's cell phone clasped on her lap, though she made no move to open it. Chaos would resume as soon as that call was made, and even though it was a false sense of normalcy surrounding us now—there *was* a dead man on the bedroom floor—I think we both felt once we made that call, our lives would never be the same.

"Gawd," Olivia sniffled, and lifted the edge of the towel to see if the bleeding had stopped. "I just have the worst luck with guys."

We looked at each other and for a moment neither of us spoke. Then we began to laugh, that crazed, hysterical laughter you see in people who've drank too much, or who've forgotten their lines on their wedding day. The laughter tore at my shoulder, probably starting the bleeding again, but it felt so good, much more acute than the pain, and I didn't want to stop. Our bodies shook with it and tears rolled unheeded down our faces.

We were both gasping, dizzy, and breathless, when I felt

Olivia jerk and inhale sharply. Opening my teary eyes, I too froze. There was a beefy arm across her throat, and her fingers clawed at it, her eyes wide and instantly somber. Butch wasn't exactly choking her, but he wasn't being gentle either. Hauling her to her feet, he squared himself behind her body in a position that made it impossible for Olivia to defend or escape the hold, even if she knew how.

"You're dead," I said dumbly, though all evidence pointed to the contrary. I'd killed him. Yet there he stood, blood staining his clothing out of a wound that no longer existed. How could that be? In fact, the only ill effect he still showed was the scoring about his eyes and a blind and total reliance on his other senses. Especially, I noted, his sense of smell.

"Not quite," he said. "Not yet."

The words *fast healer* burst through my brain, images of a wrist popping back into place on a dusty desert road, a crumpled body coming back to life. I knew then it *was* possible. Blindly, Butch backed away from me, dragging Olivia with him, his nostrils flaring widely with every breath. He was moving closer and closer to the blade I'd dropped. I had to do something quickly before it was too late to do anything at all.

"Let her go," I said, pitching my voice to the right of the bed before easing myself up and to the left. "Y-You want me, fine. But leave her out of this." My arm throbbed and the bedroom wavered as I stood, but I forced myself steady. I didn't know how long I could stand, but passing out wasn't an option. I'd save Olivia or I'd die trying.

"How'd you do that?" Butch asked, head tilted into the middle of the room.

"Do what?"

"Kill me. You're supposed to be immobile during metamorphosis. How'd you move?"

Like I knew? Instead of answering, I advanced.

"One more step and you'll watch your sister die." He'd stilled and was focused on me despite his blindness. For emphasis, he tightened his grip. Olivia's eyes bulged. "Now step back."

Death rode his brow. I stepped back. *Think, Joanna. Think!*

Okay, so Butch's sight was gone, but his other senses were flawlessly acute. It made me wonder at this transformation he'd talked about. It obviously meant something to him. He'd waited until then to try and kill me, and in that time all my senses had been shut down. But now that they were back, what about that "sixth sense" he'd spoken of? Was that what he was using to track me now?

As much as I hated to take my eyes from Butch and Olivia, I had to close them in order to transfer focus to my other senses. I did, and the difference was immediately discernable. Colors flashed behind my eyelids, accompanying scent and sound. By simply casting my mind in the direction of the objects I last remembered seeing, I could smell them.

On myself I smelled blood, Ben, and the faint scent of the soap I showered with. I turned to the dresser beside me where a bevy of beauty products rested—mint, eucalyptus, wax, powder, and a perfume that reminded me unerringly of Olivia. Turning my attention to her, I inhaled deeply, and caught lingering tendrils of that scent, as well as something sharp, which I instinctively identified as fear.

As for Butch, I didn't dare cast my mind in his direction. His scent was already overwhelming me, like being locked in a room with a pustulant corpse. I was already more sensitized to him than anything else in the room.

Except the blade on the floor between us.

My eyes flew open in time to see Butch's head jerk, then jerk again when I inhaled sharply. We scented it at the same time, or scented each other scenting it. He was closer than I. I lunged, he snarled, and we reached it at the same time.

I came up with the tip burrowed beneath my chin, Butch's laughter hot in my face. Olivia's squeal was choked off in a warning tug. "Don't fucking move. You don't think

I *know* what you're doing? What you're thinking?" He flicked the blade, a swift motion that made me wince in anticipation, but no pain came. Yet. My necklace, however, dropped soundlessly to the carpet. My jaw clenched reflexively, but otherwise I didn't move. Butch laughed humorlessly. "I can detect your thoughts before you even form them. Remember, I've been at it longer, Archer, and I've never been an innocent."

That I could believe.

"Just tell me what you want," I said, fighting to keep my voice even. "Anything you want. Me for her? Give the word and I'll do it."

"Oh, now you're making deals, are you? Isn't that noble, sacrificing everything for your sister. But you've done that before, haven't you, Jo?" He grinned that corrosive smile. "Time to do it again."

"No!" Olivia struggled against his iron grip. He just held on until she'd worn herself out. If it had been me, I could have bent forward until his weight was on my back, flipping him, or swept a leg, or scraped his shin on the way to breaking bones in his foot. But it wasn't me. It was my sweet, harmless, innocent sister, and she could only stand there and weep. And choke.

"Take out the weapon in your left pocket, and throw it out the door."

I didn't wonder how he knew about the hidden *kubotan*. Even I could smell the cold, pressed aluminum. I did, tossing it through the doorway leading to the living room.

"Now step back . . . Step back," he repeated, when I didn't move. "I can smell the defiance on you, Joanna, don't you know that? Do you really think you can do something to change what's happening here? You think you can save Olivia now like you saved her before?"

I stepped back, but instead of relaxing Butch, this seemed to provoke him. Olivia struggled, her face going red, but his grip was a crowbar wrapped around a feather. If he'd shoved that knife through my jaw, I'd have felt less horror.

"No!" My fists balled impotently at my side and fear slicked my insides and rose like a tide of tar, oiling the air around me. I knew he could smell it on me. Desperation made my words earnest. "You said you'd trade me for her! Me for her!"

"Now why would I want to trade you for her?" he asked, loosening his grip. Olivia stilled. Butch raised the blade. "When I can have you both?"

With that he began to cut.

"Joanna?" Olivia's voice was childlike, small. She looked at me as if seeing me for the first time, wide eyes filled with childlike confusion. I knew, though, that she was really viewing me through a veil of white-hot pain. I remembered how the world looked when buried beneath your own blood. Tears burned in my eyes for Olivia's sake and a strangled cry escaped my throat.

Butch began to laugh. Laughing and cutting, precise despite his blindness. Beyond the brutality, there was just something horrifying about seeing that pure beauty marked. I'd never seen Olivia injured before and it was like seeing wings torn from a butterfly, like watching a temple being defiled. It broke something reverent in my heart, and her anguished cries filled my own mouth.

"Stop! Stop!"

Butch held out the dripping blade. "Stop? Yes, well . . . why not? She's nothing to me, after all. Just a pawn, really. Just a way to get to you. Thank you, Olivia. For a job well done."

The tips of his filed teeth sparked in a telling grin. I saw it, and still there was nothing I could do. Butch opened his stance, turned his shoulders, and propelled Olivia into the arching wall of glass. I heard the sick thud of her body hitting, the hollow crack of the pane, and in what seemed like slow motion, the glass splintered, then shattered. It collapsed, and Olivia fell with it.

Her scream razored through the night, lingering after her body had fallen. An answering cry burst from my throat as I rushed the window, clambering gracelessly over the wide bed and bounding across the other side. I clawed at the jagged glass, bloodying my hands and forearms, feeling nothing.

I couldn't see her. She was already lost in the void of night; dropping like the rain, falling like a star, setting like a crimson sun.

Staring out into that cold black void, I had a momentary urge to follow. One step, a mere five inches, and it would all be over. I'd never have to move or fight or weep again. I wouldn't have the unending chore of breathing anymore, and the screams pinballing in my skull would be silenced once and for all.

I heard my name; a taunting, singsong repetition, languorously drawing out the syllables. All I could think, all I could feel, was that I'd been wrong. Wrong to believe I'd taken every precaution to protect myself. Wrong in believing nothing else could be taken from me, that I had nothing to lose. There was one last thing that I had cared about in this world. My sister.

And now she too was gone.

"Jo-ahn-naa . . ."

Sucking in a deep, steadying breath, I lowered my head like a bull readying for the charge, and I did take that first, that final, step forward.

But not before I had turned around.

I sprang forward, body low, and used my weight to take his legs from under him. There were no thoughts of weapons as I wrapped my arms around his knees. No care of injury as his bulk collapsed and toppled forward. I swiveled, fighting for his back, but he was quicker than he looked, even blind. Before he could use his fists or weight against me, I was out of reach, regrouping, and readying for a second assault.

"What are you doing?" He sounded genuinely surprised. "You don't have a weapon."

"Yeah. I do."

"No. I'd be able to smell it."

Both of our nostrils flared, and we located the weapons; his scimitar that had skittered beneath the bed when I killed him the first time, my folding knife knocked from his grasp when I'd lunged, and that now lay outside the door.

"I *am* the weapon, you asshole." And I hissed in his direction, my breath filled with the same black intent as my heart. For the first time Butch looked scared.

My movements weren't as smooth as normal, my strikes less practiced. I swung out with more adrenaline than skill, but I got a few blows in, took a few too, before pulling back and forcing myself to think. I imagined Butch's body as a grid. I overlaid it in strike zones, trying to see him as an opponent and not only the man who had just murdered my sister.

"Over here." I circled him from behind. "What are you, blind?"

"I'm going to kill you." He swiveled side to side, trying to locate me with his four remaining senses. Which gave me an idea. I backed away, edging toward my sister's dresser until I found what I needed there. "Hear me? I'm going to fucking kill you!"

"No. You're not." I located Olivia's perfume bottle by touch and picked it up. "But you're going to die trying."

Spritzing the fragrance into the air, I pumped until the room smelled like the inside of a sweet powdery seed. Then I sprayed the remainder on myself. The perfume sent Butch's olfactory senses into overdrive. He stumbled about in the center of the room, oddly more at a loss with his lack of scent than he'd been with his loss of vision. Feeling my lip curl, I thought of the three senses he had left to work with— touch, taste, sound—and decided to fuck with them all.

Pushing the alarm on Olivia's digital clock, I wrenched the knob as high as it would go. Nirvana's "Come as You Are" filled the room. Startled confusion was soon replaced by helpless anger. Butch let out an outraged howl and began to totter unsteadily in my direction. I threw the empty perfume bottle into the opposite corner where it shattered against the wall. He whirled in that direction, his chest moving shallowly with his breath. Lowering myself to the floor, I rolled under the bed and came up on the opposite side with the scimitar clutched firmly in my fists.

Two senses left.

My anger was cold now, narrowing my resolve into an icy arrow poised for release. I was the hunter; like the big cats crouched in the waving grasses of Africa, the blood-thirsty eagle swooping to rip the flesh from its earthbound prey.

And there was nothing glorious or heroic in the way I toyed with him. I'd trained my body and mind in combat too long not to recognize a rogue warrior, a vigilante bent solely on retribution. I watched Butch revolving about the room, striking out with his fists and voice as he tottered this way and that. On his face was the dawning realization that he might lose. That he might die. That I might be the one to kill him.

Kurt Cobain's voice rasped through the room, swearing over and over that, no, he didn't have a gun . . .

I waited until Butch calmed enough to remember the weapons, counting on his memory of the room's layout and the relative distance between him and my knife outside the doorway. As expected, he lunged for the closer and more familiar weapon, the one he'd brought with him. The one I held in my hand.

He knelt, thrusting his hands beneath the bed, searching frantically with his fingers. His sense of touch. He couldn't smell, hear, or see my approach. Too bad, because I saw my reflection in the dresser mirror—eyes black, muscles tensed, arms raised high—and I looked like a fallen angel.

Butch froze. I smiled. And that bowed blade sang.

The stubs Butch instinctively cradled to his chest were white with bone and red with blood, trailing strings of meaty flesh. He howled, demon's mouth opened wide, head thrown back like a baby bird searching blindly for its next meal. Obligingly, I inserted the tip of the blade, pressing lightly against his tongue. His lips peeled back in a parody of a grin.

His last point of sensory perception was at my fingertips, the sense of taste. I leaned over to take his jaw in my free hand, forcing the blade to bite into his lower lip, and he whimpered as I lowered my lips to his ear. He had lied and laughed with that tongue, and both at my sister's expense. With the gentlest press upward of my fingers, I lifted him to his feet. "Do you have something to say to me?"

He shook his head as much as he dared, tears streaming from his destroyed eyes.

"I think you do," I said, my tone dry as dust. "In fact, I think it's right there on the tip of your tongue." I pressed, felt the bite of blade into flesh. Butch gurgled, a strangled cry for mercy, and I let up. "What was that?"

"Haar-yyy." The points where his lips had touched the double-edged blade were stained scarlet. He'd said sorry. I straightened, my body deadened to emotion.

"Well that's not good enough." I whispered it, not even caring if he could hear.

I could have slid that curved sword down his throat, severing the roof of his mouth, skewering his guts from the inside. I could have twisted it, sending that tip burrowing up into his skull to flay the soft tissue encased there. Instead, with a brisk flick of my wrists, I tore the blade free.

Butch leaned forward, retching blood, and fell again to his knees.

"Don't cry, Butch. All devils speak with forked tongues. This will just make it easier for others to recognize you."

He was bereft of all his senses now, as helpless before me as Olivia had been in his arms, but instead of killing him, I lowered myself to the edge of the bed and watched. I wanted to observe the last seconds of his life, as death marched across his features. I wanted to see if he would heal.

Then I could kill him all over again.

But he did die. The sonofabitch died and left me there in

my sister's cream-colored, blood-splattered room, with a hole in the window like some large, gaping mouth. He exited this world the same way he'd entered it—squalling, miserable, and covered in a woman's blood.

I don't know how long I slouched there, bleeding and crying, and intermittently screaming with the rotting stench of this demon's death rising up around me; willing both him and my sister alive again so I could change it all.

Eventually, I stood and turned off the music. Silence buzzed in my ears as I hauled Butch's body to the window and pitched it over the side. I didn't watch his tumble, but the rain had stopped and the whole world was silent, as if it existed in a vacuum, so I heard the thud, and the cracking report of his body hitting pavement. Never say I don't learn from my mistakes, I thought humorlessly.

Then I keeled over and retched up my guts.

8

"Police! Open up!"

The words rang in my ears as I came to, lying next to my own vomit. Feeling leaden and hollow, I pushed myself to my knees, then my feet, allowing a moment for my head to stop spinning. My mouth was dust-dry, my eyes crusted over with tears. I didn't know how long I'd been laying there, but the night sky had cleared outside the destroyed window, and though the lights of the city still rendered the heavens starless, a soft, crisp breeze blew against my back.

Another knock sounded urgently at the front door, and I drifted into the living room to answer it, my feet reporting hollowly on the tile floor. My martini sat perched on the coffee tray where I'd left it, next to my still unopened gift. Tears stung my eyes again, and I had to blink them away as the pounding continued. A neighbor had finally rang the cops. I wondered why they didn't just knock it down, but swung it open anyway.

Ajax stared back at me. "Hello, Joanna. I'd have come sooner, but I was . . . detained."

Shocked, my response was delayed, and when I slammed

the door he caught it easily, wrenching it open again. I backpedaled as he shut it behind him. He made no move to attack, instead cocking his head to one side, like he'd just thought of something. "Why, Joanna, dear, there's something different about you." He sniffed delicately at the air before snapping his fingers smartly and pointing. "I've got it. You've changed your hair."

He did step forward then, and I retreated into the sunken living room. I knew he would kill me. I was injured and he was fresh, angry, and knew better than to underestimate me, unlike Butch. He also had all the inexplicable powers that Butch possessed, and I didn't know if I could fight that again . . . or even if I wanted to. What was the point? I'd never been more alone in my life.

"Now," he said, crossing his arms over his body. This time he unsheathed two serrated pokers, one in each hand. "Where did we leave off?"

Okay, so I'm alone. I swallowed hard. *Get over it.*

Pounding sounded behind me, and I turned and stared, not quite believing my eyes. There, clutching the parapet of the building, was the homeless bum I'd run over, still looking disreputable, and still popping up in the strangest of places. He was mouthing something, pointing and jerking his head toward the bedroom. I turned back to find Ajax as awestruck as I, his mouth open in obvious displeasure.

"Warren," he said, lowering the pokers. "I should skewer you through your useless Taurean heart."

"Warren?" I said.

"Shut up, Ajax, you pathetic excuse for evil. Who dressed you this morning? Certainly not your mother. You look like some B-movie cliché."

I glanced back and forth, less concerned that they knew one another than with their being able to converse between a thick plate of soundproof glass. And that I could hear every word.

"Don't talk about my mother!" Ajax said, enraged.

"She should've swallowed that load, dawg, that's for sure. Don't worry, she'll make up for it tonight." And he began to make a repetitively lewd motion with his private parts. Right there on the ledge.

It took another meaningful look from him to realize he was buying me time. Afraid of telegraphing my intent, I fled without glancing back. I heard Ajax's curse, his feet pounding across tile, but I had the bedroom door slammed, locked, and was already halfway across the bedroom before it crashed open again.

"Give me your hand!" On the other side of the glass, Warren stretched out his own.

"Shit," I said, looking down. The breeze was much stronger out there.

"Give me your hand now!" he repeated, and pulled me forward from my center of gravity. I cursed again, but was half pulled, half lifted out onto the ledge, and just out of Ajax's reach.

"Bitch!"

"Come and get her," Warren taunted. I'd rather he not, I wanted to say, but the bum was already moving away, palms against concrete and glass, back against the building. "This way."

He paused at the buttress, and held onto me until I was steadied on the ledge. Then he turned and continued moving toward the living room windows. I hesitated. "He'll see us."

Warren glanced back, his hair swirling around his head like some mad professor's. "It's the only way. There's a staircase that leads to the roof. On that side, there's nothing."

I glanced behind me, swallowing hard. There was a swatch of material hanging from the jagged glass, torn from my blouse when Warren pulled me out, but no sign of Ajax.

"Joanna?"

"Okay." The word escaped on an exhalation and I nodded. We inched around the corner, my feet a mere inch shorter than the ledge's width. I traversed the facade, gaining on him, but a gust of wind slapped at me, and Warren grinned as I hugged the facing.

The living room windows shone like gems in front of us, and the light inside was a beacon, calling me back to reality. *What the hell was I doing out here?*

"Ready?" Warren said.

I nodded, took a deep breath, and followed.

Ajax appeared inside the cozy living room, framed like a slide in a projector. He was in a warrior's stance, legs wide, arms cocked, hands fisted around the pokers. Warren seemed unconcerned and kept inching along the ledge, a turtle on a tightrope.

"What do we do if he breaks the glass?"

"Try not to get hit."

I turned around. "I'm going back."

"Joanna." His voice froze me in place. I turned to find his crazed eyes sober upon mine. "There is no going back."

He was right. What would turning from a possible death to a more certain one do for me? It wouldn't bring Olivia back, or change the fact that I'd killed a man without remorse; and I seriously doubted I could sweet-talk Ajax into changing his mind about doing the same to me. Besides, how many times had I prayed for God to take away the past? To change events so I could wake up and be happy and normal and . . . like Olivia. Never once had my prayers been answered.

Or had they?

I looked at the man leading me. Sent from the heavens or not—and I had to admit it was unlikely—I knew one thing: he was not who he seemed. He also held the answers to the events that had plagued me the past twenty-four hours. And I wanted those answers. Besides, I told myself, he was right. There never was any going back.

"I'll follow you," I said, and Warren's face lit in absurd elation. "If you promise me two things."

His brows drew together again.

"First, you have to tell me what the hell is going on, and I mean all of it."

"Done! Easy-peasy," he said, and leaned toward me confidentially. "And second?"

"And second? Take a fucking shower." I wrinkled my nose. If he stunk before, he positively reeked now.

"Such a sweet girl. Glad you're on my side."

"I'm on *my* side." I edged out, and Ajax appeared again, poised as he'd been before.

"You two finished yakking yet?" His lips moved on the other side of the glass, but his voice bloomed next to me. "Can we get on with this?"

"By all means. I've got a date with your mama. Gotta get a move on." Warren hopped from one foot to the other with a sharp, jeering cackle. This infuriated Ajax and he rushed the window. I lunged for a vertical post, clinging to it with whitened fingertips. Warren did not, making himself a target.

I squeezed my eyes shut and averted my face as the poker lanced through the window. No crash came. Whirling back, I saw the tip slide through the glass as easily as trout through water. Warren dodged, wrapped his hand in the tattered hem of his duster coat, and seized the triangular blade before Ajax could withdraw. He yanked, the blade screeching and stuttering through the glass to the hilt. Ajax's face slammed against the pane, and I gained another post before he'd recovered.

"Let. Go." He spaced the words evenly, one eye riveted on Warren.

"You let go."

Ajax must have sensed the futility in arguing with someone possessing the rationale of an asylum patient. That, or he was sick of eating glass. He pulled away and released the poker. "That's okay. I have another."

Viper fast, quicker than I'd have guessed, he had the second weapon spearing through the window, angling toward my gut. I assume everyone has a moment of terrified realization right before their death. I was no different. That sliver of a blade was the sharpest thing I'd ever seen. I anticipated pain, knew I'd be skewered through, and wondered if I'd feel the impact when I fell to my death.

Wondered, briefly, if Olivia had.

I didn't feel it. I waited, eyes squeezed tight, and still it didn't come. Having already braced myself for the hereafter, I found this relatively unnerving. I opened one eye. Ajax and Warren were staring at me, wide-mouthed and wordless. I looked down. Bending halfway to the hilt, the steel blade looked rubberized. Then its ruined tip began dissolving, dripping onto the stone ledge, and then down the side of the building like liquid mercury. Nonplussed, I glanced back up at the two men. Were supernatural beings supposed to look that surprised?

"Ah-ha! Eureka! I found her, Ajax! I found her!"

"I found her, you noxious bag of air."

"Yes, but too late. Too late, and now look. She's too strong for you! Just as we'd hoped. Just as I *knew*!"

"She's not!" To prove it, Ajax yanked the first poker from Warren's grip, which he'd loosened in his excitement, and thrust again. An inch away from my body it melted like snow. He tried again, with the same results, then dropped the stub with a cry of rage.

By now Warren was almost doubled over with laughter, tears streaming down his dirty cheeks as he wobbled precariously from one foot to the other. "Too strong! Too strong!"

"I don't understand," Ajax said to me. "You can't have that kind of strength. You're an innocent."

"Yeah, that's what Butch said. Right before I killed him."

"Butch was here?"

"What? Can't you smell him?" I asked nastily, bolder now that I was safe. Not counting the two hundred foot drop behind me. "Why don't you use your nose? Sniff him out?"

They both stared, like I was the abnormal one there.

Warren found his voice first. "You can't smell the dead, Joanna. You've erased his scent, his essence. It's as if he never existed." He turned to face the man on the other side of the glass. "Isn't that right, Ajax?"

Ajax had begun to shake. "You bitch. You fucking bitch."

"Are you disrespecting me, Ajax?" Warren said. "Are you? Because if you are—"

"I think he's talking to me."

"Oh," Warren said. "Go ahead, then."

"I'm going to kill you, you know that?" Ajax told me. "I'm going to find you and I'm going to fucking kill you."

"How?" Warren asked. "You can't scent her, therefore you can't find her."

"Temporary. When the aureole wears off I'll be on you like peanut on butter."

Stupid thing for a homicidal anorectic to say.

"Or like a cat on a mouse." Warren pointed at Ajax's feet.

Ajax screeched, and wheeled backward. Luna hissed and began to stalk him, her butt swaying in a mean saunter, tail high and shaking. Ajax continued backing away, casting uncertain looks around him to make sure there were no other feline attackers. Shaking, he made his way to the door.

"This isn't over," he said, pointing at me. "Not by a long shot." Then he fled out the front door just as Luna charged.

"We can go in now," Warren said.

Luna met us inside the bedroom window. She was licking a paw—buffing her knuckles, it seemed—as she waited for us. She moved over as I climbed through, and wound about my legs, probably expecting a treat. I scooped her up and buried my face in her fur the way Olivia had. The purr shook her body and reverberated into mine.

"I didn't know your sister had a cat."

But somehow he knew I had a sister. Had a sister, I thought again, and felt the tears well. "Yeah. She did."

Warren fell still. Inhaling deeply, he glanced at the window before turning back to me, and his expression—usually so crazed and wild-eyed—was blighted. "Oh God, Joanna. I'm so sorry."

"You don't smell her anymore, do you?" My voice was small and didn't hold much hope. Warren only stood there. I looked away. "Neither do I."

"We have to get you out of here."

"Yeah," I agreed, not caring where we went. "Let's get me out of here."

Warren didn't speak as we walked the five blocks to a roadside motel—not to me, at least—and that was fine. He did, however, keep up a babbling monologue—something about baboons on Mars—which had the few pedestrians we did encounter steering a wide berth around us.

Beneath the garish red flash of a neon sign, a clerk wordlessly handed Warren a room key, and gave my blood-soaked and torn clothing a quick once-over without the slightest change of expression.

Oh yeah, I thought, noting the way Warren's shoulder-bent stoop gradually straightened as we crossed the dusty asphalt lot, this bum had a lot to answer for.

He opened a gray door, ushering me inside, and flicked on a light to reveal an equally dismal room. The requisite bed, dresser, and bedside tables were so nondescript I barely saw them. I dropped into one of four chairs flanking a battered round table and slouched with my back to the wall, head back, eyes closed. Every once in a while a car would pass along the road behind the building, tires humming and splashing in the puddles left by the storm, before fading away again into a soundless void.

Warren picked up the phone, and speaking lowly, ordered someone named Marty to bring us food. Gone was the feebleminded lunatic who'd taunted Ajax, the one I'd hit with my car. This was a man in charge, who apparently gave orders he expected to be obeyed. I didn't understand it, but that was a pretty common state of mind for me these days. All I knew right now was that I didn't want to eat whatever he'd ordered. I didn't even want to drink . . . imagine that. Instead, I felt like keeping my eyes closed, mindlessly counting cars passing outside the room until forever itself had come and gone.

"You should shower," Warren said at last, breaking the silence. His voice was still cracked, dusty with dehydration and disuse, but his words were appropriately somber.

"You should shower," I retorted, though the usual heat was lacking from my words. They were wearied, weak, and shaky. Like my knees. Like my life.

"Fine. I'll shower."

I didn't move when the bathroom door shut, or when I heard the shower start up. I didn't move when the knock came at the door, or when a man entered, uninvited, with a tray of bread and lunch meats that made my stomach do an unsettling flip-flop. When he left, I still sat there. Finally, I pushed myself to my feet and crossed the room to stare in the mirror at a woman I no longer recognized. She was dark-eyed and disheveled. She had blood beneath her nails and a stone where her heart used to be. She had killed a man in cold blood and hadn't an ounce of regret.

"Who the fuck are you?" I said hollowly. The woman stared back. She had no answers for me.

The bathroom door opened and I turned to find Warren watching me, still bearded, but clean-faced and clear-eyed. He had on fresh clothing; a gray T-shirt and baggy blue sweats, worn but odor-free and unsoiled. His hair was snarled and matted, but it was pulled back relatively neatly. Only the uneven gait remained totally unchanged. He wobbled, crossing to the tray to make himself a sandwich. When he finished, he took a seat across from the one I'd been slumped in and looked up at me expectantly.

"Tell me what happened." He didn't baby me, and he didn't beg, just as he hadn't pleaded with me to shower or to eat. He gave me nothing to rail against, no reason to argue, and so I found myself obediently seated as before. Perhaps he could give me answers. And maybe the answers would provide some relief to the grief and guilt rising like a geyser inside of me again.

I explained as much as I could remember of the night's events, and when I was done, waited for his response. Warren continued to chew, pausing mid-bite to nod thoughtfully. "That's why you were able to resist Ajax's conduit. I'd heard of it being done before, but I've never actually seen it myself."

At my look of incomprehension, he explained. "A conduit is a weapon made especially for the individual operator, a weapon of great energy and power. A conduit, by definition, channels energy. In this case, intent."

"You mean because the user intends to kill someone else with it," I said dully.

He nodded. "Here's the thing, though. Not only can't a conduit be duplicated, it leaves no trace of existence in the physical world. You literally melted Ajax's, without lifting a finger in defense."

Even I was curious how that had happened. "And?"

"It was because you'd just killed another Shadow agent—that's what we call those in our enemy army—but it was more than that," he hurried on, excited now. "You used Butch's conduit on him. You turned his own magic against him. No agent can heal from the blow of his own weapon.

"But, most important, was your motive. Intent. You slew him in vengeance, pure and simple. An 'eye for an eye' and all that. Powerful stuff. We don't practice that much."

I frowned, not liking the way that sounded. That wasn't how it had happened. Vengeance was something requiring forethought, and cold-bloodedness. Warren didn't see the way that monster had carved into my sister's perfect and delicate skin. Or the way he'd tossed her like refuse from the side of a building. "You'd have done the same thing."

"Maybe, but that doesn't mean it wasn't hard to do. You killed a senior Shadow agent, without training, knowledge, or a weapon of your own. We work for years to instill that sort of instinct in our troops and still often find ourselves on the losing end of the battle."

I looked at him warily. "Who's 'we'?"

"I told you before. Zodiac troop 175, division Las Vegas—"

"Fucking superhero shit!" I pounded my fist on the table, a gesture so swift and violent it surprised us both. I pointed my finger at him. "Don't start that again! I just watched my sister die and could do nothing about it! Nothing! And neither could you!"

"No," he said softly. "Not this time."

" 'Not this time'?" I stood, knocking my chair backward as I stalked to the door, throwing it open. "Not any time, nutcase! I'm out of here."

"Hope your shoulder feels better."

I froze. Then backed up to look in the dresser mirror. Checked my hands. Then sank onto the edge of the bed. "No wounds."

He shrugged, almost apologetically. "Fast healers."

Like him. Like *Butch*. I dropped my head in my hands. What was happening to me? Here I was healing while Olivia lay dead, her final scream still spiraling in my mind.

"Why her?" I whispered, shaking my head. "Why not me?"

Warren didn't answer. He just sat there as I sobbed, unashamed and unable to stop, weeping in a way I hadn't for a decade. Bile rose to coat my throat, and I ran to the bathroom.

When I returned, Warren was still picking at his food, though he seemed to have lost his appetite as well. I wiped my mouth with the back of my hand and took a deep drink of water. It did nothing to erase the cloying sickness from the back of my throat.

Lowering myself to the edge of the bed, I said, "What happened to me tonight?"

Warren took a deep breath. "It's called metamorphosis. It's a transformation that marks the beginning of a third life cycle. It happens to all of us when we reach a quarter century in age. Because you were so well hidden, we couldn't locate you until you began emitting the hormones, the pheromones, that come with the transition."

"Which is why Butch was sent to kill me at that exact moment," I surmised.

Warren nodded. "It's a time of change, one that signifies a move into great power, or at least access to that power. Problem is, the exact moment of transition is also a time of great weakness. You're frozen, as unable to act or react as a marble statue, though most of our members describe it in terms of heat, a rush of energy into your core." That, I thought, jibed with what I'd felt. "We usually place our initiates in a sort of safe house, surrounded by our other members, where they can go through the process without risk to themselves or any near mortals."

Like Olivia. "Why didn't you do that with me?"

"Because the initiate has to be willing. You've been hidden so long your true nature was buried, even from yourself. We couldn't find you in time to enlist you, much less educate you."

"So how'd Ajax find me?"

"Opposites attract. You're always more attuned to that which you fear or hate."

I let out a hollow laugh that broke down into a tattered cough, and shook my head at the irony of that. So why hadn't I known what to do about Butch? Why had my instinct only kicked in after it was too late?

"So, that's how it works," Warren said, after I motioned for him to continue. "We couldn't locate you until our enemies identified you first. Then we could only hope that it wasn't too late."

Which brought me back to my original question—why me? "I think you've got the wrong heroine."

Warren leaned forward, one corner of his mouth lifting in a small smile. What was most unsettling about this was how normal, and sane, that smile looked there. I rubbed at my eyes. "You're special, Joanna, even among us. Your mother was also a member of the Zodiac troop. She was the Archer."

I looked at him sharply and my heart began to pound. Nobody had spoken of my mother in nearly a decade. "You know my mother?"

"You were born on her birthday, right?"

I nodded, both surprised and not that he knew this.

"So was I. I'm a Taurus, though, the Bull of the western Zodiac, also after my mother. Our lineage is matriarchal," he explained, sunburned hands wrapped around one knee. "I suppose you can call it an inheritance of sorts. Every generation twelve men and women are born, raised, and trained to keep order in their part of the world. When all twelve positions are filled, there is peace and cosmic balance. Every major city in the world has a Zodiac troop, though the suburbs are patrolled by independents." He frowned at that, as if the word tasted bitter in his mouth.

"Independents," I repeated, my brows raised dubiously.

"Rogue agents," he said in an exaggerated whisper.

"Superheroes?" I pressed, and he shrugged.

"For lack of a better word, yes. We live in the city of our birth, pay our taxes, and hold normal jobs, but in the meantime we scent out Shadow agents, our polar opposites on the astrological chart, and destroy them."

I shook my head to drown out the words. They didn't make any sense anyway. "I still don't see what this has to do with me. I'm not a superhero. I'm—"

"Something never seen before," he finished for me, and leaning forward, looked into my eyes. "You, Joanna, are the first sign."

I rubbed a hand over my face and did a quick calculation. "Sorry to interrupt this fantasy in progress, but Sagittarius is the ninth sign of the zodiac, not the first."

He shot me a look like I was the crazy one in the room and began cleaning the crud from beneath his fingernails. "Unless you define 'sign' as the portent signaling our ascendancy over our enemies. Your discovery means just that. It's the first sign. *You're* the first sign."

Oh.

He paused, mistook my blighted look for one of confusion, and rubbed a hand over his beard. "Think of us as a metropolitan police force, but for the paranormal."

"Then you suck," I said bluntly. "Crime has risen eleven percent in the last year alone."

Warren smiled and shook his head. "We can't control what mortals do, Joanna. Ever hear of free will? Individual choice? All those universal checks and balances set up since the beginning of time? We do what we can on the physical plane—if we're in the right place at the wrong time, that is—but our real job is to counteract the criminal activity of the Shadow side."

"Such as?"

"Like the bombing of the Catacombs casino last year, and the tear gas released through the air ducts simultaneously at five Strip properties in June. The ambush of the governor's motorcade three months ago. Oh, and the hostage situation out at the air base. I took care of that one personally." He blew on his knuckles, pretending to polish them on his shirt, and there was that maniacal glimmer I was coming to recognize as his alter ego.

"I never heard about any of those things."

He looked at me. "Exactly."

I frowned. "So what does any of this have to do with me? You said yourself members have to be raised and trained for years to fight paranormal crime." Did those words really just escape my mouth? I shook my head. "Why can't you find someone else to take up the Sagittarius sign?"

"The Archer," Warren corrected.

"The Archer, then," I sighed, uninterested in the semantics. "There has to be someone else who wants the job."

"Because you're different in one way from the rest of us. A way that's been spoken of in our mythology, taught in our classrooms, but none of us, even in previous generations, has ever seen." Leaning forward, eyes going maniacally bright, he said, "You have a characteristic that makes you exceedingly dangerous to our enemy, Joanna, and, very possibly, even more powerful than the most learned of our troops."

"Let me guess. I can leap tall buildings. Fly faster than an airplane, blah blah blah."

"You were born on your mother's birthday, true," Warren said, ignoring the sarcasm, "but you were born on your father's birthday as well."

I recoiled slightly. "My father?"

"Not Xavier. Your real father."

I crossed my arms and watched him with wariness and suspicion, and more than a little interest. "And he was?"

"Not was," he said, shaking his head, a frown overtaking his expression. "*Is.* He's the leader of our opposition. He's our enemy. *Your* enemy."

My enemy? I drew back. What the hell did that mean? I mean, up until twenty-four hours ago I wasn't aware I *had* any enemies. "You mean he's like Butch and Ajax? Some sort of . . . demon?"

"Oh, he's much worse than that." Warren's face darkened. "And much stronger. Our troops are being depleted. Murdered. Basically, he's finding ways to kill off our star signs. In response, we're having to harvest our initiates younger and younger, before they're ready. But you . . . you might be the answer to stopping him."

Because I might be this *sign*, this portent, signaling his super-troop's ascendancy over my evil, overlord father. Yeah. Sure. I rubbed at my eyes. I was fading now, this whole conversation and night blurring in my mind. "Well, what if I don't want any part of this superhero, crime-fighting bullshit? What if I just want to live a normal life like all the other . . . mortals out there?"

"Do you?"

"Yes."

"No." Warren folded his arms across his chest. "You can't."

"You said I had to be willing," I argued.

He inclined his head. "There have been those, though rare, who've chosen not to fight. They knew the facts, they'd grown up in the Zodiac, and decided to leave it while they could. There's a procedure that's somewhat painful and has minor side effects—no worse than Paxil, really—but it will clear your mind forever of any paranormal knowledge or powers."

"I want that."

"Jo—"

"I want it! Now!" I did. I didn't know what the hell I was going to do next, but I knew I didn't want any part of a world of conduits, enemies, and astrological superheroes.

"Jo, all those operations were performed premetamorphosis." He shook his head. "It's too late for you."

Too late by one day. I stood, needing to pace, to think; needing air and time, and someone to make sense of this all. I felt trapped inside a foreign world where the rules had been upended on top of me. I didn't speak this language of star signs and Shadow agents, and I didn't want to. "Look, I don't want to be a superhero freak like you, okay, Warren? I don't want to fight crime, and I don't want to smell pheromones or kill bad guys. I just want to go home! I want . . . I want my fucking life back!"

He motioned to the door. "So leave."

"I will," I shot back, heading that way.

"Fine."

"Fine!"

He lobbed his parting blow. "Just know if you walk out of here now you'll be labeled a murderer."

"It was self-defense!" I said, whirling back. "He attacked me and murdered my sister!"

Warren blinked. "I'm not talking about Butch, Joanna."

I shook my head but it came out in a jerky motion. I opened my mouth but no words fell from it. The room faded and I felt my knees buckle. I leaned against the wall, taking long, deep breaths, and waited until I could stand again. I'd been wrong, I thought, to believe this guy had any characteristics resembling sanity. He was as crazy as I first thought.

"They'll frame you for Olivia's death," the psycho was saying. "Your true father, and all his henchmen. They'll set up all the physical evidence, and there won't be a thing you can do about it. Then, after the trial, when you're in jail and awaiting injection on death row, they'll find you by your scent—by then a soured mixture of bitterness and hate—and they'll kill you cold."

"But I didn't do it," I said breathlessly.

"Your car is at the scene of the crime."

"You told me to leave it there!"

He shrugged. "Your prints are all over the place—on your martini glass, and I'd imagine on your sister's body as well. They're especially dense in the bedroom where she was murdered."

"And so are yours!" I shot back. "And Ajax's and Butch's!"

He looked at me blankly. My eyes widened and I sucked in a quick breath, remembering Butch's impossibly smooth fingertips. "Give me your hand," I said in a whisper.

Warren held it out, palm up. Though his palms were rough and callused, the tips of his fingers were smooth and opalescent, almost pearlescent as they gleamed up at me. I ran a finger over the pad of his thumb, rubbing lightly. It was like touching a marble.

"None of us has fingerprints, Jo."

I looked up into his face. "I do."

"You're different. You're—"

"Don't say 'innocent,'" I said through gritted teeth. I'd never felt less so in my life.

"I wasn't going to," he said quietly. "I was going to say you're a latecomer to all this."

I couldn't believe this. I had to get out of there. There

had to be a way. "Well, what about motive? Anyone who knows me—us—knows Olivia and I love each other. I'd never harm her."

"Not for anything?"

"No!"

"Not for money?"

"Why would I? I have money of my own."

"But she has more."

"She has—" I stopped, and felt my face drain of color.

"You lost your inheritance today, did you not?" I knew he was just playing devil's advocate. I knew it, and still I could see his point; how it would look to the rest of the world.

"How did you know that?" I asked, my voice small.

"I told you. You're being watched." He moved aside as I sank beside him on the bed. "By instruction of an unsigned note Olivia was handed the entire Archer legacy. Some people would see that as reason enough to kill."

"But I wouldn't."

"You're a fighter," he pointed out. "Aggressive. A loose screw."

"So is half the fucking population, Warren! It doesn't make me a killer!" I thought of Butch. "It doesn't make me *her* killer."

"But you had motive. And you were there."

"So was Butch!"

"You can't prove it. You *won't* prove it," he corrected, before I could speak. "Our blood is like water. It soaks into the ground, it feeds the earth, but leaves no trace of ever having been shed. That's why there won't be a trace of Butch's blood in your sister's home. There won't even be yours by now. Just Olivia's. And your fingerprints."

I swallowed hard. "I thought you were going to help me."

"I am helping you. I'm telling you how it's going to play out. By tomorrow morning this is going to be all over the television, in all of the newspapers. 'Heiress Daughter Killed by Jealous Sister.' Your face will be plastered in every newspaper in the country. You'll be infamous."

I'd have been better off dead.

"Or . . ."

I glanced up at him sharply. "Or?"

"Or I can take care of it for you. *We* can take care of it," he corrected.

"Can you bring her back?"

"No." His voice and expression gentled and the kindness softening his doe brown eyes almost killed me. I looked away. "But we can make sure the world doesn't find out about what happened tonight. *That's* our job. To protect the people of this city from those who would hurt them as Butch hurt Olivia. To make supernatural events appear normal. Ever hear the saying, 'What you don't know won't hurt you'?"

"I've never believed that."

He gave a slight shrug. "That's because you didn't know any different."

I stood gingerly, testing my legs, and returned to the dresser to study the woman I saw there. If she'd looked unfamiliar before, she looked downright foreign now.

"They were setting me up," I finally said, gazing at Warren through the mirror.

He nodded. "That's what they do."

"And what about you? Is that what you do?"

"We work to counteract their acts, yes. Usually we're a bit more successful than this."

A bitter laugh escaped me. I closed my eyes.

"Look, I know it's a lot to take in. Shit, it's a lot even if you've been raised in this lifestyle, and there's more yet"—he held up a hand when my lids flicked open—"but you have a decision to make, and you have to make it quickly. We need you, we *want* you in our organization, but you have to come willingly."

A superhero, I thought numbly. Good versus evil. Shadow agents. Paranormal battles. "I don't know."

"Okay." He blew out a long breath, and for the first time I saw the signs of fatigue weighing on his browned face and sunken shoulders. "Okay," he repeated, "there is one thing I can do for you."

I stared at him through the mirror.

"You have twelve hours before your scent returns. One thing about turning a conduit on its owner, it's such strong magic that you can wander this earth like a ghost. That's called the aureole. Neither mortals nor agents will be able to discern your presence unless you're standing right in front of them. It's a gift. Like you don't even exist.

"My team can hold off until just after dawn. That'll give you time to make a decision. Use it. Think about what I've said. You can refuse the offer, but once you do there's nothing we can do to help you."

I nodded at last. "Thank you."

"I'll wait here. Come back to me with your answer, or consider coming back to me *as* your answer. Otherwise . . ." He shrugged, and looked truly sorry. "You're on your own."

9

Even as a girl Olivia had a way of moving—through a room and through life—without settling very long in any one place, or at least never long enough to allow anything to really touch her. Some people thought her distracted, others called her flighty, but from a young age, watching her, I had named her Magic.

Wasn't it magic when a woman could maintain her childlike innocence long after her childhood was over? Or believe that tragedy was an anomaly and the world really was a good place? Or that all people, despite past deeds, were essentially good, and could be redeemed? No, no matter what happened—to me, to her, to our family—the hope in her eyes had never dimmed, and the surety in her smile never faltered.

Of course, Olivia knew the effect she had on others. On men, in particular. I think she believed if it made someone happy to look at her, her job was to give them something fabulous to look at. Despite my disagreement, I was proud of her, and proud to be related to her. She was a pure light. A beacon as bright and compelling to others as a flame was to a bunch of flimsy-winged moths.

Only one other person had burned that brightly in my life. But for reasons I never understood, Ben Traina had preferred the dark.

I stumbled through the grid of familiar side streets, my eyes swollen and sandpaper dry, images of Olivia flailing in death caught like debris beneath my lids. My fatigue was so great it felt like a bowling ball was weighted on my shoulders. All the years of sweat and training and preparation had boiled down to this: I'd been useless under pressure. I'd been helpless, ineffective, deficient . . . and, as a consequence, Olivia was dead. Olivia was dead.

Olivia was dead.

Veering away from the Strip and the garish, flashing lights canvassing the sky, I crossed into the shadows, where apartments could be rented by the week, trash bins overflowed onto the sidewalks, and alleyways were tagged with scrawling obscenities. I noticed a vagrant asleep on some folded boxes and, thinking of Warren, stopped and leaned over him. I knew he was awake by the shallowness of his breath and by the way he shivered with the cold. I could even smell the dirty blade clutched in the fist he used as a pillow. But the man didn't stir. He had no idea I was there, and the thought made me want to cry. Even here, among the darkest shadows in the city, I couldn't hide from the person I'd become.

That was when I knew. No matter how long or far I walked, there was no escaping this new reality. The scents of both the living and dead would continue to reach out to me, and meanwhile I would leave nothing of myself behind.

Spotting a cab idling beneath a lamp post on Spencer Street, I crossed to it at an intersection where the night was deep enough to hide the condition of my clothing and the smudges of fatigue stamped beneath my eyes.

"You on duty?" I asked, bending to address the driver through the open window. He jumped like a catfish yanked from the water.

"Shit, lady! You scared the bejesus out of me!"

"Sorry."

He nodded once, gruffly, swallowed to regain his composure, then stretched to see around me. "You alone?"

I nodded.

"Well, you look harmless enough." He jerked his head toward the backseat. "Where you goin'?"

I climbed in, read him the address from the back of the card Ben had given me earlier—God, had that only been this evening?—and tried to continue looking harmless. The driver glanced back at me every once in a while, as if to reassure himself I was still there, but he didn't try to talk, and the silence stretched between us, like the lights that elongated and snapped through the windows as we skimmed along the surface streets.

I wondered how harmless he'd consider me if I told him I knew he'd just finished a cigarette, and that less than an hour before he'd eaten a hot dog, with relish and mustard, along with a Diet Coke. Prior to dressing for work, he'd also had a quick, nonsweaty bout of sex, presumably with the woman whose ring he wore on his left hand. I looked at the dashboard and the license holding his name and photo. Ted Harris had a dog, but no children. He also had a gun tucked beneath his seat.

I could smell all of it on him.

"I think this is it," I said. He jerked at my voice.

We pulled up to the house and I paid him with bills Warren had pressed on me before I left the motel. A homeless man with a wad of twenties in his pocket, I thought, shaking my head. Only in Vegas.

"Can you wait? Just in case no one's home?" I asked, handing him the money through the open window. He took it gingerly, careful not to touch my fingers.

"Sure, lady," he said, but I didn't need to see the way his eyes flickered to tell it was a lie. I could smell the perspiration trailing down his neck. Sure enough, as soon as I started up the driveway, the wheels of the cab screeched from the curb and I was left in a cloud of burning rubber and exhaust.

I tried not to take it personally.

The house was not one of the newer tract homes, with their pastel stuccoed exteriors and five feet of space between one neighbor and the next. Ben couldn't have lived that close to another family, I don't think. He wasn't even that close to his own family.

No, this was one of the boxy wood-paneled homes that'd gone up in the seventies, before land was so valuable the builders halved it, then halved it again, and Ben's sprawling lawn and towering pines were a testament to that more generous era. Though paint could be seen peeling from the faux wood shutters, the window boxes were full of perennials, bright despite the winter chill, and the smell of fresh mulch—clean and damp and musky—reached out to me as I passed colorful pots of bronze and orange mums, dual sentries standing guard at the bottom of the concrete porch.

I paused when I got to the front door, wondering what I was really doing here. Sex was the last thing on my mind. What I truly wanted was sleep; to drift away on a tide of dreams, and wake to find that this night had been a nightmare. One that could be chalked up to something simple, like eating too close to bedtime. Reality, however, was that I had five hours left to decide whether I wanted to be some sort of twenty-first-century heroine—fighting crime on a paranormal plane against other superhuman beings, for God's sake—or if I could somehow prevent being convicted of killing my own sister.

Tough fucking choice.

So, I raised my hand to knock, paused again, and tried the handle instead. It gave easily, with a soft snitch of the latch, and I was admitted into the womb of Ben's home. *Come*, he had said. And then he'd left the door open so I could. Once inside, I was careful to lock the door behind me.

* * *

If I'd found Ben intoxicating before—the scent of him, the taste and the touch—my new enhanced senses sent my mind to whirling as soon as I entered his house. He was everywhere, and for a moment I grew so dizzy I had to lean against a wall to catch my breath. God, but he spoke to me. Ben Traina was so wound up in my soul, so intertwined with my past and the young girl I'd started out as—full of hope and innocence—that I think a part of me was expecting to find her here, as well as him. As I looked around his house, at his things, I knew that's why I'd come. Ben was the only person left who knew me as I was really meant to be.

I did nothing to disturb the silence of the house, moving quietly through the dining room and kitchen, knowing Ben was here, somewhere, sleeping. I couldn't help but try to scent out another woman's presence, even if it were just a whiff of perfume long gone stale as weeks, and hopefully months, had rolled by. There was none. Just Ben, and the verdant scent from the small jungle of houseplants shooting leafy shadows at me in the dim half-light. A relieved sigh escaped me as I slipped into the living room. Halfway through, however, I stopped.

Ben, it seemed, had been doing a little reminiscing. By the gray light filtering in through a large picture window, I saw an empty bottle of Corona sitting on the coffee table, and an empty glass beside it, which still smelled of yeast and—if I inhaled deeply enough—Ben's mouth. Next to these lay an open photo album, and I skirted the table to the other side and tilted my head, leaning in for a closer look.

There were twelve pictures in all, both sides of the open album filled. They'd been taken at different times and places, with different cameras, including the one Ben had given me for my fourteenth birthday, the one that had begun my passion for photography. The first photo taken with that camera lay on the page in front of me, a frozen moment that captured the girl I had once been.

"I knew you'd be here," I whispered to her.

Of the others, only one drew my full attention, and I slipped it from its sleeve, hands trembling slightly, and made my way over to the window for better light. This had been taken with the same camera, though the subject was three women instead of one. Three Archers.

Olivia was barely a teen, captured with a blinding smile, the baby fat still high on her smooth cheeks, though the woman she would soon become could already be seen peering out from behind shining eyes. I was next to Olivia, and my image was such a stark contrast to the mirrored one I'd faced earlier that night that I immediately turned my attention to the third woman, staring up at me through the glow of the streetlight.

Zoe Archer was an amalgamation of Olivia and I. Dimples that flashed, Olivia's; a watchful expression, mine. A wide and easy smile. Olivia's. An attentiveness bordering on paranoia. Mine. Her red hair was all her own, though, and sunlight flashed golden in the strands, while the freckles dotting her nose made her look impish. Despite, I thought, the flint in her eyes.

I raised the photo across from me, trying to study it objectively. By the following spring the same picture would capture entirely different women. There would be Olivia's determined innocence, a force so strong it would even outshine her brazen beauty. My physical power would be burgeoning, a strength born of total weakness.

And my mother? Zoe Archer wouldn't be in the picture at all, I thought wryly. She had left before winter even swept its chill fingers over the valley.

"I have so many questions for you," I murmured, running my finger along Zoe's jawline. "Wherever you are."

I considered that for a moment. My mother was alive, well, and someone knew her whereabouts. Yet she'd never bothered contacting Olivia or me, and that sat in my stomach like a ball of acid. I let the photo drop, let the memories drop away as well, and went into the bedroom to find Ben.

* * *

One object stood out more than any other in Ben's bedroom: the bed itself, a king-sized monster with a padded leather headboard in deep mahogany, and a chocolate-colored duvet that made the whole thing appear layered in inky clouds. In it, during this, the deepest hour of night, was the man I loved. I stole up to his bedside and peered down at his face, wondering how best to wake him. After all, he was a cop, and by all evidence, used to sleeping alone. The last thing either one of us needed was for me to be looming over him when he awoke.

So I knelt by Ben's side, breathing in the thick scent of a deeply sleeping man, and reached out to touch him. But I stopped as I caught sight of my fingers, pale in the thin light cast from the bedroom window, and I couldn't help remembering what else they'd touched that night. A scimitar. A dead man's body. Olivia.

I gasped at the last thought, jerked my hand away and stood in one swift motion. Ben didn't even stir.

Like you don't even exist.

I couldn't wake him, not the way I was now. The last thing I wanted was to soil anything or anyone else with my touch, with what I'd become, and as I backed away, I wondered if I'd ever be clean again. My skin itched with the question. If I could have removed it, taken it from my body and bones in that moment, I would have. Instead, I settled for a shower.

For the longest time I stood under the spray, eyes closed, just letting the water scald and sting my skin. It pounded the thoughts from my head, drummed the echoes of Olivia's screams from my ears, and washed away the filth that couldn't be seen or scented but was seeping into my soul even now. I shook my head and refused to think about it. My muscles relaxed, my skin grew red, almost raw, and still I remained beneath the steady stream of wet heat, not wanting to move. Not ever again.

I thought I'd be too wired to relax completely, too aware

of Ben's presence in the next room, and of dawn's steady approach, but I'd underestimated how exhausted I truly was. Somehow I managed to doze off still standing, leaning against the tiles like a beached bass waiting for another tide to come in.

I awoke to arms snaking carefully around my naked waist and a soft sigh catching in my ear. Goose bumps prickled down my neck and breasts and back, and I didn't have to inhale to know it was Ben.

"Jo-Jo," he said, feathering kisses along my earlobe, hands rising to cup my breasts as he moved in closer behind me. I tensed, realizing in some ultra-alert corner of my brain that I shouldn't be doing this. I couldn't. Not tonight, of all nights.

"Wait," I said, half turning to him, hardly daring to meet his eyes. "We can't."

Ben smiled kindly, mistaking my reaction for plain-vanilla reticence, and why not? He had no idea what kind of night I'd had. He knew only that a handful of hours ago we were climbing into each other's skin, and that now I had accepted the invitation into his home and then climbed into his shower.

" 'If we could decide who we loved, it would be much simpler, but much less magical.' "

That hit me. Not only had he just admitted he still loved me, but because he did it in the way we had when we were young, hiding behind the mask of a quotation, using someone else's words to bolster our own softly blooming emotions.

"Who said that?" I asked, slicking my hair back with one hand as I looked up at him.

"The dudes who created *South Park*."

A laugh burst out of me, strangled but strong, and I bent my head to his chest, shaking as my smile slipped into tears. For a long time Ben just held me, letting the water sluice along my shoulders and back, his hands still, chin resting on my head. He was giving me time, letting me know it'd kill him to back off now but he'd do it if that's what I wanted.

My decision, at last, came out in a single smooth watery movement. I lifted my lips to Ben's and released the weight of my own pain, just let it wash down the drain along with every other thought in my mind.

The soap had cleansed me, the water warmed me, but it was only with Ben's touch that the nerve endings beneath my skin began to skirt back to life. He ran his hands down my arms, gripped my waist, then skimmed them gently along my hips. All the while he kissed me, a soft exploring pressure against my mouth that tasted like musky sunshine and was the most solid thing I'd ever known. Passion rolled through me, quaking through my core at first, then causing my limbs to curl tightly around him. The selfish and greedy part of me that still wanted to live, to thrive, even after all I'd seen and done that night, reached out to Ben, opening to him, and overrode the numbness threatening to encase my soul.

We switched places, nearly slipped, and used each other's flesh to right ourselves again. Ben was as voracious as I was, and we laughed when we met with teeth instead of tongues, bit instead of kissed, and when we bruised instead of brushed the flesh we'd waited a decade to touch again.

He shifted, leaning back beneath the spray, and pulled me along with him. Water pounded our skin, filled our ears and our open mouths, creating trails for us to track, liquid maps laid out over our bodies. Ben followed one over my neck and down to the slope of my breast, where it paused, cresting at my nipple. There, his tongue turned lazy, lingering and teasing until I dipped my head back, moaning, and arched into his mouth and arms.

The water snapped off suddenly, Ben muttered some dark demand against my skin, and I lifted my head in time to see him blindly pushing open the shower curtain before I was lifted from the tub, wrapped in a towel, and dried in short order. He never stopped kissing me. I never stopped kissing back.

"Now you," I finally said, pulling back to offer him the towel.

His eyes lit on my face, as dark as a banked coal. "I'm not cold."

I dropped my gaze, inspecting his body. No, he wasn't.

He picked up a bottle and moved toward me. I let the towel drop.

He started from the top, kissing every place he touched both before and after slicking it with lotion. He grew distracted again when he reached my breasts and, I confess, so did I. His palms were wide and warm over the sensitive skin, his thumbs and tongue earnest in their circuitous exploration. I reached for him, but he moved away, poured more lotion, then lifted one of my legs as he leaned against the counter.

"How you doing over there, Jo-Jo?" he asked as his fingers worked my instep. I dropped back against the opposite wall of the tiny bathroom and stretched my leg toward him in reply. He chuckled, his hands moving higher.

"You going to slick my whole body?" I asked as he massaged my calf in broad strokes.

"That's the plan." His fingers slid past my knee. Our eyes locked, and I ran my instep along his hip, then his inner thigh, opening wider to him. He inhaled sharply, his eyes flicking down my body, narrowing when they returned to my face. Then my leg was thrown over his shoulder so fast I was gasping before his knees hit the ground. His hands moved over the inside of my thighs, flared over my stomach, and dropped to cup me from behind. I strained toward him, and he moaned, the echo sliding through my body, humming in my thighs. I bowed back, reaching for new sensations, and this time earned twin moans from us both. The silence in the room was punctuated only by our breaths, catching and quickening, the breathy music of lovers improvising a duet.

He was feasting. More, he was watching me as he did it, eyes so dark and filled with such desperation, it was almost fierce. He licked slowly, savoring, and touched me deeper with his tongue. I moved my body into his, offering myself to him, and came a moment later with a cry that sounded distant, like it was coming from someone else entirely.

Ben dropped his head to my belly, weight pinning me while his heart thudded between my thighs. "I didn't expect it," he finally said, the words whispering against my stomach.

"Expect what?"

He lifted his gaze up to mine. "The sight of you. In my arms again." He looked confused for a moment. "It's devastating."

I could only swallow hard at that. That, and watch him rise, our stare never breaking as he picked me up and carried me to his bed.

"I knew it," Ben said, his voice scarcely more than a whisper. "I knew you'd come to me."

He was propped up on one elbow beside me, his other hand exploring, taking his time. I nestled my head deeper into his pillow. "How? I didn't even know."

"I know things about you, Jo-Jo." He smiled, and touched a finger to his breastbone. "In here. Probably things you don't even know about yourself."

I could have laughed at that. I could have said, "You have no clue who I really am," and told him stories of first signs and conduits, and magic that allowed a person to walk the earth like a ghost. But I didn't. He was too sincere, and so sure of his quiet belief in me—and in us—that I couldn't shatter it. I wanted to believe it too.

"Like what?" I said instead. "Tell me something you know about me."

"I'll do better. I'll show you."

He leaned over, tenting his body above mine, and the hand that had been propping him up climbed into my hair. He pushed my thighs open with one of his, taking up residence in my most personal space . . . exactly, I thought, where he belonged. The sheets rustled around us, conforming to the new shape of our two bodies forming one, and I shut my eyes and inhaled deeply.

Ben's scent was everywhere; on the pillowcases, in the air, clean and warm and dizzying as he bent over me. I lifted my head, pressing my lips to his, trying to coax some of that scent into myself. He kissed me back freely, unable to know what I was really seeking, but responding to the way I dug my fingers into his back, letting me set the pace. I sighed into his mouth, lifting one leg up his hip as my palms flattened and pressed over his back, and his skin was so hot it felt like I was raking burned silk.

I squeezed his bare hip with my right hand, then ran my nails along his outer thigh, my knuckles along the inner. As hard as he was, he stiffened further, and ground himself against me with a moan, trapping that hand. He moved his own fingers along my left side, half spanning my rib cage with his palm, dropping farther to my hip before settling beneath me, lifting me to him as he pressed from above.

He closed his eyes and whispered, "I want to go back a decade. I want to go back, and never let you go."

I stilled, wondering how he could so clearly read the thoughts of my heart.

Go back. God, that sounded good. Back to being that girl who feared nothing, who was on the cusp of becoming the woman she was born to be, before God or fate or whatever personal dogma you hung your hat on intervened. I would do it too, in a nanosecond. I would go all the way back, and this time I'd protect her better. I'd never cross that midnight desert.

And that, I realized, was what I was really searching for night after night, as I snapped photos of the disenfranchised on the litter-strewn concrete streets and urine-stained walls. Ben thought I was looking for the monster who'd taken a bite out of my young life. But I was really looking for her. For me.

"Okay," I finally said, lifting my head, and freeing my hand to caress his flushed cheek as his eyes clouded. "Let's go back now."

"Yes," he agreed, and began to lead me, slowly, kissing me lightly as his chest brushed my nipples, then harder as he opened me with one gliding caress, still cupping me from below. "Yes."

He entered me smoothly, a key settling in its lock, a corner piece clicking home in a puzzle to make sense out of things not previously understood. I cried out with the rightness of it, and he dropped his forehead against mine, gasped into my mouth. And rocked.

I clasped my thighs around his waist and squeezed, then kissed him hard, and the shock I'd been in for the past few hours snapped so instantaneously that my life came flooding back to me—my life as it was meant to be, before I'd been touched by violence, or fate, or anyone and anything who wasn't Ben Traina. That was when I knew I could face the dawn. With this to come back to, I thought, I could face anything at all.

Buried in me, Ben murmured against my cheek, infusing me with his scent and life and love . . . and his hope. Starved, I shifted, rolled and straddled him in one swift motion, lifting our hands so we were linked both above and below. He gazed up at me silently, his eyes twin brands regarding me brightly in the dark. The glow of the streetlight outside sent silver light skittering into the room, and our bodies were bathed with it as we set to a gliding rhythm. I could hear him, whispering to me in the silvery light, telling me things he'd bottled up for years, and in doing so, causing those years to melt into nothingness behind us.

Then, without warning, I began to shudder, the climax overcoming me in long arching waves—claiming us both—and driving us to a place that was neither in the present nor the past, but one reserved for the possible, the inevitable. The new.

* * *

"Jo-Jo?" Ben said after a bit.

"Hmm?"

"There's one more thing I know about you."

I cracked open one eye. "Already?"

"Not that," he chuckled, and pressed a kiss to my forehead. "No . . . I know you still love me."

I looked at him fully, then just watched him watching me before nodding my mute reply.

"You always have," he said, with full confidence. "You always will."

I stared past him and outside the window, where dawn waited impatiently. "I guess that's how you knew to leave the door open for me."

"Oh, Jo-Jo," he said, sighing sleepily as he gathered me tight to his body. "It was never closed."

I stayed still for as long as I could. I had no desire to break Ben's embrace because I knew these final moments for what they were. *Stolen.* I felt it with every second marked by the bedside clock, I marked it myself with every steady exhale Ben released beside me, and I counted the moments until dawn using the pulse that beat under my fingers at his wrist.

Ben didn't stir when I swung my legs over the bed. Of course, he wasn't dreading dawn the way I was. He didn't have any heavy decisions to make about joining a supernatural underworld. I watched his eyes move beneath his lids as he battled some sort of wafting image, and then they stilled and he fell deeper into his dreams. I envied him his peace, and wished it for us both.

After dressing, I went back into the living room and called for a cab. As I gave directions to the house, my eyes strayed to the photo I'd tossed onto the coffee table. I didn't think Ben would mind if I borrowed it for a while. I could make a copy, give him back the original, and have at least one photo of my mother, my sister, and me all together. I'd long ago torn up the rest.

I found a pad of yellow Post-its, wrote down my intentions, and pressed the note onto the empty photo sleeve. There was a bookshelf along one wall, and the lowest level was lined with albums identical to the one I held. I longed to look at them all, to savor every picture and wonder at every moment captured while I'd been somewhere else. Perhaps someday. Right now, lacking the time, I simply slipped the album I was holding back into its place and turned to leave.

That's when I saw the camera. It wasn't a fancy one, not like the Nikon I used for my professional work; in fact, it wasn't even what I would consider a real camera. It was one of the throwaway kinds people bought when they forgot to bring their own on vacation with them. But it was all I had, all that was there, and I picked it up, suddenly wanting to capture this moment—the deep silence, the unsure light—everything that would change the moment I walked out of the house.

So I took the camera back to the bedroom, back where Ben had shifted to his side, his hip rising like a wave beneath the dark covers, his long legs running the length of the bed. Not wanting to risk the flash, I used the lightening sky to bring his features into relief, and when I snapped the picture, the click reported like a shot throughout the silent room. I lowered the camera to watch him sleep with my naked eye, and jumped when a horn honked outside. I should leave, I thought, before he could wake. I didn't, though. Instead, I bit my lip and paused to consider him just a moment longer.

Just one more.

Holding my breath, I moved in closer, careful not to make a sound . . . not that it was necessary. I still possessed the aureole, and for a while longer, at least, I was still just another shadow layering the night.

When I was in place, Ben's face framed by the primitive square of the cardboard lens, I stilled. Then softly, almost inaudibly, I whispered, "Ben?"

A pause, another deep inhalation, then the corner of Ben's lips lifted ever so slightly. It was a lopsided smile, like his thoughts were only half formed, but it made me want to smile too. I clicked. I tucked the camera in my pocket. Then I left.

A sliver of sun peered over the eastern ridge of the valley, illuminating the peaks of the Black Mountains like jagged bruises against the face of the sky. The air lightened, spreading pastel swaths across the wide canvas, and I sucked in the first bright breath of dawn. After a moment's more hesitation, I turned and strode into Room 8 of the Smoking Gun Inn, slamming the door behind me.

Warren was seated where I'd left him. I'd have wondered if he'd even moved, except there was another man with him, slouched on the edge of the bed. I ignored the newcomer and wordlessly tossed the photo I was carrying on the table in front of Warren. Only his eyes moved.

"I have three questions for you," I said, my voice low but steady. "If I like the answers, I'll go with you."

A smile began to spread across his face, but I stalled it with a shake of my head. *If* I liked the answers.

"First, there was something Butch said to me right before midnight. Before the metamorphosis. He said I was hidden in plain sight." I tilted my head. "What did he mean when he said 'Xavier's daughter, no less'?"

"Ah." Warren spread his palms out on the table before him. "Well, he was right. Only someone as canny and talented as your mother could have pulled it off." He leaned forward. "See, while superhuman in some areas, we still have to operate in the mortal realm. We're bound by all the natural laws—gravity, time, place—so our job is to make other, more *fluid* boundaries appear normal. And we need mortals for that."

"A front? Like when the mob used to run the casinos as a cover for money laundering?"

"Exactly! Spoken like a true Vegas girl," he said, peering

up at me in the growing light of dawn. "And in return for this guise, we give these human allies support. Sometimes it's a transfer of power, convincing other mortals to give him or her an important place in society. Sometimes it's a bit of physical strength where there was none before. I know of at least one mortal who won a gold medal in the last Olympics because of it. And then there are those who ask for—"

"Money," I finished for him.

"Money," he repeated, nodding. "Xavier is your true father's chief contact in the mortal world. His pet, if you like. He provides a cover for the Shadow side, allowing them to exist and operate on the mortal plane, and in return he is provided all the wealth he could ever desire."

"So by marrying Xavier, my mother was looking to infiltrate the wolf pack."

"By marrying Xavier," Warren corrected, "your mother was living in the wolf's den. And you? Everyone believed you were really Xavier's daughter."

It explained a lot. Xavier's meteoric and unprecedented financial rise in the world of gaming. The pitfalls experienced by anyone who challenged his supremacy. It also explained the unmarked, unsigned note he'd received earlier in the week, and his complete unwillingness to question its origin. It came, after all, from his benefactor.

I shook my head slowly. That asshole had been a part of it all along. He'd sold his soul for money, and in doing so, contributed to his own daughter's death.

"So, theoretically speaking," I said, "if I did join your forces and the Zodiac troop become more powerful as a result, this would help bring Xavier down?"

"Definitely. In fact, anything with the enemy's emblem would be open to ruin. In times of strength, like now, it's a sign of victory. Otherwise, it's a target."

I frowned. "What's his emblem?"

Warren looked amused. "He's your mirror opposite in the astrological chart, Jo. The Shadow side of the Zodiac. Anything with the word Archer on it belongs to him."

"So it's like a brand?"

"It is. It warns, and it protects." Which put Xavier under the protection of my enemy. Who knew it was possible to feel even more animosity toward the man? "What's your second question?"

I glanced down at the photo on the table before meeting Warren's eye. "Where is she?"

"Your mother?" He shrugged, though his shoulders had stiffened. "In hiding."

"But she's alive? You're sure?" and when he nodded, I said, "But you can't tell me where?"

"I don't know where. Nobody does." He paused, as if caught between two thoughts, but his expression quickly shuttered and he hurried on. "If the Shadow Archer knew where Zoe was, he'd be after her in a shot."

"He hates her that much?"

"He hates us all, but yes," he said softly, eyes filled with some memory. "He hates Zoe even more."

I wanted to know why. What had she done to incur such long-held wrath? But more important right now was my third question. I took a deep breath. If Zoe had married Xavier to infiltrate the enemy's key organization, then what had forced her to leave? I looked at the man in front of me—both crazed and sane, open and guarded, helpful and hard—and the only one who might know. Then I asked him the hardest question of all. "Was this man, my real father, responsible for the attack on me when I was sixteen?"

Warren opened his mouth, shut it again, then swallowed hard. "Yes."

Even expecting it, the truth hit me like a lead bar. Squeezing my eyes shut, I pinched the bridge of my nose between forefinger and thumb and shook my head. My blood father had had me attacked. Raped. Left for dead.

"My mother slept with this guy?" My voice cracked.

"He didn't know you were his daughter. He still doesn't. It . . . it's complicated," Warren said, in what was, perhaps, the understatement of the year. "And it's not my story to tell."

I stared at him for a long while, then nodded and returned my attention to the table. "Okay, just one more question, then. What's the worst that can happen? To you, I mean. What would happen if these . . . Shadows won? If they succeeded in wiping out your troop?"

Warren's Adam's apple bobbed at the thought, and the other man shifted uncomfortably on the bed. They shared a look, a whole conversation passing between them in that short glance before Warren turned back to me. "Chaos, Joanna. Sodom and Gomorrah stuff. What do you think happened there? What happens whenever all lusts and baser evils go unchecked? Every man for himself. Society disintegrates, mortals become enslaved to their baser emotions. And the Shadows? They are their captors."

I stood still and silent for another good minute before saying anything. At last I returned to the photo I'd thrown down in front of him and pointed to Zoe, the woman I'd once thought lost to me forever. "This man, this Archer, has cost me my mother.

"My sister," I continued, moving my finger to Olivia, who really was.

"And my innocence." I pointed to myself, then picked up the photo and handed it to him. "This city is all I have left."

Warren looked at it for a moment before glancing up. "You realize you'd be entering a whole new realm, don't you? A different reality. More than one, actually."

"My reality's already different."

"We kill these people, these Shadows, Joanna. That's what you'd be signing up for."

People like Butch and Ajax. People who sent madmen after little girls in the desert. "I got it, Warren."

"And do you think you could kill your own father if given the chance?" I nodded once. "In cold blood?"

"I've trained my whole life for it," I said, and even

though I'd always told myself my training had been for defense, this was the truth.

Finally, after what seemed like forever, Warren nodded. "I can give you that chance."

"And so the hunter becomes the hunted." I smiled wryly as I threw his own words back at him, and held out a hand to shake. "You've got yourself a heroine."

Warren ignored the hand. Instead, with tears suddenly springing into his eyes, he leapt from his chair and plowed full force into my arms. I staggered backward, and the other man, silent all this time, caught my eye over Warren's shoulder and shrugged.

"Okay, okay," I said, pulling away. "Sheesh."

"Did you hear? The first sign has come to pass," Warren said, turning to the other man. "She'll do it. She'll join us."

The man simply nodded. He was beefy, but not in the hard way that Butch had been. More like Santa Claus, I supposed, if Santa had lived in Vegas.

Warren turned back to face me. "This is our witness from the troop's council. He's just here to make sure you're joining us of your own free will, and haven't been coerced in any way."

I looked at him blankly. "You're joking, right?"

"Under any direct duress from me, I mean." He smiled self-consciously, wringing his hands. "I didn't twist your arm or knock you around or anything, did I?"

"No." I turned to the man. "He didn't."

"Good enough for you?" Warren asked impatiently. The man nodded and rose. Ah, there was the difference between him and Santa. He was nearly seven feet tall. "Oh, but where are my manners? Micah, this is Joanna. Jo, Micah."

How did I know he wouldn't have a nice, normal name like Bob or Joe? "Nice to meet you," I said, holding out a hand.

Micah, the behemoth, finally spoke. "I hope you still feel that way when you wake up."

"Wake up?"

The blow came from the side, and caught me on the back of my neck. My legs folded neatly beneath me, and as my eyes rolled into my head I saw Micah looming above me with a steel baton in his hand. I had only a second to think he was faster than he looked before Warren caught me beneath the arms, his lips close to my ear.

"Remember," I heard him say, "we all become who we need to in order to survive."

Then his voice, his image, and his scent all swam away on a final wave of incoherence and mercifully dulling pain.

10

The dreams a person has while unconscious are not the same as when they're asleep. They're more like something from a Bradbury novel, a carnival ride with ominous portents and sinister beings waiting to take siege of your soul. My dreams were like that now, shadowy, one slithering into another, carrying snatches of oblique conversations I'd never had and images of faces I'd never seen.

"More to the left," I heard someone say urgently. *"That's not how it is in the picture, see? It has to be perfect."*

A masked face loomed over me, eyes concerned and considering, before it drew back and fluorescent lights blinded me again. *"She will be perfect."*

No less unnerving were the tattered flashes of things I *had* seen, but combined in new scenes and settings, like a horror film saddled with an alternate ending.

There was Olivia, eyes shooting open to pierce me from her deathbed on the ground nine stories below me. Her skin was bleached white, and all of her blood had pooled in a heart-shaped lake around her broken body. Her gaze wide and imploring, she posed the one question I couldn't answer.

"Why am I dead?" I struggled to reach out to her, but was whisked away, her parting words ringing in my ears. *"Why me and not you?"*

Xavier caught me from above. His grip was steel around my biceps, and as much as I thrashed I couldn't escape him. He dragged me to him, opening his mouth wide to swallow me whole. *"Zoe left you too."*

Then I was running, fighting for air as I fled through a dark desert night. I felt the sharp sting of tumbleweeds against my shins, my ankles turning over on themselves as I ran blindly into boulders and stones, barely keeping out of reach of an unseen fleet-footed pursuer. He—and it was a he—didn't speak at all. Instead his voice invaded my brain by other means, slithering inside, not so much a snake's hiss as the rattle of its tail. *"I should have killed you the first time . . ."*

I woke with a start, breathing hard. The room was dim, though not completely dark, and daylight peered at me through long slats in the window shades. I spied a lumpy outline in the corner of the room, and felt my mouth twitch. Warren, I thought woodenly. I was going to kick his ass.

"You know, you're not funny," I said, causing him to jump. He straightened in his chair, rubbing a long hand over his eyes, and stretched loudly. "You think you're funny, but you're not."

He held up a hand as he rose. "Don't hate."

"Too late." Yawning widely, I lifted a hand to rub over my eyes, but discovered it was too heavy, too far from my face, and too much trouble to complete the movement. Which was odd. Yet having had the distinct displeasure of a lengthy hospital visit once before, I recognized the lethargy as being chemically induced, some sort of painkiller probably. The question was, why had they drugged me? "What am I doing here?"

"Recovering," Warren answered, standing at my side. "And hiding."

"Are they after me?" My heart fluttered beneath my breastbone. "Can you smell me again?"

"Shh, don't worry. You're in isolation. Nobody outside this room can sense your pheromones. It's like . . . you don't even exist."

I took a tentative whiff. All I smelled was hospital; drugs, antiseptic, and the type of cleanliness that erases not only bad odors, but good alike. It was a clean I'd hoped to never experience again. I looked at Warren. "There's nothing. I can't smell me at all."

"I can." He smiled, perching himself bedside. He'd taken off the long duster that made him look like some demented cowboy, wore a simple khaki T-shirt and fatigues, and his hair was pulled back, the matting tightly bound to his head. Each time I saw him, he looked a bit more reputable. Scary.

Closing his eyes, he inhaled deeply, like he was bending over a rose instead of a body. "You, but more so. The unscented thread now blends in with the rest of your genetic makeup. It's beautiful, really. Lit up like some life-saving beacon . . . if you'll excuse the visual analogy."

I closed my eyes and breathed, casting my thoughts downward, inward. Nothing. After several seconds I looked at him again. "So it's like an identifying trait? Like, I don't know, permanent perfume?"

"More like the vein that runs through a particularly strong wedge of blue cheese."

"Thanks a lot." Just when I started liking the guy. "So, when do I get to go home?"

He rose from the bed. I narrowed my eyes. It looked like he was putting distance between himself and me. "There's no easy way to tell you this, Joanna, so I'm just going to say it." My heart did that little flutter again as he took a deep breath. "You're dead. You've been dead for just over a week."

"Dead-dead?" I asked hollowly. "Really dead?"

"Well, obviously you're here, but as far as the mortal world is concerned, yes," Warren said. "Your funeral is tomorrow.

I've saved you the newspaper clippings from the last week."

He motioned to the papers stacked on the bedside tray, and I glanced over to see my face staring up from the top copy, with the headline HEIRESS JOANNA ARCHER PLUMMETS TO DEATH. The byline, dated four days ago, posed the question of whether it'd been foul play or if I'd leapt from the midtown apartment. I dropped my head back, unwilling to read any more.

I was dead, I thought numbly. I no longer existed. And I felt strangely well for the experience.

"If I'm dead," I finally said, "then who am I?"

I motioned down the length of my body, wincing when my hand brushed against my chest. Gasping with as much surprise as pain, I looked down, gasped again, and clutched both breasts in my hands—what I could fit into them, anyway. They were extraordinarily sore, with a tenderness that had less to do with the natural flux of the moon than a surgeon's steel and, apparently, some huge creative license. The drugs had kept me from feeling the ache before, but I sure felt it now.

"What have you done?" I cried, holding them tenderly. I don't think I'd ever heard my own voice so breathy and panicked. Then, brain cells and synapses firing rapidly, another thought occurred. I hadn't actually ever heard my voice this high-pitched before either. I tried it again. "La, la, la, la . . . mother fucker!"

Horrified, I glared at Warren. "You've changed my voice!"

"And your breasts," he said, pointing out the obvious with what I considered a great deal of misplaced pride. I glared, and he took another step backward. Just then Micah entered the room, halting inside the doorway. I lowered my chin and narrowed my eyes.

"You knocked me out," I said accusingly, before turning on Warren again. "And you let him!"

"Well, we couldn't have a dead woman walking about town, could we?" Warren said, like that was a reasonable argument.

"You told me you would take care of it! You said you'd clean up and make sure I wasn't in trouble."

"And we did," Warren argued, crossing his arms. "You can't be charged with a crime, because the only one dead is you."

"But I don't want to be dead!" I screeched in some other person's voice. What was I supposed to do now? Only come out at night? Suck blood or haunt the living?

Warren looked insulted. "Sorry, but it was the only thing I could come up with on the spur of the moment. We had to do something to keep you out of jail, not to mention *alive,* so we brought you here."

I looked around. Where was here? It *looked* like a normal hospital room; uncomfortable bed, machines that made beeping noises. Really bad wallpaper.

"You're in a private facility just outside of town," Micah said, confirming my thoughts. "I work here."

"You're a doctor?" I asked, eyeing his sausage-fingers and substantial girth. He looked more like a pit bull in a lab coat.

"Micah takes all the cases that might send up red flags among the mortal physicians," Warren said. "He's an absolute genius with the scalpel."

Why did I have the feeling the line between genius and mad scientist was frighteningly thin here?

I shut my eyes and dropped my head back onto the pillow. Maybe this was one of those dreams I'd been having. Any moment now I was going to wake up and be myself, and Warren would still be a bum, and Micah some bartender pulling the caps off bottles of Bud. Because I really could use a beer about now.

"That's right," Micah said, causing the dream to implode upon itself. I felt him palm my chin, turning it side to side. "I performed all the work on you myself, and did a bang-up job if I do say so myself."

"Why are you touching my face?" My eyes flew open. "Why is he touching my face?"

Warren looked chagrined. Micah looked surprised. He too glanced at Warren. "You mean you haven't told her yet?"

"Told me what?"

Warren chuckled lightly, a sound tinged with nerves, and had me jerking my head sharply in his direction. "Actually, I was just getting around to it."

"Aw, shit," I said in my foreign voice to no one in particular. "Do I dare look in a mirror?"

"It's really not that bad," Warren said, then backpedaled as Micah shot him a piercing stare. "I mean, you're gorgeous. Nobody would ever think it was you."

"Thanks a lot," I said dryly. Then, tentatively, I lifted a hand to my face to feel for myself. Everything seemed normal until I got to my nose, or whoever's nose this was. Mine had been broken in a sparring class, and the slight off-centeredness lent a sort of aquiline quality to my features, or so I chose to believe. In truth, I was deathly afraid of even the thought of surgery . . . a slight irony given the circumstances.

I let my hands trace downward. My lips were full, but still my own; my chin, however, dipped to a more heart-shaped point than I remembered. I felt for a strand of hair and lifted it, peering sideways. "I'm blond."

"The package said 'Platinum Perfection.' "

I let my head fall back again. The boobs, the voice, the face, the hair . . . I didn't need a mirror to put it all together. Unbidden tears suddenly filled my eyes. I never cried, so my guess was that it too was part of this grand prize package. God, they'd fucked with my body *and* my hormones. "You've turned me into a . . . a . . . a bimbo!"

"Shh," Micah said, patting my shoulder, trying to comfort me. "It's the perfect cover."

The perfect cover for a woman who wants her breasts to enter a room before the rest of her, I thought hysterically. One who relies on her looks to do the talking. One who doesn't even take herself seriously!

"We all have our disguises," Warren added helpfully.

"What?" I snapped angrily. "And 'Yoda on crack' was the best you could come up with?"

"I see you did nothing about her temperament," Warren muttered.

"Some things even I can't fix."

I glared at them both, then spaced my words so that even with the come-hither soft-porn voice they'd know I meant business. "Get. Me. A Mirror."

"Okay, but I'm warning you, it might be something of a shock."

"More shocking than being whacked on the head with a steel baton?" I said sharply. "Or more shocking than waking up officially dead?"

More shocking than watching your own sister die? I didn't say that. Instead, as Warren adjusted the slant of my bed, I held out a hand for the mirror. He gave it to me once I was propped up, and a fresh spasm of alarm sprung up in my chest as I felt their gazes, almost hungry, on my face. Taking a deep breath, I lifted the mirror and looked.

I felt my jaw moving, saw the reflected jaw working in the mirror, but no sound came out. I turned the mirror over, checked for a false back, pounded it against the bed twice, and peered into the glass again. Then I lifted my gaze to Micah's anxious one. "It—It's . . . Olivia."

His face relaxed into a relieved smile.

"*You're* Olivia," Warren corrected, his own smile broad and hopeful.

I returned my gaze to the mirror. I certainly was.

And this time I passed out all on my own.

When I next woke, I was alone. The room was dark, and I thought briefly about calling for a nurse before deciding against it. Instead I reached for the stack of newspapers, but yelped when I lifted the first one. My fingertips were both sensitive and numb at the same time. I felt the structure and weight of the paper, even the fibers that comprised the page, but that was a deep knowledge, one born of previous experience. On the surface it felt like I was holding it between crystal gloves. I overturned my palm and stared.

My fingerprints were gone.

I tapped the pad of my thumb against my forefinger, expecting to hear a clicking like fingernails against glass, but there was only silence. The clink was felt, not heard, as if my bones were banging brittle and cold against one another. It was an odd feeling, slightly nauseating, though perhaps that would lessen with time. For now, I resolutely reached for the newspapers, prepared to feel trees screaming beneath my touch, and began to read.

The articles were stacked by date, most recent on the bottom, and the contents of each became increasingly surreal. They went into excruciating detail, not always flattering or correct, about me, my life, and my tragic demise.

The gist of the story was this: Joanna Archer had died after a botched break-in at her sister's ninth-story apartment. I'd fought and struggled valiantly, but ultimately fell to my death along with my assailant, one Butch Lewis of Houston, Texas. However, I'd saved my sister's life in the process.

How ironic was that? Hailed a hero in death when the reality was I'd been able to save no one. Including, it now seemed, myself. I sighed and read on.

Olivia Archer, reportedly in critical condition, had been relocated to a private facility where even her closest friends and family members, including the megawealthy Xavier Archer, were denied access to see or visit her. An anonymous source—and I had a pretty good idea who that might be—disclosed only that Olivia was stable but presently lying in a life-threatening coma.

I skimmed through the papers again, and thought, there it is. An entire life reduced to black and white. Summed up in a week, old news by the week's end.

I picked up the mirror next to me and gazed again at a face I knew intimately well, and didn't know at all.

"How?" I said aloud. Olivia's singsong voice came out, but it was tinged with a weariness she'd never possessed. How was I supposed to look at her every day? It would be like facing a beautiful, accusing ghost, along with my own still-raw guilt over failing to keep her safe. But that wasn't all I dreaded, and I knew it. Others looked at Olivia and saw softness and beauty and a feminine wealth of power. But I only saw weakness and vulnerability. A potential victim.

In turning me into my sister, Micah and Warren had unwittingly turned me into what I feared most.

"I saw you moving on the monitors." I jumped, dropping the mirror guiltily, and looked up to find Micah peering through the doorway. He was waiting for an invitation. I nodded, and he came in, watching me like a keeper watches a caged lion. "Water?"

He poured from a plastic pitcher and handed me a paper cup. Then he folded his hands in front of his massive body and waited. The water was as crisp and fresh as any I'd tasted, and I finished it off at once. "Thank you."

He smiled, reassured as he returned the empty cup to the table, then perched lightly on the side of the bed. He possessed amazing grace for such a large man. "How do you feel?"

I thought about it. None of the postsurgery blahs. In fact, I felt incredibly well for someone who was dead. Or in a coma. Much less who had marbles for fingertips. "Great, considering."

"You should. You heal cleanly as well as quickly," he said. "And I was very gentle."

I knew it was his way of apologizing. "Thank you."

His fleeting smile was swept away by furrowed brows and worry-filled eyes. "I thought you'd be pleased with the changes. I never stopped to consider how it might affect you to live in your sister's body."

"No offense, Micah, but all of this is new to me. Metamorphosis, people trying to kill me, never mind this acute—and cute, by the way—new sniffer." My sigh reverberated dully throughout the room. "I had twenty-five years to grow used to my face, and now . . . I don't recognize one thing about myself."

I didn't know who I was anymore. Joanna Archer? Olivia Archer? A twenty-first-century superhero, for God's sake?

"Changing a Zodiac member's identity after a supernatural incident is part of the clean-up process. This was a bit extreme, even for us. Usually we can prepare the subject better for change, but with you there simply wasn't time. We don't want to lose you, Joanna. You're very special."

I smiled humorlessly. *Not special* was sounding very good right now.

Micah sighed. "Look, I don't know what Warren's told you, but we're on the verge of collapse. Three star signs have been killed in the past two months, and they weren't novices either. They were full-fledged professionals, the elite—this generation's Zodiac. That's why we had to act quickly to secure you and alter your identity. Nobody can know who you really are, do you understand?"

I didn't, but nodded anyway.

"And nobody knew Olivia better than you, right? You can act and walk and respond the way she did. It's a bonus really that you don't have to remember countless mannerisms and develop a whole new personality. It simplifies things for you." He paused. "It also has the added benefit of keeping you close to Xavier Archer."

"I don't want to be close to him," I said. Micah said nothing, which I was beginning to recognize as a bad sign. "What?"

"He's in the waiting room. He hasn't left in three days."

"No." I turned away, folding my arms across my stomach. He was waiting for Olivia, I thought bitterly. Not me.

Micah nodded, agreeing readily, too readily, with my wishes. When he held out a hand, I regarded it warily. "You feel up to moving around a bit?"

I didn't, but my body ached so much from the lengthy immobilization that I took his hand and stood for the first time in days. Dizziness rolled into my head, but eventually I nodded to Micah that I was okay. He led me across the room to a chair situated next to a full-length mirror. "Sit here. Just get used to being upright for a while."

I knew what he was doing. He wanted me to get used to my face, and to seeing myself the way the world now saw me. He swiveled the chair on its casters so I was in front of the mirror, and pulled a nearby table forward. Then he did something completely unexpected. Lifting a brush from the drawer inside the table, he began to comb through my hair.

How could a large man have such a gentle touch?

"I knew your mother, you know," he remarked, ignoring the way I stiffened. He just continued to brush gently from the ends of my hair to the roots, curling each section softly around his fingers before laying them aside. My eyes drifted away from my face and I began to see the dance of his fingers, that inborn surgeon's skill. "You're a lot like her, actually. You have the same cheekbones . . . well, had. Anyway," he hurried on when I frowned, "your mother was gorgeous. And deadly. She could do things with a combat cane that I never saw before, or since. To tell the truth, I had a bit of a crush on her. We all did, I think."

I still said nothing.

"She gave up everything to infiltrate the Shadow Zodiac through Xavier. It'd be a shame to have all that work go to waste now."

I shook my head, causing the waves he'd just set about my face to tumble this way and that. *You don't understand what you're asking,* I wanted to say. I couldn't face the world like this. Olivia was born feminine and soft. I was about as pliable as new leather. Instead, I muttered, "I don't know how to be a superhero."

Micah smiled gently at that. "Nobody's born knowing how. We're just born with specific gifts. Think of the things you're naturally good at, those that you loved to do as a child. When a new recruit begins his or her training, we build on those gifts. Eventually they develop into weapons, and those can be used against the enemy."

"Are there that many ways to kill a Shadow agent?"

Piling my hair upon my head, pinning strands here and there in a close imitation of Brigitte Bardot, he hummed, a melancholy sound that resonated throughout his entire wide body. "About as many ways as there are to die."

But death was easy, I thought, watching him. No more than a mere breath away. As close yet as distant as a stranger in your bed. Like my real parents. "Is my birth father really trying to kill my mother?" I asked Micah.

"I'm not sure I'm the one who should be telling you this," he murmured, eyes on his fingers. "What exactly *has* Warren told you about your birth father?"

"Only that I was born on both his and my mother's birthday, which makes me unique somehow. And that he's the leader of the Shadow side of the Zodiac. Our enemies."

Micah nodded. "And he's a powerful leader too. Before him we had no problem balancing the Zodiac. We were practically invincible."

"What makes him so different?"

"He's a Tulpa." At my blank look, he shook his head. "Cripes, you really don't know anything, do you? A *Tulpa*. A person who's been created rather than birthed."

Images of the Tin Man and the Scarecrow flashed through my head. Then a rib being pulled from a man's side, the man himself formed with clay. "Created how?"

"Someone imagined him into being."

I stared at him wordlessly.

"I know," Micah said, holding up a hand, "it's not something our western culture can easily understand but the eastern philosophers accept it readily as fact. Think about it. Take someone with the concentration of a Tibetan monk. Now have that person apply all his thought and energy into visualizing a being. The power of a disciplined mind is so profound, so mighty, that it can actually imagine that being into existence. That entity becomes their Tulpa."

"But . . . you can't *imagine* a person into existence. It's not possible."

"Sure it is. That's the power of the mind, isn't it? What you tell yourself is true becomes true for you. We all have the power to create in one form or another."

I thought of painters, writers, mothers. "Yeah, but not everybody uses it."

"Ah, but this person did use it, and he used it for evil. He imagined a being both strong and wicked. One strong enough to rule a group of nefarious beings as instructed, with no question or conscience. But the creator didn't count on one thing."

"What?"

Micah smiled wryly. "Once the Tulpa gained enough clarity and substance in the originator's mind, it became independent. It took on a form and personality of its choosing, then began acting out of its own consciousness. Began ruling and doing as he liked."

"But who would imagine such a thing in the first place? And why?" I asked, earning myself a look of ironic amusement.

"Why is simple. Power. Immortality. If you can create a living being out of nothing more than the gray matter in your mind, knowing that if you just give it enough substance it'll live forever, then a part of you will live forever as well.

"As for who?" Micah chuckled humorlessly. "Well, that was the million-dollar question. The great mystery of our world. The axis upon which all our fates hinged. It was the mystery your mother was intent upon figuring out."

And she had. It took her years to do it, but eventually she came upon a mortal named Wyatt Neelson, a westerner who was a fervent student of Tibetan lore. However, he hadn't limited himself to Tibetan studies, or Buddhism, but was a self-taught student of all world religions. His original goal was to create his own religion, an amalgamation of those things he most fervently believed in.

Very Jim Jones of him, I thought wryly as Micah went on.

"But then he got distracted by the idea of a Tulpa. I mean, why coerce, convince, and hope that people will follow you when you can create a being who will compel, even force, them to do so?"

Why, indeed. So Mr. Neelson set about creating an entity that wouldn't age, and couldn't be killed—a god among mortals. He figured it'd be much easier to convince people to give in to their weaker natures—hate, lust, greed . . . all of the seven deadlies—than to convince them to do good. He quit studying the religious doctrines and focused solely on meditation, harnessing the power of his mind, dedicating fifteen years of his life to creating the Tulpa.

"See, we don't know if the Tulpa can be killed—we haven't found a way yet, at least—but Zoe thought if we could somehow kill its creator, maybe it would sever any lingering power between the two of them. Create a gap. We could then act upon any resulting weakness, infiltrate the Shadow organization or kill the Tulpa outright."

"So my mother got close to this Tulpa in order to find out who his creator was?"

"She spent years gaining his trust, concealing her identity, masking her scent. It wasn't easy, but she was dogged." Micah shook his head in admiration. "So convincing that sometimes even we wondered whose side she was on. Yet, she always came through with some small bit of information that would give us an edge, or stop an attack, or save a Zodiac member's life along the way."

"She was gaining his trust."

"Getting in tight." Micah nodded behind me. "And she used whatever means she had to in order to get there."

Including her body. "He never thought his greatest enemy would be in bed with him."

"Most men wouldn't." Micah placed his hands on my shoulders, causing me to look up and meet his eye. "Don't think she didn't love you, Jo. You wanted to know who your father is, and I'm telling you. He's pure, unfiltered evil." I flinched. "But he bedded down with pure goodness and didn't even know it. She had the option to rid herself of the pregnancy, but even knowing that keeping you would risk everything she'd worked for, she didn't. She wanted you. More, even, than she wanted him."

She had wanted me. But she had left me too. "So what happened?"

He smiled, but it was reserved. "She succeeded."

"She did?"

He nodded. "Just in time too. It wouldn't be much longer before the Tulpa could see she was pregnant, to *smell* she was pregnant. But she found Wyatt Neelson, and immediately killed him herself. Got away clean, and disappeared like smoke.

"Problem is, every time you kill someone, not only do you destroy their signature scent, you leave your own in its place, like a calling card. Great when you want the recognition, but hell on subterfuge. When the Tulpa found out it was your mother who betrayed him, he became crazed."

"But did he become weaker?"

Micah shook his head. "Stronger. It was like cutting the strings from a puppet only to discover you'd freed it from shackles. The belief of the other Shadows was already strong enough to keep him going, so he was free to destroy and rage and run the Shadow organization the way he wanted. And what he wanted, more than anything, was to find Zoe and crush her.

"Here's the genius of it, though. While he was looking far and wide, she masked her scent, created another new identity for herself, and took up with Xavier. Snuck back in and hid right under the Tulpa's nose. You were born shortly after—Xavier's child, for all the world knew."

And then she'd had Xavier's real child too. It made me wonder if she'd ever been with a man solely for love.

"She just wouldn't give up," Micah continued, shaking his head. "A more single-minded and brave woman I've never met. She spent years with the Tulpa, then years with Xavier, and in the process forfeited any personal joy she might have had, any chance at a normal life."

"She still failed," I pointed out.

"Yes, but she was so close," he said, tucking a curl behind my ear. "A few more weeks and she would've had him."

"But?" I prompted, needing to know why she'd disappeared so abruptly, both when I'd needed her most and these people had needed her also.

"But you."

Micah looked at me with utter stillness, a bittersweet smile on his face. "You inherited more than your mother's cheekbones, Joanna. You possess her genetic makeup, and while she had the ability to hide her own scent, you weren't protected. You hit puberty, entered what we call the second life cycle, and your hormones went rampant. Shadow agents were scouring the city looking for her, and one of them—"

"Found me." I closed my eyes as the final pieces of the puzzle clicked together. No wonder her grief had been so palpably guilt-ridden.

"He tried to kill you, to kill everything that was good and pure and . . . Zoe in you. Just so you know, any one of us would have died that night."

But I hadn't. Why? I glanced at myself in the mirror. The eyes were still mine, I noticed. They'd deepened like the night at the mention of my attack. "His genes," I said. "They protected me."

Micah inclined his head. "I guess you could say the Tulpa, the creation, was now your creator. You're something new, Joanna. Something never seen before, though your existence has been foretold. See, you're the only one who's ever been both . . . certainly the only one who's ever survived such an attack. *The only one.*"

Then he explained about someone called the Kairos, the fulcrum, upon whom all their fates hinge. It was part of their mythology, both Shadow and Light, and Warren apparently thought *I* was it. I was silent for a while, trying to let that soak in with all the rest, but everything just seemed to pile up on the surface of my consciousness. "Does he know about me?" I finally asked.

Micah shook his head. "Not that you're his daughter, thus not that we suspect you're the Kairos either. He only knows that you're Zoe's. We can all smell it on you now that you've reached your third life cycle. And now that he's aware of your existence, he'll be gunning to take out his revenge on you."

So the leader of the paranormal underworld—or at least that of the greater Las Vegas valley—had a hard-on for my blood. Fabulous. I bit my lip and looked up at Micah through the mirror. "So did he do it?"

"What? Who?"

"The man. That night. Did he kill . . ." I searched for the right words, but there weren't any. There was only the truth. "Did he kill all that was good in me?"

"Yes," Micah said softly, but smiled. "But that you're even asking that question should reassure you."

"I don't understand."

"Simple, Joanna. He broke the potential hero in you. Then your mother put you back together."

The machines were silent, no dripping or beeping to mark the passage of time, and the room was painfully quiet as I pondered this. An answer to one of my life's most enduring questions was taking shape in my mind, but before I could form it aloud, Micah did it for me.

"She gave you everything she could, every olfactory blend we'd created to protect her, every personal power that kept her whole. She used chemistry to mask your pheromones and then she hid you, even from us. But that left her open to discovery and vulnerable to attack. She knew it was only a matter of time before the Tulpa found her, and if he got hold of her . . ." Micah shuddered.

"But how could she just leave? Abandon everything she'd worked for?" Abandon *us*, I wanted to say. I wondered if I hadn't said it aloud because Micah gave me such a look of disdain and annoyance that I immediately felt ashamed.

"She gave it all up *for* you."

I didn't move, not even to swipe at the curl that lay tickling my left cheek. I heard myself breathing, heard Micah behind me, and cast my thoughts in his direction, just to see what I would discover. He smelled like silver powder, rain clouds, and Old Spice. The blend fit him perfectly.

"So what am I supposed to do now?"

Find the Tulpa? Find my mother? Find out how the Shadow agents were killing off the star signs?

"Just learn to stay alive," Micah said gently, and put the brush down. "We'll never know what you're capable of if you don't at least do that."

"And you're going to teach me?"

"Me," he nodded, "and others. We'll teach you to be the person you were born to be. We'll teach you the ways of the Zodiac, of the Archer in particular, and your mother's legacy."

A legacy of star signs and superheroes. I glanced in the mirror at the finished product, an image that had emerged at some point during the past ten minutes. Blue eyes widened back at me, the rims of contacts barely discernable along the edges of my irises. "Wow."

Micah beamed behind me. "We found some great photos of Olivia in your house. You have a real talent. I was able to capture her down to the most minute detail." He reached into the pocket of his lab coat and pulled out the photo I'd brought with me to the motel the night we'd met. "See?"

I held the photo in front of me, studying it carefully, before lifting my eyes to the mirror. There was no discernable difference between the two images. I frowned. Shouldn't I, at least, be able to tell us apart?

"See how happy she is," Micah said, pointing out one difference.

"That's because someone's taking her picture," I muttered. But it wasn't. It was just Olivia. Happy, yes. And open, trusting. Innocent. "I look more like Olivia than Olivia," I said.

"I would bet," he said, nodding cautiously, "if you were willing, you could even fool Xavier."

I glanced at him sharply, then sighed. What were my options? I mean, I wanted my old body back, my own face if only so I could scowl and not have it look like a sultry pout, but I couldn't exactly ask him to change me back, not after I'd already been dead almost a week. An altogether different identity would be just that, *different*, but hardly an improvement.

Stay alive, I thought doubtfully. Survive. To do that I would have to convince the world I was Olivia Archer. One part of me thought, How hard could it be? Olivia shopped and brunched and chaired a bevy of balls and charities, and—at night, when no one was looking—ran an illegal website. I could probably just skip that part.

But what about the harder part of being Olivia? Could I really allow myself to be that soft without seeing myself as weak? That vulnerable without thinking like a victim? That agreeable without believing I was a pushover? It wasn't the things Olivia *did* that gave me pause. It was her utter defenselessness.

I pursed my lips and watched Olivia pout across from me. So that's how she does it, I thought, and smiled. Her mouth—my mouth, actually, since it'd been the same—curved upward, looking devastatingly seductive in that heart-shaped face. I lifted my eyes to Micah, who was watching, waiting as I decided.

"You did a very good job, Micah."

He took the compliment for what it was, a concession, and an acceptance of my situation. A grin bloomed in reply. "Thank you, Olivia," he said.

Olivia.

Me. Olivia. I took a deep breath, then released it slowly, until my body felt emptied of air. Perhaps this way, through me, Olivia could still live. I rather liked that idea. It was the least I could do for her . . . and the only thing now. At least it made me feel less helpless, and that was something. As for the rest, I'd just have to figure it out as I went along. "You may send my father in."

Micah held out a hand and gently helped me to my feet so that we stood eye-to-eye for a moment. "Yes," he finally said, "I think you're quite up for a visit now. A miraculous recovery, really. Your father will be so pleased."

Then it'd be the first time I'd ever pleased him, I thought sourly, but that wasn't what I said to Micah. It wasn't what he was waiting to hear. It wasn't, I thought, what Olivia would say.

"I'm so glad," I said, trying for sincerity.

Micah helped me back into bed, then turned immediately to the door. I think he was afraid I would change my mind. "I'll be right back."

So I leaned back and waited. I tried to tell myself every superhero led a dual existence. Look at Superman and Clark Kent. And Wonder Woman was a kindly secretary when she wasn't lassoing bad guys with a truth-inducing rope. There were others, I was sure, and it made me wonder how many of these stories, these fictions, were pure figments of some comic book writer's imagination . . . and how many had leaked through this thin webbing of reality that separated the Tulpa's world from our own. My own dual existence, this channeling of my dead sister as a cover in the real world, certainly had a fabled air.

I was Joanna, who was dead.

I was Olivia, who was also dead.

And I was also my mother, who had risked her life in ways I had yet to put together so that I might be safe. But if that were true, then I was also *him*. The man, the Tulpa; an entity so evil he had once both destroyed me and simultaneously kept me alive.

"I will kill you." The words hollowed out the hospital room. And that's how I recognized the Tulpa in me. But I liked the sound of that oath, and I swore it again. "I will kill you for what you did to my sister. And for my mother." And for what was left of myself.

And with that pledge still lingering in the air, I leaned back and waited for the man who both was and wasn't my father to enter the room. When he finally did, I looked up and smiled sweetly.

11

They buried me on a cold, blustery January day. I watched the live coverage on the local news from the bed of my enforced convalescence, while a makeup artist dutifully applied the pallor of the sick to my healthy complexion. It had to be Olivia lying in that casket, cold in my place, though I hadn't asked and neither Micah nor Warren had said. The anchor's voice-over seemed obscenely cheerful to me as he followed the procession of Nevada politicians, Stripside entertainers, and business associates of Xavier's flocking to pay their respects to a woman most had never met. It was big news, even in this transient and jaded city. I had to admit, it was like some overwrought adolescent fantasy, being able to watch people mourn my passing, to hear how very much I'd be missed.

Mostly, though, it was just a sad procession of acquaintances detouring through the graveyard on their way to drinks that night, and then on to the rest of their lives. Scattered among them, however, were the few people who'd truly known and loved me. Asaf, who would be quoted in the following day's paper as demanding a full-scale investigation into whether more than one person was responsible for my death. He grieved for me, and I for him.

Then there was an old friend I'd only seen a handful of times since high school, but who had such enormous tears streaming down her face, it made me want to lunge for the phone to tell her I was all right. Or at least alive. I was also surprised to see Olivia's friend, Cher, looking lovely as she stood graveside, and not a little alone.

Then there was Xavier. He stood a bit apart from everyone else, appearing dignified if a little bored at the whole affair, and the sound bite accompanying a close-up of my casket was of him saying how grateful he was that I'd saved Olivia's life. "She sacrificed herself for her sister, and this is what gave her death, and therefore her life, true meaning."

I felt no anger over the words. He had clutched me in his arms the day before, thinking I was Olivia, shedding tears as real as he was capable of producing. As useless and distracted a father as he'd been to me, at least he'd loved Olivia, and I was gratified she'd had that much.

Then another man appeared. Lean in silhouette, he flanked Xavier's left shoulder, his empty blue eyes snaking this way and that.

"Ajax." I leaned forward on my hospital bed, squinting at the image. Looking skeptical, and dangerous in an ebony trench coat, he turned his attention to the camera, nose twitching. "You bastard."

"Do you mind, ma'am?" The makeup artist, some girl named Raine, raised a pierced brow, sponge in hand. She'd been dabbing until circles appeared beneath my eyes, and creating fading bruises on my cheekbones for Xavier's visit later that evening. I'm sure she wondered why, but I knew Micah was paying her enough not to ask. I ignored her, and turned my attention back to Ajax. He was gazing to the left, the wind lifting the hair from the nape of his neck as he sucked in a big mouthful of it.

"I'm right here, you rat-fucking bastard," I said, and my

breath caught when he turned and looked directly at the camera. A look of such hatred passed over his face I thought for a moment he'd heard me. Then his eyes fired like torches and a knowing smile jerked at one corner of his mouth. The same smile he'd shown me at dinner when he claimed he was going to kill me.

But he hadn't heard me, and despite the look, he hadn't seen me either. I knew, because just then he turned and stepped from the frame to reveal exactly what—who—had caught his interest.

"Oh, God." I had to put a hand to my mouth to prevent the wail that threatened to rise from my chest. "God. Ben."

He wept openly, shamelessly, tears running over his cheeks, his mouth contorted in pain. He shook off the consoling arm of one of his colleagues, and there were more than a few, all in uniform and looking awkward around their comfortless friend. Ben, I thought, who had kissed me so passionately I'd forgotten about danger. Ben, whom I'd safely left behind to go to Olivia's.

Ben. Who thought he'd lost me yet again.

Now I was weeping, and Raine had silently retreated, uncertain what she should do next. In my searing horror and grief over Olivia, in the consuming fury that had impelled me to take another person's life, and in my shock at finding myself with a whole new identity, I had utterly forgotten Ben.

But what was this? I sucked in a breath and held it there, tears drying instantly in my eyes. Helplessly I watched Ajax approach Ben and speak words that had his head jerking in surprise. Of course the sound was muted, the anchor's solemn voice-over blabbing on and on about my place in society—my father's place, really—and Olivia's estimated inheritance now that she no longer had to share it with another. But *I* saw Ajax's mouth move. His thin lips went wide with the syllables, exaggerating the words, as if he knew I was watching and wanted me to follow, and understand.

My condolences.

Ben had already reached out to shake his hand when recognition flashed over his face, freezing it for an instant, and he didn't move while Ajax pumped his hand with an overly firm grip, a snaking smile taking the place of his faux compassion. I saw the instant Ben tried to yank his hand away, you could catch it if you knew to look for it, but Ben's friends—sharp-eyed cops though they were—didn't. They heard the words. They caught the back and forth pumping of a solid handshake. They saw only one man offering sympathy to another.

But I saw something else.

A slim silver chain snaked around Ajax's neck, taunting. I gasped, putting my hand up to my own naked throat, and Ajax shifted and smiled. The chain glinted in the thin winter air.

And Ben lunged for his throat.

The commentator interrupted his live report as Ben's friends yanked him back, hands pulling at his arms, his torso, his neck, while Ajax plastered an innocent look on his face. Ben was yelling now, his face red and wild, hair falling over his forehead, his suit jacket raised up around his chest. The commentator was attempting a play-by-play, but he must have been prompted to go to a commercial. There was enough time to see Xavier's head swivel as he observed the ruckus with a slight roll of his eyes. Then Ben was yanked from the frame. Ajax shot the camera, and me, a victorious smile.

"No!" I screamed, leaping for the television just as the picture cut off. Makeup went flying, the bedside tray clattered to the floor, and I slapped my palms on the screen once, twice, then sent a fist flying through it. Raine let out a terrified squeal and backed into the corner. "You stay away from him! You leave him alone!"

I yanked the television from its mount and sent it crashing across the room. The sound was divine; satisfying and gloriously destructive. A switch flipped inside me, and havoc coursed through my limbs. And suddenly I couldn't stop. I threw everything—the monitors, the machines, the cords, the tables and plastic chairs. All the while a voice, my true voice, was severing the strands of my new vocal cords. "I'll kill you, I'll kill you, I'll kill you . . ."

Olivia, so good and sweet and pure, never had a chance against Butch, and my heart had broken at that fact every day since her death. And my mother, who *would* have been able to fight him, hadn't been there to protect her; ever since I learned the real reason for her absence, my heart had bled for her too.

But never once had I allowed it to break for myself. I had breath, and I had life, and I told myself that was enough, and more than I deserved. But after seeing Ben's face, his all-consuming anguish, there was no stopping it. I screamed, and broke, and shattered everything around me, so it would represent how I felt, so it would match my insides; everything torn and stripped, raw and aching. So tired. And so very, very sorry.

When I'd finished—two minutes, two hours, or two years later—I found myself curled into a fetal position, rocking back and forth in the corner of a demolished and empty room; the makeup artist had long since fled, the lights busted on the walls, their counterparts swinging on bare wires from the ceiling, machines toppled and silent and dead.

"Joanna."

I looked up. Warren's appearance, as sudden as the first time I'd seen him, surprised me, as did his use of my real name. He'd been calling me Olivia for days. He was dressed the fool again; an unwashed, unwanted bum reeking of desperation and desertion, but his eyes were trained on me with a sort of sober ferocity, and that brought fresh tears to my eyes. He was really seeing me. "Now the true healing can begin."

I shook my head slowly, then harder, and covered my face with my palms. This wasn't healing. This was attack; the way antibiotics assault a foreign agent planted inside the body, though in this case I *was* the foreign agent. I was the virus inside.

"I am not dead," I told him through stiffly splayed fingers. He knew this, of course, but I needed to hear the words for myself. "I'm not. I feel more, and I smell more. I'm more alive than I've ever been."

"Olivia—" he began, crossing the room.

But I cut him off and backed away. I didn't want consoling words or generic explanations. "I'm not Olivia! I'm not weak or vulnerable! I'm not . . ." That good, I thought. "That innocent." What I was was *alive*, damn it, and I wanted someone, anyone, to know it! No, that wasn't quite true either.

I wanted Ben to know it.

Warren crouched in front of me. "It's enough that you know who you are. As long as you know, the rest won't matter. In time." And something in his tone made me think he'd had occasion to tell himself the same thing.

But he was wrong, I thought as he held out a hand. It mattered because Ben mattered. What this was going to do to him—again—mattered. But I took the hand anyway. It was the only one being offered to me.

Warren pulled me to my feet and steadied me before him. "I know who you are too. And I promise I won't ever forget."

"I'm Joanna," I said, and allowed myself to weep. I was both Light and Shadow and knew now that I always had been, but more than that . . . "I'm still me."

I remained in the hospital another week. Even Xavier's raging and threats weren't enough to get Micah to release me into his custody. I was safer there than I'd be anywhere on the outside, and Micah wanted to keep me hidden until he was sure they'd completely masked my old scent and he could provide me with a new olfactory identity as well.

"We have to make sure it's perfect. Ajax is especially

good at scenting out the identities of new agents," Micah told me one day as he toyed with my hair again. "Probably because he takes it personally."

"Personally? Why?"

Micah shook his head, muttering something about Warren and his damned secrets, before continuing, louder, "Ajax's mother betrayed the Tulpa by crossing over and trying to become Light."

I turned in my chair to face him. "You can do that?"

Micah forcibly turned me back to the mirror. "Oh, yes. Just like humans, we always have a choice in who we want to be."

I thought that was a damned ironic thing for him to say to me, but Micah had resumed flat-ironing my hair—I'd apparently become his favorite new doll—and missed my pointed look in the mirror. "We took out three of their Zodiac signs in as many weeks because of her advice."

At least I knew now why Ajax grew so incensed when anyone mentioned his mother. "So did she stay . . . Light?"

Micah shrugged. "She may have, if she'd lived long enough. We changed her identity, masked her scent, did everything we could to make her 'invisible' to the Shadows. Only one person could have located her."

Someone who'd been inside her, I realized. Someone who'd been *of* her. "Ajax let the Tulpa kill his own mother?"

"Oh, no," Micah said, putting down the brush. "When Ajax found her, he did it himself."

My own sense of smell was also blossoming in ways I'd never have imagined. The bouquets that filled my room were like floral injections into my bloodstream. The roses bled color behind my eyes, carnations spiced my palate. The first time I stepped onto the hospital's outdoor patio I almost fainted at the assault of textured scents there. I could smell emotions too; the gaseous heat of anger, the seepage of cloying suspicions into the pores, and the dry vibration of denial as the dramas of the hospital played out around me.

But Warren was wrong about the rest of the world not mattering. I grieved for Ben daily, and, though I'd never given it much thought before, found myself also mourning my old life; longing for my house, my darkroom, my clothing, my old body. I couldn't believe how much I'd taken for granted; the ability to move about in the world as myself, and speak my mind without wondering first if it was something Olivia would say.

I was a disappointment, if not a complete failure, at this last task. Xavier would frown when I automatically responded caustically to one of his remarks, leaving my bedside not long after. And Cher would fall uncharacteristically silent when I reacted to one of her bubble-brained ideas with nothing more than a blank stare. Micah explained to them that I wouldn't seem totally myself for quite some time, that hiccups in my character were to be expected, and I was experiencing prolonging trauma from seeing my sister plummet to her death. That, at least, was true. But he never explained how to recover from that.

He did, however, fill me in on the Zodiac's history, answering my questions as rapidly and thoroughly as I fired them, still feeling guilty, I think, about turning me into my sister.

When Warren first told me about the Zodiac troop, I pictured cartoon figures, hyperbolic symbols of the forces of good pitted against evil flying through the air, wearing ungodly amounts of spandex, and bright capes fluttering behind them like bulletproof banners. But Micah spoke of an organized, if otherworldly, quest for personal power, dominance over city politics and influence over community mores, and gradually the bright primary colors of Saturday morning cartoons were replaced by stark slashes of blurred action. The human drama of life and death played out in my imagination on a canvas of black and white . . . one occasionally splattered in bloodred. In other words, it was our reality of Shadow versus Light.

We'd always been here, Micah said. We weren't extraterrestrial like Superman or Captain Marvel, and we hadn't always been referred to as superheroes. But as long as there'd been humans, there'd been individuals who could access places and planes others could not. People who were faster, stronger, better healers.

"Ever wonder what a mortal would be capable of if he or she utilized more than just ten percent of their brain at any given time?" he asked me one day while fine-tuning the work he'd done on a tooth I'd chipped but Olivia hadn't.

A few mortals do use more than that, of course, and even one percent is enough to make a perceptible difference. For example, there are those individuals who can control pain enough to, say, pin themselves with a foot-long needle—in one side of their body and out the other—with no apparent damage done and no blood to show otherwise. There are others who can spontaneously inflict a sort of self-hypnosis, slowing their bodily functions enough to place themselves into an almost catatonic state. This was particularly helpful, Micah said, if there's some mortal injury done to the body and no medical help readily available.

So it was possible, in part, for humans to attain greater strength and control and ability . . . given a healthy amount of discipline and practice. "For us, though," and here Micah winked as he peered into my mouth, "it's as natural as the blood moving through our vessels."

Yet even we have our limits. We might be able to manipulate the boundaries of our minds and bodies, but we're still bound by the universal laws of gravity and physics, and a good deal of our abilities can be explained by quantum mechanics, something Micah said humans are only marginally beginning to understand . . . and which I didn't understand at all.

So, though free of mortal law, we were still confined by universal law, which is why the troops had developed ways for science to augment our abilities; chemistry to mask our pheromones, biochemistry to study how different we really are from human, and genetics, because—like mortals—we're constantly evolving, even still.

I laughed, however, when Micah claimed even astrology was considered a science. I couldn't stop myself, though I wish I had when he drew back, leaving a suction hose hanging from my mouth, his fierce expression made fiercer by the sharp dental instrument held aloft in his hand. "Myths—Greek, Roman, Neopagan—die out, Joanna. But you can't kill the stars. Astrology *is* a science. Maybe not a well-understood one, but back in the day doctors like me were called shamans. Scientists were called mystics, and these were the mediators between the visible and invisible worlds. There's no difference between the cabalistic and medical fields, not if you really think about it. Both still have impenetrable secrets, and if you can't bring yourself to believe that, just remember this: *every* life and death is written in the stars."

But I was struggling with something much more basic than that. I was having trouble wrapping my brain around the idea that I wasn't human, that I was something . . . extra. Something other. Micah, realizing this, tried to simplify things for me.

"Look," he said, a smile reaching his eyes, my insult about the science of astrology all but forgotten. "Think of us as being related to mortals in the same way primates are. We're long removed cousins, but on the opposite side of the developmental spectrum." And then he shot me a full smile. "What? You didn't think the human race was all there was, did you?"

Yeah, I kind of had. But there was no denying what had happened to me. Or the things I could do now. My lungs felt like they'd been expanded to twice their size. I could run without losing my breath . . . fast too. I could climb without fear of falling, because I could fall without fear of dying. Metamorphosis had changed every molecule, and I didn't even need Micah to explain that. I knew it as soon as I began healing from injuries any mortal would've died from.

So, I accepted Micah's explanations, and began viewing the once colorful world—of Vegas and comics and the world in all its varying shades of gray—in terms of black and white. The bruises applied by the makeup artist—a new one; Raine had refused to return—were now applied in a light dusting. I grew used to seeing Olivia's face greet me every day in the mirror. And the day would soon come, I knew, when I'd have to step beyond the sanctuary of the hospital walls and face my new life as her. And, as strange as it sounded, as some sort of superhero.

"She's going to get too muscular," Warren complained one day when I was training outside. It felt amazing to move, and I reveled in the stretch and give of my muscles as I jumped and lunged and lifted. I longed for the discipline of my Krav Maga gym, yet I knew if I walked in there like this, as Olivia, Asaf would die. From laughter.

"She's not," Micah argued from his position on the shaded porch. It was one of the few times since that first day the three of us had been together, and unsurprisingly, we'd picked up exactly where we left off. Squabbling like kids. "I've layered her in soft tissue. She's well-protected."

"What am I? A fucking Christmas ornament?" I asked, punching at the weighted bag.

"I don't know why you're bothering with your mortal skills anyway," Warren said to me. "You're faster and stronger than you've ever been. A human could never touch you. Once you acquire your personal weapon, your own conduit, you'll be nearly invincible."

I steadied the punching bag with my gloved hands and shot him a sidelong look. It was the "nearly" part that bothered me. "Invincible," I repeated, jabbing with my right. "Like Butch? That kind of invincible? Or do you mean like Ajax? If I recall correctly, his weapon wasn't so invincible."

"Don't get cocky."

Micah chuckled. "She's got a point."

"Olivia doesn't box," Warren said, ignoring Micah. "She doesn't fight."

I stepped back from the bag and wiped my face with my forearm. Then I smiled wickedly, petulant at best on this angelic face. "She does now."

"No," Warren said, stepping forward. "You have to appear to the world just like the Olivia of old. There can be nothing of Jo in your words or your actions. Your life, and all of our lives, depend on that."

I'd been alternating jabs and cross punches while he spoke, a rapid staccato of beats overlaying his words, but now I stopped, breathing heavily, and smiled. He didn't smile back, which I couldn't hold against him. Even I could smell my defiance. "Warren. What kind of person could watch her sister get thrown through a plate-glass window and not be changed in some way? People aren't static, everyone grows. I've given a lot of thought about what Olivia would do, and I think she'd start studying Krav Maga."

"Another good point," said Micah.

"You're just projecting what you'd want her to do."

"I think I know her better than you." *Knew* her, I corrected mentally, and started punching again, uppercuts this time.

"You'd better hope so," he said. "Because it's time to go."

That stilled me. I lifted my chin, sniffed. "Where?"

"Back into the mortal world. Back into your life."

Olivia's life, I thought, and looked away. "I'm not ready."

"Sweetie," Micah said, the arbitrator, "if Olivia doesn't return soon, the Shadow agents are going to get suspicious."

"Won't they be suspicious anyway?"

Warren shook his head. "Ajax saw you alive, but he didn't see Olivia die. He didn't even know she was there that night because by the time we showed up her scent had been—"

"Murdered," I said dully, and combined my punches. Jab, cross. Jab, cross, hook.

"Anyway, we always disengage," Warren said quickly. "Change our identities so even our closest friends and family won't recognize us. That way the temptation to return to the old life is eliminated. Ajax knows this, so there's no reason for him to look for you there."

"Besides," Micah added, "Olivia is Xavier Archer's daughter, and anything with the Archer insignia on it is off limits. They wouldn't dare touch her now."

I raised a brow. Hadn't my name been Joanna Archer? Hadn't I been under the protection of that insignia when Ajax first attacked me? Warren shook his head, reading my thoughts. "Who do you think wrote that note to Xavier?"

Micah nodded. "It was more of a bullet than a letter. He should have just put a bull's-eye on your forehead."

I ripped my gloves off and reached for some water. "But won't they be able to tell it's me and not really Olivia? Smell me or something?"

He shook his head. "It's different now that you've metamorphosized. You're harder to track. We've also given you an injection for extra coverage. The only time your real pheromones might be clearly recognized is when you're either injured or overly emotional. So practice the meditation exercises we've taught you every day," he added helpfully.

Warren said, "And no fighting."

No losing, I thought, but kept silent.

"Look, all you have to do for the next few days is hang around Olivia's apartment," Warren said. "If she kept a diary, read it. If she had a hobby, study it. Pillage her wardrobe, examine her photo albums, and create a past for yourself. Do everything possible to become your sister. When you're ready, we'll take you to the sanctuary."

"Where you'll meet the other star signs," Micah added. "So you can learn how to be the Archer."

"But first you need to learn to be Olivia. Only when you can fool even those who knew her best can we introduce you to the others."

"Why only then?"

"Because if you're not convincing, if you're not *Olivia*," he said soberly, "there's only one other person you could be."

"He's right, Jo," Micah said, noting my reaction. "Nobody can know who you really are, do you understand?"

I leaned my head against the nylon bag, suddenly weary. Then I tilted and looked up at the sky. It was an unending sprawl of baby blue above me, without a cloud to hide behind. "Is there no safe place?" I finally asked.

Nobody answered me. It occurred to me then that nobody could.

12

I called Cher to pick me up the next morning, which she sounded completely, frighteningly, thrilled to do, and promised me she'd be there within the hour. I'd argued about this with Warren and Micah, but in the end reluctantly agreed it was exactly what Olivia would have done. I replaced the receiver, shaking my head. "I can't stand that woman."

"She's Olivia's best friend."

"She's as plastic as a Visa."

"So are you," Warren pointed out. I glared at him in reply.

Cher showed up at noon sharp in a candy-apple-red convertible and a matching cat suit. I actually looked for the stripper's pole in the backseat. As it turned out, Cher had a matching cat suit for me in the nylon Prada bag slung over her shoulder. I shot Micah a look of pure desperation as she pressed me into the bathroom. He smiled and waved me away.

"Fucking doctors," I mumbled under my breath, and knew he'd heard when he cleared his throat loudly in the next room.

"Sorry?" Cher said, turning cornflower blue eyes upon me like question marks.

"Nothing," I said. It was obviously not the answer I should have given. Her face dropped, but an overly bright expression popped up almost immediately. I looked away, which I was sure was a relief to us both. "What is this thing, anyway?"

"It's your traveling suit, darlin'," Cher said cheerily as I fingered the shiny cloth. "Just like Evel Knievel. Or Thelma and Louise. If you're gonna go, you gotta go in style."

Note to self, I thought later, catching a startling glimpse of the two of us in the lobby windows. Get. New. Best. Friend.

"Are you sure you want to do this, Livvy-girl?" Cher said as we sped across town in the low 'vette, breaking at least three major traffic laws that I counted. Cher drove the same way she walked and breathed and lived—like there was no one else who would dare take up her sprawling southern space. "You know you can always stay with me."

"Yes," I said, thinking *No* as she took a turn at thirty-five miles an hour. No, to doing any of this. No to an apartment that reminded me of the last time I'd seen my sister's beautiful, stricken face; no to being a superhero; and—as I ate glass on the next curve—definitely no to Cher!

Maybe I could move north to Carson City. Or really north. Like Alaska. Yeah, I thought, that sounded good. What were the chances of running into evil igloo dwellers? I made a note to ask Micah about it later. Ice fishing sounded attractive right now.

We arrived at the high-rise and ascended to the ninth floor in silence. Exiting into a deserted hallway, the only sound was the jingle of the keys as Cher fumbled at the lock. I took a deep breath as the door opened. She shot me a worried look, I tried on a reassuring smile, and Cher immediately pulled the door shut again. Shit. I'd probably grimaced.

"Olivia, darlin'," she said, her drawl even more pronounced with troubled sincerity. "Come on home with me.

You know you're welcome to stay as long as you'd like."

"I know." I didn't meet her eye.

She tried again. "We can brunch every day, and get manicures and spray-on tans, and have that big guy you like, Trevor the Tank, rub *très* essential oils all over our bodies!"

It was enough to have me reaching for the door. "It's okay. I can do this."

I wanted to ignore the hurt that passed over Cher's face. I wanted to push past her and just shut the door behind me, but something about it touched me. After all, I told myself, she'd lost Olivia too. She just didn't know it.

"Look, Cher," *Cher-bear*, Olivia would have said, but I'd cut out my tongue before allowing that to pass my lips. I faced her squarely and said, "I loved . . . love this apartment. You know I do. The doctors say I have to reclaim this space for myself, and the sooner I do that, the sooner things will be . . ."

What? I thought, searching for the right word. Normal? Better? Fixed?

"I know what you're saying, darlin'," she interrupted, with a shake of her head. "But I worry about you being here alone."

"You don't need to worry about me," I assured her. "At all."

"At least let me go through the apartment with you," she said, and noting my hesitation, flushed with indignation. "Just this time, for goodness' sake. I'll leave as soon as we get you settled, I promise. Just let me come in and show you what I've done with the place."

In truth, I was grateful for the company. Olivia may have had a plethora of pleasant memories to bind her to this apartment, but I had only a few, and the very last of these kept making guest appearances in my psyche. Cher kept up a solid monologue as we moved from room to room, a cheerful din that only added to the unreality of the neat and orderly apartment. It was bright, the January sun streaming in through the wide windows nothing like the black-skied storm I'd fled weeks earlier. It was clean too; freshly aired, and redolent with flowers that floated in crystal vases everywhere I turned.

Cher explained that after the police and the repairmen and cleaners had all finished their work, she'd come in herself and added the small touches she knew I loved. Irises in the vase by the entryway. Vanilla candles for the thick candelabra on the dining room table. A cluster of daisies in the living room. Things *I* didn't even know Olivia had liked. She'd even bought a replacement cell phone for the one that'd ended up on the ground the night of Butch's attack. This one was encrusted with Swarovski crystals—bloodred lips pursed against a shining diamond background—and Cher informed me she'd already programmed it with all the numbers of "my" various contacts, liaisons, and lovers.

I immediately turned the phone off, dropped it atop a chenille throw, and felt panic skirt through my veins. No wonder Cher kept looking at me like she didn't know me. No wonder Xavier had been all too willing to let her drive me home, uncomfortable with the long silences that had never pooled between him and Olivia before.

I don't even know what kind of flowers she liked, I thought desperately. How the hell was I to know what she'd say or do? What she ate? Who she'd call? It was with a dull stab to the chest that I suddenly realized I'd never really known my sister at all.

Then I spotted the package. Still aligned on the corner of the coffee table where Olivia had left it, it seemed to have been forgotten by everyone, until now. I reached for it and clutched it to my chest, eyes squeezed tight. My birthday present. The last Olivia would ever give me.

"I didn't know what you wanted to do with it." Cher's voice made me jump. I turned to find her wringing her hands nervously, a wary expression on her face. "It didn't seem right to open it, or throw it away." She hesitated. "Was I right to keep it?"

Her uncertainty, as sweet and fragile as any of Olivia's

objects, was what broke me. I nodded, but couldn't speak, my throat astonishingly thick with tears. I hadn't realized I had any left to shed. My face crumpled.

"I don't think I can do this," I said, sitting heavily. "I don't know how."

"Why, of course you can." Cher rushed to my side in an onslaught of concern and perfume. She finally had something useful to do, some way to help. "And I'm going to help you. You're gonna reclaim this space you love so much and erase all the bad memories. Fill it with good ones again. New ones. Jo would want you to."

I wondered about that. Would I? Would I want Olivia to get on with her life? To forget that anything evil had ever touched her inside these walls? "Yeah," I sniffed, and glanced at the present in my hand. "Yeah, she would, wouldn't she?"

"Sure she would," Cher encouraged. "Why, I remember the first time I met Joanna. She kicked us outta her bedroom, and never let us back in. Remember? Never was one to look back, that Jo Archer."

"You were making out with her four poster bed." I stood, wiping away the tears with the back of my hand. "You were demonstrating how to French kiss on her headboard."

"Well, she needed the lesson. Before Ben, she was useless when it came to boys."

She was right, and that irked me enough to have my tears drying. I put the package down and stared out the window where cars and pedestrians passed below us in miniature. I felt like reaching down and picking one of those people up, then putting them down in an entirely new location. I felt like changing someone else's fate forever. I felt mean and small, and I didn't even have to wonder which side of me—Light or Shadow—was talking. I closed my eyes to the view.

"You never liked her," I said, before I even knew I was thinking it.

"Oh," she said softly, joining me at the window. "Is that what this is about?"

"This what?" I peered over at her.

"The way you've been acting. The way you keep putting Joanna between us, like a ghost challengin' my every step alongside you. Like she's still alive."

If only you knew, I thought, turning away. "I don't know what you're talking about."

"I think you do," she said, too softly. Her gaze was uncomfortably hard upon mine. "Now I don't expect you to get over something like this in a minute, but you're holding onto Jo like she's the only person you ever lost. And while she always was a strong pillar for you to lean on, she was by no stretch of the imagination perfect."

"I never said I was!"

Shit.

Cher blinked once, then again. "Well, no sugar, you're not either. But at least you don't pretend nothing's ever touched you. That no one ever will again."

My jaw clenched. "Neither did Jo."

"The fuck if she didn't," Cher said, surprising me. "She was like a clock, dropped the day she was attacked. Outside she looked normal, but inside she no longer worked."

I sucked in a breath so deep and quick that it was as if I'd been punched. "You bitch."

Cher's chin shot up, pointed and perfect. It made me wonder if she and Olivia practiced that look in the mirror together. "I'm going to ignore that comment because I know you're under severe mental stress, but I need you to keep going, Olivia. Don't stop *working*. Find a reason, a purpose, to get up in the morning. Don't you remember how good that feels? To have a goal? It used to be your computer work, or the semiannual sale at Saks, but you have nothing motivating you now. And do you want to know why?"

"No."

She told me anyway. "Because you think you are nothing. You feel guilty because she died and you didn't."

"That's not true! I have nothing to feel guilty about. I

tried to save her," I said, not knowing if I was saying this as Olivia or myself. "I tried but I couldn't!"

"So stop kickin' yourself over it!" she said, and forced me to look at her. "It's like you died that day too, right along with Joanna, who never did learn how to live again—"

I gasped.

"—after the attack." She drew away, as if just realizing what she'd said. Shaking her head, she said, "I'm sorry, sugar, but I have to say this. We swore we'd always be honest with one another."

"Honesty doesn't mean being hurtful," I shot back, knowing even as I said it that sometimes it did.

"It means being truthful, the way you wanted to be truthful with Jo. You were just too afraid she'd tune you out, or turn you off, or do whatever it was she was doing to the rest of the world."

"She'd never do that to me!" Would I have? If Olivia had pushed me? If she'd tried to get me to be more open and exposed . . . more like her? And Cher?

"How do you know? You never tried! And now that it's too late, now that you've been gravely hurt, you're wondering—"

"What are you, a psychoanalyst?"

"—if she was right," she continued, ignoring the acidity of my words. "If it's just easier to shut everyone and everything off. To feel nothing—"

"I've been isolated at the hospital if you haven't noticed!"

"—and so you're becoming just like her. An empty shell. A broken clock. Pretty soon, you'll be just another ghost walkin' around, haunting the world with your empty presence."

It was too close. Too close to what I'd felt like. Too close to what I'd believed.

"Get out," I said through clenched teeth. "Get out of my apartment."

She offered up a small, bitter smile, as if I'd just confirmed all she'd said. "That's just fine, Livvy-girl. I'll give you the space you think you want, but at least I won't regret not speakin' my mind. And there's one more thing . . ."

I heaved an impatient sigh.

"No, don't turn away. I want this to be like crystal between you and I. Your sister did not like me, she did not respect me, and she did not treat me well. I want to help you, Liv, but I'm not . . ." She pursed her lips, fighting for control. "I mean, I *refuse* to be your punching bag too."

I thought she might break there, even hoped for it a little, but she didn't. She took a deep breath and finished what she had to say.

"If you keep comparing me to Joanna, you're not going to like what you see. I'm just me, same as always. And I'm not going to change. Not even for you."

"And what would you know about change?" I said, my voice gravelly and low. "What could you change if you really had to, Cher? Your nail polish? Your hair color? Your wardrobe?"

She whitened at that. "Well, congratulations." She swallowed hard. "Looks like one of us has Joanna down to a T."

And she whirled away, heading for the door in a blur of color and scent and indignation.

I closed my eyes and clenched my teeth together so hard my jaw ached. "I don't understand what you want from me!" What *anyone* wanted from me. "I watched my sister die, Cher! *I* almost died!"

"Well, we're all gonna die, darlin'. Until then—" Cher flung the door open and threw me a hard look over her shoulder. "—you'd better learn to fuckin' live." And the door slammed behind her.

The bitch.

Though no sooner had Cher left than I wanted to call her back. Isolation crowded in around me, silently shaping itself to my body, Olivia's frame. I turned one way and then the other, sniffing, before I relaxed. There was nothing and no one there. I was quite simply alone. Just as I wanted to be. Right?

"Paranoid," I muttered, zeroing in on the bedroom. It was the one room Cher and I hadn't gotten to yet. I kicked the wall as I headed toward it. "Let's get this over with."

The room was shadowed, but pleasantly so, and there were flowers, as well as one of those spider plants even I couldn't kill. Now that I thought of it, Olivia had given me mine, and I wondered if this was its sister plant, if they'd both taken root at the same time, and if the other still lived among those things that used to be mine.

The carpeting was new. Butter cream and berber, it gave stiffly beneath my feet as I crossed to the bed and looked beneath it. Not a dust bunny to be found, never mind a scimitar or severed hand. The sheets were new too, I could smell that, and the glue that held the full-length windows in their oblong frames had only just lost that overtly pungent smell. I suppose I should have been uneasy in a room where I'd witnessed so much violence and carnage. A room, I thought, where I'd committed even more. But it was too tidy, too pink, and too benign.

I was just about to leave when I saw the closet door slightly ajar. Nothing strange in that . . . except that the rest of the house was obsessively ordered. I frowned, took a step toward it, another, and realized my heart was outpacing my feet five to one. I found myself wishing for my weapons, any weapon, before shoving the thought impatiently aside. Silly, I thought, reaching for the handle. It's just an empty closet.

She leapt the moment I opened the door. There was a growl—hers, mine?—then a blur of white fur streaked through the open door and out into the living room. Cursing, I put a hand to my chest. Luna, my new feline roommate.

"Luna-tic, is more like it." I sighed, sagging against the doorjamb. "I need a drink."

In the kitchen, I grabbed the vodka I knew lived in the

deep freeze and poured it straight over ice. Leaning against the counter, I closed my eyes and sipped, but my mind kept seeing the still-wrapped present sitting on the coffee tray. I leaned against the granite counter, fighting the urge to go to it. I both wanted to open the gift and I didn't. To know what Olivia had gotten me, yet keep not knowing. Opening it would not only reveal the object inside, but it would cement it too. No more silly surprises in my future, I thought, sipping again. No more present tense. Only Olivia, dead in the past.

I poured another glass to the rim. One thing was certain: whatever I was going to do, I wasn't doing it sober.

Back in the living room, I kicked off my shoes, the first marring of my sister's space, and wondered briefly if she'd have done that. I had no earthly way of knowing.

Letting the vodka fill my mouth, holding it there to numb my tongue, gums, and soul, I stared at the package. From the corner of my eye I saw Luna slinking behind the couch, crouched low as if that somehow encouraged stealth. The ice in my glass rattled as I sat it on a glass-top table and reached for the gift.

Thin, expensive wrapping, a girly bow, a card nestled securely beneath. I didn't rip it open as I normally might, but tugged at the ribbon until it loosened, then lifted the paper until it fell away. I put the card aside for later. Inside was a pristine white box. Why, I asked myself as I took another swig, was I suddenly noting the most mundane things? Luna sat directly across from me, gold eyes unblinking, apparently wondering the same thing. I lifted the lid and sorted through the tissue paper until I recovered the first item, and lifted it free.

The photo was recent, the last one taken of us together. The occasion was the opening of a new restaurant in Valhalla, and I remember being annoyed with my father for making us attend, and with Olivia for insisting we pose with a group of helmeted and horned Vikings. I'd felt silly already, dressed in expensive black silk. I didn't want some model with a long sword pressed up against me.

"Please, Jo," she had begged, her pout in place, lashes fluttering. "You look so beautiful . . . for once." She knew to soften any compliment for me with a mild insult, otherwise I might not believe the whole of it. No, not *might not* believe. *Would not* believe. I took another drink.

Funny thing, though, she was right. I did look pretty. Or perhaps I just missed my old face. My hair was a sleek and shining dark bob, tucked behind my ears, and a reluctant smile played at my lips, glossy and somehow knowing. That had me dropping the photo to my lap with a wry laugh.

I had known nothing.

The second gift was both smaller and larger than that final captured moment. A simple disk, something she'd probably spent hours fiddling with on her beloved computer, but not, I knew, something downloaded and burned and offered up for my listening pleasure. Olivia would never give me something that common. "How the hell am I supposed to watch this?" I murmured, closing my eyes.

But I did watch it. After retrieving the vodka bottle.

Luna had been sitting beside her. The television went from blank to bright, and she was suddenly there, absently stroking the cat, rubbing perfectly manicured fingers along its temples and ears and brow as she waited for the recorder to engage. Only belatedly did she realize it already had. I laughed aloud at her expression—surprise, pleasure, and chagrin all at once—but instead of rewinding and starting again, she simply shrugged it all away, as was her way.

"Hiya, sis! Now get that sour look off your face, this is a great idea, and just wait until you see how smoothly I've edited it. I'm an absolute star!" She giggled, sipped from a wide-bowled martini, a movement I echoed with my own drink. "So, I figure we can do this every year from now on, commemorate the year just past, and, you know, look forward to the next year and stuff. I've been doing it for myself for a few years now, kind of a video diary, and it's a great way to keep track of where you are, and who you are, you know?"

She tilted her head as if waiting for an answer. Then, shaking a finger at the camera, she said, "And no, that doesn't mean you have to make a disk for me, I already know you won't. I'll just do it for the both of us, and then fifty years from now we can have a slumber party and watch them all at once! How does that sound?"

"Like as much fun as a root canal," I said, not meaning it. It sounded fucking fabulous.

"Oh, shut up." Olivia smiled, a knowing glint in her eyes. I smiled back, and for a second I could actually believe there was a connection there; that she saw me seeing her, and was responding in real time. I opened my mouth to say something, anything to draw the moment out, but it had already passed.

"So now, without further ado, here is . . ." She did a poor impression of a drumroll, earning what I took to be a feline scowl from Luna. ". . . the first quarter century of your life!"

It was, indeed, a video diary of my life. Actually, they were just photos, a slide show running to music—beginning from my infancy to chronologically span the twenty-five years since—but they appeared to be moving because of Olivia's editing, and I felt myself caught up in the story. The story of my life. A collage of images meant as celebration.

And I saw what Cher had been talking about. One moment there was a photo of me, grinning madly as Ben and I leaned against an old oak in Lorenzi Park, shade dappling our young faces in playful patterns, and his arms wrapped firmly around my waist. The next moment the clock she'd spoken of had stopped. Me, alone. An empty shell, smiling because it was expected, but looking straight through the camera. I didn't even remember it being taken. "Jesus," I said on a sigh.

Then Olivia was back. The light in the room was different, revealing the passage of time, and Luna had left her side. She was leaning forward, gaze intent. This time she'd caught the red light flicking on and the exact moment the tape switched back to her. She caught my eye.

"I know you hate all this mushy stuff, but bear with me for a moment because, I don't know"—she looked to the side, like she was looking out the window, then back again—"I just feel like I need to tell you this now. Like tomorrow will be too late somehow, and I don't want to have any regrets."

My breath caught. God, I thought, and she was supposed to be the ditzy one?

"Please know that I love you deeply, and I admire you, and I wish . . . or I used to wish I could be more like you, but . . ." She laughed, a small and fragile sound, while motioning down her body with one fragile, manicured hand. "Well, look at me."

"Don't," I said to her, too late, dropping to my knees in front of the television. I traced her face on the screen. "Don't say that. You're perfect the way you are."

"Still," she continued, oblivious to me and my tears. "We all have our talents, right? And mine is keeping us together. You and I. I know you don't trust a lot of things or people in this life, but you can trust that. Happy Birthday, sis." And, on a teary self-conscious giggle, she blew me a kiss good-bye.

I lowered my head into my hands and shook as the screen went blank. The sound that came from my throat was that of a small animal. It shattered the room in a keening wail, like cracked glass jarred from inside me. I jerked at the brush of fur against my leg, and looked down to find Luna staring up at me, her tail straight and quivering as she pressed her lithe, white body against me.

"Miss her too, huh?" I scratched her as I'd seen Olivia do, and she fell for it. Literally. She dropped in a pool of fur at my feet, anticipation rumbling through her body. What a picture we must make, I thought. A drunken woman and her cat.

Then another voice, *his* voice, filled the room. Luna and I both whipped to attention and one of us hissed. I wasn't so certain it was the cat. I whirled around, but it wasn't until my eyes landed back on the screen that I saw him. "Fucking bastard."

Ajax's long face stared at me from the television. "Is this thing on?" he said with mock exaggeration. He leaned forward, tapping on the camera so his knuckles hit the screen, and laughed.

"Well, no matter. I don't really expect you to see this, Joanna, because I know they'll fix it—fix *you*—so you never see your sister again, but just in case . . . just in case you're stupid enough to stay nearby, in my city, *alive*, I thought I'd send my own birthday wishes. Give you a little something to remember me by too."

He blew a kiss, as Olivia had, and as I sat there, I smelled rotted cactus juice, cold ashes, and another odor in the apartment that wrapped around my neck like crimson pearls, a drop of blood for every person he'd ever killed, and there were many. I gagged. Luna raced from the room, ears flattened, and I had to cover my mouth and nose with my palms so that my voice came out muffled. "Fuck you, fuck you, fuck you."

"Just so you know, I can smell you too," he continued, and lifted a hand to his neckline where he withdrew a silver chain and began toying with it. I wanted to plow my clenched fist through the television screen. I wanted to rip that chain from his fingers and put it back around my neck where it belonged. "You're everywhere even though you appear to be nowhere. But then, we both know looks can be deceiving."

He inhaled deeply, a connoisseur musing over a glass of wine. "Yes, you're here in your sister's apartment, just as you can be scented in your own secluded, sorry excuse of a house. I've even been to the dojo where you trained for what must have been years. Your sweat and blood and fury absolutely stain that place, like the pit of a rotted apricot, all that golden juice gone to mold."

He shuddered delicately, before lifting my necklace and running it between his lips, scraping it along his front teeth, licking it with his tongue. I lowered my hands as the room cleared of his scent.

"Do you know," he continued conversationally, "that I could even smell you at your funeral? Not in the coffin. No," he shook his head, "that wasn't you they lowered into the ground, was it? But your imprint was on that poor sap who actually believes you're dead. You know," he paused again, tilting his head, "the cop?"

I rose to my knees to grip the sides of the television screen, my face inches from Ajax's. He smiled indulgently and crossed his legs. It would have been effeminate if it hadn't been so damned calculated.

"I know you're new to all this, dear, so let me give you a little lesson. Love has a distinctly pungent smell, and when it attaches itself to another emotion, such as sorrow, it acts as a bonding agent, as an enzyme does to a molecule. Processing it. Altering it. Making it other than what it was alone. I find the results particularly . . . heady." He sniffed delicately. "You can imagine how surprised I was to find that Joanna Archer had allowed herself to be loved. It's rather nice to know, actually. Restores my faith in womankind."

Ajax ran his tongue over his teeth, letting it flicker over the chain again, chin lowered as he leaned forward. "Just so you know, he'd be dead by now . . . except for one thing." The look on his face turned feral. "It's so much harder on you both with him alive."

Then he blew me another tainted kiss. "See you soon, Jo."

I was breathing hard by the time the screen went blank again. My tumbler was empty but I was perfectly sober. I tried to slow my breathing, but what I really wanted to do was punch something. The sonofabitch had been here, I thought furiously. I'd seen immediately that the room was as it was now, all of Cher's homey touches in place, as opposed to Olivia's taping session, where her surroundings looked more lived in.

He'd also been in my house. In Asaf's studio. Within reach of Ben. And I couldn't protect them, I thought wildly, because I wasn't allowed to go near them. Not as me, at least.

I lifted my head, catching the movement in the pane of glass opposite me. The sun was high in the afternoon sky and rays bounced from the windows, a tangible layer between the city and myself. Superimposed upon that, however, was a sharper image. I stared, and took in the female form reflected there. It was a body of silken curves and shining hair, hiding myriad psychic scars and a spine of steel.

"She's beautiful," I murmured, staring at myself. And that was the problem. I still looked in the mirror and saw someone else. Like the city beyond that pane of glass, my interior landscape was overlain by Olivia's image. Olivia's body. Olivia everywhere.

But this was an Olivia the world had never seen. Her full lips were pressed thin with rage. Her eyes were dark and dead, and cold with hate. I closed those eyes, breathed in deeply as Micah had taught me . . . and emptied myself of it all.

I could feel the life pulsing from the living plants around me. I sensed Luna curled into a protective ball in the next room, and I scented the lingering traces of all the people who'd recently passed through the apartment.

Ajax had been there exactly two days earlier, noon sharp. He hadn't bothered masking his scent. He wanted me to know and hate that he'd been here, and to fear him as well.

Instead, I pushed that hatred and fear and knowledge aside and imagined myself—the woman I remembered myself to be—merging with that soft shell of flesh reflected in the glass. When the room was entirely clear of emotion, I opened my eyes.

She stood as before. I glanced down at the photo of us on the couch then back up. Olivia and me in both. Olivia and me in one. "Show me," I said aloud. "Show me how to be you."

Cher claimed I had no goal and no purpose. Well, now I did. Now I fucking well did.

I put the vodka back into deep freeze, and made a pot of coffee so strong and black it burned like acid in my stomach. Then I watched the disk again. And again. I studied Olivia, and I studied the montage that was my former life with increasing objectiveness, and when I was done, I studied *him*.

Three pots of coffee later, when the sun had set and the Strip was sprawled like a glittering invitation below me, I glanced again at the woman superimposed upon the city. She wasn't quite whom she was meant to be, but she was different. Not a superhero, to be sure, but Cher would be gratified. She was no longer a completely empty shell.

"She's learning how to live," I said, and I picked up my new cell phone and turned it back on. In the light reflecting from that glowing pane, my sister and I both smiled.

13

I still had questions about my new life, but at least I knew why Warren had said not to contact him until I had Olivia's mannerisms, habits, and thought processes down pat. If I didn't wholly believe I was Olivia, nobody else was going to either. So, while Warren and Micah had promised answers, I decided to seek them out myself. With an hour to spare before a scheduled "date" with Cher, my first, I decided to use the time for research.

"Not just research," I corrected, aloud. "Mythology."

Only two blocks from the salon where I was to meet Cher was the comic book store that Micah had mentioned to me. I swung into a parking spot in front of an L-shaped strip mall that also housed a beauty supply store, a video store, and the most familiar sign of modern-day suburbia—Starbucks. As I stepped from Olivia's TT, I sniffed lightly at the wind. I'd had the nagging feeling of being watched ever since leaving the apartment, but I hadn't scented or seen anything peculiar. The cars closest to mine belonged to patrons of a sandwich shop three doors down, so I dismissed the feeling as nothing more than nerves and headed for the entrance of Master Comics.

"Oh yeah," I muttered, looking at a life-sized Aqua-Man painted on the shop's windows, "this looks like *exactly* where the answers to the world's paranormal mysteries are kept." I walked in anyway.

A jangle of cowbells announced my arrival. I briefly surveyed the place—noting the comics and animé were shelved alphabetically, and the most valuable editions were secured behind glass cases—then noticed the hanging silence. I looked down at my leather minidress and the skintight knee-high boots—which, I'd been horrified to discover, cost more than a payment on my Jag—and grimaced. It'd seemed a conservative enough outfit that morning, but I realized now it was somewhat inappropriate for visiting an establishment frequented by teenage boys.

I compared myself briefly with one of the buxom beauties on the cover of a nearby comic and found I held up nicely. This would explain why the looks I was getting from the half-dozen other patrons were less lascivious than hopeful. Too bad I didn't have a gold lasso in my pocketbook.

I settled for sauntering up to the register, manned by the only adult in the place. I gave him Olivia's most encouraging smile. "Hi."

The man didn't answer, just stood there, tongue half exposed between his chubby lips. Perhaps he was just shy . . . though the saliva pooling at the corner of his mouth couldn't have been normal. I tried again. "Hello, earthling?"

A voice popped up beside me. "You look just like Daphne of Xerena."

I turned my head, saw no one, then looked down and recoiled. Hairy ten-year-old, or large midget, it was a tough call. "Excuse me?"

"Daphne, the Xerenian princess whose shadow detaches to fight crime worldwide while she's sleeping. Do your heels turn into switchblades?" he asked, bending over to look for himself.

Ten-year-old. Definitely. "Sorry. No."

He straightened, plainly disappointed, and I got a clear look at his face. Tufts of hair sprouted from his cheeks in aberrant fashion, and muddy brown eyes peered up at me from beneath bushwhacked brows. "Let me guess, Wolf-Man?"

He rubbed a hand along his voluminous sideburns and shook his head. "Growth hormones. They just have the added benefit of making me look like a superhero."

I wanted to tell him that Eddie Munster wasn't much of a hero, but refrained when he pulled a claw from behind his back and made to lunge for me. After the month I'd had, he was fortunate I saw the nails were made of plastic. Another nanosecond and he'd have been eating my Dior handbag.

I raised a brow. "Cute." He growled menacingly.

I realized then exactly where I was. A role-playing, hormone-ridden den of iconic culture. An adolescent precursor to *Playboy* magazine and Internet porn. I studied a half-dressed heroine on one of the rags behind the case. Warren probably felt right at home here.

Turning to the man behind the counter again, and ignoring the growling noises emanating from Wolf-boy, I tried another smile. "I'd like some information on superheroes, please." I felt like an idiot as soon as the words were out of my mouth, a feeling intensified by the way the guy just continued to stare, but I waited. And waited. "Do you speak English?"

"Why do you want to know?" he finally said.

"Well," I said, taken aback by the coldness in his voice, "it's just that you weren't answering me."

A voice popped up on my other side. "He means why do you want to know about superheroes?"

I turned to find a bald-headed youth staring at me with an equally closed expression. He had a twin—identifiable as such by a T-shirt that said I'M HIS TWIN with an arrow pointed in the first boy's direction—who duplicated his expression and his stance, right down to the spindly arms crossed over his chest. As twins are wont to do, I supposed.

Keeping my eyes on the twins, I spoke to the man. "Correct me if I'm wrong, but is this, or is this not, a retail establishment? I buy, you sell. I ask, you reply. The customer is always right . . . any of this sound familiar?"

Dead silence.

Clearly the mantle of "reasonable adult figure" was being thrown solely across my shoulders. I took on a commanding stance—as one did when facing a prepubescent Inquisition—and crossed my own arms over my chest. When all eyes had finally returned to my face, I cleared my throat. "If you really must know, I'm doing a paper for school. You've heard of college, right, boys? It's where you go if you haven't ditched too many high school classes to hang out with Wolf-boy over here—"

"No!" A voice flew at me from the back of the store. I looked in time to see a head duck back behind an upside-down comic. Even if the voice hadn't cracked in the middle of the single syllable, it wouldn't have been an especially impressive show of vigor.

"No, you haven't heard of college?" I asked sweetly.

"No, we won't tell you about superheroes," the man behind the counter finally said.

I returned my gaze to him, clearly the ringleader. "What's your name, sir?"

"Zane."

"Well, Zane, I'd like to speak to your manager."

"I am the manager."

Wolfie giggled beside me.

"The owner, then."

"I'm the owner too."

"Then sell me a comic book."

"No."

Confused, I stared at him. Then, figuring I'd been given this body for a reason, I leaned over the counter and asked again nicely. Olivia, I thought, could have done no better.

"No," he said again.

Now, if I'd been in my own skin I might have given in to the impulse to take Zane by his greasy hair and slam his head into the counter so that glass became a permanently identifiable part of his features. But I was Olivia now, and Olivia would never. Besides, I didn't relish the thought of taking on Wolf-boy, Tweedledee and -dum, the town crier . . . and whoever else might be lurking in the back of the store. I straightened and sighed, reconciled to trying reason.

With a grown man who read comics.

"Well, why on earth not?"

"Because earth is all your puny close-minded psyche can fathom!" yelled the crier, rising halfway from his chair. His face was bright red and he was unconsciously crushing the comic book in one balled fist. "There's a whole universe out there you'll never grasp! A whole world that can never be accessed by the likes of you!"

"Sebastian!"

The boy dropped back into his seat, deflated, and lifted the crumpled comic to cover his face. His hands were shaking.

"Is he on medication?"

A chorus of growls met this suspicion, and I could feel the hostility rising in the room. I inhaled deeply, imagining the air passing through my limbs, my chest, every cell down to my toes. I scented deodorant, raging hormones, and a taut thread of high-strung affront, but there were no weapons, no Shadow agents, and no superheroes in the bunch . . . including Wolfie and his plastic claws.

"Sebastian is a little sensitive," Zane said unnecessarily. "We all are when people like you come poking around."

Did he mean people who brush their teeth after each meal? I wondered, catching sight of something plantlike between his front teeth. "People like me?"

"People who want to study us like bugs under a microscope—"

"You tell her, Zane!"

"Who think we're a sociological macrocosm to be dissected and analyzed, then served up in a report so you can get an A-plus in some moronic class that perpetuates the myth of modern-day society. But we don't accept your mores and values, got it? We defy your definitions of what is right or wrong, and what is truly the norm. We defy *you*!" He finished off with a pump of his fat fist, accompanied by a loud chorus of victorious accord.

I looked around the store suspiciously. Seriously, reality shows were popping up in the strangest places these days.

"Now get out of here," he said, breathing heavily, "before Sebastian really gets upset."

I glanced doubtfully at the quivering mass of nerves at the back.

"Fine. There are other comic book stores, you know." I hoped. "Somebody will take my request seriously."

"Not in that dress they won't."

I turned to leave, the derision of a half-dozen adolescent boys licking at my heels, before I paused in my go-go boots.

Did superheroes take this kind of shit from mere mortals?

I mean, if I couldn't face down a pack of Xbox addicts, then how was I going to rid the entire Las Vegas valley of twelve homicidal Shadow agents? Not to mention a being *imagined* into existence?

Turning back to Zane, I leaned my palms on the glass countertop, mostly because I knew it would annoy him, and pushed my face into his. The victory cries died off into a strangled and wary silence. "Look, forgive me for not knowing your password or secret handshake or whatever gets a person access into your labyrinth of anarchy here, but I need this information. I'm not really writing a paper. I'm not even in school. I mean, have you ever seen an undergraduate who looks like this?"

His eyes flickered, but the rest of his face didn't change. "Then why do you want to know?"

I sighed loudly, then motioned him closer. Four bodies leaned in. Sebastian strained forward from his seat in the back. "The truth is, I'm a new agent for the Zodiac troop 175, paranormal division, Las Vegas. I'm the Archer, and I need to do some research."

They all drew back as if propelled, or repelled, by a single force, but no one spoke. As Zane was nearly drooling again, I decided backing up sounded like a good idea.

"Shit, lady," Wolfie finally said, scratching his half beard. "Why didn't you just say so?"

"Yeah, man. We're big Zodiac fans. Travis here has all the trading cards."

His twin looked up at me. "I don't have you, though."

They all looked at me, wariness once again overtaking their features.

"I'm a new recruit. I didn't even know I was superhuman until I underwent metamorphosis."

Zane nodded thoughtfully. "Ah . . . a late harvest."

"Ripe, though."

I scowled down at Wolfie, who grinned.

"Show the lady where the Zodiac manuals are, Carl." To me, Zane said, "I'm going to trust you are who you say you are, even though you obviously know nothing about your microuniverse and you have no identifying symbol."

"Symbol?"

"Your glyph. You know, your Zodiac emblem? You're not marked as an agent of Light or Shadow."

Is that why they'd all been looking at my chest? I looked down, saw only impressive cleavage, then looked back up into a less-than-impressed face. I shrugged. "I'm working on it."

Wolfie tugged on my hand. "C'mon."

He led me deeper into the shop, passing Sebastian along the way. The boy peered up at me from the corner of his eye, extreme agitation marring his brow. Nothing, I thought, a little Thorazine couldn't take care of.

"Boo," I said, and he yelped and scurried away.

"Dang, this stuff itches," Carl the wolf-boy said, yanking off his mustache as he walked.

I winced. "I thought you were taking hormone pills?"

"Nah." He pulled off another tuft of his beard, studied it, then tossed it aside. "Model glue."

I watched as he worked a roll of glue from his chin. "That's disgusting."

"Yeah, my mom thinks so too. You remind me a lot of her, actually."

"Why? Is she a superhero too?"

"Nah." He shook his head. "Compulsive liar."

A quiet chuckle from behind met that remark. I turned to find Zane leaning against a nearby wall of manga titles.

"Right here." Carl stopped before a wood-paneled cabinet in the farthest corner of the shop, unlocking it to reveal an ordinary carousel of comics. Scratching at his chin, he looked from the rack to me and back again. He was beginning to make me itch. "There are two series to choose from, the Shadow side of the Zodiac, and the Light."

I looked and saw that the series was divided into vertical columns. The only difference between the two lines was the spines. The Shadow side had a black edging to each book, with titles like *Enforcing the Eclipse*, *Midnight Portals*, *The Opaque Vein*, and *Afton's Epitaph*.

The Light series had a silver spine, and included the titles *The Luminous Void*, *Shadow Slayer*, *Lambent Moonlight*, and, my favorite, *Zodiac: The Desert Ablaze*.

"You probably want the Shadow side of the Zodiac since you're such a bitch and all."

"I do *not* want the Shadow side." I glared at him. "Look at me. Do I look like . . . like . . ." I glanced at the lead title in the Shadow series row. ". . . like *Simone: The Mourning Butcher*?"

Carl scoffed. "Oh, sure, you're all Britney Spears on

the outside, with your blond hair and rack out to here . . ."

I narrowed my eyes.

". . . but looks can't hide your true identity. It's the eyes that give you away. You've got dark eyes . . . not the color," he hurried on, before I could interrupt, "but the soul behind them. The intent."

I leaned down until my face was inches from his. "Listen, you little wookie, I'm not a villain, got it? I've just had a really bad month."

I straightened and reached for the first Light title.

"Stop!" Carl grasped my arm.

"What?" I said, yanking away. This kid was beginning to freak me out.

"If you touch that book and you're not really an agent of Light, then you're going to get the biggest shock of your life, and I mean literally! I've seen it before, and it ain't pretty." He shook his finger at me, a frown marring his furry brow. "A girl like you can't walk around with those sorts of skid marks, if you know what I mean."

I ignored the innuendo and glanced behind me at Zane, who was leaning against a wall, leafing through *Spider-Man*, but listening closely enough that his mouth was twitching. He caught my look and nodded, concurring.

I turned back to the kid. "So, you're saying a Shadow agent can't read the Light comics, and vice versa?"

"That's right, blondie. Keeps the sides from cross-pollinating."

"So if I'm an agent of Light and I touch this," I said, pointing to the lead Shadow title, "I get zapped?"

"You won't," he said with surety, crossing his arms over his puny chest.

I didn't think so either, but my belief had nothing to do with what series I touched. I reached for the Shadow title, paused just to hear the weird kid's breath quicken, then yanked the title from its rack. Nothing.

"I told you!" He pointed, jumping up and down. I grabbed another, then another, and every Shadow title down to the ground as Wolfie continued to holler manically beside me. "I told her she was evil! Did you see?"

"I saw," Zane said mildly.

It meant nothing, I told myself, then said it aloud. "It doesn't mean anything!"

Zane shrugged and turned back to his comic.

"It means you're a freakin' baddie, baby," Wolfie said, jabbing his finger through the air. "A Shadow agent bent on death and destruction!"

I slid my eyes to the racks as he continued to jeer, then started grabbing more books. He stilled abruptly, mouth hanging open. I snatched the last Light title from the lower rungs of the rack, straightened, and grinned at him.

"You're not supposed to be able to do that!" he stuttered. "Zane, what's going on?"

"Guess you don't know the Zodiac series as well as you thought," I retorted, turning to smirk at Zane. "Comic books that zap you. Please."

But Zane had gone chalk white, and the comic he'd been leafing through fell heedlessly to the floor. He stared at the pile of comics in my arms, then back up into my face.

"Light and Shadow," he finally said, softly. "So you're the one."

I drew back, not entirely certain what he meant, but answered with what my gut told me was true. "Yeah," I said. "I guess I am."

Whatever that meant.

Dumping the pile of comics in the trunk of my car, I decided to walk the two blocks to the day spa despite my three-inch Christian Louboutin boots. Air was what I needed after the claustrophobic environ of Master Comics, though smog is what I got, toeing the sidewalk with cars zipping by me at forty-five miles an hour. I still couldn't shake the feeling of being watched, but it didn't take long to realize it probably had more to do with my outfit than any paranormal activity. I gamely ignored the whistles and honks aimed my way, even from the group of high school boys who raced by again in the opposite direction just to comment on specific body parts, and wondered how Olivia had handled this all those years.

Unfortunately, the catcalls from the teens had elicited the attention of a group of workers doing pavement repair just ahead of me. They paused to watch my approach.

"Shit," I muttered under my breath. "Not today."

One worker whistled as I waited for traffic to subside. I'd have to pass in the street to avoid the wet pavement. I ignored him, and spotted an opening in the wake of an enormous SUV. The same kids who'd already passed me twice. The passenger leaned out the window this time, making lewd motions with his fingers and tongue. This, in turn, seemed to embolden the three men on the pavement. Still ignoring them—a lone woman's sole defense when confronted with the pack mentality—I stepped into the street.

"Check the unit, boys!"

I kept walking.

"You don't want to miss this one, *mijos*. Sweet as a split peach."

Almost there. I gritted my teeth.

"I bet her rim jobs could oil a semi."

That one, plus the accompanying laughter, stopped me cold. Adrenaline surged, tsunami waves wracking my core and my vision turning red. The oncoming traffic was racing toward me again, and I still had time to spring to the opposite walk and continue on my way, but I didn't move. I couldn't. I didn't want to.

Whirling to face the snickering men, I caught the half-hearted attempts to cover their grins. Ignoring the horns blaring behind me—with irritation now, rather than admiration—I began to saunter back the way I'd come.

"Check the unit, boys," I said coldly, the wind of the passing cars whipping my hair into snapping coils around my head. My heels clicked sharply on the pavement as I advanced. "You don't want to miss this one, *mijos*," I said, watching the laughter die on the faces in front of me as something in my face—probably those eyes Carl had commented on—revealed something lurking inside Olivia's frame. "I bet her rim jobs could oil a semi."

I stopped in front of the man who'd last spoken. He was my height; plain, not bad-looking. He shifted, and I answered his hesitant smile with a tight one of my own. Then I stepped forward, into his face, his space. Right into his universe. Staring directly into his eyes, I ran a hand over his chest, down his stomach, and into his pocket. The two other men began to laugh, a mixture of discomfort and excitement. I kept my smile fixed even as the man began to breathe hard. Wet cement clung to his fingers, and I could smell the McDonald's breakfast he'd had that morning, the type of soap he'd showered with, the emotions seeping through his pores. I lifted his wallet from his pocket and thumbed through it.

"Hey." He shook himself, as if from a dream.

"Is this her?" I said, flipping to a photo of a brunette. "She's pretty." I pulled the photo from its plastic cover. Karen, and his name was Mark. I saw it on his ID. I looked back up at him and smiled cruelly. "Too bad you're right about her, Mark."

"What are you talking about?" He didn't quite manage the laugh this time.

"You know what I'm talking about," I said sweetly, leaning into him. "The nights when she comes home later than you. When her lipstick's too fresh, and her eyes too dark, and she smells like secrets and someone else's soap."

The other two men stopped laughing as well.

"Actually, come to think of it, *mijo*," I said, pivoting partially to face the second man, "it smells a lot like your soap."

Mark froze beside me, while the second man's eyes grew wide.

"What?" I said, mimicking his expression. "You really thought he didn't know?"

I folded the wallet and handed it back to Mark, but he didn't see. He was staring blindly at his friend, who in turn was glaring at me.

"I don't know what you're talking about, *puta*," the man finally said, his eyes full of hatred. Someone should have told him the adage about protesting too much.

"Here." I tapped Mark with his own wallet. He jolted, then took it, not looking at me.

It was then that I saw his hands were shaking.

A sudden wave of sorrow washed over me. Shock rolled into me like an earthquake, and it came from the man named Mark, who truly loved his wife Karen; and yes, who he knew, deep down, was having an affair with his good friend. What had I just done?

Looks can't hide your true identity. It's the eyes that give you away . . . the soul behind them. The intent. The Shadows.

Olivia would have never done this. I'd come over here intending to hurt these men, and I'd used this ability, whatever it was that Micah had said made me special and *heroic*, to injure an innocent. A mortal. A man.

My anger was gone. It was a small thing compared to the shame filling my lungs, strangling my breath. I had to get out of there, away from Mark's injured gaze and the pain I had caused. As the two men began to argue, I turned, passing by the third.

"Bitch," he shot from beneath his breath. And at that moment, who was I to argue? "You have issues!"

"You have no idea," I muttered, and with that, walked right through the construction zone, my heels sinking into the newly poured pavement. I knew the sidewalk, my Louboutins, and the lives I left behind me would never be the same again.

14

I hurried the rest of the way to the day spa, imagining I could hear voices behind me rising in accusation and denial, anger and refute. I found myself wondering if those three men would ever work together again, if they'd ever be a team, or holler at girls in the street again. Doubtful, I thought now, but somehow took no pleasure in that.

Light and Shadow, Zane had said. *So you're the one.*

"What have I done?" I asked aloud. Another question I couldn't answer.

"Never mind you, darlin'." Cher's voice popped up seemingly from nowhere. "The question is what have I done?"

Halting, I glanced around the street. No Cher. Her Corvette was backed into an opposing slot, but there was only one vehicle in front of the day spa, a shiny red BMW. I walked to the other side of it to find her crouching furtively by the driver's door.

"You hit a car," I said, unnecessarily. "Again."

Cher had to be infamous within her insurance company.

"It's only a little bitty ding," she retorted, digging in her purse. "Come on over here and keep watch. I'm going to fix this."

She pulled out a bottle of red nail color and began dabbing at the door.

"Cher, this is an accident. You have to report it."

"It's not an accident until you've been caught." She blew on the door and tilted her head. "Another coat, I think."

The absurdity of the moment hit me, contrasting sharply with the moments just past, and laughter—somewhat hysterical, I admit—began to bubble up inside of me. There was no cruelty here, no nefarious activity or laws of an alternate universe at work. It was just Cher. Neither Shadow nor Light. Just my sister's best friend in all her blinding shades of fuchsia. "You missed a spot." I giggled.

"Thanks, Livvy-girl."

I was smiling when *he* caught my attention. I sucked in a surprised gasp. The man stood between the building and sidewalk, too still. At least, I thought, my smile fading, I knew now why I'd felt followed.

"Hey, Cher," I said quietly. "I'll be right back."

Her head popped up halfway. Barbie-Kilroy. "Who's that?"

"A cop."

Cher squealed and ducked.

It took both forever and not long enough to reach Ben's side.

So much to say, yet no words would ever be enough. So I said the simplest, truest thing that came to mind. "God, Ben. You look like shit."

His half laugh came out strangled, like he hadn't used it in a very long time. "And you look beautiful. As usual."

He'd always been rugged, even as a boy, but now there was more sadness than toughness lining his face, and his penchant for imagining and brooding lived too close to the surface of his eyes. I sucked in a breath of salty sorrow. "I know you're undercover, but do they really let you go into work like that?"

He glanced down, shrugged. "I'm kinda taking some time off."

"How much time?"

"Just a bit. Just until I get my head together. I don't know." He shoved his hands in his pockets and shuffled his feet. "How have you been, Olivia?"

Olivia. Be Olivia. I took a deep breath. "Uh . . . not quite myself, actually."

"I know what you mean." He ran a palm over the back of his neck. "I'm sorry for your loss."

I wanted to say it'd been his loss too, but the words backed up in my throat. "How long have you been following me?"

"Just today. Well, yesterday too. I had some sort of misguided notion you needed protecting, but that's probably just my own guilty conscience at work." He laughed again, but it was too bitter to be funny. "I was going to help you with those guys back there, but you seemed to take care of them too. You must get that all the time."

Yeah, I'd taken care of them, all right. I looked at my shoes, flecks of cement on the bright red bottoms, and felt my own guilty conscience spring to life. "Did you need something, Ben?"

"I did . . . do, actually." He reached for his back pocket. "Can you tell me anything about this picture?"

I knew what he was going to show me even before he pulled out the photo. The mug shot must've been taken the night Ajax attacked me in Valhalla. I recognized the suit hanging slack on his body. I'd given him the injury that lay bandaged on his neck. Shit, I could practically smell the rot through the photo paper.

I swallowed hard and handed the mug shot back. "Terrible lighting. But at least he doesn't have his chin resting on his fist. I hate that pose."

"It's a mug shot, Olivia," Ben said through gritted teeth. "You've never seen this guy before? Sure you don't know him?"

"Oh my God!" I said in mock alarm. Ben straightened expectantly. "Puh-lease don't tell me this is one of those guys from that blind dating reality show. I knew I shouldn't have given them my number."

"Never mind," he said, sighing, and I could practically see him deflate. After a long silence he said, "I know it probably doesn't matter now, but what about that night? Do you remember anything at all about . . . anything at all?"

"I'm, uh, still working through all that." I looked away like I didn't want to talk about it—and I didn't—but I wasn't fast enough to miss the way his lips thinned in frustration. Ben had never looked at me that way before. Like he was disgusted. Like I was weak.

Then he sighed heavily . . . and I didn't like *that* at all.

"Look, Traina, don't get all huffy and impatient on me, okay?" I said, my high voice rising even higher with indignation. "I've had some memory loss. There's a lot I can't recall."

"I'm sorry, of course." His face softened. "But if there's anything you can remember about Jo, about that night, anything . . . you'll call, right?"

I nodded, a soundless lie.

"I don't know—" he began to say, then stopped before trying again. "I don't know if she told you about our date, or if she got the chance, or—"

He swallowed hard, and I watched his throat work. The throat I'd kissed and nuzzled just weeks earlier. I knew what it smelled and tasted like, and suddenly I knew the words that were going to come from it. "Olivia, forgive me for dredging up the past, but there's something I've wanted to say for a long time now."

I shook my head, felt the mass of blond hair bounce. "Ben—"

"Please, let me say it. I should have said it to Joanna, but I didn't, and now—" He broke off, face crumbling.

I bit my lip, nodded once, and braced myself for what I was sure would be a heartbreaking speech.

"I just wanted to say I'm sorry."

Genuinely surprised, I drew back. "For what?"

"Being weak. For not standing by your sister when she needed me. I caused you both pain." His voice broke again, and the words I'd been expecting came through in that awful sound.

Tears welled in my own throat and eyes. "She never blamed you, Ben."

"I know. I hated myself enough for the both of us." He ran a hand through his hair, causing it to stick up further in wild, curly tufts. "God, I think I was afraid she'd end up like my mother, just this shell who'd once been vibrant and beautiful and solid but who'd let one man change her, and hollow her out."

Ben never talked about his parents. I was so surprised he was doing so now, with Olivia, that I remained silent.

"He told me it was my fault, you know. He said that's what happened when a man couldn't take care of his woman, and as much as I know he was just saying it to hurt me, I think a part of it sunk in. Not here, but here." He pointed to his head, then his heart.

"Your father was an ass, Ben." I didn't care if it sounded like Olivia. It was something he needed to know.

"I know." He nodded. "But those words stayed with me. I let them torture me, just like my mother let his words destroy her, and I lost out on the chance to know who Joanna had become—lost a whole fucking decade—just so I could imagine her as she was."

"You were young." A tear slid down my cheek, and I brushed it away, hoping he hadn't seen.

"She was younger," he said vehemently. "So were you."

"What happened that night made us all who we are today," I said, trying to calm him. "And Jo . . . Jo liked who she was."

He nodded after a bit. "I liked who she was too."

He'd stopped ranting, but the sorrow rising off him was twined with such guilt and fury and denial that the sickly combination, oily and raw, would eventually eat him alive. "Ben, please," I said softly, moving closer. "You have to let her go."

"She did *not* come back into my life in the eleventh hour just to let me know what I was missing!" The words burst from him so fiercely, it was as if they'd been gathered on the tip of his tongue, waiting for a lit fuse to ignite them.

"Shh." Jesus, I thought, stepping back. "Okay, Ben. It's okay."

But that was a lie, and he shook his head violently, knowing it. "And there's more to this whole thing than a botched break-in and two people falling to their deaths. I know it!"

"How do you know?" I said quietly. "You weren't there."

"I know because I know Jo!"

What could I say to that? A part of me thrilled to hear those words. But if he didn't leave this one alone, he was putting us both in danger again. I hardened myself to his sorrow. "This isn't one of your mysteries that need to be solved, Ben. You can't put a happy ending on this one."

"Then I can at least get an answer that satisfies me."

"The police say she died."

"I don't care. She came to me that night, Olivia! She came to me and we made love, and she was supposed to be dead already—" Shit. He was right. "But she was in my arms, warm, alive, and—"

"I saw her, Ben," I finally said, hating to hurt him, but seeing no other way. "I saw her fall."

He was silent for a long moment. "The papers said you couldn't remember anything."

Oops. "That's the last thing I remember," I said. "I'm sorry. She's gone."

His jaw clenched stubbornly. "Then I want to find out why. Why'd she return to your apartment, huh? Why didn't she just go home? Why did she leave me at all?"

I turned away to pace, to try and think this whole thing through, though I hardly knew where to begin. I didn't know how to act because this life as Olivia, as a crime-fighting heroine, was not yet fully mine. But there was one thing I did know. I glanced back at him. "You're not working with the police on this, are you?"

"I told you," he said, not meeting my eye, "I've taken a leave of absence."

I shook my head. *My God. He'd gone vigilante.* The department said it was an open and shut case; I was sure Warren and Micah had worked hard to make it so. Now Ben, of all people, was opening that door again.

"No, Ben. This is not what she wanted," I said, before correcting myself. "It's not what she *would have* wanted."

"Oh, Olivia." He looked at me like I was hopelessly naive. For one moment I actually thought he was going to rumple my hair. "Vengeance is exactly what she wanted. And I'm going to get it for her."

"Ben," I said, my voice a sharp contrast to his overly solicitous one. "That wasn't what she was doing. That wasn't the goal."

"Really? Did you ask her? Because I did. I asked what she'd do if she ever found the man who attacked her, who attacked you both. She said she'd kill him."

I *had* said that.

"Joanna was often glib that way." I swallowed hard, thinking fast. "But what she really wanted was to face that man down and let him know she'd survived it. That she'd survived him. She wanted to look that . . . that monster in the face and let him know not only didn't he kill her, but he didn't break her."

Ben's jaw set stubbornly. " 'It is better to be violent, if there is violence in our hearts, than to put on the cloak of nonviolence to cover impotence.' "

Yeah, and thank you, Mahatma Gandhi, for that one.

I pretended I didn't hear him, and put a gentle hand on his arm. "Don't let this break you, Ben. Joanna wouldn't want that."

For a moment I thought I'd gotten through. His face

cleared and he looked young and lost, but it was only for a moment. His expression hardened again, and shadows seized his eyes.

"Stop looking at me that way," he said softly, jerking back from my touch. "Everyone's looking at me like I've lost it . . ."

You mean like the way they used to look at me.

". . . like I'm crazy, and I don't know what I know. But I know what I saw, Olivia! Joanna was in my bed and in my arms at the time they're saying she was already dead . . ." Shit. I was going to have to ask Warren how to clear up that one. "And I may be angry, sure, but I've never been clearer on what I need to do. In fact, I think I'm more in my right mind now that I've been in, oh, at least a decade."

And I couldn't help but notice his eyes did look clear. But his scent was that of futile regret, and his guilt had soured upon him.

"I'm sorry," he said, catching my look. This time he was the one to lay a hand on my arm. Olivia's arm, I reminded myself as his touch shot a tremor through me. "I shouldn't have come to you with any of this but . . . you're all that's left of her."

"I know." And at least I could give him that comfort. I pulled him into a hug, resting my palms on the hard plane of his back, and for a moment—just one—I let myself go. I shut my eyes and hugged him like I was me and nothing had changed and there was still a storm brewing on the far horizon. I pretended we'd never left the restaurant that night, and wondered if Ben could feel the regret of that decision in my arms. I squeezed harder, because maybe through the force of that hug I could put him, us, back together.

Yet the reality was we had lost one another. Again. There was no fixing this, and I should have just said to him there were no answers to be found. Only the truth, which he could never know.

"I'm going to find him, Olivia," he said, his promise warming my head, ruffling my hair. "I'm going to hunt him down, just as Joanna would have, and this time I'll kill him. I'll take away everything and everyone that means something to him. I'm going to annihilate his world so thoroughly he'll never be able to piece it back together."

"I have to go now," I said, pulling away, hating his words. Hating who he reminded me of. Hating, I thought, the scent of rot seeping through each syllable.

"Okay, but you'll call if you remember anything, anything at all?"

"I'll call," I said, practically tripping over myself to get away from him.

"Olivia!" I stopped, closed my eyes and turned back slowly. When I opened them he was standing just as before, but he didn't look as angry from a distance. He just looked alone. "You know when I first ran into Joanna again I gave her this generic list of attributes, characteristics to tell her how well I knew her . . . or thought I knew her."

I folded my arms over my chest. "I bet stubborn was on that list."

At least he could smile at that. "Yeah, and so was restless. And impatient. But I forgot one."

"Really? Which?"

"Mine," he said, his fists bunching at his side. "She was mine."

And he walked away, leaving me staring, wordlessly, behind.

Leave it to Cher to think a nice pick-me-up after a sister's death would be a spray-on tan. I was ushered indoors, signed in, and naked in such short order that my head was actually spinning, and the sight of the spray gun had thoughts of comic books, construction workers, and even Ben Traina scuttling to the back of my mind. It looked like a machine from *Ghostbusters*.

"You want me to spread what?" I dubiously asked the technician for the third time. She was Russian, heavy on the makeup, light on patience, and obviously a great fan of her own product. She muttered something under her breath, sat back on her heels and glanced in Cher's direction.

"Come on, Livvy," Cher said. "You're acting like you've never done this before. Now bend over and show Yulyia your talent."

I grimaced as the two women hooted with laughter, but did as I was told, following Cher's lead.

"Whoo! Olivia, are you getting dizzy yet?"

Inverted, I looked over at her. "No."

Red-faced, she turned an accusing gaze upon me. "You've been eating again!"

The spray hit my ass before I could reply. Perhaps, I thought desperately, it would help to try and think of something else. Fortunately or not, I had a lot to think about. I wanted to tell Warren about my strange encounter in Master Comics, and ask him what Zane had meant about me being "the one." I wanted to see if he thought it was all right for me to swing by my old house as Olivia, knowing even if he didn't, I probably would anyway. I wasn't the sort of person who took orders easily. Unless, I was discovering, there was a can of tanning solution pointed at my naked ass.

I also needed to figure out what to do about Ben. And how to do it as Olivia. I frowned, thinking of the time I'd spent studying her home. I'd been all over that apartment in the past two days; read every piece of paper, viewed every video diary, even every recipe she had written down in the place. It was possible she had a safety deposit box I didn't know about, but I'd found no key, and no mention of one. There was also her beloved computer, but that was the one place I *couldn't* access, not that I believed any of the above could help me solve this problem.

How to stop him? How to help him? How to keep him from getting killed?

"What's wrong, Livvy?" Cher said, arms raised so Yulyia could spray beneath her pits. "You're not talking much."

What to say? I'd been half listening to the conversation, and so far it had lacked any meaning, direction, or obvious import. These two seemed to pluck topics from the sky and fold them like origami into something with meaning. For instance, I now knew there were eunuchs in Afghanistan who made more money than prostitutes, that Cher's mother had decided she needed to share with her adult daughter everything she thought about sex—I had to groan with her on that one—and I'd learned that Yulyia's motto in life was, "No cheaters, no beaters, no little peters."

Call me crazy, but I had the sneaking suspicion that my concerns over my recently acquired superheroine status weren't going to score very high in comparison with these eclectic topics.

Or would they?

"I was just wondering," I started conversationally, as Yulyia tagged my left pit, "if you could be a superhero, what kind would you be?"

"You mean to have save me?"

"Not X-Man and no He-Man," Yulyia said before I could answer. She motioned expansively with her spray gun. "I want G-Man."

"G-Man?" We both looked at her.

"To help me find G-spot. That's my kind of hero."

"Good point!" Cher exclaimed.

Too much information. I grimaced and tried again. "I meant what kind of superhero would you *be*?"

"A cute one, definitely!"

"With fur-trimmed cape trailing behind as I fly through the night!"

"Fox fur!" yelled Cher, getting in the spirit.

"Marten," Yulyia purred, shuddering delightedly.

Did this spray kill brain cells?

"Okay, but other than—you know—*cute*, what kind of

powers would you have? You know, how would you use them to fight evil and save mankind?"

They both looked at me in a moment of profound silence.

"The power to make any man fall in love with me!" Yulyia exclaimed.

"I already have that," scoffed Cher. "How about the power to have spontaneous orgasms, and never grow old!"

Yulyia squealed and Cher giggled. I sighed and tried not to breathe in too deeply.

Fifteen minutes later we were in the day spa's lounge area; tanned, dried, and wrapped in short terry-cloth robes. I was reclining in a vibrating massage chair, while Cher poured us fizzy water from a pitcher filled with lemons, ice, and cucumbers. About a half a dozen other women were scattered about the room, like a bunch of seals sunning on a rock. But the melodious chatter of dulcet female tones gradually melted into a sea of serenity. I hadn't been in this environment before. I'd either shunned it in favor of a sports massage, or all chitchat had ceased when I entered any ultrafeminine domain. I was surprised to find the smell of peppermint, cucumber, and estrogen to be a heady and profoundly relaxing mix.

"Do you want to get French pedicures?" Cher asked, handing me a glass.

I sipped, and considered making up an excuse to leave, something I'd have readily done only one week earlier. I'd never had another woman look to me for companionship. I knew Cher believed I was really Olivia, but it felt good to be the recipient of her open smiles and concerned attentions. I remembered how fondly my sister spoke of Cher on the video diaries, and for that alone I would have said yes. Besides, I reasoned, what would Olivia do?

"Why not?" I said, smiling.

Cher seemed pleased to lead the conversation, and I was content to let her. She started off talking about a new pill that was supposed to shrink the waist, lift the breasts, and put color into your cheeks—being tested on mice as we spoke—then moved on to a story about a lingerie saleswoman who'd copied her phone number from her check and was making threatening phone calls about how many times Cher had sent her back for a different size chemise in magenta rolled silk. At some point, through the rhythm of Cher's narrative, I began to understand the rhythm of my sister's life in a way I previously hadn't. I also began to wonder why I'd never gotten a spa pedicure before. The foot massage alone would have done wonders after a training session with Asaf.

Of course, thinking about Asaf led me to think about all the things I'd loved about my old life. My coach and his family, the training that had started as an outlet for my youthful anger and turned into a daily comfort, not unlike prayer. I thought of my home, my darkroom, and the camera that had been as much a part of me as another limb. Why couldn't there have been, or still be, a merging of the two lives? And that thought led me back to Ben—

". . . I mean, can you believe she said I was high-maintenance?"

Uh-oh. It was the first time Cher had stopped to ask me a question. Quickly, I thought, what would Olivia say? "That bitch."

Cher drew back, looking at me blankly. Her pedicurist did the same. Mine stopped massaging the balls of my feet.

"What?"

"Did you just call my mother a bitch?"

"No! No." Shit, I thought, and cleared my throat. "I thought you were still talking about the lingerie girl."

"No, darlin', my *mother*. But I told her that *she* was the one who was demanding. I mean, at least I can make my own appointments."

I looked at her. "Do you really tell your mother everything?"

She raised a perfectly waxed brow. "You know I do."

"It's just I can't imagine that," I said, and leaned my head back in the cushioned chair. I thought about everything I'd learned of my mother lately. The truths that had been lies, the greatest lie being our lives together.

Cher placed a hand on my arm and, surprisingly, I didn't shake it away. "Mama's been asking about you, you know," she said softly. "She has this idea of fixing you up with a—how did she put it?—'a very well-to-do southern gentleman.' She wants to know when you're going to come by again."

I fought off a full-body shudder and thought, Never.

"Of course you could avoid her blatant matchmaking attempts if you'd bring your own date," she said, pausing. "That guy you were talking to looked like he might clean up well."

"Ben? Not my type, and I'm definitely not his."

"Olivia, honey, you are every man's type."

"Not Ben Traina's. He was always into Joanna."

To my surprise, Cher said, "Oh, *that* Ben! Well, I have to say, he didn't look half as unhinged as people say. A little dangerous perhaps, but who doesn't like a strong little chaser to wash things down. An ex-cop might fill that bill nicely."

I glanced at her, too sharply, and looked away quickly, feigning interest in the color being applied to my toes. "What do you mean 'ex'? He's just taking some time off."

Cher lifted a hand, studying her nails. "That's not what they said on the tube, honey. And I don't blame the department. You should've seen him at the funeral. He went absolutely apeshit. Attacked some poor, innocent man who was just offering him his condolences. We can't have a guy like that patrolling our streets."

I couldn't believe what I was hearing. "Poor? Innocent?"

Cher rolled her eyes. "Okay, so they did say the guy cheats at craps. Either way, I know what I heard. Ben Traina has been put on an indefinite leave of absence."

"But he said—"

"But he lied. It happens with the mentally unstable."

But he wasn't mentally unstable. He happened to be right. And I, for one, wasn't going to give up on him. I *knew* him. That boy who saw things as black and white, right or wrong, was still there. Besides, I was partly responsible for this . . . this transformation. Both of them, I decided. Both times.

"Ben's different," I muttered. "He's been through a lot, and he never stopped caring for Joanna."

"Well, don't you think that's precisely why he might go right on over the edge?"

I wanted to shake Cher so hard her teeth rattled.

Something of my thoughts must have shown in my face because her own softened. "Oh, don't listen to me, honey. I have such bad luck with guys . . . what do I know?" she said, sighing. "I always look for the one thing that'll make them run. Then I do everything I can to make sure they do." She practically deflated on the next sigh, showing a vulnerability that surprised me.

I let the subject of Ben drop, filing it away for later. Like when the smell of bubble gum and acetone wasn't coloring my every thought. "Maybe it's because you don't let them see the real you."

"Darlin', all of me is real," she said in that haughty tone I used to hate.

This time I only snorted and leaned my head back into the neck rest. "Then maybe that's the problem. Maybe all they see is boobs and hair and nails . . . oh, and a really great tan."

"Thank you. I think."

I smiled over at her. "I'm just saying. There's a lot more to you than meets the eye." And I was surprised to realize I meant it. "You just need to find someone who will look at your internal beauty first."

"Really?" she asked softly.

"Of course, really."

She lifted her chin. "You're right. That would be my kind of hero, anyway . . . you know, when you were asking earlier? I've been thinkin' about it, and I've decided I wouldn't need someone from the pages of a comic book. He wouldn't have to leap over buildings for me, or even surprise me with the latest designs from fashion week. I have a personal shopper for that. But if somebody would just . . . be there."

"Girl, that ain't a hero," one of the nail techs put in. "That's a prince."

Cher tilted her head and thought about that for a moment. "You think Wills or Harry would be interested in a slightly experienced southern woman?"

We all laughed, but a small part of me sighed. *Be there? Ben would have done that.*

Later, as we lounged in the dressing area, now surrounded by a comfortable silence, Cher said, "Thanks for letting me take you out today, Livvy-girl. I've really missed you."

"I've missed you too. This was . . . the most normal thing I've done in a long time." I ran the back of my hand over my eyes, mortified to find myself close to tears. All this girly stuff was getting to me. I probably just needed to hit something.

"I'm sorry we argued before."

"It was my fault," I said, shaking my head. "You were right. I had shut down. Thank you for being a good enough friend to say something."

On a sob, Cher opened her arms for a hug. Thrilled—it was an indisputable sign that I'd passed this test—I held open my arms too. I'd no more than taken two steps toward her when she gasped so violently I jumped and whirled to defend myself against . . . anything.

"What?" I said, whirling back. Then I realized she was pointing at my chest. "What?"

"You're streaked! The bitch streaked you!"

I turned to the full-length mirror and looked for myself.

Sure enough, there was a medium-sized white blotch right in the middle of my chest.

"Shit." Would this have happened to Olivia?

"Now you don't have an even, all-over tan!" Clearly more distraught than I was, Cher had tears rolling down her face. "You're not going to look cute naked! Oh, sorry."

"It's okay," I said doubtfully. I wasn't planning on anyone seeing me naked anyway. "How long did you say this stuff lasts?"

Cher wasn't listening. She was moaning and cursing—delicately, of course—and pulling at her hair extensions. "I wanted this to be perfect!"

"It has been," I assured her. "Really. I can't think of the last time I've had this much fun."

"Truly?" She sniffed, and stared at me through tearstained eyes.

I nodded. "This is the most fun I've ever had naked with another woman."

"Except for that time in Cozumel."

I'd puzzle that one out later.

"But now you have to wear turtlenecks for two whole weeks!"

Facing the mirror, I sighed. That answered that question.

"It's not right!" Fresh tears welled in her eyes. "First you ruin your Louboutins and now you're marked for life!"

"It's not for—" I broke off, whirling to face the mirror again and looked closer. *Marked.*

"I think I'm faint," Cher continued behind me. "I need a drink with something stronger than cucumbers in it."

"It looks like . . ." I found I couldn't finish. I cleared my throat and tried again. "It's a . . ."

Cher gasped as she came up behind me. "I see it!" Her amazement, my horror, and the symbol on my chest were all reflected clearly in the glass across from us. Cher was the first to find her voice, and it was reverent. "It's shaped like a stiletto!"

Shit. She could be right.

It was blurred, smudged around the edges, and not entirely drawn in—like a half-finished tattoo—but dammit, Cher just might be right. If I angled myself just so, squinting . . .

Damn. My glyph, I thought, turning to view it from another angle, was a fucking stiletto. But at least this time I didn't have to wonder what Olivia would say.

"Well," I said, and blew out a sigh. "At least it's cute."

15

I'd once thought myself a stranger to darkness, but as I drove back to Olivia's apartment I thought back to my encounter with the construction worker earlier that day—cursing myself for remembering his name, Mark—and of the pain that had bloomed in his face as realization struck. At my words. Words Olivia would never have uttered. I shifted in my seat, uncomfortable with myself. Darkness, I was finding, came in many forms.

And what about what had happened in the comic store? Carl had seemed not only genuinely surprised that I could pull from both the Light and Shadow series, but I'd recognized that flash of fear as he looked from me to Zane and back at the comics in my hand.

So you're the one, Zane had said.

The only one. Micah's words hurtled back at me.

And then Warren's, *you're the first sign.*

I parked in Olivia's spot in the underground garage, grabbed the comics from the trunk, and decided to read through them all tonight. I needed to fill in the holes

Warren and Micah had left in my supernatural education . . . and in my life.

The phone was ringing as I slid the key in the door, and smelling nothing out of the ordinary, I jogged to the bedroom and grabbed the portable from its hook. Luna wound her silky body between my legs, nearly tripping me up.

"Hello." I perched on the edge of the bed and leaned to stroke Luna's head. She arched fluidly under my hand just as Warren's voice reached my ear.

"Olivia, it's time. We've got to get you out of here, to the sanctuary." He sounded panicked and out of breath.

My hand froze on Luna's back. "You said I wasn't ready."

"No choice. Every agent is ordered off the streets."

"Why?"

"I don't have time to tell you . . . hold on." There was a muffled sound, like he'd placed his hand over the receiver or muffled it against his chest. After half a minute he was back. "Remember when I told you the Shadows had found a way to kill off our star signs? One by one?"

I nodded, though he couldn't see it.

"Well, they're tracking us; I don't know how, but they have their next target. That's why we all have to go."

"Who are they after?"

There was another silence. "Me."

I stood and paced to the window, where shadows, once again, were soaking into crevices along the valley floor. "But why do I have to go? You said I wasn't ready. And remember, Olivia is an Archer. They won't touch her, or me, right?"

"Joanna Archer," he said, surprising me by using not only my real name, but my full name, "they don't want me for my sterling personality. They want me because of you."

Oh.

"Meet me at the Peppermill on the Boulevard. Walk, don't drive. We don't want Olivia's car anywhere near the pickup point. There will be a cab waiting out back. Pack like you're going to summer camp, and bring only what you need."

I looked around the room, with no idea where to start. "How long will I be gone?"

"Long enough to learn what you need to, but not long enough for anyone to miss you."

"That narrows it," I muttered to myself. "What about Luna?"

"She'll be taken care of."

I paused as the image of Mark and his naked pain and disbelief crowbarred its way back into my brain. "I need to tell you something, Warren. Or ask you—"

"Later. There's a window of opportunity for the crossing, but it's short. We must hurry."

"The crossing?"

"From your world into ours," he explained impatiently. "It can only be executed the exact moment day turns into night, or vice versa."

I drew back and actually looked at the receiver. "That's called dusk, Warren. It lasts more than a moment."

"Not the point at which the light and shadow are divided evenly in the air. Be there, mid-dusk sharp." He hung up in my ear.

I scowled at the phone, then down at Luna. "Bossy for a homeless man, isn't he?"

I packed swiftly, only throwing in items I was comfortable with . . . or relatively so, considering Olivia's wardrobe. Nothing silk, nothing with heels, and no lace. Sure, the jeans I stuffed into the duffel bag were Sevens rather than Levi's, and the sweats were velour lined with satin rather than simple cotton, but at least they were items I could move in. I could run. I could fight.

Figuring discretion was the way to go since Warren had been specific about not using Olivia's car, I donned a turtleneck and loose slacks, both black, though I decided to bring her crystal-studded cell phone along; after all, Olivia couldn't just drop off the face of the earth, could she? Then I started throwing in the usual toiletries.

Underwear, socks, hairbrush, toothpaste, lotion . . . camera.

"Oh, my God," I whispered, freezing with the cheap cardboard camera in my hand. I held it in my palm as gingerly as I would a baby bird. On it were the last images I'd taken as myself; the images I'd snapped in those early morning hours before returning to Warren to tell him that yes, I would accept his offer to become a superhero.

The ones of Ben, smiling in his sleep because I was alive.

I looked at the clock. Did I have time? My heart thudded at the prospect of viewing these photos. I'd have liked to develop them myself, to play with the shadow and light in the confines of my own dark space, but I knew that wasn't an option. My home was being watched, and even if it wasn't, Warren would never agree.

Still, there was a one-hour photo shop located inside a Quik-Mart only one block east of the Peppermill. If I drove that far and hurried, I might be able to make it.

The drive was a short one. I parked a block away, then crossed an intersection and three stop signs on foot to get to the store. I was only harassed by one motorist and one panhandler, so I figured my day was improving markedly.

I was greeted inside the Quik-Mart by a sleepy-eyed girl who looked barely old enough to vote. Perhaps greeted is too strong a word because she actually looked disappointed to see me, like I'd interrupted her life-in-progress and she wanted only to go back to her regularly scheduled programming. I wanted to tell her I could relate.

"How fast can you develop this?" I asked, handing her the camera.

"The sign says an hour."

"I need them in half that."

"So does everyone else, lady. Can't do it." She pushed the camera back at me and turned away.

"This says you can," I said, sliding a hundred beneath the box. She looked from the money to me, and returned to the counter.

"You'll have 'em in twenty."

She may have been lazy, but she wasn't stupid.

I decided to wait outside, thinking twenty minutes was enough to get started on at least one comic. The November air was sharp, but freshly so, and comfortable enough with the turtleneck on. I sat with my back against a stuccoed pillar and pulled the stack from my duffel bag, wondering where to begin.

Light, I decided. Definitely. I chose the one with the earliest date—volume two, number twenty-five—and flipped it open to learn more about the "independents" Warren had so distastefully mentioned the night of my metamorphosis. Apparently independents—also known in less flattering terms as rogue agents—were a constant threat to a troop's equilibrium. In a world where lineage meant everything, the competition for open star signs was fierce, and even those of the Light had been known to take out their matching star sign just for the opportunity to usurp them in the Zodiac. That meant the independents weren't liked or trusted by established troop members, and were rarely tolerated within city boundaries.

Fortunately, most of the time there was no disputing a star sign's lineage; it went from mother to daughter, or if there was no younger female left, to the eldest son. But every once in a while a sign opened up with no obvious heir, and according to the manual, that's when things got "interesting."

I grimaced and flipped the page, remembering the way Warren's mouth had curled when he spoke about the independents. Why did I get the feeling "interesting" was a euphemism for "deadly"?

I also had to wonder how my ascendancy into the Archer sign would be viewed by the star signs in his troop. If the Archer sign had been empty since my mother's disappearance, might some of them liken my sudden appearance to that of a rogue agent? At the least, wouldn't it be seen as "interesting"?

Not having these answers, and not liking the direction my questioning was taking, I quickly flipped that manual shut and picked up another. This time I ignored the chronological ordering and just snagged the one with the best-looking superhero on the cover, shoving the rest back into my pack. *Stryker*, it was called. *Agent of Light*.

"Stryker is striking," I murmured, settling back. The rating on it was PG-17, and I could see why; leather clung to the man's thighs, snug in all the right places, and a loose-knit cashmere sweater revealed tremendous biceps . . . as well as the glyph pulsing like a heartbeat on his chest. It was, in fact, pulsing on the page. Though no expert in astrology, I thought it might be the glyph for Scorpio, the sign and month before mine. Stryker was holding what I assumed to be a weapon, bent like a crossbow, but with a chain attached. Its use was totally unfathomable to me.

"I'd be willing to find out, though," I said, my eyes grazing his figure again. Note to self: side benefit of being a superhero? Getting to know other superheroes.

I paused as my eyes caught the author's name stretched across the top band in black stencil. Zane Silver. The same Zane who worked in the shop? I wondered, before my eye caught the second name illustrated there. Carl Kenyon, penciler.

"Wookie-boy?" I wondered aloud, shifting so the comic was lit from the streetlight above the store.

Ten minutes later I had a tenuous grasp on some of the events that had plagued me recently. I followed Stryker—a character, or a real person?—through a series of events leading to his metamorphosis. He'd been taken to an empty warehouse on Industrial and Pollack, and was surrounded by eleven other men and women, though it was difficult to tell one sex from the other. Each person wore a loose-fitting robe, white and dotted with what I took to be golden-threaded constellations.

"Nice job, Carl," I said, placing a finger on one of the sparking star clusters. It pulsed warmly beneath my hand. I smiled and continued reading.

"Your first life cycle ended at puberty, and the second ends tonight." The words bubbled up from a man who looked suspiciously like Warren. Only it couldn't have been Warren, I thought, tracing the image with my fingers, because Warren had never been this clean-shaven. *"To enter the third life cycle, you must go through metamorphosis and be willingly initiated into the seventh house of the Zodiac, under your mother's sign of the Scorpio. Do you accept?"*

"Crap dialogue," I muttered. "Who wrote this shit?"

"I accept," Stryker said with dignity befitting the gravity of the ceremony. *"As my mother did before me."*

"And you do so of your own free will?" the man asked, a slash of lightning outside the warehouse sinking him into silhouette. The storm clouds, I knew, were gathering outside. I could almost hear them erupting in my head the way they'd once erupted around and above Olivia's apartment.

"As my mother did before me," Stryker repeated, inclining his head. Behind him the windows had begun to streak with rain.

"At least you knew what you were choosing," I muttered, turning the page. A shaft of light shot up from the pages. It was like a paranormal pop-up book! The manual trembled between my fingertips, and the words, panels, and dialogue bubbles dissolved in an explosion of thunder. I watched as Stryker was pummeled by the same force that had entered me not long ago, dropping him to his knees and turning him into a helpless supplicant. The other star signs made a tight wedge around him—their bodies shown from above to create the symbol of his star sign—Stryker at the center. The book was more of a screen now, revealing images that flashed and burned away in turn, only his bright star immobile in the middle of the page.

There was a crack so great it shook the pages between my fingers. I almost dropped the whole thing as the sound of the sky rending in two joined the stabbing light, and with it a cry as horrible and intensely feral as I'd ever heard.

"No!" I heard a voice, perhaps Warren's, scream in response.

The symbol was broken, its bright points—the other agents of Light—splintering and turning outward to face an invasive red glow. I couldn't follow, the action was too chaotic and confused; like I too was caught in the turmoil. Blows rained down around my head, the air filled with words I'd never heard before . . . and screams I wished I hadn't. Every so often the action would slow, like a tape being caught in a recorder, and a clear image— one more reminiscent of a traditional comic—would pause, burning on my retina, before being swallowed again into chaos.

I saw Warren slaughter a man with nothing more than a rope and his fists.

I saw Micah use his surgeon's hands to slice first the scalp and then the face from an attacker's falling frame.

And I saw, with a sort of disbelieving numbness, the man who'd attacked me as a teen. A name bubbled up through the air in long capitalized letters—JOAQUIN, followed by SHADOW AQUARIAN—then it popped, the lettering cracked into shards and shooting out beyond the confines of the pages, gone.

"Joaquin," I said aloud. I knew him. I knew the look of death on his brow.

And I knew, as I turned the page, that he would kill Stryker.

And there he was. Gorgeous and helpless and immobile in the center of this maelstrom, his head grasped between Joaquin's large hands. The Shadow Aquarian began to pull, and I watched, horrified, as the strong but tenuous cording in Stryker's neck stretched, the tendons beneath straining, a cry catching in his throat. Then, in what seemed like slow motion, his flesh gave. A horrible gurgle was yanked from a newly rent hole in that throat, and his head, popping, was hauled from his body. The light in the center of the page blinked out and was no more. The red glows dissolved and were simply, suddenly, gone. And the cacophony of martial voices died until there was only one.

A woman, dressed in the same robe as Stryker's, rushed forward and sobbing, lifted Stryker's head—just the head—into her lap. It lolled there, and she bent to it, crying and stroking his hair. I could see the familial resemblance through the tears and faint lines webbing her face.

Our lineage is matriarchal.

"God." Unable to bear the scene any longer, I turned the page.

The woman was still there, but she was standing now, fists clenched, eyes burning, her shift sodden with her son's blood. *"There's a traitor among us,"* she said in a destroyed voice.

Jesus, I thought, slamming the comic book shut. This was a Light comic?

And was that what I was up against? Beings who appeared out of nowhere to rip heads from bodies? Off of superheroes?

"Ex-Excuse me." Jolted, I looked up to find the photo clerk staring at me, eyes wide, face pasty, a scattering of photos at her feet. She swallowed hard, and I didn't have to wonder how long she'd been standing there. "Th-These are the f-first few. I thought you might want them immediately."

I tried out a smile on her. She took a step back, not that I could blame her. I sat forward, gathering the photos. "Go finish," I said.

She ran back inside with a whimper, all the teen defiance gone. I leaned back again, wondering how I'd explain this away, and tried to catch my breath. Good thing too, because one glance at the handful of photos from the ground had the air fleeing my body again in an involuntary cry.

These images didn't flash. They didn't blur or glow or shoot light from the paper they were printed on. My photographer's eye saw a dozen different ways to improve the composition, but there was absolutely no way to improve upon the moment. I lifted the top one close to my face, unable to keep my hands from shaking, and studied the one-dimensional and utterly heartbreaking image captured there.

I knew my man.

I'd known how to angle myself in the encroaching dawn so as to maximize the lighting without using the flash. I knew every angle and smoothly sculpted plane of his sturdy face. I knew the length and breadth of his fingertips, and the way they felt stroking my own. I knew what color his eyes were in the morning, their intensity deepened by dreams.

And I knew, at the moment this shot had been taken, Ben Traina had been thinking of me.

It had been just before full sunrise, and dawn was breaking beautifully over his face. The smile was secretive, too small to cause his eyes to crinkle up at the corners in the way I loved, but it was the contented smile of a man who was expecting to wake up and face the first day of the rest of his life. He thought I was alive. He didn't yet know of a man named Butch and bodies tossed out plate-glass windows. I compared the image with the man who'd stopped me earlier today, and knew he'd never be this happy again. And neither would I.

A gust of air, carrying the scent of a nearby Dumpster, brought me back to the present. I looked up, mildly surprised to find myself still in front of the Quik-Mart. I'd been unaware of the passing time. I glanced at my watch, heard laughter—probably a man stumbling from the bar down the street—then shut it out, sighing over the sound.

Perhaps Warren could help Ben, I thought, turning my attention back to the photo. If he could change an identity, maybe he could erase a person's memory so they no longer mourned a loved one. I bit my lip. Did I want to be forgotten? Did I want him to get over me, and turn those smiling morning eyes on someone else?

I recalled kissing him and I didn't. Then I thought of how I'd seen him look after he thought me dead and I did. I thought of the lust that had ignited so effortlessly between us again, and I didn't. Then I recalled the fury I'd seen on his face this afternoon, and I did.

"God, Ben," I said, pressing the photos to my chest as I closed my eyes. "We're never going to be this innocent again."

Laughter sounded behind me again, closer.

The fear that punched at my heart was a physical blow. I rocked into a standing position instantly, my legs braced wide, head up, and I sniffed. Rot on the air. Decaying hate, bloodthirsty hunger. "Fuck, fuck, fuck."

Ajax. I don't know how he'd found me, but he was coming, and quick.

I shoved the photos and comics into the duffel bag, zipping it as I raced into the store. I ducked down the first aisle and zigzagged to the back of the store, past cosmetics, lotions, shampoos, candy, and condoms, the security globe above capturing my every move. I fled past aisles stocked with visors and cheap T-shirts, there only because the words *Las Vegas* were splayed upon them in some manner, and quickly discovered that among the mundane and the kitsch and the items that made life oh-so *convenient*, there was one thing missing. A place to hide.

I should have run, I thought, blood churning. I should have taken off in the opposite direction of the stench and laughter, and run all the way to the Peppermill. To the safety of Warren or someone else who might know what to do.

Nobody can know who you really are, do you understand?

I looked again at the mirrored globe, and cursed Olivia's reflected image. If Ajax didn't kill me, Warren was surely going to do the job.

The automatic doors at the front of the store slid open. Through the security globe I saw a figure slide inside like a wisp of smoke, then disappear. He was following my scent, the fear now, and whatever emotion or pheromone that had alerted him to me in the first place. Seconds ticked by like bombs, and I felt the frantic despair rats must feel in a maze. There was, very simply, nowhere to hide. Then my eyes fell to the clearance bin in the middle of the aisle. Nowhere to hide, I thought, except in plain sight.

Tossing my duffel aside, I dove for the mishmashed items; remaindered Halloween costumes made of colored felt and cotton meant to wear away in one washing. All I needed was a mask. I tossed aside bear bodies, bumblebees, superheroes—ha!—and butterfly wings, and finally unearthed a cheap plastic mask. It would only cover half my face, but it'd fit. Fumbling it over my head, I snagged a baseball cap sporting the famous *Welcome to Las Vegas* sign on it, and tucked Olivia's golden locks up inside. Then I turned, breathing hard, and waited.

His laugh, the one I'd mistaken for drunken mirth, was the first thing to reach me. But if Ajax were drunk, it was with the intoxication of anticipated success and unrestrained violence, not hard alcohol.

When he appeared, the first thing I noticed was his Adam's apple bobbing in his throat, then the anticipatory twitch of his long fingers; those effective, effeminate hands. His lanky skeleton pressed beneath his skin as he moved, and I was almost surprised his bones didn't clack together when he walked. Already in place, his feral grin widened when he saw me.

"I have to hand it to Warren. This is his best disguise yet . . . other than his own, that is," and his laugh was so cruel it was clear he wasn't speaking of Warren's vagrant persona. "I'd have never guessed it was you."

My eyes, beneath the slit of plastic, flickered up to the mirrored ball. A pink pig's snout protruded from beneath the rim of the hat, but my face—Olivia's face, and her hair—were perfectly hidden. Dignified it wasn't, but it did the job.

"I'm guarding my identity," I said, unnecessarily.

"I see that." Ajax took a step forward, his long coat swirling around his ankles. I mirrored him, taking one step back. "But, very soon, neither your plastic mask nor your veil of flesh and bone are going to matter. I'm going to rip your head from your body and swim in your blood."

I thought of Stryker and shuddered. Ajax laughed. "God, but your fear is delicious! It's like an aperitif . . . a promise of delights to come. Can you see it the way I do? Every emotion emanating from your body in a silvery wave, rolling in sheets of phosphorescent emotion. See, there goes a particularly strong one. Like the tide rushing from the sea, nice and foamy at the edges as it roars for escape."

I clenched my teeth and brought a mental barrier slamming down in front of me, the way Micah had taught. I held my breath until I was sure I could control it, then exhaled slowly. Ajax frowned. "Quick learner, aren't you, Jo? I didn't expect you to find your glyph so quickly either, but of course you've had help."

I glanced down. The symbol that had been sprayed on my chest earlier that day was suddenly pulsing with light, a white heat throbbing beneath my black turtleneck. Damn it, I thought. I bet that Yulyia bitch wasn't even from the Ukraine.

The rip of steel through air had my head whipping up.

Ajax had his poker gripped in both hands, point down, poised in front of him like a walking cane. One with extremely sharp teeth.

"Tell me, do you also have your conduit?"

"Yes," I lied.

"Let's see it."

I swallowed hard, motioning with my chin. "It's in that duffel bag."

Smiling, he sheathed his weapon and lifted the bag by its soft handles. "Never leave your conduit unattended, Joanna. You, more than anyone, should know the power in turning an enemy's own weapon against him."

He lifted the bag, but hesitated, brows drawing in closely, nostrils working like a rabbit's. He was sensing my lie. I had to distract him, fill the air with an emotion other than anxious hope.

"Powerful," I agreed, "and Butch's scimitar was particularly fun. Do you know I began by chopping his hands off at the wrists? I think the majority of blood loss occurred there, but I also forked his tongue and watched him choke on his own blood. I've never seen so much blood," I said, shaking my head, and that was true. Remembering, I was able to conjure up the taste of molten vengeance in my mouth. I exhaled the memory in Ajax's direction.

He reflexively lifted a hand, shielding his face, and glared at me from over the top of it. "He was like a brother to me."

"Well, Ajax," I said, and leaned forward, "your brother pissed himself when I used his own blade against him. Now *that's* what I call a wave of fear."

I braced myself in case he was going to rush me, but rage had him ripping into my duffel, blindly searching for a weapon that wasn't there. It also had his fingers inadvertently running across the weapons that were.

Carl, the little wookie, had been right. Getting zapped by an enemy's manual wasn't pretty. I had the five agent of

Light comics stacked on top of the Shadows, and Ajax, it seemed, got a good handful. He dropped the duffel bag immediately, but the damage was already done. The skin on his right palm charred before my eyes, his eyes rolled so far back in his skull that they were snowy white orbs, and his hair sizzled down to within a half inch of his skull.

I was already turning, ready to run like an Olympic sprinter, when I saw the photos of Ben scattered in the aisle.

Shit. Ajax would recover. Ajax, I thought, swallowing hard, would see them. Then he'd hunt down the one man I'd ever loved, and torture him the way I'd tortured Butch. He'd do it to spite me, or bait me, or lure me. And I, of course, would come.

The fingers on Ajax's good hand were already beginning to twitch to life, and his eyes were rolling back into place, independent of one another, like twin reels on a slot machine. He'd have himself a jackpot if I were still kneeling at his feet when they hit home.

I lunged for the photos, gathering them quickly. He groaned and staggered forward. He bumped my arm with his left foot and I cursed as he fumbled for his weapon. Springing forward from a crouch, I wrapped my arms around his spindly but strong legs and sent his body crashing forward. His chin landed with an audible crack on the hard linoleum, and he nearly impaled himself on his own poker. Nearly, but unfortunately not quite.

Pivoting, I reached for the poker, but his hand closed around the grip first, so I redirected and kicked the duffel from his reach. I leapt over his body just as three feet of barbed supernatural steel came arching my way. Scooping up the bag, I felt fire graze my right hamstring, but I was already moving away, stumbling, then breaking into a full-fledged sprint.

I was nearly out the door when a fresh scream sliced the air in two. Safety was feet away, but there was no escaping the horrible stuttering sobs behind me. There was nothing heroic about it; just a slight pivoting of the feet as I turned back around, and the still-fresh memory of the way my sister, also an innocent, had died at the hands of another Shadow agent.

The photo girl's eye makeup ran down her cheeks in black streaks. Her blue eyes would have seemed transparent in comparison, but they were weighed in their sockets with tears and congealing fear. I probably couldn't save her. I hadn't been able to save Olivia, and I sure as hell didn't know how to save myself, but if I ran from this—and God knows I wanted to—I wouldn't be able to live with myself anyway. The duffel dropped from my hand with a dull thud, and I stepped back in the store.

Ajax began to laugh.

"You move fast, Archer," Ajax said, his voice merry with observation. The girl whimpered.

"Don't," I said, taking another step forward.

"You should've run when you had the chance. It's one thing I can't quite understand about the Light signs. Putting your lives at risk for mortals when there are just so many of them about." He waved his poker in the air like it was a wand. "When are you going to realize they're expendable? They're nothing. Just flesh, weakness, and stench. That the agents of Light would care for them at all boggles the mind . . . and makes you so much easier to kill."

I read his deadly intention before he moved, and dove half a second before he flipped the poker in his hand. The weapon, a missile now, sank home exactly where I'd been standing, its steel tip buried in a pyramid of Coke cases, sending sodas exploding in the air as it burst into flame.

I began to sprint toward him before the smoke could clear, darting across aisles with no particular plan except to close the distance between Ajax and me and bring that terrified clerk within arm's reach. I crossed two aisles and raced up a third, to end up behind him. He pulled another poker from beneath his jacket, and this time there wasn't enough distance to duck, dive, or even blink. Ajax laughed.

"Yes, you're very fast," he repeated, turning the hilt of the blade over and over in his hand. "But let's see if you're fast enough."

He didn't throw it. I knew he wouldn't, even before he inverted the tip and plunged it into the teenager's heart. Her screaming cut off into a gasping whine, then a gurgling sigh, and finally an irregular sucking noise, like she was breathing through a bent straw. Ajax twisted the poker, making no move to dislodge it from her chest cavity, just twisting and turning like he was stirring soup. As she died, his eyes never left mine.

"Why?" I asked, my breath, body, and mind going utterly numb. I pulled my remaining energy inward, knowing if I didn't that I'd collapse right there, weighed down by guilt and revulsion, and the knowledge that I'd caused this. Again. "Why do you kill innocent people?"

He dumped the girl's body on the floor and wiped his hands on his jacket. "Pain amuses me. Death amuses me."

"Then you're going to find this hilarious." Ajax found out just how fast I was, and it was fast enough.

We hit the floor with a loud smack, rolling together behind the photo counter. Smells became colors behind my eyes; yellow-tinged chemicals, dusky blood, tar-thick smoke, and Ajax's breath, putrid as pus, audible in my ear. The taste of him was sour as my teeth found flesh and bit down hard. He howled, anger laced with pain, and pulled away, his blood joining the noxious feast. I smiled as he cried out again, only vaguely aware in some still sane part of my mind that I was still wearing the pig's mask, and with another human's blood running down my chin, I must have looked like an animal indeed.

We leapt at each other again.

He should have been too fast for me, at least the "me" I'd been nine weeks earlier, but I was countering his moves; meeting blow with blow, and each parry with feint. My training, coupled with the strength I'd been gifted with during metamorphosis, was the most delicious melding of power I could ever imagine. Aggression fused with streaming adrenaline, unadulterated hate, and manifested in a speed I never knew I possessed.

I reveled in it. My strikes were preemptive. I landed punches first and hard. I gained stronger footing. I swung out with my legs. I was confident . . . and that, of course, was my mistake.

I landed a blow to the thigh designed to take out his left leg and Ajax seemed to stumble. When I moved in for the follow-up, he wrong-footed me, and plowed a right hook into the exposed part of my lower face. He was on me before I recovered, and we hit the ground again, this time my body taking the full impact of our combined weight.

My breath was driven from my chest, and a hollow snap accompanied by an acute shot of pain told me at least one rib had cracked. Ajax flipped me easily, mounting me at the waist and settling his weight on my tender midsection. I struggled for breath, but it wasn't coming. Ajax laughed . . . as he had upon scenting me, and upon killing the young, innocent clerk. I was getting sick of that dry, bone-rattling sound.

I swiped the back of my one free hand over my mouth, and came away with blood. When I repeated the motion, it came away dry. I was healing faster than ever. Unfortunately, Ajax noticed this too.

"What? No more tricks, little Archer?" He placed his palm on my chest in what could have been mistaken for an intimate gesture . . . until he leaned forward. I groaned as pain bloomed behind my lids and the freshly healed rib popped again.

He chuckled under his breath, and I could see where this was heading. Sitting back, his weight still pinning me down, he tilted his head and considered me more closely.

"Did you know, I almost felt sorry for you when we

first met? I remember thinking, 'This poor little girl has no idea why she exists, never mind what she can do or who she might become.' It was pitiful, really. All that ripe, raw power beginning to glow beneath your skin. All that pent-up ability straining to burst free, trapped instead by that stupid, ignorant mind. Not to mention this fragile wall of flesh." He popped the rib again, and my head swam with pain. I closed my eyes, afraid I was going to pass out. Ironically enough, his voice kept me anchored in the present.

"I am not, as you might expect, totally void in my feeling for others." I opened one eye to see if he was serious, but had difficulty seeing through the slits in my tilted mask. His voice sounded serious. "Butch, for example. I cared for him."

Great. He'd once cared deeply for another psychopath. I wanted to tell him it didn't necessarily qualify him for sainthood, but I could actually feel my rib stitching together again in my chest and didn't dare.

"I went on that first date," he continued conversationally, "intending to kill you quickly. Mercifully."

"So what changed?" I asked, trying to keep my voice even. Trying to breathe through the pain so I could think of something else to do.

Ajax wasn't fooled by my question. Leaning forward again, he popped that fragile rib easily. "You opened your mouth."

He caved in another of my ribs just for pleasure. I cried out at the fresh break, unable to stop myself this time.

"Look at me, Joanna. Look at me," he repeated patiently, like speaking to a child. He sunk his fingernails into my jaw, forcing my gaze straight. His face was somewhat obscured through the mask, but I caught his eyes probing mine. "I want you to know who I am, deep down, when I kill you."

"I know who you are," I managed as his fingers sunk

deeper into my cheeks. "I've seen you without your mask before."

"In the restaurant, yes, but seeing is not knowing. Observation is no match for experience."

Oh God. This didn't sound good.

"They lied to you, Joanna." He almost looked pained as he said this. "There is no precious balance between good and evil. No yin and yang. No good or bad. Light or Shadow."

"Apparently your mother disagreed with that."

Ajax froze momentarily, then patted my cheek, hard. "She was wrong. Misguided. She never learned, or must have forgotten, that all there really is in this world are varying degrees of evil. That, and the point at which every human being breaks."

"She didn't believe that."

He grinned sadistically. "She did in the end."

"Well, I don't."

He leaned closer, eyes gleaming. "I'll make you a believer too."

I recoiled, but there was nowhere to go.

"Let's both remove our disguises, shall we?"

He gouged his fingertips through the eyes of my mask so forcefully only the narrowness of the slats saved my eyesight. Just as quickly as he lifted the pig's snout away, however, it snapped back into place, the plastic edges stinging my skin. His weight was gone so suddenly it was as if he'd been lifted straight into the air. A wild war cry, accompanied by a flurry of wind, swept through the building.

Freed, and desperate to stay that way, I backpedaled until my head slammed against the photo counter. Ripping the mask from my face, I strained to see where Ajax had gone, as well as who, or what, was in here with us. The answer was immediate. I was lifted to my feet, none too gently, and found myself facing an angry set of brown eyes.

"Warren," I gasped. My eyes darted away from him, searching for Ajax, finding him in a crouch atop an aisle barrier facing two other men. The first was stocky but obviously strong, the other lithe as he leapt the entire seven feet in height to square off against Ajax. Both were armed, and both their chests were glowing, pulsing vibrantly. I pushed at Warren's hands, but he jerked me back into place, yanking my ball cap low.

"Don't let him see your face." Cuffing me by the neck like a mother cat with her kitten, he forced my head lower again. Then he half dragged me to the exit, shielding me with his own body. Even so, I felt the moment Ajax's eyes lit upon my back. I felt their probing, their impotent fury, and the oily slickness of his thoughts just behind that stare. Outnumbered, he turned away with an outraged cry.

"I'll find you out, Archer!" he called out. "I'll discover your true identity and when I'm finished with you, you will *believe!*"

Warren's fingers tightened on my neck, squelching my instinct to turn, and he blew what I took to be a raspberry at Ajax while ushering me out the door. The last thing I heard was the report of feet pounding across linoleum, a back door slam, and two other pairs giving chase. We headed in the opposite direction, back toward the Strip, where the light bled into the street.

"My duffel!" I said, halting suddenly.

"Don't stop," he ordered, pushing harder. "Felix will get it."

"Can you at least let go of my neck? I'm getting a kink."

Warren released me so abruptly I stumbled. He glanced side to side, pivoting so he was walking backward, then turned again before taking off in a trot. "Hurry. The time of crossing is near, and we're not safe yet."

We ran, Warren openly vigilant, and me trying to

breathe through the ache in my side which was finally, if slowly, receding. The silhouette of the Peppermill loomed closer, contoured from the other side by the setting sun, and I could see people dining through the long plate-glass windows, oblivious to our plight. It was unsettling how normal everything looked. The foot tourists hardly glanced up as we wove between cars in the restaurant's asphalt lot. Perhaps they thought it normal in Vegas for an unshaven bum in a leather trench coat to be jogging with a girl whose sweater was half singed from her chest.

"This way." We darted around the building's far corner and into a narrow alley that reeked of urine. A cab waited there, lights off, and a couple stood at the window, arguing loudly with the car's sole occupant.

The man loomed over the driver, one hand propped on the hood, irritation coating his voice. "Look, are you on duty or not?"

"I want to go to the Luxor," the woman whined.

The headlights flipped on to illuminate us in their beam.

"He's waiting for us," Warren said sharply. The woman took one look and whimpered. I didn't know what I looked like, but Warren was striding toward them at a decidedly aggressive pace, limp exaggerated, his coat billowing around his ankles. The couple backed down the alley, not exactly the safest choice of exits, but at least it was away from us. The cab inched forward, and the doors on each side swung open.

"Get in," Warren ordered, skirting to the opposite side. I did, wordlessly, wincing as the leather seat caught the gash in the back of my thigh. Leaning my head back, I closed my eyes, and sighed as the door shut and the car began to move.

"I smell Ajax," the driver said, singsonging the name. I peeked to find him regarding me through the rearview mirror. All I could make out of his face were his eyes, but they were wide and crinkled at the edges as he laughed at some private joke. I didn't see what was so funny, and neither did Warren.

"That's because Ajax somehow tracked her," he answered, shifting to face me. "Tell me, Olivia, because I feel like I'm missing something here, but what part of 'meet me at the Peppermill' means 'go fight Ajax at the corner drugstore'?"

I turned my head away. "He started it."

"Do you know what you've done? What you could have undone?"

I clenched my teeth and my jaw ached where Ajax's fingers had dug into bone. I knew the feeling would fade, that I would soon heal, but the knowledge alleviated nothing right now.

"What did you do to call him?"

I glanced at the driver who was still staring at me, a lucky rabbit's foot swinging beneath his mirrored image, his eyes still amused, then turned to Warren. "Nothing."

"You did something," he said, squaring on me in his seat. "He found you despite the masking agent we administered, and in less than two weeks. I want to know how."

Apparently I hadn't gotten to that comic yet. I shrugged.

Warren stared at me, his face stony and cold, eyes unblinking. "Did you invoke his name?"

I shook my head.

"Did you go after him yourself?"

"No." I clenched my teeth again. The pain was gone.

"Damn it, Olivia!" He punched his fist into the seat in front of him. "You're not going to keep getting this lucky! What did you do?"

I leaned toward him and spaced my words evenly. "Don't. Yell. At me. Anymore."

"Warren's right," the driver said conversationally. "You are lucky."

"Not just lucky . . . *stupid* lucky!"

I looked at him, and I swear his outline was singed in

red. This manipulative fruitcake thought he had reason to be furious with *me*? While my sister was dead, my life was over, and my bones were stitching together inside of me, again?

"I said don't fucking yell at me!"

The words ricocheted like shots off the inside of the cab, shaking it on its wheels. The driver gripped the steering wheel, eyes on the road and no longer smiling, and the smell of singed hair hung in the air. I glared at Warren, and realized he'd backed up in his seat.

I knew then my Shadow side was showing. That hadn't been my voice. It was deeper, lower than my natural range, the vocal cords scorched by fury. I swallowed down the anger, the heat scalding my lungs, and turned away again. Tears boiled in my eyes. *Shit. Shit! What was happening to me?*

"Jesus," the driver said, exhaling deeply. It was the last thing anyone said for a long time.

"Did you kill someone?" Warren finally asked.

I looked at him in blatant disbelief, shocked to the bone. "Well, it was on my to-do list right after *get pedicure*, but, no, I hadn't quite gotten to it yet!"

Warren shook his head, looking a lot older than I'd ever seen him. "This isn't a joke."

"Wrong, Warren! This whole thing is a joke! A supernatural organization is protecting Las Vegas? Give me a break! Information passed on through comic books . . . and m-my goddamned chest lights up like a Christmas ornament when someone wants to kill me!" Now I just sounded panicked, frightened rather than frightening. "It's all a fucking joke, and guess what? Me—my life!—is the fucking punch line!"

I felt laughter bubbling up in my throat, bitter as bile, and I held it back because I knew it'd come out in a scream, and I was afraid it would never stop. Swallowing hard, feeling light-headed, I said, "Don't tell me what to think about what I've seen since you entered my life.

Don't tell me what to laugh at, or what's funny and what's not. I'll fucking howl at the moon if I feel like it. And," I added, pointing my finger at his chest, "don't ever, *ever* tell me how to feel!"

And then I really did start laughing. I laughed and laughed until the manic sound soured and turned to tears. Then I cried and cried.

And then I cried some more.

16

The rest of the cab ride was spent in stony and uncomfortable silence, and as we sped up Industrial, heading under Flamingo Road, I dully watched the sun setting behind the Palms and felt the darkness rising, eyeing me from the east. Gridlock had set in on I-15, parallel to us, and I could see people singing and talking from behind their windshields, suspended on that strip of highway, momentarily delayed on the way to the rest of their lives.

Meanwhile, as the world went on revolving around me, I tried to answer Warren's questions for myself. How *had* Ajax found me? Had I done something to call him to me? I tried to think back, but my memories were blighted by screams and pain, and Ajax's particular scent had slithered beneath my skin to suck at my pores. The questions continued to pile up before me, and like those drivers on the freeway, I felt stuck in eternal gridlock.

And why would Warren ask if I'd murdered another person? Could he really believe I could do it? Did *I*, in some chipped and faulty corner of my heart, believe it of myself? I thought about the construction workers again, and how power-drunk I'd felt as I used my senses and words to blow holes into their worlds. I had tried to justify it in my mind, telling myself they'd deserved and asked for it; but the truth was, even though I hadn't killed that man named Mark, or the other man who was sleeping with his wife, I had altered their lives in a horrible and irrevocable way. And wasn't that a death of sorts? Wasn't that a way to murder Mark's hope, in his own fallible heart, that he was wrong in suspecting his best friend and wife?

I put a hand to my mouth and stared blindly out the window, deciding I didn't want the answers to all my questions.

We pulled abruptly into a half-empty parking lot behind Tommy Rocker's Cantina, a favorite hangout for locals who wanted to be near the Strip but not necessarily the tourists. Two men emerged from the bar, looking innocuous, just colleagues enjoying an after-hours drink before facing the drive home, but I recognized them as the men who'd chased Ajax. The shorter was dark and severe-looking, but the taller appeared happy and light, bouncing on his toes as he approached the cab. The paranormal world's answer to Laurel and Hardy.

The doors opened for them. "Is it taken care of?" Warren asked as they slid in.

"Of course," the first man said. He slouched low, not even glancing at me. "The place was absolutely stinking with *her* scent."

"It's fine," the other man countered sharply, and they both fell silent.

The cab began moving again, but this time my view of the freeway was blurred by fresh tears. The "it" Warren referred to was really a "she." I wondered what the headlines would read in tomorrow's paper. *Teen Dies In Botched Hold-Up.* Or, *Tragedy At Quik-Mart.* One thing I was certain it wouldn't read was *Novice Superhero Destroys Yet Another Life.* Warren and his friends would see to that.

I sniffled involuntarily at the thought, and the tall man—the one I'd seen leap to face Ajax across the aisle dividers—turned to me with a small, sympathetic smile.

"Here," he said, holding out my duffel bag. I swallowed hard, took it, and clutched it to my chest. The first man had turned too, but there was no kindness in his face. He rolled his eyes at my tears and turned back around.

"And Ajax?"

"The usual," came the answer. "Smoke, mirrors, all that Shadow shit."

The kind man was still watching me. I wanted to tell him to turn around, but right now he seemed to be the only friendly face in the cab. I tried to look nonthreatening. He held his hand out over the back of the seat. "I'm Felix."

"Here we go," the other one muttered.

Felix smiled. "So you're the new Archer. We haven't had an Archer in the Zodiac since your mother."

I lifted my hand. "I'm Jo—"

"This is Olivia," Warren interrupted, and I flushed, feeling his glare.

I dropped my hand back in my lap and turned away from them both. The other man in the front seat mumbled something I couldn't quite hear, but I had the distinct feeling it wasn't complimentary.

"Shut up," the driver said, and we all did.

There was a sense of urgency to the way the cab maneuvered through traffic, around—and in one case over—barriers, and something about the way the light shone through the windshield really did make the city seem divided in two.

"Are we going to make it?"

"We'll make it, but someone else is going to have to drive."

"You're staying on this side, Gregor?" Felix asked. The others also seemed surprised.

"Just until dawn. Someone has to watch the city. Besides,

nothing interesting is going to happen with her," he said, jerking his head in my direction, "before morning."

"That'll be a nice change," I murmured to no one in particular, though Warren grunted.

"Be careful, Gregor. We don't know if they have intel on you or not."

"I think if they did they'd have gotten to me by now. I'm not exactly the strongest of the star signs." Gregor held up his right arm for my benefit. It ended just above the elbow. "I found a lucky penny today, though, and I have my trusty rabbit's foot. I'll be fine."

Warren turned to me. "Like I said on the phone, you can only make the crossing at the exact moment where light and dark are divided evenly in the air. Something to remember if it's midnight and you've been tracked. You'll have to survive for six more hours before seeking sanctuary."

"Gawd," the man up front crossed his arms and mumbled, "she doesn't even know that?"

I shot forward in my seat, feeling the anger rise in me again. So far I was a complete failure as a superhero, and had a pretty dubious self-image as a human being, but I still had a grasp on my pride, if a tenuous one. "Look, mister, I don't know who you are or what you've got against me, but I've never seen you or any of your Kryptonite-fearing buddies before Warren over here jumped in front of my car—"

"Was run down, technically."

Felix turned to Gregor. "I don't fear Kryptonite. Do you?"

"So let's get something stick straight between us. I didn't ask for this. I'd be more than happy to never know anything about crossings or metamorphoses or any of this other weirdo, paranormal bullshit, but here I am. So get over it. Apparently I have to."

The man had turned in his seat and watched me through

slitted eyes. There was something odd about the texture of his anger; odd, and familiar at the same time. I felt like I should recognize him, or one of the components that made him *him*, but I didn't.

At the end of the long silence that followed, Gregor eased the car over to the side of the road, shifted to neutral, and swiveled in his seat to face me. "Olivia, this is Chandra. She's one of our best blenders in the chemistry lab. She made your new signature scent for you."

She.

I felt the anger drain from my face and body, along with the color. I did a mental head slap, thinking the familiar thread in Chandra's genetic makeup was her sex. Female. Hello.

It was definitely one of those days.

"I'll drive." Chandra flung open the door.

"Well, *that* was the wrong thing to say," Warren muttered as she stalked around the cab.

"Chandra hates being mistaken for a man," Gregor explained as he opened the driver's side door, but his eyes were laughing again. And at least I knew I wasn't the first to have done so. Unfortunately I also knew women. They rarely forgave a slight like this, and Chandra didn't seem terribly forgiving in the first place.

"Don't wait up for me, kids," Gregor said, exiting the car.

"Call if you're gonna be late," Warren said.

"Nag, nag, nag."

The doors shut behind Chandra, and she slammed the car into gear.

"Shit," I heard Felix mutter.

"Got your belt on?" Warren asked. The car revved, tires squealing and spinning over gravel before finding purchase and jolting forward. I was thrown back into my seat, my gaze fixed straight ahead, but from the corner of my eye I saw Gregor's diminishing bulk in the sideview mirror. However, the solid concrete wall standing twelve feet before us seemed a more pressing issue.

"Women drivers . . ." Warren said, sounding weary.

Perhaps the car could fly, I thought as the wall loomed closer. Or maybe the wall moved or disintegrated or we'd disappear right through it like it wasn't even there. But then Warren braced himself beside me, and I knew that wall wasn't going anywhere.

We struck it going at least sixty-five miles an hour. The impact propelled me into the seat in front of me, and the angry screech of metal kissing concrete married burning rubber and dust-filled air. Bricks scraped against the sides of the car, slamming atop the roof before we came to a halt as violently and abruptly as any normal car would. When I opened my eyes, however, I saw the shell of the cab was undamaged.

"I hate that part," Warren muttered, unbuckling.

I pressed the back of my hand to my mouth and came away with fresh blood. "What the hell was that?"

"What?" he said, raising a brow. "You thought crossing over to an alternate reality would be easy?"

"You'll get used to it," Felix said, smiling as the doors swung open. "Helps if you have a cocktail first."

"You mean I'll have to do that again?"

Chandra smirked at me through the rearview mirror. "Welcome to our world," she said, and got out of the cab.

Bitch, I thought, watching her stalk away through debris.

"Come on," Warren said, waving me along. I sighed, shook my head, and went ahead and followed him into his world.

I stepped from that cab in the same way other adventurous humans once stepped onto the moon. A small step here, another tentative one there; gravel and cinder block and glass crunching beneath my boots. It seemed we were in a dusty, debris-scattered courtyard, with oddly shaped sheet metal stacked and leaning at every angle and high walls ribboned with whorls of cyclone wire. Glancing back, I tried to see Gregor through the breach in the wall, but all the dust stirred by our vehicle's impact had wafted toward that opening like smoke to a chimney flue, and it was congealing there somehow, as thick and unyielding as cinder itself, swirling like concrete being poured through air.

The others were in front of me, walking single file, Warren's gimpy gait even more pronounced as he picked his way around the sheet metal. As I rushed to catch up with him I realized the steel pieces in the yard weren't scraps of metal at all, but signs sporting words like Normandie, Photo Shop, and Le Café. There was a life-sized cactus with chipped green paint and holes where bald and broken bulbs protruded like thorns, and a six-foot martini glass outlined by clear glass tubes. There were acres more of shattered incandescent lamps, fluorescent paint, and the historic signage that had dotted the Vegas skyline when Italian men were still running the city and flashing neon drenched the streets from dusk to dawn.

"Where are we?" I asked, glancing at scripted individual letters someone had lined up to spell Casino.

"Neon Boneyard," Warren shot over his shoulder, picking his way past the Landmark and Dunes signs. Each letter was larger than he.

"Where the lights go to die," Chandra said, smirking as she twirled to face me.

"Where the Light goes to rest," Felix corrected, suddenly appearing beside me. He smiled again, and I was gratified. "It's as close to home as you're ever going to get again."

We followed Warren past the Aladdin's original genie's lamp, and took a left at a sign that said Thunderbird in script. About an acre in we stopped in front of the largest, gaudiest piece in the yard, still magnificent, even with all its lights busted and burnt out. "Here," Warren said.

I gazed upward, nonplussed. "The Silver Slipper?" Next to the Foxy's Firehouse and the hundred-foot clown still standing in front of Circus Circus, the Silver Slipper had been my favorite neon landmark as a kid. As I got closer, I saw the bulbs that had once studded the bright evening shoe were long gone, their threads rusted, maintenance halted after the property was demolished. I was surprised to see it was only fifteen feet high—it had always seemed larger looming above the property on its rotating axis—but it looked to weigh at least two tons, and I watched as the others crossed to the back of the giant shoe and began to climb a rusted staircase attached to the heel.

At first I just stood there, craning my neck upward, gazing from the ground as three superheroes became silhouetted in the waning evening light. Chandra was first. She didn't look at me or anyone else as she reached the top, but sat down unceremoniously and slid down the great, bulb-stamped pump. Just before she slid off the front of the curved toe, a light flashed and she disappeared.

"Come on," Felix yelled down to me. "You'll fall behind."

Which was the last thing I wanted. Slinging my duffel over my shoulder, I scurried to the staircase and began to climb. I arrived just in time to see a path light up, much like a landing strip for an airplane.

"What do we do?" I asked, though Felix was already kneeling for his slide, which meant I was about to find out.

He smiled at me over his shoulder. "Just follow the light. It'll lead the way." And he let himself go, sliding down the giant slipper until—flash!—he disappeared into the toe.

"It's like anything else," Warren said, stepping onto the narrow platform. He extended his bad leg out in front of him first, then the good. "You take the first step with the faith you'll end up where you want to be." Without waiting for a reply, he too disappeared.

"Where I want to be," I repeated, though there was no one left to hear. I was no longer sure exactly where that was . . . though I was relatively certain it wasn't a hole in the ground beneath the Silver Slipper in the Neon Boneyard where discarded Las Vegas signage went to die.

Just take the first step. I did, and a preternatural landing strip lit up before me. That had to be a good sign, I thought, eyeing the beacon at the end. I took another step. Suddenly the Slipper exploded with light, the small landing strip disappearing into a void so bright I had to shield my eyes, locking them tight. If anything, the light grew brighter.

I stepped back, trying to feel my way off the platform. I was afraid I'd fall but I couldn't take my hands from my eyes long enough to look because they were tearing up in defense. I heard a sizzling sound and smelled burning. Then I tasted it, hot and cloying at the back of my throat, and realized it was coming from me.

Agony jigsawed through my skull, drilling at my temples, and I cried out and rushed forward blindly. I had no choice but to move. I was incinerating on that platform, like I was shut in a microwave, organs heating within me, roasting from the inside out.

I stepped, slipped, and slid into oblivion. The incline was like a greased luge run, and me without a sled, I thought hysterically. And while the drop into the toe was not unexpected, my breath was sucked away. Light, brilliant but miasmic, streamed past me, surrounded me . . . and instead of illuminating me, infected me.

I choked on the white-hot heat as it rolled like lava into my mouth, rising into the soft tissue of my brain as I fell. I was being vacuumed down into a trough of invisible flame, fire biting at my cheeks and ears, sinking in like pokers behind my eyes. I screamed, but the sound was wrenched from my mouth.

"What's taking her so long?"

The sweltering words slid past me as I continued to fall. More heat invaded me, radiation now; attacking my fevered flesh, piercing my veins, seeking bone.

"She's coming now. Hear that?"

Hurry, I thought, knowing I was near to blacking out. *Charred.* I grew dizzy and my lungs felt close to imploding. Only when I landed with a hard thud did I realize there was any air left in my chest to lose. I crumbled, but sucked in air like I was Nessie coming up from the bottom of the loch.

"That was graceless," I heard Chandra say.

I rolled onto my hands and knees, facedown, gulping down air, thinking I'd never breathed in anything so crisp, cool, balmy, or sweet in my life. It set the sores in my mouth to drying, and they crackled as I winced. They were on my lungs too, where they remained wet and aching.

"Olivia?" Hands on my shoulders. I whimpered and jerked away, and not just because my flesh sizzled at the contact. I was pissed off and feeling vulnerable; exposed and lost, dizzy and disoriented, and betrayed by the very people who were supposed to be protecting me.

And I was so very fucking hot.

Why hadn't anyone told me what to expect? Or what to do? Why had they just left me up there, alone and burning? I couldn't get the question out, though; not past the air I was trying to suck in. I started shaking, an improvement over the stinging paralysis, but not by much.

"What's wrong with her?" Felix this time, voice hesitant and low.

My eyes, scalded, refused to see—I couldn't even tell if they were open or closed—and my head throbbed where it had whipped back against the top of the slide. But that was nothing compared to the pulpy blisters I felt rising in my brain. I knelt on my haunches, curled into myself and wished for death.

"A little dramatic, don't you think?"

"Shut up, Chandra."

"Olivia?" Warren's hands again. This time I let him turn me over. There was a collective gasp . . . which probably wasn't good.

"What happened to her?"

"God. I've never seen anything like it."

"Get Greta," I heard Warren say. "Hurry."

"We could have killed her ten times over by now," Chandra muttered, and I felt Warren shift. "I'm just saying! It's a weakness. The Tulpa will find out about it. He'll use it against her."

"He won't find out if nobody tells him. Besides, he shares the weakness."

"What happened?" I finally managed. The words were catching like splinters in my throat. I pushed them out anyway. "Why did that hurt so much? Why won't my eyes stop tearing up?"

"They're not tears," Chandra said, and this time she sounded apologetic. "It's blood."

I touched a hand to my face.

"I'm so sorry, Olivia." Warren's voice was low but panicked, and alarm beat at my chest as I felt him hovering over me uncertainly. "It's my fault. I forgot, and it's my fault."

"Forgot what?" I asked, raising my face, as blind as a baby chick. I could only imagine how I looked.

"The Shadow in you. It can't take the Light."

I didn't know what to say to that.

And then there was another voice, a scent like rainwater and sage, and a cool, feminine palm on my shoulder. A wet cloth with herbs was pressed gently over my eyes. "Shh, honey. I'm here. It's going to be all right."

"She's hurting, Greta." Warren sounded scared.

"I know," the woman answered. "Bring her to my rooms. I'll take care of her."

Strong arms lifted me. There was the click of heels leading the way. And there was Warren's breath, cold and small, in my ear. "I'm so sorry."

I felt a tear fall, imagined its crimson path as it trailed over my cheek, and thought, So am I. I leaned into Warren, still smelling burning flesh. *So was I.*

17

The woman, Greta, asked if she could give me something to knock me out, and I whimpered my agreement, thinking she could knock my head clear from my shoulders if it would just stop the pain. Such drastic measures, thankfully, were not needed, and she administered a shot that had me slinking blissfully into the ether within moments.

When I woke, the room was pitch-dark, but crowded. The darkness I quickly attributed to cloth bandages wrapped loosely around my head. The crowdedness was because . . . well, there was a crowd. But over the voices rising and falling around me, I thought I heard birds chirping—did the Silver Slipper have an aviary?—and I knew I smelled at least two dozen roses, which I identified as Double Delights from the slight spice wafting from each petal. My eyesight might have been questionable, but the sniffer was still in top form. Yippee.

"We can't let her leave the same way she came in," Felix was saying. "It could kill her."

The thought of crossing through that big, rounded, silver toe again immediately set my pulse to throbbing.

"Well, she can't stay here forever."

"Greta never leaves the compound," Micah pointed out.

"Greta's a psychic," Chandra muttered. "Not a superhero."

They'd been going on like this, I took it, for a while. The forces of evil may have been hard at work in Vegas tonight, but the superheroes of Zodiac troop 175 were arguing back and forth like opposing teams on a baseball diamond. They were also speaking about me as if I wasn't there. Worse, like I was, and couldn't understand a thing they were saying.

I did understand, of course. I was a superhero, and superheroes didn't die. I almost had, and they were all scared to death because of it.

I shifted against what felt like a veritable sea of pillows, and all chatter ceased. "So basically what you're all saying is that I'm trapped here?" Five pairs of eyes, felt rather than seen, landed on me. "Trapped in the Silver Slipper, right?"

"Uh," said Warren, after a bit. "Yeah."

I nodded as if to myself and pursed my lips. "But I'm safe?"

"Safe, but not very useful," Chandra muttered from my right.

"Safe and useless sounds just fine right now," I replied.

"The point is, we can't let her out of the sanctuary anyway until we figure out how Ajax found her so quickly," Micah said. "I implanted her new olfactory scent myself, right after Chandra blended it. It was fresh, and completely enshrouded her natural scent. I even underscored it to link her to Warren."

I hadn't known that.

"Micah's right," Warren said. "I still say we should hypnotize her, find out that way—"

"Warren, we've already discussed this." Greta's voice grew sharp. There were steel edges behind that soft exterior, it seemed. "She's been through enough."

"But Ajax should've had to go through me."

That statement was met by silence. I remembered Warren's angry words once we'd safely reached the cab. *What did you do to call him?*

"Well, I didn't ring him up and ask him to meet me there, if that's what you're thinking." I could just hear that conversation.

Ajax, darling, let's begin again. I need to make a quick stop first at the Quik-Mart, but we can murder an innocent girl while we're there, just for old times' sake. I know how you like that. Got anything sharp and pointy to play with? Something that bursts into flame upon impact, maybe?

Cool fingers touched my skin, and the bandages were gently lifted away. I blinked like a newborn into the light. Actually it was quite dim in the room, but my vision felt raw. It worked well enough, at least, to fix upon the two wide brown eyes smiling into mine. Attached to them was the scent I'd already mentally filed under *Greta*.

"Thank you," I told her.

She responded by alighting on the bed beside me, her weight barely making a difference. "Perhaps you can tell us what exactly you *were* doing when Ajax found you. Start from when Warren contacted you, all the way to Ajax's appearance."

I glanced around the room, frilly and feminine and filled with roses, and saw that the others, save Gregor, were all gathered at the foot of my bed. The chirping I'd heard earlier came from a large gold cage on a pedestal across the room, two bright lovebirds resting inside.

"Well, I packed and walked over to the Boulevard like Warren instructed, but there was this film that I needed to develop, and there seemed to be enough time, so—"

"So you disobeyed direct orders," Chandra said.

"I'm not a Green-fucking-Beret," I said, shooting her an annoyed glance, "and no, I didn't disobey. I was one block from the pickup point. I was early. I didn't know how long I'd be gone—here, I mean—and I wanted to take the pictures with me. That's all."

"Where are they?" Warren asked quietly. I looked at him closely for the first time. He'd already looked perfectly disreputable with his grimy clothes and greasy hair, but the rivulets of my dried blood on his shirt added a certain *je ne sais quoi*. I swallowed hard.

"My bag. Wherever it is."

It was lying forgotten in the corner. I thought about letting Warren rustle through it, but stopped him as he yanked the zipper back. "I wouldn't do that if I were you," I said. "There are Shadow manuals in there, mixed in with Light."

Warren held the duffel out to me. "Open it," he ordered.

I snatched it and unzipped the bag. All eyes were heavy on my hands as I removed the Shadow side's comics, then filled with curiosity as they tried to read the titles. I yanked out the Light series as well, putting Stryker's on top.

"I was reading this one just outside the shop when I first scented Ajax."

"May I?" Warren asked. I handed him the comic, and he began leafing through it.

"It's about a guy named Stryker who was ambushed during his transforma—"

"We know about Stryker," Chandra snapped, eyes hot. "Don't speak about him like you knew him."

"God, just leave her alone, Chandra."

"Fuck you, Felix!" she shouted, then swung around the room, daring anyone to speak. When her gaze landed again on me, she curled her lips and shook her head in sharp disbelief. "She's the first sign? What bullshit." She whirled, and the lovebirds started in their cage, crying out as the door slammed heavily behind her.

"Go after her, Felix," Warren said quietly.

"Fuck her."

"Felix."

Felix sighed, but left without another word. Micah shifted uncomfortably. "I'll go too. They might need a referee."

Micah left, and after a moment Greta put her hand on

my arm. "It was only six months ago," she explained in her calm and kind voice. "The wounds are still fresh."

I nodded, understanding. After all, I'd seen Stryker's death. Neck cords ripping, blood staining his mother's robe, her heart-wrenching cries. Chandra was still a bitch, but I couldn't fault her her grief.

"I'm sorry," I said, meaning all of it.

Greta patted my hand, then stood to pour tea from a ceramic pot warming on a hot plate. "It's all right, dear. Drink this. I pick and bag the herbs myself."

"What's this?" Warren asked, holding up the photo of Ben. I must have snapped it shut in the pages of the comic when Ajax had found me.

"Oh, my," Greta said, staring at me sadly. "No wonder."

"What?" I asked, looking from her to Warren and back, the steaming teacup forgotten in my hand.

"Anyone could have felt that," she answered, shaking her head. I opened my mouth to ask what she meant, but I suddenly knew. It was so easy to grasp, I thought, when someone pointed it out to you.

Greta, reading my mind, answered anyway. "Your sorrow, dear. Such deep grief. That's how Ajax knew where you were. Strong emotions—love, hate, grief, joy, hope—give you away if you don't know how to control them."

"That's why we ordered you to stay calm," Warren said, lifting his eyes from the photo. He still looked annoyed with me, but at least the muddy suspicion had cleared from his eyes.

Greta leaned in. "Who is it, anyway?"

Warren rudely snapped the comic shut, photo inside. He rolled it and pointed it at me. "We'll talk about this later." Then he too strode from the room, waves of fury left in his wake.

"Well," I said finally, "can I clear a room or what?"

"Yes, well done," Greta said primly, and I had to laugh despite myself.

She was a small woman, this Greta, with slim fingers and

wrists, and tapering legs and ankles beneath a pencil skirt and lab coat. She wore sensible heels, sensible jewelry, and her chignoned hair had begun to gray at the temples. I'd have put her in the early fifties but for the knowledge hardening her caramel eyes. Greta was older, I decided, and probably tougher than anyone looking at her heart-shaped face could imagine.

"You seem to be healing fine," she told me, returning to my side. "There shouldn't be any permanent damage beyond the wound on your thigh."

I touched the back of my thigh where Ajax's conduit had nicked me as I ran. It had been stitched, and was only mildly sore.

"It'll leave a mark—all supernatural weapons do—but the cut wasn't very deep." She resettled the bedsheets over me. "Your eyes were the more serious concern."

"Has this ever happened before?"

"What? An injury while trying to enter the sanctuary?" she asked. I nodded. "Not to an agent of Light, no. One time the Ram on the Shadow side tried to enter the sanctuary by force. I heard by the time he reached the bottom of the chute there wasn't enough left of him to wheel on a rotisserie. That was three years ago, though, before I got here."

Before she got there? I leaned forward as she studied my eyes. I suppose she liked what she saw because she stopped squinting and smiled. "I thought you had to be raised in the Zodiac in order to be a part of the troop?"

"Oh, no. I came to it late, like you." She propped a hip on the side of my bed. "My mother was mortal—gifted, sure, but mortal all the same. My father was the Gemini of the star signs. If troop hierarchy were patriarchal, I'd hold that star sign right now. As it is I'm lacking certain . . . physical gifts. Technically speaking I'm not really a part of the troop." She smiled wryly but didn't sound bitter at this twist of fate. "Still, between the two of them, I possess enough insight to contribute in an ancillary form. The other star signs come to me when they're afraid their emotions—and therefore their pheromones—might get the best of them. And sometimes they just come to talk."

"So . . . you're like a shrink?"

She wrinkled her nose at my word choice. "A supernatural psychologist, if you will."

"A . . . an independent?" I asked, remembering the manuals' distinction between troop members and all others.

She laughed, then whistled from the side of her mouth. "Be careful how you use that word. Some would take great offense to being lumped in with the rogue agents."

"I'm sorry."

"Oh, I didn't mean me. Like I said, I'm just an auxiliary member of the troop. My mother left when I was a child. My father died not long after—supernatural causes, of course—and I've been on my own ever since. Still, the Taurean Shadow targeted me about two and a half years ago. Apparently he and my father had some longstanding territorial dispute. Gregor found out about it, found me, and thought it his duty to bring me here. Eventually he convinced Warren of the same."

"That was nice of him," I murmured, wondering why no one had done it with me. Or Olivia.

"Oh, nice has nothing to do with it. Duty comes above all else for those raised in the Zodiac. Above family, spouse, or anything comprising a normal life. If something's not good for the organization, then it's simply not done. If it is, then everything is done to make sure it succeeds." Absently, she toyed with the small pearls circling her neck. "That's why Warren's so concerned about you. He's put a lot of hope into you, you know. He doesn't trust easily. Not to mention he's risked a great deal."

I hadn't thought of that, actually. I'd been so preoccupied with my own worries and loss I hadn't even considered what defending me might have cost him. "Like what?" I said, really wanting to know.

She gestured at me, letting the pearls drop. "Well, consider for a moment, what if he's wrong? Then he's brought a wolf into our midst. A Shadow among the Light."

"I'm not a Shadow," I said irritably.

"But are you Light?"

I didn't answer. How could I know?

She smiled kindly and laid a hand over my own. "Look, I can only imagine what this has all been like for you, but if Warren seems a bit brusque it's because his primary concern is keeping this troop safe. He's looking for reasons his star signs are being killed off. His duty as a leader is to protect them, and so far he's failing."

"Tekla said there was a traitor."

Greta look startled, then relaxed when she realized what I was saying. "You mean in the manual you read? Right before Ajax found you?"

I nodded, and she rose to pour us more tea. "Poor Tekla," she said as she took my cup from my hand. "She's not even with the troop anymore."

"She's not?"

She began shaking her head, then paused. "Well, she's here, of course—she'd be a danger to herself and the entire troop were she to be released outside the sanctuary—but Warren's had her tucked away in the sick ward since shortly after Stryker was killed."

Something in her tone caught my attention. "You don't agree with that?"

Greta shrugged, but it wasn't smooth, and she absently fingered her pearls again. "She rants whenever she sees anyone, of course. And she says the most awful, accusing things. Still . . . I don't know. I think she's in there somewhere, desperate to get out. I'd rather help her than lock her away. Maybe someday I can."

So there was no traitor. Just a heartsick woman who'd had to watch her son die before her eyes.

She returned to my side, again handing me my cup, sighing to herself as I accepted it. "You seem like a sweet girl, Olivia. But if there's one piece of advice I would give you, it's this: nobody's really what they seem." She stood motionless as she looked at me hard, willing me to understand. "Take Warren, for example. When he's out there in the real world he looks and acts and, unfortunately, smells like a career bum. You look at him and see exactly what you'd expect roosting on the corner of Casino Center Drive.

"Meanwhile he's working day and night to stop the Shadows from injuring or influencing mortal lives and thoughts. If he can't do that, he works to hide the resulting destruction. Covers it under a veil of confusion or bad luck, so there's nothing or no one to strike out at—because, you know, that's what the Shadows ultimately want. For their handiwork—destruction and chaos—to snowball. For human emotion to turn sour so they can feed off that negative energy."

"But what he does isn't right either," I said, frowning because Warren had done the same to me; set me up—or, at least, let me be set up—to take the fall for Olivia's death. "He tricked me into choosing all this. He played with my life just as much as the Shadows play with others'."

"Ah," she said, pulling her sweater tighter across her chest. "Now you've hit on the crux of what makes Warren tick. See, he cares more about the whole of humanity than he does about the individual person. To him the universe is a scale that must constantly be kept in balance. Choice, mortals' and ours, is a secondary consideration."

I drew back. "But that's . . . ruthless."

"Well, there are things in Warren's past that make ruthlessness a virtue," she said, and before I could ask what those things were, held up a hand, shaking her head. "Not my story to tell. Besides, the point is, what else can you be but ruthless when dealing with enemies who toss mortals around like pawns on a chessboard?"

She frowned, realizing that was exactly how I felt, and shot me a small, apologetic smile. "For what it's worth, there are others who feel as you do. Their thought regarding humans is, 'But for one step down on the evolutionary chain, there go I.' But Warren's the troop leader, and they're not."

And Warren's actions made a sort of twisted sense now that I knew more about him and his responsibilities. Would I have put the troop before myself? Probably not, which was why he hadn't given me the choice. Would I agree that ruthlessness could be deemed a virtue? Probably not, which was why Greta wouldn't share with me the particulars of Warren's past. I sighed.

"Look," Greta said, watching me carefully, as if reading my thoughts. "The deaths of our senior troop members have everyone rattled. It means we're vulnerable. It means change. It means we might have to take on rogue agents, and there are some who are vehemently opposed to that."

"And Chandra is one of those," I guessed.

"Ah, Chandra." She nodded slowly. "She's painfully obvious, isn't she?"

"I mistook her for a man when we first met."

Greta winced. "Well, she wouldn't have liked you in any case . . . even if you'd mistaken her for Miss America. Before your whereabouts were known, she was next in line to be the Archer. Your arrival has thrust her into a sort of no-man's-land, and she now has to carve out a new place for herself in this troop. But first we must allow her to mourn what she's lost."

I made a surrendering gesture. "Hey look, if she wants it that badly, she can have the honor."

"No, she can't," Greta said, shaking her head as she forced me to meet her gaze. "Your lineage is stronger, and the laws are clear. We only go outside the existent bloodline if the entire house has been wiped out. Your mother was one of us, and the manuals have foretold your arrival. Read them, you'll see. Your duty now is to fulfill that legacy. Ours is to show you how."

I wanted to believe her, but her words and their meaning were having trouble getting past my own muddled thoughts. With the fall down the Slipper, the warm tea settling in my belly, and the shock of being attacked by Ajax again, it was too much. Thankfully, Greta sensed that.

"Sleep now," she said, getting to her feet. "You need rest. Tomorrow you'll see the grounds."

I leaned my head back against the pillow and let out a deep sigh as she took the teacup from my hand, then set a corner lamp burning low. The birds had settled again and were chirping softly to themselves, and the scent of roses clouded my brain even after I heard the soft snick of the door clicking shut behind her. By then my head was too heavy to lift, and I gladly let myself drift away from thoughts of duty and legacies and women who looked like men, and into the safety of my own mind.

I slept that night with more soundness and peace than I had since awakening in my sister's body, and it was probably due to Greta's soft words, her tea, and the sense that even though I'd nearly been fried in the process, I was finally in a place where I was relatively safe. I know I dreamt, but there was nothing of reason or memory or meaning in the dreams, only my body healing itself in the long midnight hours, and the scent of warm roses overlying it all.

Then I crawled into the second half of the night.

I heard them yelling from my room in the opposite wing of the house, their voices stacking up on one another's just as they had that first time a decade earlier. The novelty of hearing my mother actually standing up to Xavier had been enough to have me tiptoeing through the halls to their bedroom, and the interest sparked when I heard my name ping-ponging between them kept me there. I centered an eye between the gap in the door and leaned forward, careful not to bump it with my growing belly.

"I'm talking about the way you look at her!" my mother said, and I heard Xavier take a breath, but Zoe cut him off cold. "Like she's filthy inside, Xavier. Like she should be ashamed."

He paused before saying, "She's carrying a monster's child."

My hand stifled my gasp and I drew back in the hallway, as I imagine my mother did in their bedroom. Then, in a new voice, she said, "Well, like mother, like daughter, I guess."

I heard a crack then, an open palm ricocheting off bare flesh, and my mother's surprised cry before an almost unearthly length of silence. Then, slowly, silently, almost deadly . . .

"There is nothing wrong with *my* daughter." And she said it like I belonged to her alone. And though I was sixteen again in the dream, I carried with me the knowledge that Xavier was not my father. And deep down he must have known it.

"Zoe!"

His call had me rushing to hide in the portico of the adjoining hallway just before my mother appeared, and I watched from there as she strode away, seeing her with new eyes. It was like the bandages Greta had peeled away hours earlier had really been blinders, and in this dreamy reenactment I didn't just see the sheen of tears on her cheeks, I saw the determination beneath them, and the hands clenched into able fists at her sides.

"Zoe!" Xavier followed, stopping right in front of the bisected hallway, giving me a clear glimpse of the bewilderment and anger muddling his normally composed face. The part of me that knew I was dreaming wanted to laugh. I'd forgotten all about this argument. She'd been gone the next day, and that's what I'd been focused on. But it all made sense now, and my dreaming self did laugh as I continued to study Xavier's confusion.

He heard me.

Xavier's head swiveled as if it was ratcheted on his neck, eyes finding me squatting in the dark like twin lasers fixing on a target. I froze awkwardly, smile dying on my face as his chin lowered and his top lip lifted in a sneer, and I swallowed hard. I didn't remember this part.

"Think it's funny, little Archer?" he asked, in a voice throatier than his own, one raspy with age and power. He pivoted stiffly to face me, and I fell back, hampered by my belly . . . though I knew this was a dream and I was no longer pregnant. I wasn't even there.

But those eyes remained fixed on me, colder and darker than I'd ever seen them, and they followed my frantic backpedaling pitilessly. I scrambled away as he began to stride toward me, each of his steps faster, crisper, than the last, but then my back was cornered, the stunted hallway dead-ending into a laundry chute, and I had nowhere to hide.

I took a large breath, intending to wake myself up—because I knew this wasn't real; it hadn't happened this way, and it wasn't happening now—but a fat palm slapped over my mouth, and I tasted blood as my teeth cut into my top lip. I felt like a butterfly pinned to a board. I struggled, my limbs wheeled, the baby tumbling madly in my belly, but my head was immobile beneath that iron-straight arm. Then the hand shifted and my head was lifted, forcing me to look in his face.

There was a summer during my childhood that I remember being particularly hot. I took refuge one day beneath a giant pepper tree, brushing aside the long flowing branches to enter a shaded chamber, the spicy scent of those living limbs heavy on the searing air. I was just about to lean back on the peeling bark of the old tree when I saw the cicada shells dotting the trunk. There were dozens of them, all empty dead husks marking where life had once been lived.

That's what it was like looking into Xavier's face. All life had been extinguished in that giant shell of a man, and death itself stared back at me from those black orbs. I had time to wonder if his skin would crackle and crush into dust beneath my fingers, like those cicada husks had, but then Xavier's bullish features began to contort.

It was as if a giant invisible hand was pressing putty; his mouth and nose switched places, swirling grotesquely on his face, and his eyes and brows slipped to the sides of his face, ears disappearing altogether. Then the putty thinned, tearing high along his cheekbones and forehead, and peeling away to reveal blood, muscle, and finally gleaming white bone.

His eye sockets were black pools, dark and swirling and alive with something that could only be called unyielding rage. "So are you going to pick up where your mother left off, Archer? Will you come after me too? Think you're ready to take me on?"

He poked me in the belly with his free hand, and I gasped against the palm still clenched against my jaw. The bony finger poked again, and this time I felt it in my gut, separating my intestines, scraping precariously close to my unborn child. The jaw of his skeletal smile click-clacked gleefully as I struggled beneath his invasive touch.

"Because I'm ready for you. Oh, yes I am." He was getting riled up now, and smoke escaped through the bone of his nose to make my eyes tear, as embers flew from his mouth. "Ajax tells me you're strong, as strong as Zoe even, but I can smell you on the winter wind, and do you know what you smell like to me?"

His finger stirred inside me, scratching and grating, making me whimper, and when he leaned closer, his breath reeked of minerals and the deep, fiery core of the earth. He opened his mouth and I nearly gagged on the rot of his blackened soul. "Prey."

And I jerked awake, gasping for air, nearly choking as the powdery scent of Greta's room mingled with the scent of the grave. "Fuck," I rasped, gulping for air. "What the fuck?"

My hands went protectively to my belly, and I looked down, past the glyph that had lit on my chest, glowing through my skin as hotly as it had during my run-in with Ajax. The heat was lessening now, though, and that was reassuring, as was the smooth, flat skin on my belly, unmarked by violence or pregnancy, or anything more alarming than the imprint of the sheets I'd been tangled in. I was about to breathe a sigh of relief when something wormed inside my gut. It felt like a finger, or a piece of one, was still lodged there. I screamed and backed up, head cracking against my headboard as an explosion of laughter boomed inside my skull.

Then the room was silent, but for my ragged breath and the fading volley of the laughter. I cursed again, and pressed one hand against my belly, the other against my face. I must have bit my lip while dreaming because I came away with blood there, but at least this time nothing moved inside me.

I glanced at the gilded clock beside Greta's bed, 9:18, and rubbed at my eyes. Surely the headache behind my sockets was just because I'd slept in late. And the sheets were tangled and soaked for the same reason. Because I wasn't going crazy.

And the Tulpa, I told myself on another steadying breath, had not just entered my dreams.

18

One of the lovebirds whistled as I swung my feet out of bed and made my way on shaking legs to the wardrobe mirror. There was a note attached to its beveled edge, a flowery scrawl on scented paper. *I'm off to work for the day. Make yourself at home. Warren will come for you at ten. G.*

I yanked it down before studying my reflection in the mirror. There was a clump of dried blood by my temple, sticking out from my blond tresses like a spot on a Dalmatian, but I picked it free, then leaned forward and pulled down the lower lid of my right eye. Bloodless. Perfect. Whole. Other than the new wound on my lip, I had totally healed. And even that, I saw, was already smoothing over.

I exhaled the breath I'd been holding, and gave thanks to any deity who might be listening. The most extensive repair work needed on my body would be a hot shower and food in my belly. But my mind might be a different story. The remnants of my dream clung like quicksand, threatening to overtake me with every new thought.

Grabbing a change of clothing from my bag, I pushed out a deep breath and headed to the shower. A half hour later I was steady again, and had donned a racer-back tank, hooded jacket, and terry-cloth pants—all pink, of course— my hair slicked into a low ponytail, face scrubbed shiny and clean. He'd said we were going to train today, and that, I knew, would go a long way toward helping me feel more myself again.

I'd considered telling Warren about my dream, but was shocked into silence when I opened the door to find him dressed in pleated khakis, a blue button-down shirt tucked in at the waist. His face was clean, brown eyes clear and rested, hands still callused, but smooth. Were it not for the snarls gathered back from his face, I'd have pegged him for a businessman headed off on his long morning commute.

"A full recovery, I see." Warren looked me up and down appraisingly but didn't meet my eye. The man who'd been so flippant and ridiculous when we'd first met had been replaced by a serious, almost severe leader, and looking at him I could suddenly name the question that'd niggled at me since I woke up with bandaged eyes in Greta's room.

If there was no traitor inside the sanctuary, as Warren so fervently insisted, why was it still so important to him that no one know my true identity?

I couldn't ask him now, not when he was still obviously angry with me, so when he held out the studded cell phone Cher had given me—obviously dropped on my fall into the sanctuary—I just took it from his callused palm and pocketed it as I followed him out the door.

As Felix had said the day before, the sanctuary was a place of respite, where beleaguered star signs went to re-plenish their energy, gain knowledge, and train for whatever force or enemy they were currently facing. Most of the time it was peopled only with the support staff, children, and initiates who dwelled permanently beneath the Neon Bone-yard, but now it was brimming with the remaining star signs, and the rest of the compound was buzzing with the apparent novelty of that. Warren told me the others were in a meeting, no doubt about yesterday's events, but would soon begin the day's combat training in a place called Saturn's Orchard.

For me, however, the first stop was the barracks.

"Home sweet home," Warren said, flipping a light switch and motioning me into the room. It was clean and shaped like Greta's, but the similarities ended there. Gone were the feminine touches; the laces and frills and pastel-colored doilies. The concrete floors, like the walls, were bare and painted an unrelieved white. A queen-sized platform bed was pressed tightly against one wall, mattress naked, and a chunky coffee table in chocolate hardwood flanked one end. A wooden tray filled with rocks, all white, was the only item on the table, and a trio of white paper lanterns floated from the ceiling above it, the only lighting in the room. Twelve palm-sized floating wall shelves, also in mahogany, were suspended over the bed, and echoed the lanterns' rectangular shape. They held clear glass votives, which no doubt lent warmth to the clean, modular room when lit.

Though sparse and utilitarian, it was still warm and sexy . . . though it said nothing about the person who lived there. I loved it.

"It's perfect," I told Warren, though what remained unspoken was that the three-hundred-square-foot room had better be perfect because my stay looked to be a lengthy one.

"What did Micah mean when he said he'd designed me so that Ajax couldn't find me?" I asked, trying to keep the question casual as I peered into the adjacent bathroom.

"Micah's a gifted doctor," Warren said, joining me at the doorway. "Just as he can alter the nose on your face, he can also alter the makeup of your genetic template—your pheromones. He used science to create a synthetic formula, one different than your own, and his own magic as a fixative to secure it in place. Ajax didn't know the new code, so he shouldn't have been able to find you so quickly."

He had, though, due to my distress over Ben. But I didn't want to get into that yet. "And when he said that I was linked specifically to you?" I stared at his reflection through the bathroom mirror because it was more comfortable than facing him head on.

Warren looked marginally wary, but answered. "After inoculating you, he withdrew the essence of that compound from your bloodstream, then injected it into my own."

I wasn't sure I liked that. Was Warren trying to keep me safe, or was he just trying to keep tabs on me? After his accusations the day before, the latter seemed more likely. "So it's like a tracking device . . . ?"

"Of the emotions, yes," he finished for me. He caught my frown in the mirror and turned toward me, forcing me to do the same. "I know it sounds intrusive, Jo, but you're more vulnerable than the other agents. I'd never have gotten to you in time yesterday if I hadn't been able to track you through this linking agent."

I folded my arms. "So, basically, I've been bugged?"

"*I'm* bugged," he corrected, tapping his own chest. "It's like I have a second heartbeat. I know when your pulse accelerates or slows, if not why. The blood running in your veins is like a current rushing through my ears. If you break out in a sweat, my body attempts to cool it. Basically I feel any metabolic change you go through. And yes, the sense of smell is that much greater."

"A magnified sixth sense, then?"

"More like a seventh. An eighth." He folded his hands in front of him. "Try it now, if you like. Think of something that unsettles you, and I'll tell you the moment it enters your mind."

"Okay." I closed my eyes and kept my body very still. I thought of waking that morning in Greta's scented room, the birds chirping softly on their perch, the relief that washed over me as I escaped my dream. I thought of giggling with Cher over fizzy water and peppermint lotion.

Then I zeroed in on the memory of the man across from me, asking if I'd killed an innocent, somehow entirely certain I could.

"There." My eyes shot open to find him pointing at me. "My second heartbeat accelerated, my palms broke out in a sweat beneath my own skin, but the overriding sense was one of anger. Maybe a touch of fear." He angled his head. "What were you thinking of?"

"Xavier. How he used to treat me," I said, well aware Warren could smell the lie on me. I didn't care. The man was *inside* me, or I inside him, and with these sudden questions about his intentions, I was determined to keep some things to myself. "So could you feel what I felt when Ajax found me?"

"I scented your fear when he entered the building. Your anger when he killed that girl . . ." He paused, before adding, "And the sorrow before all of it began."

I'd known it wouldn't take him long to circle back to that. I avoided his gaze and moved from the doorway, opening the closet to peer inside.

"You have to stay away from him, Jo," he said, but I wasn't paying attention.

"Whose room is this?" I asked, jerking back from the closet in surprise.

"Yours now," he said, joining me to stare at the evenly spaced clothing filling the racks and shelves, the shoes and boots lined along the floor. All black, all female. "But it was once Zoe's."

Our eyes met.

He said nothing about the eagerness texturing the air in lacy patterns between us, instead using the opportunity to pull out the photo of Ben he'd taken from me the day before. I inhaled sharply as he held it up in front of my face. "You don't want Ajax to find him, do you?" he asked softly.

Ajax who would track him, torture him, and skewer his innocent heart. And enjoy it.

I lifted my eyes, laid them dead on his. "No."

"Then train your mind. Don't even think Ben's name." He spaced these last words so evenly it was as if he bit them off. I found I couldn't meet his gaze. "If you don't control your emotions, you're putting both of your lives in danger. Mine too."

This time I heard the plea in his voice. I wanted to tell him he didn't know what he was asking, but he did know, and deep down I knew he had a right to ask it. What was my personal sorrow compared to the greater welfare of the troop? The city? The universe?

We stared at one another, tension spiking between us. Desperation oiled the air, as much his as mine, and finally I nodded. No more lives would be lost because of me. I could at least promise him that much. Warren sighed and leaned back on his heels, and as if by magic the air seemed clearer, fresher around us. It sparkled invisibly, and I sucked in a deep breath of it. Now things could be right between us again. Almost.

"One more question," I said, and held up a hand as the guarded look returned to his face and the air glimmered less brightly. "Could you sense what it was like for me when I penetrated the sanctuary?"

His hands fisted at his sides. Now it was my turn to feel and scent and taste raw guilt in the air, and it went a long way toward soothing my anger. "I tasted the atoms splicing in your body. I felt the sizzle of them on my tongue. Your boiling blood reeked in my nostrils, and I could smell the marrow melting in your bones."

I swallowed hard. I hadn't exactly realized that *that's* what had happened.

"Come on," he said, palm reassuring on my shoulder. "I'll show you the rest."

We strode along corridors just wide enough for two bodies side by side. A strip of red neon, like a racing stripe, ran along the walls near the floor, lighting our footfalls and marking our progress, before dimming again behind us. In the brief volleys of light I could make out symbols on the walls—runic, perhaps, or some long-dead language I didn't recognize—but we walked so quickly their shapes were nothing more than a flash burned on my retina, replaced in the next second by another, then another. Warren, used to them, took no note.

"Warren, what if I don't gain any more power? I mean, what if I just tried to control my emotions and live a mortal's life. Would they leave me alone?" These questions were more rhetorical than anything. We both knew I was beyond letting sleeping dogs lie. I'd seen too much. And there were too many deaths on my hands.

Warren shook his head. "They'd find you eventually. In the end you'd just have fewer ways of defending yourself. Crossing over into the Neon Boneyard via an alternate plane was the first step in gaining more power, a necessary one, because now you have the knowledge, even when you return to the mortal world. Entering the sanctuary was the second step because now you'll be able to enter any portal closed to mere mortals."

"Which means?"

"Which means," he said, squaring on me, "you now have front row seats and an all-access pass to the supernatural realm." I regarded him, unblinking. "What? Haven't you ever had doors that won't open when you twist the handle, though you could have sworn you saw someone else disappear inside only moments before? How about elevators that won't come when you call them? Or the feeling that someone is watching you, only to turn and discover nobody's there? Well, those doors and elevators—portals is what they really are—will now be open to you."

He motioned to the wall in front of us. I looked closer, spotted a discreet seam running from ceiling to floor, and pushed. Nothing. I pushed harder with the same results, then looked at Warren. He ushered me back, then with another flourish of his hands the barrier separated and the walls folded back on themselves like a Japanese fan. Beyond lay a steel elevator, doors already open wide and inviting.

"Neat trick," I muttered, getting in. "I thought you said they'd open to *me*?"

"You need a little practice. And patience."

I scowled and looked away, ignoring the censure in his voice. The elevator panels were mirrored in a smoky gilt frame, and revealed the strangest couple staring back. A fashionista in a dashing pink warm-up, and an indigent dressed up in someone else's hand-me-downs. Barbie goes slumming.

"So these . . . *portals*, they're a part of an alternate reality?"

"Exactly," he said, pushing a button marked DOWN. The doors whisked shut behind us. "You'll have to be extremely careful at first. You won't know what's waiting on the other side of any given entrance, but you'll learn."

Visions of monsters lunging from the closet and from under my bed had me sighing. Dammit. I'd only just gotten over that phobia.

The elevator slid open and we stepped into a stunted hallway leading to a set of double doors, again in smoked glass.

"Hold the elevator!" The glass swung open and a figure rushed past before halting and backpedaling. "Oh. Hello, Warren."

"Vanessa." Warren inclined his head. "This is Olivia, our new Archer."

"A new Archer? I hadn't heard." She feigned shock, then held out a hand. Her grip was surprisingly firm, and I could feel her too-smooth fingertips pressing against my palms, but the rest of her was amazingly normal.

Bronzed skin of middling color, she was of middling height, also, and average weight. Her hair was dark with soft wisps of fringe escaping the bun she'd piled on her head, and revealed a natural curl. There was the taste of the exotic about her, some lineal bent that darkened and thickened the lashes around her honeyed eyes; a cast on her heritage that would allow her to tan easily in the faintest beam of sun, but it didn't immediately step forward. She could have been anything from African to South American to Middle Eastern. Which meant, I realized, that she'd disappear easily in a crowd. "Vanessa Valen. I'm the Leonine force around here, your sister sign in the Zodiac."

"Also a fire sign," Warren offered.

I looked from one to the other, feeling stupid. "Which means?"

"It means you two should make quite a team."

"It means we kick ass," Vanessa corrected, smiling, and that's when everything average about her disappeared. Her smile was wide, brilliant, and infectious . . . or would have been if it had blanketed her eyes. This smile merely lifted the corners, like light blazing through a drawn curtain before being shut out again. Warren didn't seem to notice, but knowing about such things, I wondered what past sorrow was presently denying her the right to smile. She turned her half smile on Warren. "Speaking of fire, I heard about the one at the federal building on Friday. Two Shadows, five innocent hostages. What'd you do, smoke them out?"

He nodded. "And sang 'This Little Light of Mine' at the top of my lungs."

"Then they fled willingly. I didn't know you were religious."

"Recovering Southern Baptist," Warren said.

"My brother," she said, and they high-fived. Vanessa smiled wryly at me. "A style all his own, our Warren."

"Different drummer and all that," I said. "Yeah, I noticed."

"So, see you in the Orchard?"

Warren said, "We'll be right there."

"Nice meeting you, Olivia."

"You too," I said, and watched as the elevator doors shut behind her. "Seems nice."

"Vanessa's one of our most dangerous agents. Sure, she's nice, but nice like a sleeping cobra. Nice like the calm before a storm. Nice like you."

"I can be very nice when I want to," I said, following him into what looked like a dim foyer, though larger, more like a theater-in-the-round.

"Let me know when the urge hits. I'll log the date and time."

"Har, har."

"Now, every city needs all the star signs, a full Zodiac, to be in balance." He turned in a circle, centered in the middle of the bowed room. It was actually more octagonal than round, a large star stamped into the pavement where Warren stood, motioning to the steel paneled walls. Some of the panels were marked with brightly lit emblems that even I, with my spotty astrological knowledge, knew represented different signs in the Zodiac. "I won't lie. Our ranks have been blighted in the past year. Either the enemy is getting stronger or we're getting weaker. In any case, we're missing five signs, and that's with you taking up the Archer."

"And how many star signs does the Shadow side have?"

He bit his lip, and worry swirled in my gut. "All twelve."

"But Butch is dead."

He shook his head, eyes clouding over darkly. "They've replaced him by now. Whomever it is simply hasn't revealed themselves yet, and while the new Shadow won't be as strong, not at first, their initiates are fast learners too." His voice echoed through the cavernous room as he turned and approached one of the panels. I glanced up at the domed ceiling, a single speck, like a star, binding the corners of the room at the apex. I was sensing a theme here.

"Here," Warren said. "This one's yours."

I lowered my gaze, latching onto the symbol he pointed

out, an etching of a centaur; the half-man part of the mytho-
logical beast looking suspiciously half woman.

"Go ahead," Warren urged. "Touch it."

I did, laying my hand flat on a palm plate, and the emblem flickered, blinked on, and remained glowing in a
steadily pulsing heat. It made my eyes ache to look at it.
Still, my stomach jumped, and unexpected pride swelled at
seeing it, glowing there with the others. Then my eyes fell
to a latch, waist height. I jiggled it, and felt an incredulous
expression bloom on my face. "It's a locker?"

"Well, Superman had a phone booth, didn't he?" he
asked, brows raised. "This is much more useful."

A superhero locker? I drew back. I mean, what was in it?
A cape? A mask? Not those gawdawful tights, I hoped. I
turned back to Warren. "So, what's the combination?"

He shrugged. "Only you know."

I felt my brows climb my forehead. I did? "No, I don't."

"Sure you do. Push the button next to the middle slat
and speak into it slowly. Think of a password, a phrase,
something meaningful to you. Something symbolic."

I looked back at the locker doubtfully, then grudgingly
pressed the button. "Open up, motherfucker."

"Colorful," Warren commented.

"Open Sesame!" I tried again. "Abracadabra! Hocus-
pocus! Shazam! Shalom! Anyone home?" Then I smacked
the panel a few times with my palm.

I straightened and smiled innocently at Warren. "Still
not opening."

"I can't imagine why," he said dryly, before suddenly
shooting me a smile of his own. Quickly, before I could
react, he pulled the photo of Ben from his pocket and
shoved it through one of the tilted openings in the locker.
My cry of protest was met with a stone hard stare. "When
you can open that locker, you'll be ready to face, and mask,
your emotions for Ben."

Ruthless, Greta had called him . . . but this was just

downright cruel. I clenched my jaw, preparing to argue, but in the middle of my first eye roll my vision snagged on something peculiar, on something that wasn't there, actually. "That's the sign of the Scorpio, right? Stryker's sign?"

My question knocked him off balance. Warren swallowed hard, the cords working in his neck like the breath had caught there. "It was."

I stared at the symbol; vacant, dark, dead. And though Greta had already explained it, I wanted to hear what Warren had to say. I needed to discover for myself just whom I could trust. "You said the lineage of the star signs was matriarchal. Didn't this sign revert back to his mother when he was killed?"

"Stryker's death . . ." He paused, searching for the right word. ". . . unhinged Tekla. She's been in solitary confinement, recuperating in our sick ward for months."

And he'd put her there. Left her there. I pursed my lips at that. "So the Scorpion sign remains empty? Even though she's alive?"

"Half alive, and not especially happy to be so."

This time I felt a sorrow that wasn't mine coursing through my core. It felt like raw onions curdling in an empty stomach, and I touched a hand there, surprised. I didn't know it worked both ways. I also didn't think emotion that strong could be fabricated. "Well, maybe that's because she's alone, and has no one to talk to."

"Maybe it's because her son was torn apart in front of her eyes," he said shortly.

I swallowed hard and thought of Olivia, limbs pinwheeling into the night. I nodded. "Can someone else take her place in the Zodiac even though she's alive?"

"Only if she's willing to relinquish it to them, but for reasons unknown to all but her, she's not. We've asked her, begged her, even, but she just starts spewing obscenities, making illogical accusations, tries to injure anyone who approaches."

I remembered the first of these accusations from the pages of Stryker's comic. *There's a traitor among us.*

"So, did my mother relinquish the Archer sign to me when she . . . left?" I asked, changing the subject.

Warren inclined his head, looking relieved. "Your mother believed that when the time came, you alone would be able to create this house anew."

The house of the Zodiac. The first sign. The Archer, agent of Light.

I shook my head, only able to grasp one thought at a time. I voiced the one I thought most pressing. "But she's still out there, right?"

"She's alive, we know that much. Her power is muted, diminished because she gave it all to enshroud your identity, so she's essentially a mortal. It's a dangerous position for a member of the Zodiac to be in, but one that has, ironically enough, kept her safe."

I folded my arms over my chest. "I want to see her."

He shook his head, began to open his mouth.

"She's my mother!" I pounded my fist on the locker with a sudden fierceness that surprised even me. It had been growing there, I guessed, ever since I saw her belongings hanging in a closet. I had *smelled* her on them.

"There are some doors, Olivia, that are closed even to us."

I stared at him, thinking that of all people, a superhero shouldn't have to hear that.

"Come on," he said, turning. His limp made an exaggerated slap-and-drag sound on the concrete floor. "There's more to see."

Something other than Stryker's fate, or Tekla's, or my mother's? I wanted to ask. Of course, Warren—the bum—could give me no assurances. It seemed that even a supernatural life, for all its benefits, didn't come with guarantees.

"Okay, Warren," I said, walking, walking right past him. "Then just promise me one thing."

"If I can," he said gravely.

I shot one last glance back at the unyielding locker and the centaur glowing with six other star signs. "Shoot me if I ever grow hindquarters."

19

We bypassed another series of hallways on the way to Saturn's Orchard, Warren pointing out the children's ward—the tinkling of bell-like laughter punctuating the air in confirmation—and then made a quick stop by the animal habitat, where cats of every shape and size were striding, sitting, playing, or sleeping purposefully around the room.

"We breed them," Warren explained, lifting a pure white Persian kitten from behind the guard gate, his face softening as the two wide blue eyes stared unblinking into his own. "Cats are wardens. They're naturally territorial, so good guardians of our space. They can also identify a Shadow agent no matter what they've done to mask their identity."

"I wonder if Luna came from this bunch," I said, inching closer.

"Did Zoe give her to you?"

"To Olivia." I ran a finger along the soft fur tufting from the kitten's cheeks. "For her eleventh birthday. She's had her ever since."

The kitten's eyes slitted shut and she pushed her cheek

against my hand, a purr rising from the little body that could have shook the entire building. Warren chuckled, then dropped a kiss on the ivory head and returned her to her litter. He blushed when he saw me watching.

"They *are* wonderful little gifts. And fiercely protective."

"You don't have to tell me," I said, an image of Butch's sheared eyelids and gouged retinas popping into my head. Just then a young boy darted into the room, scrambling nimbly between us, an outraged cry rising in his wake. He lunged for the gate, climbing so quickly I knew this wasn't the first time he'd hatched this particular escape plan. Warren plucked him up with one hand, and I stared down at the blond crown of his head as he proceeded to wiggle and squirm, struggling toward the kittens that lay just beyond his reach.

"Marcus!"

A tall woman in a simple white robe reached around me and snatched the child from Warren, pulling him to her in a possessive and practiced grab. An immediate screech rose from the child, but the woman only smiled up at us as if to say, *Sorry for the inconvenience, but you understand.* I'm sure this would have been accompanied by an eye roll . . . except that she didn't have any.

"They're so boisterous at this age," she said, smiling tightly.

"They are that," Warren replied, his own smile a bit wider.

I said nothing, just continued staring at the skin, shriveled and wrinkled and scarred, where her eyes should have been.

Marcus, however, had no interest in her looks. When he saw there was no escaping her grasp, and no chance of retrieving one of the kittens, his face turned a bright shade of red, a howl like winter wind rose from his throat, and then his face, literally, burst into light. "Give me my warden!"

I whirled away, covering my eyes with one of my forearms,

clutching my furry little charge to my chest as heat from the child's anger slammed against the back of my neck. The rays of light blasted past me into the concrete walls, and his voice did the same. I heard a muffled smack, a howl of outraged pain, and then a scuffling before the light disappeared, like a wick snuffed between wetted fingers.

When I uncovered my face, the boy was gone, but the woman remained. She shot us an easy smile and serenely folded her hands together in front of her. "Somebody made the mistake of telling Marcus he was next in line for the Virgo sign, and he's bedeviled us ever since. Wants his warden, wants his conduit. He's a bit headstrong these days."

That, I thought, was an understatement.

"Need some help?" Warren asked, inclining his head toward the hall where chattering, screaming, shrill little voices rebounded off the concrete interiors. The sound cut a path straight to my lingering headache.

"I might," she admitted, with a frazzled lift of her brows. "There's only Sondra and I for the lot of them. The other ward mothers are in classes. But first . . ."

She angled herself toward me, raising her brows.

"I'm sorry," Warren said. "Where are my manners?"

"I've been wondering the same for years."

I smiled at that, instantly liking her, and held out my free hand. "I'm Olivia."

She found my hand, and held fast as she tilted her head, regarding me in some unknown way. "Rena," she offered. "Ward mother of the Zodiac offspring, charged with overseeing their development until the first life cycle. As you can see, Marcus has a way to go in the control department."

"Is that why . . . uh—"

"My eyes?" she asked, smiling. She would have been beautiful, I realized, if not for those dual scars blooming where said eyes should have been. "I'm afraid so, though not him. Another child of Light, long before little Marcus came along. I've been ward mother here for nearly forty years now. Saw Warren here through his first life cycle."

"Really?" At closer glance, I saw light wisps streaking away from her temples to mingle with the ginger hair she'd secured into a low bun. Creases that had to do with age, not scarring, also lined her face, though I noticed the ones where she smiled were deepest of all. Given her words, I placed her around sixty. A very young and vibrant sixty.

"Er, let's not get into that," Warren said, wedging between us.

"Another time, then," she told me in a conspiring whisper, then waved good-bye and headed back out into the melee in the hallway.

"I'll be right back," Warren said, following. "Then we'll head to the Orchard."

I nodded, but he was already gone, and soon so were the crisp, bell-like voices of the children and the slap-and-slide of Warren's uneven gait.

"Well, now what?" I asked the fur ball snuggled tightly against my chest. With no answer but a soft purr, I decided to look around while I waited.

The hallway was empty, but as before, the strange symbols and strips of light marked my progress as I strode away from the habitat, still stroking the kitten's cheek. I soon came upon a separate hallway I hadn't seen before, blocked by heavy double doors, closed, but without a lock. "A clear invitation to enter," I muttered into the soft, spiky fur.

But this hallway, if possible, was even more stark and cold than the rest. No lights lit up as I entered, and the rooms lying diagonally to one another were laced with viewing windows and bars, each dark inside. The kitten stirred restlessly in my arms. I took this as a sign that maybe I shouldn't be there, and was backing up when one of the doors suddenly bounced open. Greta appeared, murmuring softly, and I would've called out to her except that she was followed by Chandra. Both women were focused on a third, whom they had by the arms and were gently coaxing into the hallway.

I recognized her immediately. Her robe was grimy, and she looked thinner than she had in the manual, but it was Tekla. Shuffling forward almost reluctantly, her head was down, eyes moving over the floor vacantly, seeing nothing. The two other women continued to murmur soft encouragements, and I did back away then, not wanting to interrupt.

Then Olivia's cell phone went off in my pocket. The kitten startled awake in my hands, and I scrambled to soothe her as "Viva Las Vegas" continued to chime from my thigh. I fumbled for the phone as tiny claws burrowed into my chest and Chandra cursed at me from down the hall.

"Olivia Archer," I answered, shooting Chandra and Greta an apologetic smile. But whoever was on the line, and whatever they were saying, was lost on me as Tekla lifted her head and frowned, staring directly into my eyes. "I . . . I . . ."

I didn't know what I was saying so I flipped the phone shut and swallowed hard as Tekla regarded me with utter clarity. "I'm sorry," I managed, not sure which of the women I was talking to. Greta had noted the change in Tekla too, and her eyes were darting from her to me and back again. Chandra just continued looking pissed.

"I see you."

We all froze, except Tekla, who'd uttered the words and was uttering them again, over and over, her voice cracking as it grew louder and louder. "I see you."

"Tekla, love," Greta soothed, taking her more firmly by the arm and trying to guide her the other way, "calm down now. Let's go this way."

But Tekla's eyes had narrowed on mine, and she was suddenly heading my way. "I see you," she said, and Chandra cried out in surprise as Tekla broke free from their hold, while Greta fumbled in her pocket. She came out with a syringe, but Tekla was well out of reach by then.

"Get back, Olivia!" Greta yelled, but I was afraid to exit the sick ward. If I stayed where I was, she'd be contained, and Chandra and Greta could regain control.

In fact, Chandra had recovered enough to catch up to Tekla, but when she laid her hands on her this time, Tekla wheeled and struck out blindly, her arm crushing Chandra's nose. Chandra fell backward, Greta yelled again, and Tekla began to run.

"Traitor! Traitor! Traitor!" She was on me so quickly I could only release the kitten. Hissing, it escaped out the double doors as I fell into them. Tekla tripped me up, fell on top of me and climbed my chest until her face was inches from mine.

She smelled of unwashed skin and sour memories, and I swallowed hard, not wanting to fight or hurt her. Thankfully, Greta was suddenly there, a syringe prepped and already angling toward her shoulder. Tekla whimpered when it struck, whipping her head around to face Greta before slumping without another peep.

I relaxed beneath her as Chandra reached her other side and she and Greta began lifting the unconscious woman to her feet.

Then her head jerked back up, and *he* was alive in her face.

The skin and even the bones of Tekla's face stretched, and the Tulpa leered out at me. "I see you," she repeated, but it was his voice, rotted and threatening. "You think you're safe in there? You can't hide from me. I'm your bogeyman . . . I'm your poisoned fate."

"Jesus!" Warren was suddenly there, pulling her—him, it—away, and it took all three of them to do it as the Tulpa's face continued to leer at me. Halfway back to her room, Tekla's head again dropped, bobbed, then lifted, her gaze returning to mine. It was imploring again, as was her whisper. "Traitor . . ."

Then the door to her cell slammed behind them all, and I was left lying alone on the floor, my glyph once again burning a hole through my heart.

20

An hour passed before they got Tekla settled. Afterward, Chandra was sent to tell the others the training session in Saturn's Orchard would be postponed, and the rest of us gathered in Greta's office, where she busied herself with making yet more tea, though her hands shook as she stole nervous glances back at me. For the longest time Warren didn't look at me at all.

We were trying to figure out what had happened to Tekla. I was relieved because they too had seen the Tulpa leering from Tekla's vacant face, but my relief was diluted because even Warren didn't know how it'd happened. But after I told them about the night before, and how a memory had turned into a nightmare—the Tulpa speaking to me as clearly as if he'd picked up a phone—he was pretty clear on the why.

"Obviously Ajax has told him about you," Warren said, pushing his teacup aside. "He knows you're his opposite, the new Archer. He's letting you know he's targeted you."

"He wants vengeance for Zoe's betrayal," Greta said softly, shuddering.

"Okay," I said slowly, not liking it, but following easily

enough. "But how's he getting in my dreams? In the sanctuary?"

"Well, he's not really in the sanctuary, dear," Greta answered, steadier after my explanation, the suspicion that Tekla's accusations had raised in her seemingly tucked away, if not entirely forgotten. "Dreams are simply psychic energy, and the one you had last night was linked to a particular past trauma. My guess is that you had a hard day yesterday, and like Tekla, that left your mind more open to his influence."

"So he can get to me? At any time?"

"Not physically." Warren shook his head adamantly. "You're safe in here."

"So why was there a woman with a demon's face straddling me, Warren?" I said sharply.

But he merely stared back at me, and the suspicion was still clearly alive in his face.

"Look," I said, rising from my chair so quickly it nearly tipped backward. "I didn't do this! I didn't even touch her. I said my name and she charged me. She looked right at me and she told me . . ." I trailed off, remembering exactly what she told me.

"That she 'sees' you," Greta finished for me, almost reluctantly. "And then she called you a traitor."

She had. And though Warren was silent as we left Greta and headed toward Saturn's Orchard, he didn't need to say anything. His anger arrowed inside of me in white-hot flashes that burst in my core, rippling outward to die in my limbs. What remained, though, was a shard of well-hidden guilt that the anger had encased like a hard, protective shell.

Warren shot me a quick glance as we ascended a stout stairwell, his jaw clenching, and the feeling immediately subsided.

I looked away, pretending I hadn't noticed, but it made me wonder. *What did Warren have to feel guilty about?*

There was a single door facing us as we reached the top of the landing, and Warren stepped aside so I could peer through the window. After a moment, despite it all, I felt a smile slip over my face. There were people; a few I recognized, a few I didn't, but that wasn't why I was smiling. In a room of unrelieved white, mats lined the floor and lower walls, and punching bags dangled from steel beams set at cross purpose to one another. Along the far wall were baskets of ropes, pads, and mitts, full to overflowing. It was a dojo. Sure, it was shaped like a pyramid, and its walls were mirrored from floor to pointy little tip, but it was a dojo all the same. For the first time since yesterday I felt at home.

The tight handful of people—and tight they were; you could read it in their closed expressions, their crossed arms, their wary attentiveness—seemed to have been waiting for us. Greta's tea turned acidic in my belly as I looked at them, the mirrors in the room making it appear there were more of them than there were. I didn't even have to sniff at the air to know Chandra had already relayed what had happened in the sick ward.

"Attention, please," Warren said unnecessarily. "This is Olivia, the new Archer of our Zodiac."

Nods and murmured greetings met this, which I answered with one of my own. I let my eyes pass over Chandra, who'd begun scowling the moment we'd stepped through the door, and settled on Vanessa's face, open and friendly by comparison, though I noted a wariness there that I hadn't seen in the locker room.

Micah was hunched in the corner, on a bench that looked like it might give at any moment under the towering bulk of his weight. Felix was stretching, and he sent me a little hand wave from the center of the mat. There was another man I didn't recognize leaning against the incline of the far wall, one leg propped behind him, arms folded over his chest as he openly studied me with dark eyes.

One by one I began to do the same, sizing each of them

up, quickly filing them into three categories. Possible allies; Micah, Felix and Vanessa. Adversaries; certainly Chandra. And the X factor, the man I had yet to meet. There was Warren, of course, but sometimes I just couldn't tell with him.

"As Olivia hasn't been raised in the Zodiac, she doesn't yet know where her talents lie, she doesn't have a personal conduit, she can't track Shadow agents, and for now she can't leave the sanctuary . . ."

"Some superhero," Chandra muttered.

"We've already found her to be athletic and a quick learner, but she knows nothing of our history or the way we wage war so she has a lot of catching up to do. I expect all of you to help her, and in time I have confidence she'll live up to her . . . potential."

He'd been about to say something else. I caught the syllables wanting to form on his lips, but he'd changed his mind at the last moment. Still, we were connected, and the words neatly formed themselves in my own mind. *Lineage. Legacy. Legend.*

So he still wanted to believe, I thought, glancing over at him. What'd happened with Tekla hadn't changed that, at least.

"If she's so helpless, how'd she kill Butch?"

All heads turned to the man across the room. His brown eyes flickered when they met mine, but his face remained otherwise expressionless, no emotion skimming the surface of that still exterior, no judgment one way or the other as he looked at me to answer.

Well, two could play at that game. I batted my eyelashes, folded my hands in front of me, and answered as Olivia would. "He tripped."

"Tripped?" Chandra repeated coldly.

"Over my cat."

It was more in keeping with Olivia's image than, say, *Oh, I tortured the bastard until he keeled over and bled out at my feet.* To my surprise, they all began to nod. Except for the lone man I didn't know. He just continued to watch me with that cool and steady gaze. Probably not in the ally category, I thought wryly.

"So, you had a warden even before you knew you were a member of the Zodiac troop?" Felix asked. "That means you're highly intuitive."

"Intuition is a talent we all share," Chandra muttered.

Vanessa, either missing or ignoring the venom in her voice, added, "We augment that with other talents that complement our place in the Zodiac."

"What other talents?" I asked, fighting to keep my eyes from straying to the corner man. With him, I couldn't even fathom a guess.

"Start with your talisman," Micah said, standing. "What is it?"

"Your glyph," Warren said, nudging me.

"Okay." I unzipped my fitted jacket.

"One guess where her talents lie," Chandra muttered.

I faltered, cheeks flushing hotly, and began to zip it up again.

"No, it is a talent," the man told her, and this time when I looked at him, I saw something other than mild disinterest. He pushed off from the wall, moving lithely, almost sliding toward me. In the way of most alpha males, he took up a lot of space.

"People will underestimate you," he said, coming to a stop in front of me. "They'll see only the shape of you, the curves and swells and softness. It's as much a camouflage as fatigues and face paint in the Amazon, because people will see what they expect to see." He gave me a smile that said, *But we know different.*

I had a sudden urge to slap that look off his face. Whatever he thought he knew about me couldn't compare to the reality of who I was, or who I'd been. He didn't fucking know me at all. But I held still, watching carefully as he reached out and lowered my zipper for me. "And you are?"

"Hunter," he supplied, as respectfully as a man could when he had a hand on your top. His skin, I noticed, was that pale gold that couldn't be bottled or bought; the hair, glossy and black and gathered in a low, blunt ponytail. As contained, I thought, as the rest of him. After opening my jacket, he moved to the side so the others could see. I kept my hands steady as I stretched the sport tank down, but it was an effort. The places where his fingers had skimmed my flesh were warm, like little pilot lights had been ignited beneath the surface.

I kept my eyes firmly away from Warren. I didn't want to see his smirk, or that knowledge in his eyes, because I knew he could feel the effect this Hunter was having upon me. So I just kept my head down as I revealed the skin just above the point where my cleavage began to rise.

"Hunter's our weaponeer and head tactician," Warren supplied, a smile in his voice. Bastard. "Anything martial lies in his sphere of expertise."

I decided a little animosity would go a long way toward helping me regain my equilibrium, so I tilted my head and glanced back up at Hunter. "Anything?"

Hunter shrugged, the slightest of movements. "I'm Aries. Physicality is where my talents lie."

"Hand combat?" I asked. I tried not to sound challenging. Really, I did.

Okay, no I didn't.

"Why?" he said, rising to the bait, and I saw what he meant about his physicality. He'd barely moved a muscle and yet there seemed to be less space between us than before. "You like to fight?"

I ignored Warren when he cleared his throat next to me, and shrugged, just an innocent lamb waiting to take instruction from Mr. Martial Arts. I quirked a brow at him. "I like to win."

"At what? Candyland?"

I whirled to give Chandra a fist-sized example of "at what," but Warren was there, blocking me with his body, eyes burrowing into mine. "I have to leave now. I have a session with Greta. I trust you'll be fine without me, *Olivia*?"

The memory of Warren's suspicion as it roiled hot in my gut flashed in my mind. One guess, I thought, pursing my lips wryly, as to what this "session" was about. "Then trust must be one of your major talents," I said, so low only he could hear, turning my animosity on him.

He shot me a look of bland disapproval, which I returned with a wrinkle of my nose and a little finger wave. Just like Olivia.

"So what is it?" Micah said, leaning forward to look at my glyph after Warren's strange slap-and-slide gait had receded from earshot. I used the opportunity to back away from Hunter, glancing down as the others crowded in closer. The shape of it was pale against my skin, a birthmark in reverse, and I shuddered, recalling how it had burned on my chest, pulsing there like a second heart. "It's a stiletto."

Chandra scoffed. "It's not a stiletto. It's a fucking bow and arrow."

I looked again and saw that she was, just possibly, right. *Oh, God. Peroxide poisoning. Already.* I glared at Micah as embarrassment washed over me. This was followed by a surprising flash of disappointment. A part of me, it seemed, had wanted it to be a stiletto.

"It's just smeared," I said stubbornly, and turned to the mirrored wall behind me.

"Chandra's right," Hunter said, slipping behind me. Studying him through the mirrored surface, I decided my first impression of him had been wrong. He wasn't devoid of expression at all. The quirk of his mouth gave away a little spark of humor, and intelligence swam beneath hooded eyes. There was something commanding in the way he'd used up the room when he'd crossed to me, noting everything and nothing at the same time.

And despite the warning bells pealing through my mind, I had to wonder, Was there anything more alluring than a dangerous man?

Hunter reached out, broad shoulders blocking the view

of the others, and lifted a hand to trace the lines of my glyph, lighting little arrows of fire along my flesh. "It is a bow and arrow. See?"

Olivia's voice, a happy twittering bluebird, bounced off the soft tissue of my mind. *How lucky am I?* It sang. *First day on the job and I get a superhero boyfriend!*

Meanwhile my own voice had fled me entirely. I just stood there, staring at my chest. Total nipple hard-on. Great. I glanced up into Hunter's face, now clearly amused. "And what's your talent?"

He smiled. "I have many."

I'll just bet.

"A bow and arrow is a strong talisman," he continued, his gravelly voice louder now. "Obviously it's the Archer's symbol, but it's a personal motif as well. I'll bet one of your talents is honesty—"

"To a fault," Micah chimed in.

"Determination. Loyalty. Pride."

"Don't let Hunter charm you," Chandra broke in. "All Archers have those qualities."

I turned to find myself facing hollow eyes, and knew then that she and I would never be friends. I raised one slim brow. "Do you?"

"In spades," she said, her upper lip curling.

"What do you know so far about conduits?" Hunter asked, moving to stand between us.

Conduits are conductors of energy; conductors of the agent's express will. Each conduit is specifically made for its handler; to compliment his or her talents, and channel his or her will through means of violence, death and gore. Though Olivia, of course, would never have put it that way.

"Uh, well, most of them are pretty sharp," I said, drawing laughs from Micah and Felix. Hunter narrowed his eyes, Chandra rolled hers. "I know they come in different shapes, sizes, some of them are pyrotechnic, and each one is made to complement the strengths of its owner."

There. That was a nicely balanced answer. Not too embarrassing.

"That's right. When I design a weapon, I take into consideration the agent's particular physical and mental strengths, then fashion a conduit specifically for their hands. It takes on a life of its own that way. Becomes your companion, your match. Of course, that means I need complete honesty if the weapon is to maximize all your gifts. Do that, though, and I'll create something to suit your temperament, your mind, and your heart."

"Something that blows bubbles from its tip, perhaps?"

"Jesus, Chandra." Felix dropped his head into his hands. I could tell he, and the rest of them, thought I wasn't going to be able to handle this angry little hermaphrodite. Laughable, though it meant I was doing my job at being Olivia. I picked lint off my jacket, as if I hadn't heard.

Hunter unsheathed—or unraveled, rather—his own conduit, and offered it to me. It was a twelve-foot-long whip, with barbed tips studding the lower half of the slim black leather.

My heart began to pound. *Down, girl.*

"What else do you know about their use?"

I took the whip in hand, studying it carefully, and this time pride had me elaborating a degree. "I know if you're struck by an enemy's conduit, you'll die, even if you're more than human. But if you use a conduit against its own agent, its companion," I said, using his word for the weapon wielder, "you win a little something in their death. A bit of their power, and a rush of energy, a temporary high. They die, and you have twelve hours to walk this earth undetected. Nobody can find you; human, Shadow, or Light. It's like you don't even exist."

Hunter held out his hand. I glanced at it as I handed his conduit back. You could tell a lot about a person by studying their hands. His were tanned and elegant, despite the calluses studding his palm.

"Butch?" he asked, coiling the whip.

I nodded.

"How did it feel?"

I glanced at Vanessa. "I felt invisible. Invincible."

The room was silent. "No one else has ever done that. Used a conduit against its own Shadow companion. It's a powerful magic."

"It fits the legend—" Felix said, looking at Hunter.

"Oh, come on," Chandra said abruptly. "This? This . . . cream puff is the Kairos? The gifted individual on whom all our fates hinge? I mean, get real!"

Nobody said anything, though, and she folded her arms over her chest. "Didn't any of you hear what I said about Tekla?"

"And didn't you hear me say that if you were going to start that up again you should do it in front of Warren?" Micah answered sharply. "You know how he feels about . . . her." He motioned my way, and for the first time I saw a shadow flicker across his gaze. I straightened with a jolt as it struck me that Micah might not fully believe in me himself.

"Warren was there! He saw Tekla accuse her!" Chandra said, challenging me to deny it. "She did, didn't she? She called you a traitor!"

"Oh, and your perception wouldn't happen to be skewed in any way, would it, Chandra?"

"Shut up, Felix."

"Shut up, Felix," he mimicked.

I'd stopped paying attention to the two of them, though. The room had darkened, and I felt a shift as though the ground itself was moving. Then color swirled over the mirrored walls, psychedelic waves turning the room into a cavernous love shack. Charles Manson's love shack, I thought, shuddering as an onyx wave washed over me.

"It's a mood room," Vanessa said in answer to my unspoken question. "It reacts to emotion. When we train it follows the battle, tracking who's winning. See those circles over there?"

I did. Through the colorful spears of light bounding across the mat, two diametrically opposed ovals faced off against one another.

"Go stand on one," she urged.

I stepped forward and found the surface spongy, rather than firm like a normal dojo mat. But there was no risk of twisting an ankle. It just seemed to move with my feet, reaching up through my arches to support my movement. Gaining the first circle, the colors suddenly whipped away from the floor and walls, replaced by infinite blackness, as if I was standing on a platform in the middle of the universe. Thus, I realized, the spongy floor. If not for the support, I'd have lost all sense of equilibrium. Then tiny lights popped up, stars pricking the universe, and floating among them was a tilted cross with an arrow on one end.

"Huh. The Archer's glyph," Felix said, looking pointedly at Chandra. "Never seen that before."

"Fuck yourself . . ." she muttered, but the jab seemed to take some of the wind from her sails. "You didn't see it. You didn't see *him*."

"All right. Enough." I stepped out of the circle and the universe flickered, then died away. The mirrored walls of the pyramid reappeared, blinding, but only for a moment. "How can I possibly be a traitor? I just got here. I didn't even know about the Zodiac or this troop until a few weeks ago . . . right, Micah? I certainly didn't know about Stryker."

"It doesn't matter," Chandra insisted before Micah could speak. "Tekla is psionic, and she's psychic . . . or she was. She can see what you're going to do. She knows it even before you do."

"So she was telling the future back there? That I was going to betray you all?" I looked around for a reaction. No one answered yes, but no one said no either. I shook my head in exasperation and disgust. "Why would I? I have nothing to gain from it."

"Your father does."

"You mean the being that's trying to kill me?" I shot back, whirling toward Chandra. "The one that just used Tekla to attack me in the hall?" I scoffed. "Yeah, I'm totally working on his behalf."

"Well, I believe you," Felix said, coming to stand at my side. "We knew the Kairos was going to be both Shadow and Light. It was foretold. So now we deal with it. Besides, Warren wants you here."

Well, he *had*, I thought wryly. But I didn't share that with Felix. It felt good to have someone on my side.

"Too bad it doesn't matter what you believe or what Warren wants," Chandra said, and a blue-green spark shot out across the ceiling. It bounded overhead, and her grin looked gaseous, evil in the receding light. "We still get to vote."

"Vote?"

And that was all she needed to shore up her confidence. She lifted her square jaw and fisted her hands on her hips. "That's right. You weren't raised in the Zodiac, and you learned nothing in your first two life cycles. Your mother's actions, or inaction, has displaced you and unbalanced the rest of us. Just like a rogue agent."

"This is Zoe Archer's daughter!" Vanessa sounded outraged.

"Yeah, what's your lineage, Chandra? And drunken pity fucks that follow failed assignments don't count."

My brows rose at that, and I expected another "Fuck you, Felix," but Chandra simply clenched her jaw against the jab—one she'd obviously heard before—and kept her ire trained on me. I'd have tolerated this—until she stepped into my personal space.

"All I'm saying," she said, angling her head up so she was staring me dead in the eye, "is that the Kairos should at least be someone who can track the moon's rise and fall without first referring to a map."

"Someone as handsome as you perhaps?"

The oxygen was sucked from the room on a group inhalation. Clouds coiled over the walls, gray building upon gray, until the slanted ceiling was thick with them, walls obscured, the floor snaking with mist. Mood room, indeed.

"I'm going—"

"To kick my ass. Yes, I know. Then what? Climb a tree and start thumping your chest? Scary stuff, She-Man. If you can back it up."

I thought I'd have time to brace and block. But apparently I still wasn't up to superhuman speed. Chandra slapped me so quick and hard—palm flat, but nails curled to score my left cheek—that my head whipped to one side and I staggered back. I lifted my hand. My face throbbed in burning ribbons and I came away with blood. "You cut me."

She sneered. "You'll heal."

I stood for a moment, hand pressed to my cheek, doing nothing. Then I burst into tears. The loud, snuffling kind with crocodile tears and a wide, open mouth. Through one slitted eye I saw Chandra drop her arms, half turning to the others with a bemused expression. She'd probably never faced a tearful superhero before.

Hunter's warning cry was only half uttered when my foot plowed through her chest. I leaned back, putting my hips and thighs into the motion, and Chandra flew the entire length of the mat, crashing against the opposite wall, the back of her skull kissing her reflection with a gratifying crack. Greta had said Chandra needed time and space to grieve over the loss my arrival had cost her, but I decided a little ass-kicking would take her mind off it as well.

I touched my hand to my cheek. Chandra was right. I'd healed before she even hit the floor. I began to advance on her, but found myself blocked by Hunter's not insignificant frame.

"Like to fight dirty, Archer?" he asked, backing me into the circle again. The Archer glyph shot across the walls again . . . until he stepped into the circle opposite me. Spearing from the apex of the pyramid came a giant glyph of curling horns that arrowed down into a sharp V. It exploded into a shower of smaller horns, the quantity instantly overtaking the Sagittarian glyph.

Definitely not on my ally list.

"I use the weapons available to me," I told him, and this time I didn't back down from him as he used up all my space.

His eyes narrowed to earthy brown slits. "Want to try them on a full-fledged star sign?"

Let's see . . . a straightforward street fight versus an emotional game of "he says/she says"? I didn't even have to think about it.

My palm shot out, but he was ready and caught it, twisting so it would have broken if I hadn't relaxed and flipped with the motion. I cartwheeled through the air, landed again on my feet and sent him a jab, a knee, an elbow, and a bitch slap . . . all met and blocked in turn.

We disengaged, circling; me breathing hard, Hunter barely breathing at all. The room was a kaleidoscope again, the emotions of the onlookers merging with the glyphs now wheeling around the sky like mad fireflies. I took a moment to steady myself, then tried another tactic. Inhaling deeply, I threw a line of energy around his body like Warren had taught me, an invisible lasso between his intent and mine. No emotion crept up the invisible rope. If my eyes had been closed I wouldn't even have known he was in the room. Impressive.

He knew exactly what I'd been doing, and white teeth flashed as he smiled. "Figure out my talent yet?"

"Yodeling off-key while standing on one foot on a pile of hot coals?" I sidestepped as he changed directions. The walls shifted with us, and the night sky above was clear again, cloudless.

"Close," he said, and lunged. He was as lithe and compact as a mountain lion, as single-minded as well, but I'd convinced myself long ago that it was better, safer, to fight a skilled warrior than a street brawler. Less chance of accidental injury. Of course, there was a greater chance of calculated injury, but that was what defensive skills were for. I threw myself backward and kicked out a leg. Our shins met with a resounding crack. The knowledge that I'd heal made me a bit more reckless than usual, so I pivoted immediately, stayed close, and crushed his left cheek with a flying elbow as he turned.

A chorus of surprise lifted from the others as arrows shot over the walls and we disengaged again, him retreating this time. His exertion was coming off him in waves, manifesting itself in a coppery-smelling band that wrapped around me, linking me to him for as long as I remained his target.

He wasn't holding back either. He really wished to overtake me. One part of me was thrilled with this deadly dance, the chance to test myself against someone strong, someone new. I was a fighter, that hadn't changed, and this is what fighters did. Asaf always said the first encounter with a new foe was the most exciting, the most heady and the most dangerous, and he was right. I swam in Hunter's adrenaline. I floated in my own.

Another part of me, however, was wondering how I'd ever thought this man attractive. He was looking at me like Ajax had; a quick sizing up of body and limbs, a predator searching for the weak, old, or inexperienced in the pack. Hunter was like this: patient, and absolutely feral as he waited for his opening.

He was also uncoiling his whip. The room was suddenly painted in giant ram horns again, not a Sagittarian glyph to be found.

"That's cheating," I said between breaths. He knew I didn't have a conduit yet.

Pitiless, he shrugged and snapped it at his side, his wrist flicking expertly. "I use the weapons available to me." *Asshole.*

I didn't even need to see the walls to know I was in trouble. Bodies, even male against female, were one thing.

Surprise could still be used to my advantage. But this was too much like my encounter with Ajax; ominously one-sided, frightening, and full of unknown risks. Alarm prickled along my skin, and was released, to my chagrin, through my pores.

I backed to the center of the mat to give myself room to maneuver away from the length of the whip, noting nobody else had spoken up in my defense. No *That's enough* or *Leave her be*. Not even Micah, and that hurt. If there'd been any question before as to my place among these people, it was answered now. Hunter stalked me, and the others merely watched.

"You're afraid," he observed, lifting his arm.

"No shit," I said, and jumped as the whip licked at my heels, a barbed tongue. Landing, I glanced around for some sort of shield, finding only a practice pad that covered the length of my forearm and not much else. I secured it as he swung at my head, and lifted it in time to have the whip shearing off the top of it with only a flick from his wrist.

The next snap coiled around both pad and forearm, grazing my shoulder on its second rotation. I whimpered as a barbed tip sunk deep into my flesh, then braced myself and pulled, surprising Hunter by dragging him closer. Using my other arm, I yanked, and closed the distance between us. I had no idea what I was going to do. I only knew the farther I was from his body, the more dangerous it was for me.

"Look! Her glyph's engaged," Felix said, pointing. I felt the pulsing in my upper chest cavity, but kept my eyes on Hunter. His eyes flicked down, and I saw surprise shadow them before it was erased, the expressionless mask returning. His arm wavered, then lowered. The walls cleared abruptly, stark whiteness blinding us all. He had disengaged.

I ripped the barbs from my flesh before I could think too much, and smelled my own blood flowing freely.

"That's only supposed to happen when facing a true enemy," he said, tone low and suspicious.

"Then you might want to put the whip away," I said coolly. I let the barbed end drop, tossing the destroyed pad aside only when he began to coil it. I rubbed at my arm and backed away from them all, feeling achingly vulnerable.

"How are you doing that?" Felix said, looking at my chest.

"It's the Shadow, see? She can't control it."

"Shut up, Chandra, you had that coming." Vanessa sent her a steely glare, and came to stand next to me before also turning on Hunter. "And you. You've wanted to test the new Archer ever since you heard she defeated Butch . . . something you never managed to do. What do you expect when you gang up on her like that?"

Hunter turned so stony he didn't even blink. "I was making a point."

Yeah, I thought, rubbing my arm. Literally. But suddenly it was clear why no one had intervened on my behalf. Why a whip had to score my flesh and I had to bleed. They needed to know I could.

"I get your *point*." Only Hunter would meet my eye, and that was fine; I'd focus on him. "Here's Warren, telling you I'm this . . . this Kairos, that I have more potential than regular star signs, that I'm more powerful than the rest of you because of who my father is. I guess you just decided to see for yourselves, huh? But you didn't have to whip me, you know. All you really had to do was ask."

And, though they hadn't, I opened up a little and let them see what I'd felt when I'd gone up against Butch. How the dark side of moonbeams could bathe the soul too. How freeing it felt to let go of what was right, and think for once only of what you wanted. How vengeance burned like sulfur in every pore, and hatred like an ulcer in the stomach. And how death drew closer with every passing moment, and fury was the cancer that could take you there. They needed to see it, I thought, because they needed to know the difference. I let it go on for a time, then I sucked it all back in.

"Happy?" I asked all of them. "Scared?" And I turned back, pressing my face into Chandra's, invading her space this time. "Or do you wanna take a vote on it and get back to me?"

Chandra took a giant step back, jaw clenching tightly, and the others shifted on their feet, none looking at me, and barely looking at one another. I laughed hollowly and figured if they wanted something to mistrust so badly, I wasn't going to make them search for it.

So I turned back to Hunter, forced him to meet my eye, which he did with an empty gaze of his own. "You're going to have to do better than that," I told him.

"Better than what?"

And with the same power I'd used to punch holes in the life of a construction worker, I told him. "If you don't want the Shadow side to know about *her*—the one you love and cherish above all others—you're going to have to control that thread of desperation coiling in your psyche. I can taste it on my tongue, as fresh and sweet as sherbet. What's her name, anyway?"

I felt surprise sprout throughout the room and realized I'd just sensed something no one else had known. So even the full-fledged star signs kept secrets from one another, I thought wryly. So much for a unified troop. *Hypocrites.*

"Her name is Lola," Hunter finally answered, and his voice was steady, though a shudder had gone through his able body. At his admission, in fact, it had gone through them all. "And if you go near her, I'll kill you."

I looked around then, forcing every person in the room to meet my eye. "I thought I wasn't the enemy. Don't any of you trust me?"

"I don't know you."

"I don't trust the Shadow in you," Chandra said.

"Micah?"

He swallowed hard. He, whom I'd once thought was so firmly on my side. "I think you'll be presented with a choice before Ajax and the Tulpa are done with you. A real test, made in the heat of battle, and one where you're forced to choose what's right or . . ."

"Or?"

He looked away. "Or what you want."

And with those words I realized Chandra was right. No matter what Warren wanted, I could be cast out of the troop and sanctuary, left in the city, unguarded and alone. I'd be saddled with powers I didn't know how to use or control, more of a target than some unnaturally gifted hero.

"There's only one thing I want."

"Revenge?" Hunter asked. "For your sister's death?"

I nodded, unsurprised that he could sense it, knowing they all could. It was the one thing, I thought, that I could never hide.

"And what will you do to avenge her?"

"Anything," I swore. "Everything."

He nodded slowly, and then turned away. "And *that's* what I don't trust."

We obviously didn't train that day. In fact, all the members of Zodiac troop 175, paranormal division, anti-evil, gave me a wide berth after that. The easy camaraderie between Vanessa and I dissolved like a sugar cube after I'd shown my Shadow side, and she left the room frowning with uncertainty. Felix still grinned at me, but it was tight around the edges and didn't quite reach his eyes. Micah mumbled something about lab work before disappearing, though he did give me a gentle once-over just to be sure his handiwork had held up against Hunter's whip.

Even Chandra, so full of sting and swagger, couldn't muster a glare, and just shoved her hands into the pockets of her fatigues, shaking her head as she exited the room. Hunter followed without a word or backward glance, which left me alone in the spacious dojo, staring at my foreign and baffled reflection in the mirror, the emblem on my chest still pulsing gently.

So that went well.

I thought about finding Warren and asking him when he'd planned to tell me about this democratic little voting process, but he was probably still in his so-called session with Greta. Besides, while we were seated in Greta's office, pretending to be civilized as we glared at one another across our teacups, I'd decided there was something Warren wasn't sharing. Either that or something in his recent past that he didn't want to face. Something, I thought, remembering the guilt sitting like a cold stone in my belly, that had to do with Tekla. So what was it he was unwilling to face, or know? More, what didn't he want the rest of us to know?

These questions consumed me as I wove alone through the hallways, halting every so often to scratch the heads and cheeks of escaped cats. Wardens, I thought, correcting myself. None of them hissed or growled or swiped at my hand as I'd seen Luna do with Butch, so that was a small comfort. They just looked at me with unblinking eyes, pushing against my fingers with their lithe little bodies, and moved on when they were finished, tails raised in a parting salute.

Finally, I returned to my mother's windowless, concrete room to regroup, thankful there was at least one place in this underground labyrinth where I could be alone and feel safe. Unfortunately, it wasn't until I'd tucked myself into bed, drawing my knees high to my chest, that I realized trust couldn't even be extended to my own mind.

The dream was like wind gradually picking up in slack sails, so I knew it was coming. If I'd acted early enough, I might even have been able to stop it. Still, I wasn't braced for the feeling of invasion; like someone was picking through the folds of my mind, searching and excavating the forbidden parts. And what they found was bedrock; granite, and caliche, and a petrified memory I'd never dared touch before. But it chipped free now, sharp-edged, banging around inside of me. Slicing at my sanity. A nightmare come back to life.

The biggest nightmare *of* my life.

I was a teen again; fifteen, to be exact. Sneaky and smart, and needing to escape a world that neither knew nor understood me . . . as all teens feel the need to do, I suppose. But there was one person who did understand me, and he knew and loved me better than anyone else.

Ben Traina lived across a narrow but elongated patch of desert, long since converted into another thoroughfare for impatient motorists, but marked at the time by a sole footpath which bisected the desert floor. Ben and I probably wore that one away in this summer alone.

Though relatively close in proximity, our homes were worlds apart. The Archer mansion fanned coldly across an entire city block, a massive complex with so much faux work and gaudy detailing it looked like a Victorian ballgown. In contrast, Ben's house was like an old tattered sweatshirt. Low ceilings, small windows, a fireplace made out of rock they'd, thankfully, stopped making in the seventies, and the original green shag carpeting blanketing the concrete floor.

For all these differences, though, our families were remarkably similar. There was the overbearing patriarch—gaming mogul versus military man; the mousy wife—society maven and the housefrau; and the two point five kids, two girls on my side of the tracks, three boys on his.

His parents were out of town for the weekend—one brother was already out of the house, and the second was in basic training—so, unsurprisingly, their vacation had become ours. We were in love, a first for us both, and we experienced all the firsts that go along with that. We hid from the world that entire weekend; talking, laughing, eating. Watching movies. Kissing. Stroking. Making love for days.

Sunday morning marked the end of our lovers' tryst. His

parents would be home by noon, but it was my sister who arrived first, breathless and fresh from a predawn flight across the desert. We were forced to leave our cocoon of sheets and limbs and flesh just to silence her insistent pounding at the door.

"Mom's looking for you," Olivia announced, without preamble. "She's so freaked she wants to call the police. And Dad says this time you're going to juvenile hall."

Regretfully, I turned to Ben. "I have to go."

He sighed sleepily, smelling like me. "Will you get in trouble?"

I smiled. "It was worth it."

"Come on! I am not going to juvi with you," Olivia said, then shuddered delicately. "They make you wear paper shoes."

We fled as fast as our limbs would carry us, into the abyss of darkness, across the swath of hard desert earth I knew as intimately as the vein at my wrist . . . or Ben's. Olivia was younger than me, and at the time quicker too. I can still see her flying through the night, golden hair lit by the moon's eye, streaming behind her like ribbons cutting wind. Even at thirteen she'd been beautiful, the woman inside her already outgrowing the child. I, though older, still looked like a girl.

The man came from nowhere, hurtling from the darkness like a dust devil, catching Olivia from the side. She didn't even have time to scream before she struck the boulders and tumbleweeds of the desert floor, pinned helplessly beneath the weight of her stronger adversary. Then there were only sounds of struggle. Clothing torn. Flesh beaten. Anguished cries for mercy.

A voice, twisted and irrational, snaked up from my subconscious. *You deserved what happened that night.*

Even as I groaned in my sleep, shaking my head, I knew I did. Olivia was only there because of me. Those meaty fists rained down on her body and face, knuckles reporting like shots as they made contact with her soft flesh, pummeling fragile bone. And because it was my fault, I reacted the same way again.

"Run!" I screamed, latching onto the man from behind. I didn't have the skills then that I did now. I didn't have the strength to overpower a man of any size, and nothing to enable me to stand up to a human predator. Olivia ran, and even after I'd lost sight of her I could still hear her feet crunching over gravel and rock, her sobs streaming, like her hair, behind her. Then I heard nothing at all.

But that was then.

"I should've killed you the first time," said the man I now knew as Joaquin. I felt my eyes open—eyes like Rena's, there but not—and I stared into a face as cruel as I remembered. Thin lips wrapped around a full set of evenly spaced teeth; a smile for me, I realized, as the smell of rancid honey spilled out of his mouth. A five o'clock shadow, too perfect and precise to have been by accident, studded his cheeks and chin, and despite his position, looming over me, not a hair on his head was out of place. It was slicked back, tight and sleek, the individual lines from the teeth of his comb clear in the meager moonlight.

"No," I managed, before his fingertips dug into my windpipe, strangling me again. His other hand ricocheted across my face, whipping it to the right. On the returning backhand, I felt my nose collapse. How had I ever forgotten that sound?

"Oh, yes," he replied, arching into me, mimicking orgasm, writhing above me like a rattler. "Yes, yes, yes."

I head-butted him, causing him to jerk back, his face registering surprise as blood began to seep from his nose. I hadn't done that the first time. He slapped me again, but it was too late. A new thought had already burrowed into my mind.

"I don't have to be this again. I don't have to do this

again." And I shifted my hips, forcing space between us, and managed to free a leg long enough to ram a knee into his ribs.

"Oh, but you do," he said, and he planted himself widely over me, like a Greco-Roman wrestler, doubling his weight on top of mine.

I almost gave in. I felt my lungs creaking with need for air, felt his hands fumbling between my legs, but my training and my will kept me struggling. "No . . . I'm not that girl anymore. I'm the Archer."

"Yes," he snarled, face leering into mine, "I could tell by your stiletto."

I blinked, then felt a smile spread over my broken face. "I'm the Archer . . . and this is my dream."

"But we can reach you in your dreams," he said, grinding into me again. "I can fuck you in your dreams."

"No," I said, struggling. "I don't want this."

"Fight all you want, but you can't change who you are . . . who I've helped you become."

"I'm not like him!"

"Oh, look in the mirror, dear girl," he said, giving me a sly smile. "You're exactly like him."

There was a rustling from behind us, and Joaquin looked behind him, then jerked his head back to look at me. "Fuck," he said, and disappeared.

And feeling lighter, the weight of both his body and sleep being yanked from me, I really opened my eyes.

The blankets were tangled around my feet, sheets soaked in the outline of my body, and as I sat up I immediately saw the one thing that hadn't been in the room before; the item that had called me from my sleeping state. A newspaper had been slipped under my door, the sound somehow sneaking through the web of my not-dream. I rose, left it lying on the floor, and opened the door to peer into the hallway. No one was there.

Running a hand through my hair I noted my nose felt tender, though not broken, and my throat was raw, and probably red. But I bent to retrieve the paper, silently thanking whoever had used it to chase away my demons . . . until I saw the lead article.

"Oh, my God," I said, and the words from my dream raced again through my head. *You're exactly like him.* Slowly, I sank to the side of the bed. Oh, my God, I thought again. Maybe he was right. Maybe they all were right.

The article was brief, a dispassionate assemblage of facts and figures; time of death, the age of the victim—God, only seventeen—what officials thought had happened. I read over it half a dozen times, trying to reconcile the memory of my confrontation with Ajax with the words appearing on the page. A meaningless and random attack, it reported, by what was, most likely, a gang of teens. One of whom had a blade. The statement from the girl's mother was no more than a single sentence, but it summed up the only real known fact: "My daughter is gone, and my life will never be the same."

So maybe they were right.

I knew this was what whomever had slid the newspaper under the door wanted me to feel. It was spiteful and obvious, yet it still made me want to bury my head in my hands and never look up. I had failed this girl. I'd put her in danger, just like Olivia, and they'd both paid the price with their lives. So maybe they were right. I was exactly like him.

I was about to toss the paper aside when another column caught my eye. I was holding the whole of the Metro section, the bulk of the day's bad news in my hands, and today it featured a story of an early morning shooting, a love triangle gone wrong. A woman named Karen was shot by her husband as she tried to leave their apartment. Moments later one Mark Davis had turned the gun on himself.

I closed my eyes, and for a moment I didn't even breathe. I just sat there, chaos swirling inside me like some nauseating psychedelic drug. The store clerk had been an accident, an innocent I'd never meant to injure. But this. Ajax had nothing to do with the dissolution of this marriage, these lives. This was all me. I had fired up my new powers and blasted through the walls of Karen and Mark Davis's lives.

I managed to stumble into the bathroom, and splashed cold water onto my face over and over, until I gasped, and realized I was crying. Leaning heavily on the sink, I lifted my head to face the mirror. Olivia's lovely face, with my haunted eyes.

And the dark shadows that lingered beneath them? I'd created those—and the reasons behind them—myself.

"Who do you think you are?" I whispered at the mirrored image. I watched the reflected lips move, then fall still, with no answer.

I returned to the bedroom, picked up the newspaper and studied the image of Karen Davis smiling up at me from an undated photo. After a moment I shoved it in my duffel bag for safekeeping and left. I wanted to find out for sure if, maybe, they were right.

Even while hoping against hope that they were wrong.

21

My emotions were under control by the time I reached Greta's room. My eyes dry, face serenely composed—which, I knew, on Olivia only looked blithely unaware—and my energy carefully controlled. I didn't want to run into any of the others without all my barriers in place. I half expected to find Chandra lurking around each sharp corner, sure she'd been the one to slip the paper under my door, but she was nowhere to be found. If it had been her, then she obviously thought her business with me complete.

I heard a shot of laughter from the direction of the children's ward, saw a sole female cat out on patrol, two kittens stumbling along behind her, and increased my pace, intent on arriving at Greta's undetected. I'd just turned the last corner, casting a final, furtive glance behind me, when I slammed into something, someone, who grunted and gave with the impact.

"Warren." We both stepped back, each startled by the other, and I frowned when I saw the color drain from his face. "Are you okay?"

"Of course." His words were as jerky as his movements, and he swallowed hard. "I'm fine."

But I'd never seen him looking more disoriented. He was sweating, pale, and bleary-eyed, and all the crazed self-assurance I so readily associated with him was gone. In its place was a man who looked tired and old and scared. Whatever had transpired in the hours since I'd last seen him, it had left him uncertain and shaky.

"You don't look fine. You look funny." I sniffed lightly at the air. "You smell funny."

"Well, we can't all look as good as you, now, can we?" he snapped, a thin hand rising to rub at his face.

"Geez, Warren." I drew back. "What happened? What did Greta say?"

"I'm not at liberty to discuss my therapy sessions with you." I must have looked as injured as I felt because he cursed beneath his breath and tried to soften his words. "Look, Gregor's been out there, alone, for over a dozen hours. I'm just . . . worried. I'm going after him."

"But . . . why can't someone else go? The Shadows have targeted you." Because of me, I thought, and guilt speared through me now that I could see the toll it was taking on him.

"I'm the most *experienced*," he corrected, standing taller. "We can't lose Gregor. He's the only one of us—other than myself—who's held his place in the Zodiac for more than twelve months."

"What about Micah? Or Hunter?"

He shook his head. "Talented, both of them, but they're both new recruits. Micah's not even supposed to be a star sign. He's support staff, like Greta."

"So it hasn't just been five agents killed in the last few months—"

"It's been ten. Ten of the finest," he finished, voice weary.

"Jesus," I said under my breath.

"We replenish the signs only to have them destroyed again. One, our Virgo, the very next day." He looked at me, and his face was hard again. I'd seen this kind of determination before. I'd captured it with my camera on the faces of street people who knew all was lost but were determined to go on anyway. "I won't lose another. I'm going out there, I'm going to retrieve Gregor, and then I'm going to shut down the Zodiac. We'll wait until the troop is whole again, strong again. Then we'll take on the Shadow warriors as a team."

"You mean . . . leave the city vulnerable?"

He closed his eyes, and they moved like minnows beneath their lids, as if he were already watching the outcome of that decision. "We have no choice."

"For how long?"

"As long as it takes to train up a new Zodiac force. A year. Maybe more."

"A year!" I exclaimed, thinking of all the damage Ajax and his ilk could do in that amount of time. Thinking also of young teenage girls being attacked in Quik-Marts and the desert, and left there to die. "That's too long."

"Got a better idea?" His eyes snapped open, fired on me.

"Hey, don't take it out on me! I'm just saying—"

"Well, just don't!"

"God," I exclaimed, balling my fists. "Why are you so upset with me? What did I do?"

"I'm not—" He cut off his words as he realized he was yelling, and inhaled deeply. On the exhale he continued. "I'm not upset with you, okay?" he lied. "Greta and I had some things to discuss and they've put me on edge. I'm sorry for yelling. I've got to go."

His fear reached out to burn the lining in my nose. "Wait a minute. Things? Like me?"

"Things," he mimicked sharply, "that are confidential. It's not your business what I discussed with Greta."

"It's my business when you come out of that room treating me like a stranger. Like an enemy." I folded my arms as he opened his mouth to deny it. "The conversation lingers on you, Warren. It smells like an industrial solution. It's metallic and cold, and it's heightening as we speak. Why were you discussing me with Greta?"

"I don't have to tell you anything," he whispered. "I've done enough for you."

I drew back, surprised. Who was this man? I angled my head, exploring the air around him with my thoughts; nasal receptors probing like centipede legs.

"Stop it," he ordered, and an invisible mental wall rose like a tower around him. He pushed past me and began stalking away.

"What the hell is wrong with you?"

"It's you!" he yelled, whirling on me with hot and furious eyes. "Don't you get it? It's not me, it's you!"

I stared into those angry eyes, watched as they banked, smoked, then dimmed. Unfeeling now. Apathetic. Dead. He's shut down on me, I thought with injured wonder. He just closed me out, turned me off.

I felt my eyes grow wide, and my breath stuttered out of me on a whisper. "You bastard. You're the one who brought me into this, remember? You yelled 'Eureka!' and jumped in front of my car! You knocked me out and made me into this," I said, motioning up and down Olivia's body.

"You want your life back, Joanna?" he asked, surprising me by using my real name so openly. I looked around but whipped my attention back to him when he took a step toward me. "Or, excuse me, I mean that empty excuse of an existence you called a life? Well, fine. Once we find a way to get you out of here, we'll cut you loose. Physically. Mentally. Completely. Happy?"

I would have been; a handful of days, or even hours, earlier. But this was abandonment, and even less of a choice than he'd offered me before. So why now?

I tilted my head and took a step toward him. "You're afraid of me."

Alarm lashed through my gut like a whip, and Warren's jaw clenched. He hadn't wanted me to feel that, and tried to cover the slip with words. "We were wrong. *I* was wrong. We should have never approached you, never introduced you to the Zodiac at such a late age."

I ignored his words, paying heed only to the emotions rippling like hot oil beneath the waxy exterior. "You don't trust me."

"I don't trust the Shadow in you!"

My body jerked before I could control it and my heart skipped a beat. A wire of panic began to spread outward from the core of my belly. He'd been the last person in this subterranean hell I'd have expected to utter those words. Even though I suspected Warren of hiding secrets, I thought they'd had to do with Tekla or some troop dynamic I had yet to understand. But not me. Somehow, I'd taken it for granted, from the beginning, that he'd always be on my side. "And what about the Light? What about my mother's side?"

"Your mother," he scoffed, bitterness oozing like venom to coat the walls around us. "Zoe's gone, Joanna. She's so gone she's never coming back. Perhaps she lived with the Shadow side so long that she began to enjoy it. Who knows? She could be there now, living a life of ease, because it is so much easier, you know . . ." I did know. "Shit, for all we know *she* could be the one feeding the Tulpa information about our star signs—"

"No." I shook my head hard. "She wouldn't."

"And how do you know what she would or wouldn't do? You never knew her at all."

My mouth trembled closed. He had me there.

"We'll forget Zoe ever existed, and soon we'll do the same with you. Then we can all just go back to living in our separate realities."

My heart cracked at that, and I knew Warren sensed it. He could feel and smell and hear the echo of it in his blood . . . if only he wanted to. "So . . . just like that?"

He looked me over, his face softening momentarily, and he blinked. Then it hardened again, his emotions petrified, and it turned him into something other than a crazed bum and a leader of the underworld. It nullified him. "I have to go."

"Just like that, Warren?" I repeated, raising my voice after him. "You're going to turn your back on me like I didn't lose my entire life, my identity, my sister? Like nobody's trying to kill me too?" He kept walking and I raised my voice. "Like my eyes didn't bleed from their own fucking sockets?"

No response, just the silly little slap and slide of his gait. Suddenly, though, it didn't look so silly. It looked resolute. Defeated. Final.

"What about this special connection we're supposed to have, huh? What about that?" He rounded the corner without looking back, hearing me but not listening. "Don't turn your fucking back on me!" I slammed my fist against the wall. "Warren!"

My voice echoed emptily down the hall, then trailed away in a choked whisper. "Don't . . . don't leave . . ."

Slumping against the wall, I tried to catch my breath. How could he? He *knew* me, who I was and why. Hadn't he held me while I lay sobbing on the floor, watching my own funeral play out on the local news like some sick reality show? He knows me, I thought, the real me. He knows . . .

"That I don't even know myself."

Shaking, I pushed away from the wall. I didn't want to break down here in the hallway where anyone could see me. Where Warren's mistrust lingered like a virus.

So I lunged for the closest escape, Greta's door, and it swung open so quickly I was two steps inside before I realized I'd forgotten to knock. Half blind with shock and self-pity, I barely registered Greta's surprise or the way she jolted before she could control it. Her hands disappeared behind her back and she backed into her dressing table, my reflected face pale and ink-eyed behind her.

I seemed to be having that effect on people these days.

She put a hand to her chest. "Olivia!"

"I'm sorry. I just . . . I'm not—" I'm not Olivia. I'm not a superhero. I'm not anyone. I'm not going to cry, I thought, even as the first tear fell. "I just needed someone to talk to."

"Oh, dear. Of course you do." She rushed to my side, though I saw her hesitate before wrapping her arms around me, and that made me cry even harder. She urged me toward her flowered settee. "Come, sit."

"I'm sorry," I repeated, accepting the tissue she pressed into my palm. I made a tentative dab at my eyes, then gave up and let my face crumble upon itself. "I didn't know who else to come to and I needed to talk and I saw Warren and he won't . . . he just . . . and he . . ."

"Shh," she said, pulling my head to her chest. I rested it there. Rested, it seemed, for the first time since my mother had left me a decade ago. I closed my eyes, slumped against her soft chest, and inhaled deeply. I knew her now, I realized. The twin bouquets of roses and the herbs she brewed for her own teas were fused upon her breath and skin, her signature scent stamped like a star on the surface of my temporal lobe.

Gradually, the distress and misery left my body, sliding away through my tears, and I relaxed. My sobs were replaced by blessed nothingness, my body went limp against hers and, after one final sniffle, I lay silent. Greta continued to rock me, and though I knew she still feared what'd happened that morning, still feared me, I was so grateful for the momentary kindness that I didn't care.

"Thank you," I said, swiping the back of my hand over my face. "Again."

"One of those days?" she asked quietly.

"One of those lives," I muttered, a bitter laugh hiccuping out of me.

"You're overwhelmed, dear. You've toured the sanctuary. Met the others—"

I held up a hand and cut her off. I shot her an apologetic glance before lowering my palm and sighing. "What I am is tired of people either treating me like some chosen deliverer or an evil pariah. Mostly, though, I'm tired of pretending to be someone I'm not."

"What do you mean?"

I mean that I am so fucked up you wouldn't be talking to me now if you knew who I really was. You'd run and hide and cower in the corner. You'd scream for help, you'd flee for your life. I met my gaze in the mirror. *Isn't that right, Joanna? Olivia? Whoever you think you are.*

Greta was watching me through the reflection too, but her face slid out of focus like in the movies, dissolving into the background as my own grew sharper. It was like my skin was thinning out, the bones beneath beginning to jut through the meticulously sculpted image reflected there. I swallowed hard.

"Everyone I've ever been close to in my life is either dead because of me or I pushed them away long ago. Even my mother ultimately left because of me."

"That's not true. That wasn't your fault."

"And I like violence," I went on, ignoring her, hands clasped tightly around my knees. "I've never admitted that before, but I do. I like to inflict it, I like the power of having inflicted it. I go into dark places searching for people to harm me, just so I can mete out justice in my own twisted way. With my fists, Greta. With the hatred that fills my heart."

She smiled, deflecting the seriousness of my words. "So, what you're saying is you're not perfect?"

"You don't understand," I said, whirling on her. "I can't do this! I can't be the person you all expect me to be!"

"But you're Zoe Archer's daughter."

"I'm the Tulpa's daughter too."

She tilted her head. "Is that what's bothering you?"

"It's what's bothering everyone else," I said, and told her about my run-in with Warren in the hall.

Greta let out a weary sigh. "We had just finished a session. I hypnotized him, and he lived out his greatest fear in his mind. Your fates are deeply intertwined."

That brought my head up. "What do you mean?" I asked. "What fear?"

Her eyes grew sad, the edges tightening as she shook her

head. "That you, the woman he's pinned all his hopes on, may betray him."

I could only gape at that. Warren's actions made sense in the light of her words, but the words themselves didn't quite compute. Me? Betray him?

Greta tried for a reassuring smile. The tightness in her jaw kind of ruined it. "When your mind is that vulnerable, every sense is amplified. Seeing you so soon after he felt, watched, heard, and scented your betrayal—"

"But I didn't betray him!"

"But his mind believed you had." She leaned back on the settee and waited for my eventual nod. "Think of an athlete visualizing success for himself on the playing field. The mind can't tell the difference between what's imagined and what really happened. Warren lived out your betrayal, or the possibility of it, up here." She pointed one delicate finger at her own head. "Don't worry. He'll be back to normal soon. As normal as Warren can be."

She was joking, but I couldn't manage a smile. It did, however, get me thinking. "Do you think this hypnosis might help me?"

"What do you mean?"

I tried to keep my voice steady, but my hope trembled out in the words. "I mean, would you be able to draw out more of the Light in me? Bring it more to the forefront? Make it stronger than the . . . other side?"

She picked up her glasses from the small table at the head of the love seat, putting them on as if to examine me closely. "You're concerned about the balance of Light and Shadow inside of you?"

And she was watching me so expectantly that I found myself telling her; about the construction workers, and how I used my senses to plow through their lives. What it had cost them. And how it made me feel.

"Powerful. Superior. Untouchable." I swallowed hard, not wanting to go on, but afraid if I didn't things would remain the same between Warren and me. Between us all.

"I couldn't predict what would happen, and, believe me, if I had I wouldn't have done it, but I did do it, Greta. I did it on purpose."

I paused for her reaction—revulsion? disgust?—but got only silence. Then a slow, rising interest that grew as Greta tapped her finger against her thigh and considered me over the rim of her glasses. "And you want me to rid you of the impulse to play God, is that it? So that if this ever happens again you won't feel the need to stand in judgment?"

"It's not my job to put anyone in his place. I know that now, and I . . . I don't want to be like *him*." And I didn't. I didn't want lashing out at others to be my first instinct anymore. It was a defense that'd served me well after my attack, and in the years I'd had to live under Xavier's disapproving stare, but it was different now. Because I was different.

"I can't plant anything in your psyche that isn't already there, Olivia," Greta said as I rose to pace the floor in front of us, my boot steps muffled beneath her Persian rug. "I also can't remove Shadow impulses. It's part of who you are."

I stopped before her. "But can you teach me to control it?"

Greta pressed her lips together in a look so scrutinizing I was afraid the answer would be an immediate no. But after what felt like forever, she nodded, and motioned for me to recline where I was. A sigh rocketed from my body as tension uncoiled in my belly, and gratitude for this small kindness, when kindnesses had been so hard to come by of late, teared up in my eyes.

Drawing a chenille blanket over my lower body, Greta loomed over me like a benevolent angel, and the last thing I saw were her earnest gray eyes, cloudy with intent. Then she slid a cool palm over my face and began to count. The numbers formed beneath my lids—cloudy and ephemeral and ghostly—and I began the backward spiral into the recesses of my own mind.

* * *

I'd never been put under before, and therefore wasn't sure that I could, but I listened to the soft lilt and direction of Greta's musical voice and let her words settle into me, bone deep. My arms grew heavy at my side and my heart-beat slowed like an insect being caught and trapped under the sap of a weeping elm. My skull was light in contrast, thoughts floating there like feathers, as disconnected and random as if they belonged entirely to someone else.

Warren's baffling treatment of me was forgotten, as were Chandra's cruel remarks and Hunter's probing ones. All of these thoughts were like papers cluttering a desk, quickly swept aside as light and insignificant, the real work etched more permanently on the surface beneath.

Greta's words were fingers pushing against the shadows in my mind, into soft, pulpy places I had never known existed. Or at least, never acknowledged. A few words floated in these deep morasses of thought—*raped, vengeance, Tulpa*—alligator heads lifting above the brackish surface before sinking again beneath my subconscious, and no matter how hard Greta tried she could not raise them again.

She had better luck sweeping aside the thinly veiled curtains of my Light side; where, from behind the safety of my lids, I could stare directly into the blaze of an imagined sun. Golden light singed the edge of brain tissue, and the neon of the city I was born in set my blood buzzing, heating the crimson liquid to a lively pulsing glow.

While Greta probed, I lived in the center of this glowing womb; warm and cleansed, safe and guarded. Peace bloomed in my heart, and I sank, deeper still, into a state of contented relaxation. The secrets living inside me began to whisper to her. Whisper, as they'd been whispered to me long ago. Greta whispered back.

"I'm going to ask you some questions and you'll answer me with the first thing that comes to mind, all right?" At my sleepy sound of assent, she continued. "We'll start out easy. Do you know your name?"

"They call me Olivia."

There was such a prolonged silence after that, the nascent heat began to ebb.

"It's not your true name?"

"No."

"Who are you, then?"

"Secret. Can't tell." A sigh heaved out of my body, hollowing it. "I no longer know."

"And . . . who's Olivia?"

"Dead. She's dead. It's a dead girl's name." A whimper escaped me, inhuman, but for the sorrow that laced it. "I'm so sorry, Olivia."

"It's okay. Just stay with me now, listen to my voice." She kept talking until my breathing had returned to normal. "What would you like to be called?" she finally asked. "What should I call you?"

"I have to be Olivia in order to survive. No one can know differently."

"Does Warren know?"

"Of course. He made me. So did Micah."

A tapping, like a considering click, fingernails against wood. "All right. Olivia. You have a duty to do. Do you know what that is?"

"Return balance to the Zodiac."

"Return it? Or . . ." She left the question open.

"Not return it. Unbalance it. Hunt them down. Obliterate the enemy, destroy them all. Use my gifts to do it, but I don't know how."

She ignored the rising question in my last remark. "And who is the enemy?"

"Ajax. A man named Joaquin. The Tulpa. There are others. I've smelled them, but I don't know them. And . . ."

"And?"

"The enemy is inside of me also."

"No, Olivia, it doesn't—"

"Yes, Greta. It does." My voice deepened, like an instrument someone else was strumming. I stirred, jerking my head side to side. "I must destroy the Shadow within and without."

"Shh. Let's take a step back now. Listen to my voice, and follow the words. Are you with me?" She paused for my sleepy nod. "Good. Now, think. What experience will most help you in unbalancing the Shadow? What will allow you the vengeance you spoke to me about? What will help you restore the agents of Light to the Zodiac?"

"Krav Maga," I answered without hesitation. "The skills I learned after Joaquin destroyed me the first time."

Again, that press of questioning silence, before she went on. "And what was that like?"

I shivered, the memory sweeping through me. "Cold. So cold after, when the scorpions crawled over me, but didn't sting. They knew I was dead. They scuttled away, legs mired in my blood." I shivered again, then stilled. "But she found me and warmed me. She gave her own power and gifts over to me. So I would survive it. And avenge it."

"Who, Olivia?"

"My mother." I smiled. And I remembered. *One day, when the time comes, you'll understand I didn't leave. I fled.* "Ah, I see now. I understand."

"Focus, Olivia. Listen to my voice," Greta commanded. "What gifts did she give you? What will allow you to battle the Shadow side?"

I didn't answer. Instead, I saw my mother's face floating directly above me, her hair falling like golden-red curtains over her cheeks, eyes burning with hot, furious tears.

"Olivia?" Greta questioned.

My mother's mouth moved, three words fired like shots over the bow. *I love you.*

"Olivia!" Greta again, panicked now.

"Love," I answered simply, realizing I'd carried it with me all this time. "She gave me complete and unconditional love."

And the dam gave way. The memories I'd blocked so successfully for so long flooded my brain, the rush of them deafening in my ears, and I was borne on their tide back in time. Back to the hospital again; to the machines, tubes, painkillers, and stitches. Back with the bruises and the swelling, the torn fingernails and the rope burns still buried in my neck. Back to birth of my second life cycle. Back, I thought, when I was sixteen years old.

I turned my head and she was there, next to me. Not just hair and haunted eyes, but the whole of my mother; body and essence, skin and aura. I stared, drinking in her features; the freckles standing out defiantly on a button nose, the pressing of delicate bones beneath too-pale skin, a scar I'd always meant to ask her about. She swept shiny fingertips across my face and gently smoothed back my hair.

"Sleep," she said, and somewhere in the back of my mind I knew my mouth had moved, the command and voice issuing from my throat, my memory. I settled deeper into myself, obeying her.

"Olivia?" Greta's voice was far off and wary, no longer authoritative or sure. She was right to be alarmed. My mother's voice had taken over.

"I'm going to show you who I am, who you are," I said in my mother's voice, as she had once said to me, "who you will be someday."

She leaned over me, hair swinging delicately over my bloodless cheeks, blue eyes boring into mine. "Because you will survive this. It has been foretold. You will fulfill the first sign of the Zodiac. You will rise again as our Kairos."

Then she put her soft lips to my chapped ones, and re-suscitated my soul. Desert sage—blooms sagging, but stalks strong, as though wet with a summer monsoon—infiltrated my senses. The juice from a fig cacti, which kept knowledgeable predators alive in the desert, trickled down my throat, coating my belly. I breathed in a homey spice, like cinnamon but stronger, and it numbed my skin from the inside out so that every muscle in my body simultaneously relaxed.

Then there was the exotic and redolent scent of the womb where I'd once lived. It smelled like night-blooming flowers, and the wind across the bright side of the moon. I recognized it immediately, and inhaled deeply. She gave me more. As all great mothers do, she gave me all. "See? You can taste the Light in another person. Now store this power deep inside of you. Because he'll come for you again."

"Olivia!"

Greta's voice had my mother looking up. She frowned, annoyed at the invisible interruption, before rising and heading toward the door. She looked back at me only once, one hand braced on the door frame, a petite and powerful figure eyeing me with fierce love and resigned determination. "Watch Olivia. She'll show you how to survive."

And she was gone. Again.

"Tell me your true identity," Greta demanded, entering the hospital room through the portal she'd opened in my mind. Her outline snapped with power, like sparklers bursting to life along her skin, but I merely looked at her, words tumbling like dice through my mind. *Goddess, bitch, whore, mother, daughter, sister, friend . . .*

I could be any and all of those things, but I picked out my titles like selecting fruit from a vendor's stall. *Enemy*, I thought, picking it up, taking a bite, finding it sweet. *Huntress*, I thought, adding it to the other. Once the prey, now the *predator*. I pocketed that one, saving it for later.

"Tell me who you are!"

"Can't you see?" I turned my head to face Greta, still lingering uncertainly by the doorway to my hospital room, and I smiled. I knew from her gasp that I wasn't supposed to be asking the questions, but I suddenly had all the answers. Hearing footsteps in the hall, I leaned to peer around Greta. "Look, see how my aura precedes me? See the barbed texture of my soul? The vessel is fierce, is it not? My mind is bathed in crimson."

In a full panic now, the mind-Greta whirled, shifting so

her back was to the wall. Her whisper wobbled. Her hands fumbled, doing something behind her back. "Tell me your name."

The answer was heavy in my mouth, numbing the tip of my tongue. I gasped with its weight, and my eyes burst open with my mouth. "I am the Archer!"

And like an arrow loosed from a bow that'd been held too taut, too long, the woman I should have been winged past the last ten years like a fiery comet, plowing into me with all the knowledge I'd been born—and buried—with. The knowledge of the Archer, the Zodiac . . . and my place in it.

A second pair of eyes opened up behind my own, blinked wonderingly, then crinkled as a smile lifted one side of my mouth. Alternate ears, with drums tunneling down into my soul, popped as if the pressure on them had finally been released. New taste buds exploded on my tongue, and every pore in my skin hummed to life, making me more attuned to the particles weighing down the air than I'd even been before. My sixth sense had returned. It had taken a decade, but I was finally healed.

I rose.

A crash, the sound of glass shattering on the floor, and Greta was backed up against the far wall of her room, a vial shattered at her feet. The transition from the hospital room I'd been imagining and Greta's chamber was abrupt, but I was still my dream self, my real self, a predator haloed in red. I smiled as I turned my head to meet her eyes. She looked afraid, and I was sorry for that, but I wanted a mirror. I wanted to see for myself.

"How did you do that?" Greta asked as I swiped a damp tendril of hair from my cheek. She nearly had her face under control again, a mild sort of worry pressing in on her delicate brow, but her voice was searching, and just sharp enough to cut through the thin webbing of resistance left by the hypnosis. "I put you under. You're not supposed to be able to come out of it without my assistance."

"I've been under for a long time, Greta." I stretched, like awakening from a long nap, and studied my reflection in the dresser mirror across from me. The color was still there, not the vibrant crimson of my dreaming state, but a banked flame like a burner set to low. It was warm and steady, and this time I knew it would never go out. "It was long past time to wake up."

And I felt refreshed. My pores drank in the air, and the room appeared brighter. Greta was tinged in a sallow green, though; her fear, I guessed, and again I was sorry for that. I inhaled deeply, then jerked back, frowning. "What's that smell?"

"I—I couldn't reach you. I was drawing a syringe to bring you out of the trance chemically." She waved a hand at the glass littering the floor, one side of her mouth lifting wryly. "Turns out I didn't need it after all."

I wrinkled my nose. "I can smell the enzymes in it. I can also smell your perfume without even inhaling. Isn't that funny? It's like I can breathe through my pores." I turned from studying the glow of my aura in the mirror, and caught the fear in her eyes. Smiling, I went to her and took her face in my hands. "Don't be afraid, Greta. I no longer am."

And I left the room after that, with Greta gaping as I trailed confidence and knowledge and power like a silken red cloak behind me.

22

Doors that won't open, elevators that won't come when you call . . . they'll come now.

Intending to test this theory, I entered a locker room almost oppressive in its silence, my heels clicking sharply on the cement floor. The lockers fanned around me like sentinels guarding the perimeter of the circular room, and there was the faint hum of energy coursing through the illuminated emblems. My eyes went immediately to the centaur, glowing steadily and reassuring in a soft green neon.

I tried to ignore the five dormant signs, but Warren's admission kept sneaking up on me—ten agents, not five, had been murdered in the past few months—and the unlit glyphs belonging to those agents looked like bullet holes to me. Soundless, colorless, empty voids where no light could penetrate as long as their deaths remained unavenged.

Dragged from the recesses of a broken mind, the true memory of my mother made me believe that I could do that. Avenge them. I turned my attention back to my locker. Whatever was inside this steel trash bin was going to help me be the woman she'd given her life for me to be. It would teach me how to be the Archer. It would help me create a safe place for myself in this world again.

So forgetting about the empty eyes of the fallen star signs bowing around me, I put my hand to the palm plate. The button in the middle lit up in a red, inviting square.

"Just so you know," I said, whispering into the locker's horizontal slats, "the answer to my own life's mysteries aren't inside of you. They're inside of me." I pressed the button, a bittersweet smile touching my face. "My name is Joanna. I'm the Archer of Light."

And as easy as that, a click, and the latch released. I shook my head. All I'd had to do was take a trip down into myself . . . and come back as a different person.

The photo Warren had shoved in the day before wasn't lying at the bottom of the locker as expected, but was taped to the inside of the door, along with three others, and my breath caught as I viewed the four together.

The first was of my family as I once knew it. My mother, bent forward, one arm around Olivia, another around me. We were all wearing matching smiles, and it looked like we were at Disneyland. Xavier was in the picture too, but he was relegated to the background, arms folded resolutely across his chest, studying the domestic scene as if wondering who those people were. His impatience with the moment was set in his shoulders, though I couldn't read his expression. His face had been cut from the photo.

The second was of my mother alone, obviously taken at the sanctuary. She wore a black bodysuit that clung to the muscles of her able body, her bright hair gathered high atop her head, arms stretched forward as she aimed some sort of weapon at an invisible enemy. Her face wore an expression I'd never seen before—determination, hatred, strength—and I smiled looking at it.

Then Ben's picture, a smile lifting one side of his mouth as he slept, dreaming of a future that would never be. I traced his jaw in the photo, remembered how it'd felt beneath my fingertips. This photo would also serve as a reminder that some loved ones had to stay tucked safely away. My mother had taught me that much.

Finally, Zoe with another woman. Their arms were thrown about one another's shoulders, and they were laughing into the camera, looking impossibly young. It meant nothing to me, but it obviously had to her, so it would remain.

The only remaining item was nestled in the corner on the floor, a small package wrapped in brown postal paper, secured with aging twine, with a note tucked between the folds of the paper. I weighed it in my hand. Sturdy and small—the length and width of one palm—it was weighty for its size. Removing the note for later, I ripped open the packaging.

"Ha!" I laughed in triumph. My mother's conduit. I glanced back up at the photo, compared the two weapons, and mimicked her stance. *My* conduit. Thumb-sized arrows were lined in a chamber much like a gun's, waiting to be cocked. Flat-headed, the bowstring was made of some shiny and supple wire, while the body of the weapon shone like onyx stone. Anxious to see what she'd said, I fumbled with the accompanying note, addressed to: The Archer.

They're coming for me. I've foreseen it. To keep me from speaking truth they'll take away my voice. Help me. My eyes for your voice? Speak, and I'll show you the way to redemption. To the outside world. To the traitor.

I gasped. This couldn't have been written by my mother. I started over, noticing this time the crispness of the paper before my eyes fell to the signature, an initial only, the letter *T*. It was followed by a postscript.

Look behind you.

A hand fell on my shoulder. I yelped and whirled around, automatically tucking the conduit behind me.

"You got it open," Vanessa said, jerking her head at the locker. Chandra, to her left, said nothing, but her jaw clenched convulsively.

I shifted to stand in front of her, and she stiffened when I shot her a knowing look. "Well, *someone* delivered a little package to my room earlier, and it kept me from sleeping. So I thought I'd come up and give this a try again. Funny, isn't it? That something meant to hurt me led me to this?"

Chandra's cheek twitched. "Congratulations," she said, but I could tell by the dark violet hue ringing her body that she didn't mean it.

Vanessa cleared her throat and pointed at the note clutched in front of me. "What's that?"

"Just a note from my mother," I lied, turning away to tuck it back into the wrapping with the conduit. I settled the package in the locker and was swinging the door shut when Chandra stopped me.

"Hey! It's Tekla!" She pointed to the photo of my mother and her friend, which answered the question as to who the other woman in the photo was. And, I thought, might answer who the note was from as well. Who else but a woman with the Sight would speak of lending me her eyes?

In exchange for my voice, I corrected mentally, as Chandra and Vanessa crowded in closer. But what was I supposed to say on her behalf? And to whom? The knowledge was emerging inside me, I could feel it like the stirring of bees in a hive, but it was deep still, too remote to be understood. But . . .

There's a traitor among us.

I swallowed hard. That wasn't just the babbling of a madwoman, I thought. Tekla had known this was coming, and wanted my help.

"Your mother was beautiful," Vanessa said, turning to me. "I've always loved that photo."

My brows lifted before I could stop them. "You've seen it before?"

"Oh, sure. That's one of her trading cards." She shrugged, and tucked a loose curl behind her ear. "I guess she liked it as well."

"It seems so," I agreed, while nervousness grew inside me. I didn't really know either of these women, and since I was still trying to figure out what was so important about the items in this container, their studied gazes made me feel exposed. As if they were looking inside of me as well.

A traitor. Among us.

"What's that?" Chandra asked, pointing at the package, providing the opening I needed. With a flick of my wrist I slammed the locker shut.

"Nothing," I said coolly, and leaned against the door. It was nicely symbolic, if I did say so myself. "What're you guys doing up here?"

"Nothing," Chandra said, her voice like arctic ice.

"You guys," Vanessa sighed wearily, and left to open her own locker.

"I don't have time for this," Chandra muttered, heading back to the exit. "Meet you down there, okay, V?"

Vanessa nodded and rummaged around in her locker. "Tell the others. Just because Warren's gone doesn't mean we shouldn't do it."

"You got it." Chandra left, and now I was staring at Vanessa.

"What do you mean he's gone?" I asked, coming closer.

Vanessa shot me an irritated glance, and waved me out of her light. She'd sunk to the floor and was holding a rag in one hand and a can of oil in the other, alternately polishing and squirting at a steel club the width and length of my forearm. There was another piece of metal at her side that looked like nothing so much as a large nail file, but I didn't know for sure. More superhuman toys, and I'd had my fill for a while.

"I mean, he left an hour ago to retrieve Gregor," she said, bending close to her work. "If he's made the crossing, they'll be back soon. Otherwise they'll wait for dawn."

I bit my bottom lip, wishing I'd gotten to see Warren one more time before he'd left. I could've shown him this note.

And with us linked the way we were, he'd have known what happened to me in Greta's office as soon as he saw me. With just a look, one sniff, he'd know I was someone he could trust. We could have figured this out together.

Instead, I stood in frustrated impotence before Vanessa, all the newly acquired power and energy swirling in my bloodstream, flowing in my bones, straightening my spine . . . and with nothing to do with it. I sighed, attracting Vanessa's attention.

"You look different," she said, peering up at me as she picked up the large nail file. "Did you do something with your hair?"

I shook my head, and glanced toward the door. "He's really going to leave the city without protection?"

"Warren?" She shrugged, looking down, and pressed a button I hadn't noticed before. Five steel claws burst from one end of the bar. She began sharpening them with the large file. "That's what he said."

"But what about all the innocents? What about the city?"

"It'll just have to survive without us."

"It's Las Vegas," I said, drawing the words out.

"I know." Vanessa rolled her eyes as she tossed her rag back into the locker. "Kinda makes you wish you were born in Kansas, huh?"

I forced thoughts of Warren, and trust, aside and tried to decide on the most logical next step. Unfortunately, I hadn't thought that far ahead yet. "So what do we do now?"

"Nothing to do but wait," she said, standing and moving a safe distance away. With a deft flick of her wrist the steel bar arched open, a yawning half smile followed by the curling claws. It was a fan, similar to the kind used in the Victorian era, but far more deadly. She fanned herself delicately and glanced at me from behind it. "My conduit. You like?"

"It's beautiful," I said, allowing the touch of jealousy I felt to tinge my words.

That stunning smile lit her soft, round face as she flipped

it closed, pleased. Then she snuck another glance up at my face, and cleared her throat. "Listen, a few of us are meeting over in the cantina for drinks. Want to join us?"

I wrinkled my nose. "A cantina? You mean . . . like a superhuman kegger?"

She laughed at that, flipping her fan open and closed, slicing it through the air in a deadly dance of familiarity. "Yeah, I guess so."

I hesitated. I certainly didn't want to walk into a repeat of the day's earlier performance, me against them . . . because even though I sensed mistrust swirling between them, they were still unified in their uncertainty about me. Then again, going would give me a chance to study each of them individually. Nobody knew about my note from Tekla . . . or about my session with Greta. Vanessa was right. Why wait for Warren?

"You did really well today," she said, glancing over at me as I continued to remain silent. She put away the file in a large tool chest, and tucked the fan into the small of her back. "Not just against Chandra, but Hunter too. Most people find him too intimidating to effectively spar against."

"He *was* intimidating," I said, not adding: *Right up until the moment he pissed me off.*

"Well, you didn't look intimidated," she said, then paused. I could feel her choosing her words carefully. "You looked powerful. Frightening."

And there it was, out in the open. She shut her locker door, turning to me, and unlike in Saturn's Orchard, she met my eye. "Look, today, when we did nothing . . . I just want you to know we're not like that. We protect our own. We stick up for one another. We were just reacting, or not reacting, to the Shadow in you. I'm sorry things got out of hand. We all are."

I glanced at the double doors Chandra had just disappeared through and made a disbelieving sound.

Vanessa answered it with a sigh of her own. "Look, Chandra's one lifelong ambition has always been to serve this troop as the Archer. Every child of the Zodiac grows up dreaming of what it's like to be an agent of Light." She touched my arm, willing me to understand. "Your arrival here was a big blow to her, but she'll come around in time."

I remained unmoved, refusing to look her in the eye as I said, "She wants to vote me out of this troop. She called me a . . . an independent." *A rogue agent.*

Vanessa's impatience got the best of her and she snapped, "Yeah, and in doing so revealed her greatest fear. Because if you're this generation's Archer, what does that make her?"

I opened my mouth, before closing it again. Vanessa was right. Chandra might have the trust I so coveted from the rest of the troop, but she'd never be the person she aspired to be as long as I was living. I knew what that was like, not getting to be who you truly wanted.

I looked down, finding I was unconsciously rubbing at my arm. The puncture marks from Hunter's whip could still be seen there. Injuries from conduits, I remembered, always scarred. "I don't know if I can handle too many more training sessions like that," I said, letting a trace of my own vulnerability show through. It'd be interesting to see what Vanessa did with it. Interesting . . . and telling too.

"It's not just you, okay?" Vanessa glanced at the door to make sure Chandra had really left and no one else had arrived. "Things have been boiling over for weeks, months now. It's never been like this before, we were all raised together, and we keep putting on a front like everything's okay, but it's not. It's just . . . not."

"Because Tekla said there was a traitor?"

She hesitated before nodding. "And no matter how much Warren denies it . . . well, look around."

She gestured at the dormant glyphs, and the feeling of emptiness reached out to snag my attention again.

"Look, just come to the cantina," she said, voice soft and imploring. "Let us start over."

I'd have liked to have just said yes, but I had to wonder why she was being so open and friendly. I'd probably have jumped at the chance if only there wasn't one big question mark surrounding her. Could she be the traitor?

Only one way to find out, I thought, and because of that I gave her a nod that had her smiling as she led me from the locker room.

"What are you guys celebrating, anyway?" I asked, our heels clicking in tandem against the stone floors.

"We're not," she said. One hand on the frosted double doors, she sighed, and turned her head to stare past me, back into the cavernous room. Her gaze landed on the dead Scorpionic glyph, so dark her eyes were almost smudged. "We're remembering. It's been six months to the day since Stryker was killed." And she pushed open the door and disappeared.

The cantina was probably the most surprising room in the sanctuary so far, with couches in cubes of midnight velvet clustered around silver tables, the silver accenting echoed in the corner bar. As Vanessa made herself at home behind it, I looked up to find a ceiling glowing with stars, and shapes in the form of constellations—the Big Dipper, the Little, and others I recognized but couldn't name.

There was a fish tank spanning the length of one wall, its occupants floating around in colorful, blissful ignorance. The opposite wall held a flat screen television. Sting was crooning softly about watching every step I took, and I smiled as the steel candles on each table shot to life as Vanessa pushed a button. It was more ultralounge than cantina, I thought, sinking into a velvet chair and the feeling of being enveloped in a futuristic womb.

"The four elements," Vanessa said, gesturing around the room. "Fire, earth, water, air."

I frowned. I saw the air amid the stars above, fire in the slim candles, and water, obviously, represented by the fish tank. But earth? I looked to Vanessa.

She smiled wryly. "From dust to dust."

Us, I thought. We represented the earth, and the passing of all beings from it. Well, it certainly lent poignancy to the occasion.

"Maybe I shouldn't be here," I said, watching Vanessa stir one of two pitchers she'd filled with vodka, some sort of syrupy schnapps, and at least three other juices. The liquid was turning a disturbing shade of brown, like overbrewed ice tea, though Vanessa didn't seem worried.

"You're one of us now." Taking in my skeptical expression, she tapped the spoon on the side of the sink and set it down. "I mean it. You just have to let the others get used to it . . . uh, you. That can't happen if you seclude yourself away."

I knew that, of course. But somewhere from the locker room to here all my I-am-the-Archer-hear-me-roar power had trickled away, and the thought of sitting in this intimate little enclave with five people who needed to "get used to me" was less than inviting. "I don't want to intrude. I didn't know him."

"Well, I did, and he'd have liked you. Not just your looks, but your spirit." She placed one pitcher in the stainless steel refrigerator to chill, and brought the other, along with two tumblers, over to me. "Stryker said we reinvented ourselves every time we stepped outside the sanctuary. Your effort, he would say, just your intention in being here, should be met with respect for what you left behind. He'd want you here."

Her words settled me, so when she poured me a cup and held it out to me, I accepted it and sipped, tentatively. I took a larger swallow when I found it fruity and bright on the tongue, and it left my palate to settle gently in my belly with a low, glowing warmth. I'd stay. I'd watch. For a while anyway.

Then the door swung open and Chandra strode in, her brows burrowing down when she saw me. "What is she doing here?"

I didn't snap back because what Vanessa had told me about Chandra had softened me a bit . . . and the drink was slowing my tongue anyway.

"Looks like she's drinking," Felix said, following her in. He flashed me his boyish smile, but I could see the worry lingering beneath it. Worry over the occasion? Or, like Vanessa earlier, worried about me, frightened of me? I couldn't tell.

Micah wasn't far behind, and he beelined for me, bending over to check again that his handiwork had survived the afternoon, his own worries about me apparently resolved. But after a moment he cupped my chin, eyeing me curiously. "You look different somehow. Can't put my finger on it, though. Are you feeling okay?"

"Actually, I feel great. Like I just woke up from a long nap."

"Sounds auspicious," he said warily. I went ahead and watched him back. After a moment he blinked, then shrugged as he lowered himself into a seat, the bulk of him barely fitting between the armrests.

"If you believe in fairy tales." Chandra dropped her weight into a chair across from me, but I was saved from having to think of an Oliviaesque reply by Hunter's sudden appearance. He too paused when he saw me, and colors around him shifted from black to silver to gold as the energy spiked between us. I had no idea what that meant.

He settled himself next to Chandra, and I had a moment to think he'd be a joy to photograph. He was so composed in the flesh that a still shot wouldn't have made much of a difference from what I was seeing then, but at least I could study him at length—searching for what exactly ran beneath that still facade—without him knowing I was doing it. If, that was, I ever had the nerve to point my camera his way. "So. We're all here."

All save Warren and Gregor. And Tekla, came the unbidden thought, even though she wasn't supposed to count.

I took another sip of Vanessa's concoction, and looked around at what was left of Zodiac troop 175, paranormal division, Las Vegas.

"What do you all do?" I asked, suddenly curious. I wasn't just trying to ferret information out either. I really wanted to know. "On the outside, I mean?"

Warren was a bum, Gregor a cab driver. Olivia had been a socialite—I supposed that's what I was now—so it seemed the point was to plant Zodiac agents within the entire social spectrum of the Las Vegas valley; matched, I was sure, by the Shadow agents in one form or another. So what about everyone else? "I know Micah's a physician, but what about the rest of you? Who are you when you're not being . . . you?"

"College student," Felix offered, saluting. "UNLV."

"Yeah," scoffed Chandra. "For the past eight years."

"Hey, it's not my fault! Warren keeps making me change my major." He turned back to me and winked slyly. With his tousled hair and ready laugh, I could imagine him as the most popular guy on campus. "I keep an eye on our initiates, those close enough to metamorphosis to give off strong olfactory signals. I'm also on the lookout for the Shadow initiates. Fraternities, parties, clubs, that's where the young ones are most likely to be."

"Stryker was a crime scene analyst with Metro," Vanessa offered, lifting her cup, reminding us all why we were there. Cups were lifted all around. We drank to his memory, and Vanessa refilled the cups. "It was the perfect way to gain access to fresh kill spots."

Nobody spoke for a moment, and I knew they were remembering the warehouse where Stryker had been ambushed. A kill spot. I drank some more.

"Well," Micah finally said, shattering the silence. "We're not the only ones who've lost star signs this year. Chandra alone is responsible for two Shadow kills."

"Not me," she retorted, tipping her cup back. "I'm not a star sign, remember."

"You identified the suspects," Vanessa soothed.

"But Hunter took them out."

"We partner well together," he replied modestly. "Most fire signs do."

Spotting my confused expression, Micah expounded further. "Chandra works at Sky-Chem, the largest chemical lab in the state. She can use DNA to identify the Shadows or initiates who go searching for a job."

Chandra's lips pursed as her eyes went from Micah to me; she was fighting the urge to tell the story herself—doing so meant she'd have to speak to me—but pride ultimately won out. "I found the first one, their Capricorn star sign, through a urine sample when he applied as a bouncer at a strip club. It was easy for Hunter to go in after that, pretend he was there for the girls. The other was a hair test, the Shadow Virgo."

Hunter saluted her with his cup, a look passing between them, and as much as I disliked Chandra, I had to admit it was a brilliant cover. Every hotel in town sent their employees—and there were thousands—for mandatory drug testing; as did the government agencies, the police department, and the entertainment venues. Still, I wasn't ready to compliment her. I turned to Vanessa.

"And you?"

She leaned back, crossing her long legs. "Reporter for the *Las Vegas Sentinel*. Crime beat. See, Stryker would be first on a scene, analyze the evidence, and if it looked like a paranormal hit, he'd call me. He'd cover the case, search and bag all the otherworldly evidence, and I'd write it up in a palatable version for the mortals. So 'Agent of Light Takes Out the Shadows' Twelfth House' becomes 'West Las Vegas Man Hangs Himself in Garage.' That was one of my better ones." She toasted herself, draining her cup.

"I see," I said slowly, swirling my drink, watching as a small whirlpool formed there. I stilled the cup and glanced up at Vanessa. "Or 'Shadow Agents Track New Archer' turns into 'Heiress's Sister Plummets to Death.' "

The laughter immediately died from Vanessa's eyes. Shoulders slumping, she touched my arm, and I could see the others noting her acceptance. "I'm sorry. I shouldn't be joking. But it's all for the greater good, you see."

I nodded finally. It wasn't her fault, after all. I was just being overly sensitive, sentimental, and probably getting a little drunk. I needed to slow down and focus. "Well, it's a dirty job, but—"

"Yeah, something like that." We tapped our cups together. Chandra scowled, dipping her face in her own cup. The others also seemed well on their way to being truly shit-faced, but my own drink seemed to be turning on me, the sweetness now cloying in my mouth. I pushed my cup away and turned to Hunter. He was the only one not drinking. He was also the only one who hadn't answered yet. I raised a brow.

"Director of Security," and before I could ask, he added, "Valhalla."

I gaped at him, and now my mouth went dry. "You're trying to infiltrate the Archer organization? Like my mother did?"

The drink might have been making me a little slow, but I immediately recognized how easy it'd be to act as a liaison between the Light and Shadow sides if he literally worked for the Tulpa's organization.

"Not trying," he said, steepling his fingers. "I'm doing it."

And I didn't know if that was a jab at my mother or at me. He tossed me a half smile, also unreadable, but was clearly pleased at my obvious confusion.

"Someone has to," Chandra said.

"Chandra," Micah said in a warning voice. I sighed inwardly, but was careful not to let my fatigue show. I was getting better at hiding my emotions too.

Chandra's mouth quirked slightly at one side, but she gave no other sign of having heard him, and unlike Hunter and me, she wasn't trying to hide anything. Her eyes were swimming with drink, but that wasn't all. Deep pockets of hatred and resentment covered her entire psyche. I didn't even have to probe to see the mossy plum color radiating sickly around her. In her eyes I hadn't just usurped her place in the Zodiac, I'd stolen it out from under her. And her dreams of becoming this troop's Archer floated, dead and bloated, on the surface of her gaze whenever it lit upon me.

I caught Vanessa, her own silent gaze imploring me to let it go, so I stood, ostensibly to retrieve the other pitcher of alcohol, and with the half-drunken hope that when I returned with it, Chandra would do the same, or at least have found something more interesting to look at. But she was still there, sneering as women had sneered at Olivia so often before. Judging as they had. She held out her cup for me to serve her, then had the nerve to say, "Your mother failed us all when she deserted her star sign. And look who she deserted it for. What a waste."

The contents of the pitcher I was holding—fruit bits, sweet and sticky, citrus-infused alcohol, ice chips—were poured over her head. It was my turn to sneer, but she was standing and had slapped the satisfaction off my face before I even saw her move.

"Girl fight," I heard Felix say.

"Superhero girl fight," I corrected, and wheeling back, steered an elbow into her temple. The force of my action turned me around on myself, so I followed it up with a backward elbow to the nose. Chandra staggered, as surprised at this as I'd been at the slap, but she didn't fall, and the drunken brawl was on.

She lunged, but Felix was quicker, intercepting her just as neatly as Hunter stalled my own forward motion. Chandra and I both struggled and cursed, continuing a bit just for form's sake, though neither of us had a chance of getting loose.

"Ladies, ladies," Hunter said, sounding bored.

I slammed my head back against him, satisfied when I heard him grunt. Petty, but pleasing. And he let me go.

"I am finished apologizing for who I am," I said, jerking away from him and whirling to face them all. Chandra wasn't the only one who needed to know this. I was breathing hard, and I knew my aura had turned red with anger. "Your discomfort with me is your problem, not mine. Got it? I know who I am."

And I did. I could be beautiful without being soft, and I could be tough without being bitter. Without becoming Olivia, without experiencing the world through her body and eyes, I would have never realized this on my own. I folded my arms across my chest and silently dared them all to speak.

"Finally," Micah murmured from his corner, lifting his drink.

"Yeah." My eyes flickered to meet his. "Finally."

A gurgle sounded in my stomach. Then a rising of heat in my gorge. Suddenly, I shuddered, and my intestines seized. Pain wracked my body, and I screamed, collapsing and clutching my loins. A searing pain shot from my thighs to my chest, paralyzing my lower back, and I whipped forward. *God, what was in that drink?* The thought swam away as another series of slashing incisions, like hot pokers, scored my flesh. I felt singed and sliced as I curled into myself, my rasping cry dying out in breathless pain.

"What's happening to her?"

I gave an uncontrollable twitch, then puked vodka, citrus, and blood.

"Jesus!"

"Olivia! What's wrong?" Felix was there, but his outline blurred above me, tears and agony ruining my vision.

My organs felt skewered, like they'd been ripped out from inside me. I had to be dying, I thought. I *hoped.* "God," I cried out, and this time arched backward as an invisible blade bumped along my spine.

"It's inside. It's my insides . . ." I looked at my hands, which had been clutching abdomen and thighs, expecting to see them drowning in blood, but there was nothing. Surprise had my mouth closing momentarily. The pain abated, no longer acute, but the spasms and heat lingered. A groan spiraled out of me, filling the cantina.

Micah had reached me at some point, and I regained my sense of self long enough to realize he was cradling my head in his lap, his physician's hands searching, inspecting my ribs and stomach and legs, and finding nothing.

"It's not me!" I doubled over again, a fresh wound cutting me open from sternum to pubic bone. It wasn't me, of that much I was sure. This was a power outside myself, outside this room too. Still, waves of nausea built again in my stomach. I took a deep breath, but the air was metallic with the taste of blood. I groaned, writhed, and finally, near unconsciousness, lay still.

"It's okay. Just stay where you are, take a minute." Micah shifted, turning to the others, though I couldn't see them. "Somebody go get Greta." There were footsteps, then the report of the door.

"She's not bleeding." Hunter's voice, laced with concern, which would've been gratifying if it didn't scare the shit out of me.

"Maybe she drank too much."

The pain had subsided, but the echo of it was still in my bones. I swallowed hard against the vomit souring my throat and the brighter scents of pain and fear.

"Maybe she's allergic to the masking pheromones?"

"No, I tested the solution on a small patch of skin before I applied it. They're a perfect match."

It didn't feel perfect, I wanted to say, but a tongue of swollen sandpaper inhabited my mouth. It was as if I'd been denied drink for a week instead of imbibing only minutes before.

Then the roil in my gut again, a tight coil of fear that wasn't really mine. I couldn't understand it. It was like the core of my body belonged to someone else. I managed to sit up with Micah's help, his large palm warm and supporting on the small of my back.

"Maybe she—"

The door to the cantina swung open with a resounding bang. A figure was silhouetted in the shadows of the hall; a man of great bulk, middling height, and only one arm. The dim lights of the cantina made him appear a ghost, and bent at the waist, he wavered like one as well.

"Gregor!" Vanessa abandoned me for him. "God! What happened?"

"Ajax," he managed, before bending over himself. My body froze, even my shuddering stopped for an instant, and my eyes darted to the hallway behind him, half expecting to see Ajax there, the tip of his flaming javelin already pointed at my heart. "He found me last night, just after dusk. I don't know how . . . I didn't do anything . . . I didn't—"

"Shh," Vanessa said, arm over his shoulders. "Of course you didn't. Come sit down."

"I can't . . ." He looked up at us with as pained an expression as I'd ever seen on another human being. "I can't keep them in."

I glanced down, unprepared for what supernatural beings could do to another nonmortal. His guts spilled forward, bulging from the hollow of his body, pink coils of twisting organs snaking from the cavity. His one good arm was plastered with blood.

"Oh, my God!" Micah left me so quickly I wobbled, then puked again, this time with shock and revulsion.

"I'll take care of you," I heard Micah say over my retching. "Don't worry about a thing."

"Did you see Warren?" Hunter asked. He was the only one who appeared remotely calm. I wondered if he was still reclined in his seat, ankle crossed over his knee, a detached observer. I couldn't look, though. My eyes—like everyone's—were fastened on Gregor.

His face collapsed upon itself, and red-tinged saliva bubbled from his mouth. "They used me as bait. He tracked my pheromones."

The room fell dead silent.

"And Warren wouldn't listen." He was sobbing now, mouth wide. "I tried to tell him no, not to do it, but he never listens."

"What? What did he do?"

"He traded himself for me." Stunned by this news, nobody moved. Another helpless sob escaped him. "They let me go, but I was followed. I'm so sorry. I couldn't close off the entrance to the boneyard by myself. And there was nobody to close it behind me."

I gathered it was no small thing for a Shadow agent to infiltrate the boneyard. Still, what did it matter? Any enemy who tried to enter the sanctuary would fry, right? I opened my mouth to say as much, but another fiery assault wracked my body. My eyes bulged painfully from their sockets, my throat stretched and burning in a soundless cry. And I no longer cared about the sanctuary.

"They're torturing him," Micah said, kneeling next to me. "He and Olivia are linked, remember? She must be experiencing the residual effects."

If this was residual, I never wanted to feel the real thing. Another slice, and I squeezed my eyes so tight spots danced there. I came out of it in time to catch the end of Gregor's words. "—because he knows her true identity. We have to hand her over at dawn—"

"Or they'll kill Warren," Hunter finished for him. This time I did turn, arching my neck to find him. He sat back in his chair, eyeing me dispassionately, sizing me up like I was a sow to be sold at the country fair. I closed my eyes, wondering how I had ever thought him handsome.

"We can't send her up, even if we wanted to," Vanessa said. "She'll incinerate herself before she even breathes fresh air."

"Wha . . . ?" Gregor grimaced. Felix quickly filled him in, and Gregor dropped his head back, groaning. I doubled over again.

"Stop it!" I screamed, to the sky, to Warren, to the

torturers, and to a God I didn't even know existed. I screamed until my throat was raw, and when I finished, a chuckle whispered like a heavy, bouncing wind across the room. Then the torture stopped. We all stared at one another.

"Your voice," Hunter said quietly, eyes narrowed on my face. "Ajax heard it."

"They're linked," Micah repeated.

I thought of Warren, the way he'd left that afternoon; agitated, angry, afraid. *I won't lose another!* And I realized this must have been foretold. Of course, a man who believed the good of the troop came before that of the individual would do just that. He'd have known, and he'd have gone anyway.

"Oh, my God," Micah said, realizing the same thing. He lowered his head into his hands, Gregor's blood staining his temples and forehead and ears. "Ajax has been one step ahead of us the whole time."

I conjured the image, my last, of Warren striding down the hall, trench coat billowing at his ankles, the need to do the right thing driving his limbs. My heart sank as I looked at everybody's face. If this was a game, I thought, clutching my gut, we were one move away from losing it all.

23

Felix and Micah helped me back to my room, where Greta lit candles and some spicy incense to thicken the air, and gave me a pill to block the connection between Warren and me.

"You need your rest," she told me as I swallowed it, feeling both relief and guilt as I did so. "Concentrate on building a mental wall between Warren and yourself. Protect your thoughts and feelings from those who are probing at him to get to you. That's more important even than blocking the pain."

Easy for you to say, I thought, eyes following her from the room. But the smoke from the incense interceded after that, floating between the synapses in my brain, taking the edge from my worries.

"Warren would want that," Rena added, and I glanced over to where she sat in the corner, rocking in a chair she'd brought in from her own room. "You can bet he's doing the same."

The destroyed craters where her eyes should have been had turned to black pools in the candlelight. All her other charges were tucked in bed for the night, and she'd offered to tend to me while what remained of the troop convened in the briefing room. I knew what they were doing; talking about me, around me, but—once again—not to me. I wondered hazily which of them would cast the deciding vote . . . and how soon before I was kicked out of the sanctuary. Sacrificed for the sake of their leader.

"You should be meditating," Rena said, as if that would solve everything as she leaned back in her chair.

"The meditation exercises aren't working," I told her, managing to work up a snarl, but paid for it when my intestines filled with fire.

"That's because you're not doing them," she said lightly as I pressed back into my pillows, writhing until the burning subsided.

When it finally felt like all I had was a mean case of heartburn, I glanced back at her with watery eyes. "They're going to vote me out, aren't they? They hold me responsible for Warren's capture."

She shook her head, but it was a defeated rather than reassuring gesture. "No, Olivia. The Shadows orchestrated this, just as they've orchestrated every heartbreak we've ever had to endure." She dropped her head back, seeming to deflate where she sat, before adding, "And Warren did this too. He always does."

This last bit was said with a sort of long-standing resignation, and I'd have tried to read her aura, but I was too tired, groggy with the smoke rising in the air between us, and too afraid it would cause me more needless pain. I also wanted to ask what she meant, but was afraid I'd get more mumbling about Warren's secrets—as Micah had done—or protestations that it wasn't her story to tell, as Greta had claimed. So, instead, I asked a different question.

"How'd Warren get his limp?"

Her rocker creaked to a halt. I swallowed hard, but didn't fill the silence lengthening between us. Rena had seen

Warren through his first life cycle; if anyone knew about him and his past, it was she. And though there were larger questions than this niggling at me, this one seemed innocuous enough to start with, so I waited silently for her to tell me what she would.

"His father gave it to him."

I'd jolted, causing fire to light along my spine. It reminded me that sudden movements were a bad idea, but I'd been expecting anything but that. "But . . . but only . . ."

"Conduits can leave lasting disfigurement, yes." She grimaced, rocking harder. It didn't look comforting. "Have you noticed Warren doesn't carry a personal weapon?"

She went on, though she couldn't see my nod.

"He wouldn't touch the Taurean conduit after his father used it against him . . . and after he, in turn, used it against his father."

And what she told me next was more than I'd ever have guessed about the man who was so absurd one moment, so serious the next.

Samson Clarke hadn't been the first choice for his generation's Taurus. Another agent, a woman named Mia, had possessed that star sign, though Samson gained it after the Shadows ambushed her in a drainage tunnel leading to the Las Vegas wash. He avenged Mia's death over the next few years, taking out two of the Shadows who'd trapped her in that tunnel, and helping his peers kill a third. Meanwhile, he'd taken up with the younger sister of the Arien Light, and Warren was born shortly thereafter.

The birth of a son, rather than a daughter, had been a disappointing blow to Samson, one he never hid from the scrawny child growing up, literally, in his father's shadow. Never one to let a little thing like monogamy stop him, Samson cast Warren's mother aside and set his sights on someone who'd already proven herself capable of producing a daughter. The leader's mate. When she rejected him outright, rather than deciding it had anything to do with him, or her distaste for the way he'd so faithlessly treated Warren's mother, he decided it was because he wasn't powerful enough for her. Yet.

Rena sighed, and if she had eyes, they'd have been unfocused, looking through the present and the smoke from the incense filling up the room, while vividly reliving the distant past. "So he tried to take the position of troop leader for himself."

But Samson Clarke talked in his sleep. Warren, who'd been charged with straightening his father's room and tidying his belongings at the end of each day—including sharpening his conduit—discovered the details of his plot over a period of several days. His fear of his father's wrath, plus a desire to please him despite the years of neglect Samson had shown him, kept him from saying anything to the other star signs. But on the night his father attacked the troop leader, Warren suddenly discovered the courage to stand up to Samson . . . and nearly had his legs cleaved out from under him for the effort.

"The leg wound is a reminder of the night he killed his father," Rena told me, her voice carefully absent of emotion, "and, though he doesn't ever say it, it's also a reminder that he failed to save the real troop leader."

And yet the others still rewarded him with the Taurean star sign, and later with the troop leadership, ironically giving Warren what his father had been so desperate to possess.

I laid where I was, mind still hazy from the incense, but more numb from the telling. Warren's own father had betrayed him. After a moment more I found my voice, though my mouth was sandpaper dry. "Why couldn't Samson just have worked for the title of troop leader? He was obviously a good agent. Couldn't he have made it there, eventually, on his own?"

"He wasn't lineally qualified," Rena said, her chair squeaking beneath her as she rocked. "He was born an independent."

"A rogue agent?" I blurted before I could stop myself. "I mean—"

She smiled wryly and waved off my stuttering. "He absolutely personified the term."

Because though the Shadows had technically killed Mia, Samson Clarke was the one who'd pointed them her way.

"Ah, Olivia," Rena sighed, when my horrified gasp filled the room. "Just because agents of Light are . . . super, other, *more*, if you will, doesn't mean we don't have the same shortcomings as the humans we protect. Warren's father was abnormally ambitious for an agent of Light. Being stronger than mortals—than most agents on either side of the Zodiac, even—wasn't enough for him. He'd ascended from nothing into the position of the Taurean star sign, but he wanted more."

And he'd wanted it enough to go from merely wishing for leadership to maiming his own son.

I thought of the way Warren nearly snarled each time someone mentioned the independents. "It's why he couldn't trust me fully, even though he wanted to."

Rena made a sound of agreement, before adding, "And it's why every death he fails to stop is a sign in his eyes that he doesn't deserve to be leader. That his lineage—the son of a vicious rogue agent—means he's a failure before he's even started."

No wonder he was so willing to sacrifice himself for Gregor. For us all.

"What about the rest of them, then?" I asked. "What are they going to do now?"

"What they were born to do, of course," Rena answered, folding her hands and leaning back. "They're going to save him."

"But the Shadow agents are waiting for them in the boneyard." My eyes roved over her face. Surely there was a better plan than that. Even I could see that turning me over to the Shadows was a far better alternative. "They said themselves that the entire Zodiac will be completely wiped out."

"Without Warren, it is anyway," she said, a sigh floating from her. She patted her hair, an unconscious, nerve-filled gesture, since not a strand was out of place.

I frowned, because a woman so protective of her children shouldn't sound this defeated. "And what do we do?"

"We hope. Pray. If that's not enough, we wait until the next batch of initiates is ready." Her voice was soft, almost drowsy, but the scent of nightmares accompanied it, not dreams. "Not long, half a decade at most. Then we rise again."

"But they'll die!" I said, catching myself before I sat up.

"Yes." And her own head fell. "They'll all die."

And now I did shoot up in bed. My diaphragm burned and the heat rose like smoke to my gorge, but it was bearable. "How can you sit there so calmly and just let them go?"

Stiffening, Rena's rocking abruptly stopped, and I swear if she had eyes she'd have been glaring holes through me. "It kills me to think of Warren out there now, suffering. He's a favorite of mine. Always was. But there's nothing I can do save discipline and train the next batch to be stronger and better and smarter than the last. To teach them where this group went wrong . . . and where I went wrong with them."

I stared at her in disbelief. "You blame yourself?"

"A mother always does." Then, more softly, "Even a blind old surrogate like myself."

I didn't know what to say to that, and so the minutes ticked by, marked by the clock next to my bed, the soft glow of numbers finally blurring as my fatigue rose. The candlelight was relaxing, the incense finally doing its trick, and I would have fallen under, probably waking when it was all over, if it weren't for the sob that escaped the darkened corner.

"I always have to let them go," Rena said, voice cracking in naked emotion. "Just sit here. Sit on my hands, even if those hands are clenched in fists."

I swallowed away my fatigue and turned my head back to her in the faint candlelight. She looked like a battle-scarred angel in her shapeless robe; lost and, for a woman with so many charges in her care, entirely alone. "Would you go? If you could, I mean?"

"I would sacrifice myself for each of them, over and over," she said, every word solid and sure. She straightened in her chair. "I would take that pain in your gut and wrap it around myself so tightly it could never get loose and touch one of my children again. I would burn my eyes from my sockets every day from now to death if it meant saving even one."

"Because you're a mother, and that's what a mother does," I said, nodding, thinking of my own. Not that any of her sacrifices had ultimately mattered. Here I was, trapped, and as much at the mercy of these people as I'd been at Joaquin's hands years earlier.

"No," Rena said, surprising me. I squinted at her in the dim light. "Don't you get it yet? It's because I'm Light, and that's what we do. That's what Warren did for Gregor, what he's doing for you. It's why the rest of them are willing to sacrifice themselves for him."

Because he was Light.

"Oh, my God." I blinked once, my heart thumped twice, and I slowly rose to a sitting position in bed, careful not to let the dizziness pooling in my head topple me again. "That's it."

Rena started, and her rocking faltered. "What?"

I felt a leap in my belly as I leaned over and flipped on the light, and I felt my own excitement transmuted, knowledge registering with Warren. I snuffed what remained of the incense, reached for the water on the nightstand, and touched the glass to my cheek to cool the skin. Then I drank deeply to clear my mind, dousing what I could of the flame in my belly and ignoring the rest. Snagging my duffel bag, I rifled through it, pulling out the first dark article of clothing I could find. It was a black cat suit, half cotton, half nylon, and deplorably low-cut, but that couldn't be helped.

"He's of the Light. *They're* of the Light."

They'll take away my voice.

The pieces were coming together rapidly now, but it felt like a slow progression, like the evenly spaced ticking of a clock when I was already running out of time.

"My God, why didn't I see it before?" See it, I thought, and almost giggled.

My eyes for your voice.

"Where are you going?" Rena asked, leaning forward when she heard the rustling of my clothes. I rushed past her into the bathroom, where I knotted my hair messily at the nape of my neck and splashed cool water on my face, clearing my senses further. I was going to need help, I thought, glancing back at her through the mirror. What I had to do was near impossible. What I had to prove was unbelievable, even to me.

"Not me. Us," I said, returning to the doorway. I stared down at her, and she was so focused on me I would've sworn she could see me. She rose, face inches from mine. "It's time to stop your rocking and praying, Rena," I told her, grabbing her hand. "We're going to go save your favorite son."

24

Sneaking across an entire compound of supernatural beings was a tricky business, though simplified by the knowledge that the handful of people I most needed to avoid were either sequestered away like a hung jury or taking turns in last minute sessions with Greta, mentally preparing them for the battle to come. It was this that gave me confidence as I steered down a sick ward as empty and hushed as a morgue. This, I thought, and a note I was sure Tekla had written me just after her son had died.

Obviously I didn't have a key to her room—her cell—but the viewing window on the door should help, and my plan was to get her attention by tapping lightly on that. Not loudly enough to draw anyone else's curiosity, I hoped, but sufficiently hard to call her close so she might tell me what to do next. I just prayed she'd respond to me a little more favorably than last time.

I pressed against walls, crouching around corners, and narrowly avoided running straight into Hunter, apparently on his way to his session with Greta. I watched as he knocked on her door, and had to duck back around the corner when he whirled to sniff suspiciously at the air. Then I heard the door open and Greta's voice welcoming him inside.

I peeked again. The only light in the entire corridor was the glow eking from the office's shaded window. Tekla's room, diagonal to that, was utterly dark. I suspected I had ten minutes, perhaps less, before the next agent arrived for their session, and while it seemed enough time, I'd be standing in plain view for the duration. Even ten seconds was enough to ruin it all.

When the light in Greta's office dimmed, I made my move. My boots echoed on the tile like gunshots, but keeping my nervous energy contained so no one would detect my presence through anything but direct sight was a far greater concern.

Reaching the door, I shook the handle. Locked, of course. For a moment I considered taking it as a sign. Who knew what I would find beyond that door? Tekla might be completely mad by now. Frothing at the mouth, rocking in a corner. I was taking a big chance on what amounted to nothing more than a hunch on my part. Then again, as Rena had said after I told her what I intended to do, if what I thought was true, I'd be taking a bigger chance by doing nothing at all. So I took a deep breath and turned to peer into the window.

Two great brown eyes stared back, inches from my own. I screamed, muffling the sound with my palm, hoping it wasn't too late. The brown eyes rolled in response to my girly reaction, and I dropped my hand, embarrassed. Not only was Tekla not frothing, she had apparently been waiting for me. I swallowed my fear and embarrassment and stepped back up to the glass.

Clarity. That's what I saw there. Not the lunacy I'd been told to expect, or the grief immortalized on the pages of Stryker's comic. Not the helplessness and pleading that'd shadowed her gaze the day before. There was a hint of fury, and bitterness, I saw, pulling her mouth tight, but more than anything there was a ferocious lucidity. In that singular look I saw exactly why Tekla had been locked away. And what my role was in all this.

"Can you hear me?"

No, but I can read lips, Tekla mouthed back. She went on, her mouth exaggerating the words so I could read them, but I was distracted by the sound of pounding feet and looked away.

"Shit." I pulled my conduit from the top of my left boot, palming it, wondering even as I did what I intended to do with it. Tekla must have wondered too. Her large, expressive doe eyes widened and her mouth moved again.

"What?" I asked, leaning closer. The pounding, more than one pair of feet, was growing closer.

She pointed at me, her index finger tapping on the glass, and repeated herself. It looked like she wanted me to shoot myself. I shook my head, indicating I didn't understand. Just then Micah and Chandra rounded the corner, their own conduits held out in front of them.

"Olivia!" Micah shouted at me. "Get back!"

Chandra, holding what looked to be a normal gun, had drawn on me. Her eyes were expressionless, but still cold.

"We have to let Tekla out."

"What you have to do is get away from that door," Chandra ordered. "Now."

I swallowed hard, but didn't move.

"Olivia, Tekla is sick."

"No, she's not."

"You looked in her eyes, didn't you?" Micah lowered his weapon, which was good, but took a step toward me, which wasn't. I sighted on him, and he took back that step. "Damn it, Olivia. That's why we don't want anyone down here. That's why the doors to the sick ward are supposed to be kept shut." He and Chandra both glared at one another. "She's ill, but she's still powerful enough to influence a weaker mind. She can make you believe she's all right, but as soon as we release her, she starts ranting again."

"Maybe she's telling the truth."

"Just step away from the door." He was speaking to me in the same voice people used to coax jumpers from ledges, and it made me grind my teeth. I might be insane, but it wasn't because I'd looked at Tekla.

"Maybe she's not crazy," I continued, concentrating on keeping my arm steady, "and she's really just pissed off because no one will listen to her."

"Get away from the goddamned door!" Chandra yelled, voice deepening as she dropped into a shooter's stance, and I knew she would shoot me.

Because if you're this generation's Archer, what does that make her?

A rogue agent, I thought, swallowing hard as I stared down the barrel of her gun. And rogue agents killed their matching star signs, just so they could usurp them in the Zodiac.

"Chandra," Micah said, turning toward her.

She didn't look at him, just continued staring down her arm at me. "Put down your weapon and get away from the door."

I flicked my gaze at the window, but Tekla had disappeared. Back to Chandra, then, whom even Micah looked wary of. "Okay," I said, which had her looking surprised . . . and not a little disappointed. "Just answer one question first."

"What?"

"Micah injected Warren with a compound containing my pheromones. That's how we're linked, right? Chandra, are you able to create such a compound?"

"Of course."

"That's what I thought," I murmured, and lowered my conduit.

Micah tilted his head. "What are you talking about?"

"She doesn't know," Chandra snapped, taking a step forward. "And she isn't supposed to be here."

"With the chemicals from your lab and a little knowledge, could I do the same?"

"Yes," Micah said cautiously, brows drawing low.

"No," Chandra shot back. "It's not just a little knowledge, it's the *right* knowledge. This isn't like makeup application. It's called chemistry."

I nodded absently. "How did you know I was here?"

If Micah was perplexed by my quickly shifting subjects, he didn't show it. In fact, he seemed to sense direction behind the questioning, which there was, though I was making up the details as I went along. "We were alerted the moment you touched the door."

"Alerted how?"

"What's going on here?" Greta emerged from her office, followed by a heavy-eyed Hunter. "Chandra? Micah?"

"Alerted how?" I repeated, louder, eyes lingering on Hunter for a few moments. He rubbed a hand over his face, hard, then studied the rest of us like we were part of a dream he expected to wake from at any moment.

"We have a sensor on the door handle," Chandra said to me. I could tell she was humoring me, answering my questions until they closed the distance between us. They weren't too far off now. "Greta decided it would be the surest way to keep the general population safe."

"Greta did, did she," I murmured, and my eyes locked on hers.

"What are you doing down here, Olivia?" she asked, her voice a tad too sharp. "You're not well."

"Not well?" I repeated, as if the words made no sense. "Not well like Tekla? That kind of 'not well'?"

Chandra made an impatient sound in her throat, almost a growl. "Olivia looked her in the eyes. I told you we should have covered that window."

"Tekla can 'see' what's being done with Warren," I said, noting Hunter had regained his bearings. He was watching me in that silent way of his, eyes narrowed as they moved from my face to the conduit in my right hand. "We need her in order to locate him."

"Nonsense," said Greta. "She hasn't spoken any sense in months."

"Because somebody ordered her to be locked in a five-by-ten-foot cell, not to be seen or heard by anyone! Somebody has taken away her voice!" And with four people looking at me like I was crazy, I was beginning to understand what that felt like.

"You're confused, dear," Greta said, her voice soothing and light. "Looking directly into Tekla's eyes will do that to you."

"No. I'm not," I said evenly. "Just the opposite, in fact. I looked into Tekla's eyes and for the first time everything became clear."

She looked at me for a long, silent moment. They all did.

"I should have figured it out sooner. But, you know, everyone here trusts you so much." I laughed at the irony of that. "Trusts you more than they even trust themselves."

"What are you talking about?" Greta was forced to ask, but I could tell she knew. I explained it anyway, so the others would know too.

"I'm talking about the way you suggested to *someone* that I might like to read the day's news, news that contained information that would hurt me. News that would send me running right to you." I started walking toward her, my footsteps a deep and even beat, projecting more confidence than I felt with Chandra's gun still pointed at my chest. "You wanted to hypnotize me, get in my mind just like you've done with everybody else. But there was only one problem. My mother was already there."

"You bitch. We don't have to listen to this!" Chandra was rattled, her eyes traveling between Greta and me, and I knew I was right about the paper. But she'd also raised her arms again, and mortal weapon or not, at that distance it would make her point. As the hallway filled with the remaining star signs, however—Vanessa supporting Gregor as they emerged from his sick room, Felix just behind—Chandra became less and less of a threat. So I remained focused on the woman who'd been a threat to them all.

"I don't think I'd have put it together if it weren't for the nightmares. I've never had them before. I've never seen the Tulpa, so I couldn't fear him enough to have him lunging out at me in my dreams. I certainly haven't ever allowed myself to dream about my past. But you opened all that up with your own special blend of alchemy. Chemistry, some call it. Let me ask you, when was the last time someone visited your office that you didn't offer them a spot of tea?"

Greta's mouth opened, but I didn't let her answer. It wasn't really a question meant for her anyway. I could see the others puzzling it out as I began inching her way, though. "It's so easy to plant mistrust in the minds and psyches of people who have full trust in you, isn't it, Greta? They come to you after their greatest fears have erupted in their nightmares, and you cement those fears with your little *sessions.*" I halted, directly across from her, and folded my arms, my conduit still at hand. "You're all looking at the reason your Zodiac has been depleted. Greta's true role here is as a mole."

"Bullshit!" Chandra exploded, and her trigger finger trembled.

"Olivia." Micah's patient voice barely masked his annoyance. It was the voice a parent would use on a naughty child. "Greta has never left the compound. Not in two years."

I lifted a shoulder. "The perfect cover."

Hunter moved in, clear-gazed now, which would've been a good thing if he weren't eyeing me like a hawk. "You're going to have to give us more than that."

"Hold the hermaphrodite off long enough and I'll give you much more." The pistol was precariously close to my temple. I swallowed hard and waited, knowing my fate swung on these next few moments alone.

"Chandra. Stand down."

"What?" she exploded, whirling on Gregor, who had straightened as much as he could. "I can't believe we're listening to this! In less than two hours we're going to battle with every Shadow in town." Her breathing was ragged as she cocked the gun. "I say we start with this one."

Holding still as stone, I fixed my eyes on a point just above her head, not wanting to see when she pulled the trigger.

"What you're going to do is stand down," Gregor said, his words spaced as deliberately as notes on a music sheet. "I'm in charge when Warren isn't here, and the reason he's not here is because he traded his own life for mine. If Olivia has something to say that'll help get him back alive, then you will damn well stand down! Now!"

His voice had risen, and ricocheted down the cavernous hall, echoing before dying away. I looked at him, standing there with only one arm protruding from his shapeless hospital gown, and the humor I so readily associated with him was nowhere to be found. He would've looked more the part of ailing patient if his stocky legs weren't spread wide and his single hand weren't curled in a fist. I thought of what Warren had said about him being the most senior agent left, and knew if I could get him to hear me out, the others would follow suit. Chandra's barrel shook as it slid away from my body.

Then, from an ally I'd never have expected, I heard, "All right. I'll play."

Hunter shot me a raw, distant smile as I turned to him. "Your hypothesis is that Greta never leaves the sanctuary, therefore she can never be suspected of betrayal, right?"

"Never leaves," I corrected, "because she can't. Like me, she's unable to exit through the chute. The Shadow side is too dark inside of her now."

"I can't leave because I'm totally vulnerable up there."

Greta's voice was reasonable, as if she were leading a group therapy session. My gaze flickered her way, narrowing at the way her hands played uncertainly with the pearls around her neck, but I had to give it to her. She had her role down pat. "They would find me and hunt me down within a week."

I blinked at her. "If you haven't noticed, Greta, this is a suicide mission. And no one else seems particularly concerned with their own lives. Aren't you the one who told me that duty comes before all else? If something's not good for the organization then it's simply not done. If it is—such as going after our troop leader—then everything is done to make sure it succeeds." I shot them all a mirthless smile. "A true follower of Light, agent or not, would sacrifice everything if it meant saving this troop. Rena convinced me of that."

"Would you?" Chandra said, arms folded across her chest. It looked like she was fighting to keep from reaching out and strangling me.

I looked at her coolly. "I'm doing it right now."

"So how'd she get down here?" Hunter continued, with his usual single-mindedness, something I was grateful for at the moment. I blew out a hard breath as I turned back to him, and chose my words carefully. He didn't look like a man who gave people a second chance.

"She's half mortal. The other half is Light. Choices, however," I told him before turning back to Greta, "can be made for either side."

I saw Felix shaking his head from the corner of my eye. "So how does she tell the Tulpa who we are, then?"

Chandra frowned and turned on him like he was traitorous, but he just shrugged as he met her gaze, his eyes quickly returning to me. "She doesn't. She marks you. After she gets you into her office, she alters your scent during hypnosis so the Shadow agents can locate you when you've left the sanctuary."

"Not possible," Chandra spit out, shaking her head.

"You just said it was possible. You said with the chemicals from your lab and a little knowledge—"

"The *right* knowledge—"

"Which you and Micah have," I said, anger overtaking my fear for the first time. She was just opposing me as a matter of course. Well, fuck that. I jerked my head at her. "Where do you keep it? Notebook?"

"No. Nowhere anyone can find it."

"Folder? Filing cabinet? Microfiche?"

"No, you idiot!" she exploded, brows slamming together. "In our minds!"

I raised my chin. "And who has access to your minds?"

Her mouth opened, faltered, and closed. I looked around, meeting every eye, letting the silence grow heavy in the hallway. "Not just your minds, but your laboratories, and not just your labs, but the sick ward. And in the sick ward is the one woman who knows the truth." I turned away from Chandra to face Greta again, whose color had risen to spot her cheeks in uneven blotches. "Why don't you tell them the real reason you locked Tekla away?"

She twisted her pearls in her hands like she was counting off rosaries, and her voice was deliberately meek when she spoke. "She broke, inside, when Stryker was killed. Her mind weakened and she couldn't discern reality from fantasy."

I shook my head, said to the others, "She didn't get weaker. She got stronger. More intuitive, more talented. The Zodiac lineage is matriarchal, so the power released when Stryker died reverted back to Tekla. So, isn't it interesting this was when Greta had Tekla committed? Locked up in a soundless room, not to be seen or heard by anyone. Nobody, that is, but Greta herself."

"Warren put her away!" Greta said, that cool voice rising.

"Uh-huh." I nodded my head. "And who planted that suggestion in his mind?"

I waited, but nobody spoke. A good sign, and I turned

back to Greta with a grim smile. "You waited two years, biding your time, gaining confidences, winning trust. Learning what you could from Chandra and Micah, preparing for Stryker's metamorphosis. Then, after you used his death and Tekla's grief to secure her position for yourself, it was easy to mark the rest. You had access to all their files—their horoscopes, their natal charts and lineages—so you knew how to enter their minds. Ply them with a little tea, get their own imaginations stirred up, and you ensured they'd come to you for hypnosis."

"God," someone breathed.

"You took away Tekla's son and then you took away her gift, her talent." I found I was breathing hard. "You took away her voice."

There was a long pause, silence while each person took this in, considered it, and while Greta looked around, waiting for someone to speak up in reply. I couldn't read anyone's aura—emotions were too high, the air a roiling mix of gaseous color—but I didn't have to in order to watch Greta's color rise. She squared on me and took up her own defense.

"If I took away her voice," she said, her own growing hard, "then how was she able to accuse you of being a traitor just yesterday?"

"She wasn't accusing me. She was using what was left of her faculties, after being pumped full of enough drugs to fell an elephant, to beg me to find the traitor. Funny how she had to stop after you pumped her up yet again. Funny how that's when the Tulpa was able to use her psionic powers to get through to me."

The first flicker of fear crossed Greta's face, and her voice was child-light. "How can you say these awful things to me?"

I looked again and saw it wasn't fear. It was Shadow. I smiled. "Because *I'm* her voice now."

The false outrage dropped from Greta's face. She spun to face the others. "Tekla was the Seer. A full-fledged member of the Zodiac troop, and far more powerful than any half mortal. Why didn't she speak out against me? Why, if she knew who I was, would she say nothing?"

They all looked to me.

I pulled Stryker's comic from behind my back, lifted it and opened it to the page I'd already marked. They'd all been there, of course. They knew what had happened. But I watched as fresh grief spread through their faces, and on the page Tekla rose in a gown bloodied by her son's death, screaming in grief. I couldn't see the page myself, but, just as they had outside the Quik-Mart when I'd heard them the first time, the words boomed clearly from its pages. *"There's a traitor among us!"*

I shut the comic and the voice died, leaving only silence, and the thud of my heart beating loudly in my ears.

"That person, that traitor," I said softly, "can only be someone left alive in this sanctuary. It's not me because I just arrived. It's obviously not Warren. Is it you, Hunter?" His expression tightened, and I spoke before he could answer. "Nope, can't be. Because it's not the weapons that malfunction, is it?

"Perhaps Gregor's the Judas. After all, he's the one who left the boneyard open to infiltration by the Shadow side. Then again, I seriously doubt he'd have cut open his own bowels just for good effect." I turned to the next star sign. "How about you, Micah? Granted, you could have handed me over to the Tulpa when I was lying unconscious under your care . . . or better yet, even killed me yourself."

I shifted again. "I suppose it could be Chandra. She has the chemicals, the talent, the opportunity. But she's not a real part of the Zodiac, and that means she's nothing more than a tool for the real mole. A dupe. A pawn to be used, then discarded."

"Fuck you," she said, but she sounded more hurt than angry now.

"Or," I said, whirling so I was facing all of them again, "is the mole the person who had access to us all? To Warren, whom I saw leaving Greta's office right before his capture. Who risked all to bring me here, then suddenly—after one brief session—no longer trusted me. No longer trusted himself."

"This is ridiculous. So far-fetched!" Greta said. "How can any of you listen to this? You know me . . . and she's of the Shadows!"

But it was too late to effectively play that card, and I continued on as if she hadn't spoken. No one stopped me. "Warren was disoriented. He told me you'd just hypnotized him, and when I came in after him you tried to do the same to me. But it didn't work, did it? I awoke before you finished and there was a funny scent in the air, like metal ground into a fine powder. Something frightened you and you panicked and dropped the vial."

"It was you. I saw the Shadow in you."

"Saw it?" I asked coolly. "Or recognized it?"

She couldn't hold back any longer. Her scream hit my face. "You don't know any of this for a fact! You're making it up! My father was an agent of Light!"

"Your father was a Gemini. Dual-sided, dual-faced, right?"

"Are you questioning his loyalty?" She spit in my face. I was guessing from the shock around me that this was a side of Greta none of the others had seen before. "He gave his life for this organization!"

I wiped the spittle from my cheek. "And I bet that really tore you up, didn't it?"

"Excuse me," she said, folding her arms over her chest, "but as long as we're speaking of fathers, need I remind you who yours is, Olivia? Oh, but that's not your real name, is it? Who's the one keeping secrets now?"

I made sure my breathing was controlled, then said softly, "No, you don't need to remind me. But might I remind you that neither goodness nor evil is inherited. Both must be chosen."

She lifted her chin, her heart-shaped face hard with

defiance. "If I'd *chosen* to betray the Zodiac troop, then the people I've lived with for two years—the supernatural people!—should have been able to scent the shadow in me. They specialize in detecting intent."

"You mean they can't?" I asked, feigning surprise. I already knew why this was, of course, but I didn't want to explain it. It was important they discover it for themselves.

"I don't smell anything," Felix said, shaking his head.

"Neither do I."

"Greta's right," Hunter said at last. "At least one of us would have been able to recognize something wasn't right about her."

The others shook their heads as I met their eyes in inquiry. When they landed on Greta, she smiled smugly. I returned the smile, causing hers to shake at the edges.

"Well, I can. It smells like the earth's core; sulfur and heat. It smells like things buried deep; rotting flesh, gorging worms. Evil at work." I was moving across the hallway as I said this, and I ended up in front of Hunter. I leaned into him, an almost seductive move; one knee bending into his body, the flesh of my forearm brushing his, my breath warm on his neck. I inhaled deeply. "Not like you. You smell like the smoke rising from a living campfire. Like the green wood and the grasses and the wild things that spice embers bursting in the air. Don't you think?"

"If you say so."

"What?" I drew back and looked in his face. "Can't you smell yourself?"

He stared back at me, unblinking. "I can smell emotions, sure. I smell adrenaline and perspiration when I work up a sweat, but the basic compound that makes up my molecules is too familiar to me. I can't identify it."

"So you can't identify it on, say . . ." I looked around, as if searching for a target. Found it in Greta. ". . . her?"

Hunter looked from me to Greta and back again, frowning.

Micah stared at me, openmouthed. "I can."

"I can too," Vanessa said, and furrowed her brows. "I smell Gregor as well."

"This is ridiculous," Greta blustered.

"Micah too." Gregor nodded. "And Warren."

It was my turn to smile smugly. "Scents are attached to emotion. When Greta discovers something deeply personal through hypnosis, she tags it. When you think of that particular emotion, you emit a pheromone that calls to the Shadow agents.

"But as she's marking you she also takes a vial of your essence and injects it into herself so that her true scent becomes invisible to each of you."

"Anosmia," I heard Felix whisper.

"She binds herself to you the way Micah bound Warren and me. The way she was trying to mark and bind me when I woke up in her office." I saw a movement at the end of the hallway. It was Rena. "Of course, you don't have to take my word for it."

They all turned, sensing the movement, except Greta, who kept her eyes hard on my face.

"There's a reason she keeps lovebirds in her room and office . . ." Greta turned too, then. "And it ain't love."

We all watched Rena's slow approach, and I heard Greta's breath quicken. After that I could only sense the growing curiosity of the others as Rena drew closer.

She held a kitten. Black and white, with tufts of wild fur, it was sleeping peacefully, its breathing easy as it lay cupped in her palms. A small smile was fixed on Rena's destroyed face as she stopped a foot in front of Greta and held out the slumbering animal.

For a moment nothing happened. Then, on the next tiny intake of breath, the kitten's body stiffened, its eyes flipped open, flickered once, and registered Greta standing there. Its back arched immediately, every hair standing on end, then it hissed and lunged for her with tiny, unsheathed claws.

Greta smacked at the bottom of Rena's cupped hands and sent the kitten flying.

Hunter lunged, catching the flipping body just before it touched concrete. Greta ran for her office, Gregor tripped her up, and she sprawled like a spineless scarecrow.

"The birds were an excuse to keep the cats away," I said when the shouts in the hallway had finally quieted. "Her office and her room are the only places she can't fully mask her true scent."

Greta rolled, eyes dry. Wide, but with madness, not fear, they locked on me with unfettered hatred. Bilious blackened color, like smoke, pooled to surround her body. One by one she studied the others as if coming face-to-face with them for the first time. "Your precious leader will be dead by morning."

"We should send you up the chute," Felix said. "You deserve to fry for what you've done!"

Greta spit in his direction, not bothering to hide her Shadow side now. She reeked of maggots and rotted eggs, a fetid blend that literally spilled from her pores.

Vanessa advanced on her, nose wrinkled in disgust, eyes fired with fury. "Maybe we'll just let her loose in the cat ward. Her and her little lovebirds."

"I raised your father," Rena said, shaking her head. "He'd be so disappointed."

"He'd be used to it," Greta retorted, but I don't think anybody felt sorry for her.

"But there's no way he'd—" A sharp pain slashed through my chest and I bent, legs buckling. My mouth opened in a soundless cry as I hit the floor, and Hunter tried to lift me, but I resisted, needing to feel the ground beneath me, anchoring me. "They're hurting Warren again."

Greta started to laugh. "The Tulpa knows you've found me out! They'll kill him now . . . and it's all her fault!" She pointed at me.

Warren screamed in my brain, agony wracking us both, but nothing came out of my mouth. Then a sickening spiral, down, down into myself, and I knew that Warren, wherever he was, had passed out. That didn't stop Ajax. He laughed, and the sound resonated in my mind. A boot-shaped sole slammed into my kidney, I retched, and Greta's laughter joined his when my jaw cracked with a finishing blow, even though nothing had been touched on the surface. I gave thanks that Warren was unconscious, but shuddered knowing he'd have to wake again.

Around me the others were trying to figure out a way past the Shadows in the boneyard.

"Even if you figure out a way to hide your marks," Greta interrupted, sneering, "and you *won't* because those marks are fresh, Hunter was the last—"

"Bitch," he murmured.

"—it'll be too late for Warren." She bared her teeth, and it was hard to see where kindness had ever lived on that face. "You'll never get to him in time."

It was the last thing I heard for a while. The questioning and confused babble continued ruminating up and down the hall, and the voices laughing and groaning in my head fell into the background. I tuned them all out, but at length became aware of a dull but insistent tapping. I pried one eye open to find Tekla pointing at me from the other side of the glass again. Only I got it this time. She wasn't pointing at me. She was pointing at the glass.

"You're all lost," Greta was screeching from her position across from me on the floor. "Hear me, Archer? They've already won!"

There was the report of flesh meeting flesh, a palm arching across Greta's face. Then Chandra's voice, as angry as I'd ever heard it. "Tell us where he is!"

She cackled. "I won't, no matter what you do, and I'll have the satisfaction of knowing I did my job! You're all marked! Do you hear me? Targets! You'll never even reach his kill spot."

Warren stirred inside me. He was alive, and if I wanted him to stay that way, I knew what I had to do. As my fingers searched, found my conduit sprawled next to me, the tapping on the window ceased. Forcing myself to keep my hand steady, I pointed it.

"Hey, Greta," I said, and watched the satisfaction fall from her face as she turned to find herself staring down the pointed shaft of my arrow. "I'm not marked."

I shifted and shot fluidly, and though it was the first time I'd fired this weapon, it was as if I'd been born to the motion. Greta shrieked and ducked, though she'd be lying in her own kill spot had I still been pointing it at her. Instead, the arrow cleaved through the window of Tekla's cell, shattering the glass into hundreds of tiny pieces that fell like diamonds onto the hallway floor. Tekla's face appeared a moment later, but her voice came first.

Warren's voice.

"Come to Paradise, the Hall of the Slain, also the dwelling of those who never die. Where virgin warriors guard the gates of eternity. The palace with five hundred and fifty doors. Where dead warriors feast, where gods abide."

"What is he saying?" I heard someone ask.

"Valhalla," I said, and sunk back to the ground. "They're holding him at Valhalla." And I doubled over as Tekla cried out, Warren's skull splitting inside of me with a blow meant to silence him forever.

25

Tekla, it seemed, had always spoken for the others. Before Stryker's death, and Greta's betrayal, she had been able to see, via flashes and images, when an agent of Light was walking into danger. It had been a marvelous, if disconcerting, gift. It was during one of these moments, Micah surmised, that Greta must have bound herself to Tekla, and thus began the downward spiral of Zodiac troop 175, and of Tekla herself.

The past six months had stripped her of her voice, and like a rewound tape, she began spouting all she'd seen while locked in her five-by-eight cell. It would take a while to catch up, but time was something we didn't have.

Warren's voice had fallen quiet inside me, and I didn't need a psychic to tell me that Ajax was behind the stillness. I felt it as clearly as if I possessed the Sight. He'd silenced Warren to try and keep us from tracking him further, but hadn't killed him outright. No, that was still the carrot dangling on a stick.

Which meant there was only one thing to do.

"Find a way to get me up the chute without frying," I told Hunter, "and I can find Warren."

A short argument ensued between those who thought I should stay put versus those who believed I shouldn't, but ultimately what it came down to was this: the others were marked, and I wasn't. I was linked to Warren, and they weren't. And, finally, if I really was Warren's beloved Kairos, I couldn't be killed today, or anytime soon.

But if he was wrong? I thought as I headed back to my mother's room in the troop's barracks. If I wasn't the person they all thought I was? Well, then they'd need Warren far more than they needed me. He was the troop leader. He could train the next generation. He could find the true Kairos.

But that didn't mean I'd go down without a fight.

Sliding open the closet doors, I decided my mother had the fiercest wardrobe ever. Literally. Arranged on evenly spaced hangers were tops, slacks, and single-piece stretch suits in varying weights of silk, spandex, and leather. The uniformity came in two colors only, black or charcoal gray, with a hand that shimmered at the touch. This material, Warren had explained, would not burn through at the flaring of a glyph.

"Olivia would tremble with jealousy," I murmured, running my fingers over the fine material. I wasn't exactly steady myself, though that was probably nerves rather than reverence. After all, when my mother suited up, she at least had an idea of what she'd been about to face. I simply assumed I was facing the worst.

With the thought that this ensemble would be featured on the next series of Light and Shadow comics, I picked a long-sleeved V-neck T-shirt and fitted cargoes. Though comfortable enough, they fit me like they'd been sprayed on. I didn't recall my mother being quite as curvy as Olivia, but then I didn't remember her ever wearing a leather bra either, and here it was.

I dressed and looked at myself in the mirror. Other than my hair, which floated around me like a wavy bleached cloud, I looked like a shadow. A smudge on reality. Fitting, I thought, since that's what I'd be.

Standing before the small square mirror, I slicked back my hair and rolled it into a tight club. I found a pair of chopstick combs, similar to the ones the Chinese used to secure their own glossy locks but sharper and steel-tipped, more lethal. A most fashionable backup weapon, I thought, studying myself from the side. The street fighter in me approved.

"Thanks, Mom," I said, pocketing my conduit. There was only one item missing from my supernatural arsenal. Unfortunately, I had to go to Greta's holding cell to get it.

You had to give it to her, I thought, peering through the cell's window. For a woman facing imminent death, she was admirably composed. Though chained to a concrete floor, hands and feet bound in front of her, she sat with her back straight against the stone wall, head back, eyes closed. She even looked relieved. Like she'd been performing the same play over and over and had been longing for some new dialogue. With a crisp turn of the key in the lock, I entered the room, intending to give it to her.

She didn't look up.

"How's it feel, Greta?" I asked, closing the door behind me, my voice reporting hollowly off the stone walls. "To be helpless, locked up, wondering what's to become of you?"

"You should know." She motioned with one hand, chains clanking as she indicated the entire sanctuary. "Your cell is just a little bigger."

I advanced upon her, showing her that even a confined place could shrink upon itself. She just leaned her head back and closed her eyes again. "Tell me, what was it like knowing you were sending Warren to his death?"

"What, you're the psychologist now?" She sneered. "Savior of the Zodiac didn't fit quite right?"

I shrugged. "Just wondering."

She pulled her knees into her chest. "Keep wondering."

I shifted to lean against the wall, crossing my legs at the ankles. "You should tell someone, don't you think? I mean, otherwise your deeds won't get written down. You'll be just one more stiff in the body count at the end of a comic book."

She glanced up at me with disdain. Her chignon had fallen loose, and her skin was smudged beneath overly dark eyes. The Shadow sat on her features like a defiant child. "You think that's why I did this? To gain recognition for infiltrating the Zodiac troop when I was fated to be nothing more than a talented mortal? A mere half-breed?"

The detail in her answer told me that was exactly why she'd done it. "You tell me."

She was silent for nearly a minute. "No. I don't think I will."

"You'd better," I sang the words softly.

That got her attention. She studied me carefully for a moment, then snickered. "Or what? You're going to kill me?" She tightened her arms around her knees. "That doesn't frighten me."

"Death doesn't frighten you?" She pursed her lips, but otherwise ignored me. "But insignificance did. It frightened you enough for you to betray your father's people."

"Oh God, don't try that psychological shit on me! You're no good at it." She shifted irritably, chains rattling like pennies in a glass jar. "That's not why I did it."

"Then why?"

"You know why!" she bellowed suddenly, and I could see in her fevered gaze she really believed it. "You told me yourself this afternoon."

I thought back. Then began to nod slowly. "Ah."

"Yes, ahhh," she said mockingly. Madness danced in her once kind eyes. "Power. Having it. Using it. Controlling others with it. I was more powerful than the most powerful. More powerful than all of you."

I raised a brow, taunting her without words.

"I'd have cracked you eventually too," she said quickly, too loudly. It made me smile, and she went on in a rush. "I'd have found out who you really were and used that knowledge to plant the mark so deep no one would ever find it."

I shook my head. "I don't think so."

"I did it to everyone, even Tekla, the so-called Seer. And me, a half-mortal." I looked at the pride on her face: there wasn't even a trace of regret for the lives she had cost.

"No," I said in a low voice, "you're not even half that."

Her eyes narrowed to black pinpoints and she studied me, looking up my body and back down again. A slow smile began to thread from one side of her face to the other.

"You're going after him. You think the mark Micah planted will lead you to him."

"It will," I said flatly, "and I'll bring him back safely."

Abruptly, she howled with laughter, throwing her head back like a wolf to the moon. When she was done, finally, she wiped the tears from her cheeks. "You *are* your mother's daughter. Always thinking you can do the impossible. Always wanting to be the hero. Always doomed to fail."

"I won't fail," I said, tucking my hands into my cargo pockets, finding what I needed in the right-hand side. "You're going to ensure that."

She hooted again. "Don't count on it."

I slipped an ugly smile over my pretty face. Her malicious grin wavered, then fell.

"Have I ever told you about my sister?" I asked, pushing off from the wall to stand in the middle of the room. Greta didn't answer, giving a good imitation of a person at ease. "She was similar to you in that she was half Light, half mortal, though I always thought of her as being entirely good. All innocence. Completely pure of heart."

"Not like you, then," Greta murmured, taunting me with what she knew.

"Not like you either."

There must have been something jagged in my voice, something I couldn't hold back, because she did look at me then. She studied me for a moment, then shrugged and fixed a petulant expression on her face. "She sounds like a bore."

I didn't rise to the bait. My love for Olivia had lain plain on my face, hanging like ripened fruit to be plucked. It was an easy target for Greta, and I couldn't be angry she'd taken it. Besides, I was hoarding my anger, letting it build inside me until later, when I'd call upon it. When it'd be most needed.

I closed my eyes and conjured up the clearest picture of Olivia possible. I wanted Greta to be able to see. "She was anything but boring. She was beautiful. When she walked into a room, people used to stop just to watch the magic in her movement. She was so blond the sun could have taken lessons in shining from her. So voluptuous the mountains around this valley shook with envy. 'Too much woman,' I used to think. Too much hair and flesh, too many curves and softness. It was overwhelming."

I could sense Greta's interest despite herself. "So she looked like you. So what?"

I opened my eyes and smiled. "Yes. She looked exactly like me. Exactly."

Greta's brows furrowed, then rose in twin surprise, eyes going wide as realization dawned. "You're the sister! You're her, the one who died!"

"What? Didn't you do your homework, Greta?" I asked, head tilted. "Don't you even know my name?"

She looked at me, her face bleeding one emotion into another—fear, amazement, doubt, surprise—eyes zipping around my face like furious flies, never landing. "But you're *her*! I studied Olivia, and you're her!"

"I studied her too. And, remember, I had a lifetime to do so." She had no response to that. "You want to know what I learned in becoming someone else? Something you apparently never picked up?"

She flinched at the insult.

"I learned it doesn't matter what mannerisms you pick up, or what clothes you wear," I said, sweeping my left hand down my body, "or what mask you try to hide behind . . . be it beauty or psychology. The shadows inside you can't stay hidden forever."

We both knew I was talking about her, but she jerked her head at me. "You remember that when what you've tried to keep hidden becomes unearthed like a rotted corpse."

"That's the difference between us," I said. "I'm not trying to hide my shadows anymore."

And I pulled back the curtain on my one-woman play, just enough to let her glimpse what lay beneath—anger and pain over Olivia's death; hatred for the Tulpa, Ajax, and anyone aiding their side; disgust over the wasted lives of people meant to be super . . . and the inherited and shadowed urge to take it all out on her.

"I'm not afraid of you," Greta said, voice shaking.

I didn't answer, but turned instead toward the door like I was ready to leave.

"You never told me your real name," she said quickly, thinking I'd leave and she might never know. "Who you really are."

"I did," I said, not turning. My hands were busy in front of me. "When you tried to hypnotize me. I told you it depended on who was looking."

She scoffed, annoyed with the answer. "So who are you right now?"

How to answer that? All the qualities I'd mentioned while under hypnosis still existed inside of me—the bitch, the goddess, the daughter, the sister, the friend, the enemy, the huntress, the predator, the Archer—and needed only to be called upon. But I wanted to give her the truest answer of all. I owed her, and all of us, that much.

So as I slowly turned to face her, one of her slim needles, pumped and primed, spiking from my hand, I slid open the curtain, revealing to her the whole of the shadows inside of me. "Right now, Greta? I'm my father's daughter."

And Greta screamed, finally afraid.

26

I met the others at the launch pad near dawn, approaching by stealth, testing myself . . . and the weapon Greta had given me, albeit unwillingly.

"Jesus!" Felix jumped as my hand landed on his shoulder.

"Olivia!" Vanessa whirled next to him. "I didn't hear you arrive."

"Neither did I," Hunter said, narrowing his eyes suspiciously. I tried out Olivia's most innocent smile as they all looked at me.

"Are you all right?" Micah asked, brows drawn, studying me.

"Peachy," I said, my blood still whirlpooling in my veins, power still screaming through my ears. I didn't try to read anyone's aura. I didn't need to now. "Though you guys seem a bit wound up."

"You look different."

"Brushed my hair," I said smartly.

"Not physically," Felix said, beginning to circle me. "Different beneath that. Under the skin." He ran a finger along my nape and I stiffened visibly. I was strung drumtight. "Feel different too." After a moment he let his hand fall and, though it was almost imperceptible, backed away.

"We were just discussing tactics," Gregor said, oblivious. All of his energies were focused on healing, but the others felt it. They'd begun to circle the wagons, so to speak, and were standing shoulder-to-shoulder across from me, a half-moon to my lone star.

"I'll be staying behind for obvious reasons," he continued, managing a wry smile from where he sat in a wheelchair. "Chandra will remain as well."

I glanced at Chandra, who didn't meet my eye. She couldn't go, I knew, because as long as I was alive she couldn't be a real and active member of the Zodiac.

"I'm staying too, because if you—" Micah cut himself off, clearing his throat. "I mean *when* the rest of you return I may be needed in a medical capacity. We've deemed that more important than my offensive skills."

He meant he expected most of us to come back wounded. If we came back at all.

"So here's the plan," Hunter said, stalking over to me, his movements once again reminding me of a cat. A very large, very patient cat. "Felix will flank your left side and Vanessa your right."

"Provided I can get out of here, you mean."

His mouth quirked as he pulled his arm from behind his back, holding out an answer to my challenge.

"What is it?" Felix said, inching forward.

"A helmet?" I asked, taking it. I flipped it over in my hand. It was pliable, made of distressed leather on the outside, but with a strange crisscrossing of wires woven tightly beneath. It was designed to cover the eyes—twin mirrors shot my reflection back at me—and arched across the temples and over the soft tissue behind the ears. A leather toggle secured it around the base of my skull, or beneath a low bun like the one I was wearing now.

"A mask?" Micah said.

"No," I said. Not a mask, though it would probably be

drawn that way in Zane's comics. My eyes lifted. "It's a shield."

Hunter inclined his head. "Try it on."

Securing it over the bridge of my nose first, I slid it along my skull and fastened it below the bun. I shook my head side to side.

"How does it feel?" Vanessa asked.

"Like it was made for me," I answered, thinking Warren would approve. Not only would it shield my eyes from the lights within the chute, but it would conceal my identity for as long as I wore it.

Spotting a full-length mirror to the left of the launch pad, I stood in front of it and studied the reflection. It smiled. For the first time since taking over Olivia's identity, I recognized myself. "It's perfect."

"Of course," Hunter said with his usual arrogance. You can also use it to freely enter and leave the sanctuary in the future, just like the rest of us."

"Good thinking," Vanessa said.

I inclined my head, giving him his due credit, and because I was grateful. Now I could hide my Shadow side, at least in this one small way.

"I just don't get it!" Felix exclaimed, and began circling me again. "It's like there's a wall around you. I can see you, but I sure didn't hear you come in, and no matter how hard I try, I can't scent you, even though you're only two feet from me."

"Doesn't bode well for tracking down Shadow signs, does it?" Vanessa said.

Felix gave her a steely look.

Hunter stepped closer. He leaned in as he had in the dojo, crowding my space, taking up all the room. I unlaced the shield and lowered it from my eyes as he scratched his chin.

"Figure it out yet?" I asked in a low voice, gaze steady on his.

Vanessa gasped just as understanding dawned, widening

Hunter's hooded eyes. There was an uncomfortable shifting in the room, like wind lifting suddenly in a tree.

"Greta?" Hunter asked, face unreadable.

I smiled.

"Oh, my God! You possess the aureole again!" Micah said, up to speed now. "The needles?"

"You used her own weapon against her," Hunter said, his voice considering. "Like you did with Butch. So you could walk the mortal world like a ghost. That's why none of us sensed you."

"God," Felix breathed from behind me. He had backed away.

"You killed Greta?" Vanessa asked, her voice small. "In cold blood?"

"No. I was still pretty pissed when I did it." Then I held out a hand to stave off any more comment. "The point is, I have the ability to walk around completely undetected for the next twelve hours."

"All night," Gregor said, and excitement lined his words.

"No, the point is she *murdered* someone who was half Light in order to gain power!" Vanessa pointed at me, and I was surprised to see her hand shaking.

"You've got it wrong, Vanessa," I said, turning on her. She swallowed hard but didn't back away. "What I did was take the power from someone who *used* to be half Light, and now I'm going to use that to battle the Shadow side. See the difference?"

She opened her mouth to argue, then let it snap shut again. After a moment, she nodded. "You're right. It's a powerful weapon."

"Wish I'd thought of it," Felix said, his voice wistful.

"If you're all done chatting," Hunter said, moving back to the launch pad, "perhaps we can get to the fighting now?"

"Isn't there a way to test this first?" I asked, holding my shield out in front of me.

"No time," Hunter said, flexing his fingers, rolling his neck. There was no hesitation in his voice, but I was gratified to see his movements actually appeared nervous. Even superhumans were human. "Fifteen minutes until the light splits."

Felix clapped his hands together. "So let's go kick some preternatural ass."

"On my signal, cowboy," Hunter said, earning a scowl. "Once you're through the chute, move aside because I'll be coming up fast. Vanessa, take the left flank. Olivia, you go up last."

"But—"

"Last," he repeated. "They won't sense you so maybe they won't see you. Besides, when was the last time you felt Warren stirring inside of you?"

I thought about it. It'd been a while.

"I don't want that connection severed. He may be too weak without you."

"Thanks for your concern," I muttered, earning nothing more than an arched brow.

"Whatever you do, don't hesitate. These bastards are fast."

"Not as fast as we are," Felix said, earning a high five from Vanessa. He rubbed his hands together, his boyish enthusiasm turned deadly.

"Wait," I said, suddenly nervous. "What if I accidentally shoot one of you? I mean, what if I can't tell the difference?"

"Can't tell the difference between Shadow and Light?" Felix scoffed. "Impossible."

Have you looked at me? I wanted to say. *Have any of you really seen me?*

"It's too late to worry about now," Hunter said, and motioned Felix forward to stand on a large X. Raising his left hand, Hunter placed his right on a chrome lever. "Felix, go."

With a whoosh of air, he was gone. Hunter took his place and, without hesitation, or even a backward glance, shot from mid-crouch up the chute.

Vanessa flipped open her conduit, the blades of the fan locking violently in place. Then she whipped it shut again, holding it ready in her right hand. She looked straight up, back slightly bowed, like she was beseeching the heavens. Throwing back the lever, she whispered a final word. I couldn't hear it, but I read her lips, and it was, indeed, an invocation. Stryker's name.

And suddenly I was alone.

I swallowed hard, and tried to think of my mother—what would she think if she could see me now?—but she and all of my other soft memories had been locked up tight, and to access them now would mean revealing my light to the world. I touched my chest where Warren's second heart had, until recently, resided, but he too seemed to have abandoned me. Or did he think we'd abandoned him? The thought put some resolve into me. I didn't know what I was about to face, but at least I knew why.

Finally, I knew why.

Slipping the shield over my eyes, I let Greta's fresh death course through my blood, and the other death I'd caused poked its head, Butch-shaped, above the murky swamp of my darkest thoughts. I let the images surface, and my palms itched as I recalled slicing a tongue, severing hands, pushing a syringe. I let the darkness swirl inside of me, upsetting the hate that had settled like silt on the bottom of my soul. Hand on my conduit, I mainlined adrenaline and stood as the others had, on the giant X, knees bent in anticipation. Then I threw back the lever, and my body was shuttled into space.

They were fighting before I ever made it up the chute. I could hear them, their cries tunneling past me as I rose to the surface, the wind screaming in my ears, my eyes and temples cool and untouched beneath the shield. If the breath wasn't being whisked so rapidly from my body, I would have sighed in thanksgiving.

My arrival above was announced by nothing more than a hiss, and that masked by the combat around me. I crouched atop the Slipper and took a quick inventory. The boneyard was awash in shadows. And Shadows.

Felix had been right—it was physically impossible not to discern the difference between the two. Agents of Light were like overgrown fireflies, zigzagging in the air, easy targets were they not so damned fast. Stars trailed in blinding streaks behind them, the air sparkling in their wake. The Shadows—trailing smoke behind them like downed bombers—had the best chance to nail one by anticipating their moves, striking the air marked before them. But the agents of Light anticipated this too.

I watched Felix swivel, a maniacal shooting star, all lithe limbs and bowing core, a frustrated Shadow warrior roaring murderously behind him . . . then crying out again as he was struck from the back. Vanessa wheeled away, trailing off-pink lights like a whipping tail, the smoke of a Shadow warrior obscuring them as he followed close.

Then I saw Hunter. Suspended ten feet in the air and dropping fast on a Shadow, his loose hair flew madly about his head while his whip wheeled behind him. I knew then why they made him their tactical leader. Black stars, glittering silver in the predawn light, were camouflaged, like a trick of the eye, and his whip struck out like a feline flicking a deadly tail.

But the Shadows weren't exactly sluggish, and there were more of them. I picked two off with my conduit from the top of the Slipper—piercing one to a giant letter N, and catapulting the other through the air to drop behind the one-dimensional outline of a martini glass. Still, I considered these kills nothing more than luck since neither they nor the rest had seen me yet.

The Neon Boneyard was quickly becoming a cloud of smoke and flame. I scurried to the ground, taking cover behind a rusting depiction of a slot machine, and waited for an opening in the melee. Problem was, most of the fighting was taking place in the thick of the smoke. I decided to wait it out, take only a sure shot . . . but when the yard finally cleared again, my breath caught and held.

All movement had ceased. The remaining warriors, both Shadow and Light, were frozen in place, chests heaving, a weapon at every back. They looked like a human Scrabble game, one piece linked to another by conduit; brutal hinges on the verge of swinging open at the slightest provocation. Hunter's whip was lashed around the neck of a woman dressed like a prostitute, but who had the creamy complexion of an eighteenth century debutante. He had only to give one great yank for the barbed hook to cleave her larynx from her throat.

But there was another Shadow behind Hunter, and he had an ax arched over Hunter's head. Felix had him covered, an edged boomerang cradled on his windpipe, but a normal-sized woman with an abnormally large machete had lodged her grip beneath his breastbone, and his other hand was clutched beneath it to keep the weapon from sliding and rending him in two.

Vanessa had her steel fan arched across the woman's neck, but the first woman—Hunter's whore-debutante—had circled around, and had a slim steel brand poised just beneath Vanessa's left eye. I was the sole independent actor, but I was afraid to move. Nobody else moved either.

"Give it up," Hunter said, sounding unafraid.

"You have an ax resting at your temple and you're telling me to give it up?" The man behind him laughed, but it died away as Felix shifted his boomerang, nestling in closer. Like a snake eating its tail, I thought, watching the circle of people. The beast was going to destroy itself.

"You're surrounded," Hunter told him.

The man laughed. "Not true, Ram-head. The Tulpa claims we've already killed off five of your star signs. There's only three of you here, the Libra's captured, and Micah is probably still helping Gregor scoop his bowels from the floor." The Shadow women began to snicker. "That leaves no one."

Hunter stole their laughter for himself. "What? And the Tulpa's never lied to you before?"

The man's smile fell. Light flashed beneath his skin, his bones burning briefly, then he was himself again. "The Tulpa tells us all we need to know."

"I see. I suppose he didn't think you needed to know we planted ten initiates in the boneyard before you ever arrived." He was good. Even I couldn't sense the lie.

"Perhaps he didn't know," Felix said, the usual cockiness in his voice somewhat strained. Who could blame him with a machete at his heart?

"You're bluffing. The Tulpa knows all."

"So when this cactus sign explodes behind me, he'll know it?"

That was my cue. I cocked an arrow back in my compact bow and took aim.

"We've been camped outside your doorway all night. If there were even one initiate out here we would have found him by now."

I fired a shot past his head, the arrow whistling past his hairline before imploding the pictorial sign on impact. I was moving again before it hit. The Shadows cringed.

"Initiates can't scent out Shadows," the gorgeous hooker said, sounding unsure.

"Well, they don't have to if you're standing in plain sight, do they?" Vanessa answered. "I'd watch the gold horseshoe over your left shoulder. It's going to explode. Now."

I slammed the arrow home like I'd practiced it my entire life.

"And I'd drop your conduits if I were you," Hunter said once the dust and flame died again.

"No. You wouldn't."

"Then we all die." Hunter shrugged, like it was a small thing. "It's okay. Our initiates are anxious to prove themselves."

"Initiates are no match for star signs, and you know it.

They try to rescue Warren and they'll all be dead before sunrise."

"Unless some of us are also star signs." I entered the clearing from the base of the Silver Slipper, the opposite direction from where I'd just fired. I smiled as the Shadows shifted. None of them had sensed me at all.

"Say hello to our new Archer."

"Then drop your conduits," I added, smiling.

"The Tulpa didn't say anything about a new agent of Light."

"Apparently they're on a need-to-know basis," Vanessa said to me.

"Too bad they needed to know. Now drop 'em." I drew back my notched arrow and sighted right between the middle woman's eyes. Mine narrowed as hers widened. She was the belly of the snake. Worse case scenario, they didn't drop their conduits and I cleaved the snake in half.

"You'll kill us if we drop them."

"We can't kill you," I said, and they looked surprised. "Ajax has our Bull. Our guns are at your temples, so to speak, but his is pointed at Warren and we want him back. Five Shadow warriors die, and it'll produce such a jolt of energy that he just might pull that trigger."

"Like dominoes," the man said. "You kill us and Ajax kills your leader."

I shifted, my arrow pointed between his eyes. "Just don't forget who dies first."

"She's new, but she does have a knack for summing up a situation." Hunter smiled like a proud papa. "Then again, she should. It's been prophesied that an Archer will rise to cast her shadow or, if you will, her light, over both sides of the Zodiac."

I looked at him. It had?

"The Kairos? A myth," the hooker scoffed.

"You mean the Tulpa told you it's a myth," Vanessa corrected.

"The legend is that the woman who bears both sun and

moon inside of her will have to choose her allegiance. Like a fulcrum, her fate is not fixed. She begins by belonging equally to the day and night," the man said.

"Which means," added Dawn, "that we have as much chance of spawning the Archer as you."

"Is that what your manuals say?" Hunter said. "Interesting. Because ours tell us that one night in the season of Jupiter, eight Shadow warriors will infiltrate the Neon Boneyard, and battle there until dawn breaks over the Black Mountains. Some will die, but the rest will be given a choice to lay down their arms and live, the first time in history either side has offered a truce. If the Shadows don't accept, however, they die en masse, along with the warriors of Light. Either way, one star sign walks away. This marks the rise of the Kairos."

Hunter motioned to me, and I took a small bow, though more because he expected me to than out of any belief in what he'd said.

The Shadows looked at one another. Then the man said, "Prove it."

I glanced at Hunter. He shrugged. "Zell wants you to prove it."

So I squared on the Shadow agents, and without removing my shield, allowed my bones to rise from beneath the shroud of my skin, rearranging themselves on the surface; elongating, gleaming in the light of the full moon, revealing the face of my father. I blew him a kiss as I sucked the bones back in. It came out on a scalding wisp of breath, and I smiled prettily.

"Shit," one of the Shadows said softly.

The man behind Hunter lowered his ax, then tossed it on a pile of scrap metal. Vanessa, in turn, folded her steel fan. Dawn removed her machete from Felix's middle, hand shaking, and threw it aside. Felix doubled over, clutching at his stomach.

"Felix!" Vanessa rushed to him.

"Oops," Dawn said, laughing. She shrugged at Vanessa's

upturned glare. "Well, don't look at me. I did that before the deal was made. Though it was a good strike if I do say so myself."

"Get him to Micah," Hunter ordered Vanessa.

She gave a sharp nod, her face gone pale. "I'll catch up with you guys later."

"You can't come alone," Hunter argued, then jerked his head at the three Shadows. "This isn't all of them."

"Then wait for me."

"There isn't time."

Vanessa looked at the lightening sky, then back at him, frustrated resignation clouding her face.

"Bad luck all around," Zell said, shaking his head. "Was that in your manual too?"

Felix straightened long enough to slam a fist into the guy's mouth . . . then collapsed in a heap.

Vanessa caught him, gathered him up, and Hunter motioned for me to guard the Shadows while he assisted them to the base of the Slipper.

Zell chuckled, licking the blood from the side of his mouth, then turned to me. "Why the mask, sweet cheeks?"

"It's not a mask. It's a shield." I hesitated, then said, "My Shadow side won't allow me to enter the sanctuary without it."

"What happens if you try?" the whore-debutante asked, sounding genuinely curious.

"Same thing that happens to all of you. I get microwaved from the inside out."

They all shuddered.

Zell, whom I took to be some sort of leader, folded his arms as he studied me. "So if those two are going back into the sanctuary, and you and Hunter are going after Ajax, who's supposed to keep us all rounded up here like good little sheep? Those invisible initiates you were talking about?"

I shook my head. "They don't exist."

"I thought not," Dawn muttered.

"Don't worry," Hunter called down from the top of the slipper, "we have something far more frightening in mind."

Before the Shadows could ask what, Hunter called out, "They can come up now, Rena."

There was a moment when we all wondered what might exit the mouth of that slipper. This pause was followed by a deep internal rumble that had the Shadows glancing around them, looking ready to bolt. Zell caught me watching him, glared at my smile, and stayed put.

Seconds later two dozen children of the Zodiac tumbled out like ants pouring from the mouth of a mound. They were screaming gleefully, zipping to the far reaches of the boneyard and back, their faces alight, literally, with joy. Rena followed closely behind.

"I don't approve of this, you know," she said to Hunter. "It's past their bedtime."

"It's good practice for them," he replied, watching as more children tumbled over the Slipper. "Have they eaten?"

"Double chocolate banana splits and espresso. They'll be up all night."

"Shit," the woman next to me muttered again, squinting against the residual zips of light.

Little Marcus raced past me, his face an intense chocolate-smeared mixture of joy and determination. As he passed the Shadow man he leaned in and gave a ferocious growl, his expression so fierce it sparked the entire boneyard to life. Zell cried out and covered his eyes with his arms.

Marcus, of course, thought this hilarious. He circled the Shadow warriors, leaning in and leering at them so that his face blinked on and off like a little bulb. The other kids, shrieking, began to do the same.

"Brilliant," I murmured, squinting even from within my mask. Like baby rattlers, the children's strength was in their inability to control their power. If the Shadows found the rest of us hard to bear, then the children's raw and undiluted power was insufferable. And the little vessels of pure light, I thought, smiling, could keep these Shadows immobile for as long as they wished. I heard a howl of pain as one of the kids poked their quarry in the stomach. Sparks flew as flesh met flesh.

"Linus! Stop that this instant! What did I tell you about torture?"

Hunter was suddenly beside me again. "You ready?"

I nodded, backing from the raucous melee and the cringing Shadow signs. "Guess we don't have to worry about these guys for a while."

"Don't worry. There will be more where we're going."

"The Hall of the Gods," I muttered, following him toward dawn and another reality. Toward Valhalla.

27

As we circled the casino, looking for the best place to stage our entrance and Warren's eventual extraction, the Strip was coming to life. Early morning joggers bounded up the near-empty streets, dodging slower pedestrians who'd emerged in quest of sunlight or breakfast buffets. Life, I thought, went on. I studied the building before us, the faux castle facade, the lush landscaping that surrounded it like a moat. It was no longer a mere casino, I realized, but a guarded fortress. And I was trying to scale its walls.

"I have an idea," Hunter said, and headed toward the casino. "Give me five minutes."

"Wait! You can't go in alone!" The Shadows, were they there, would scent him. And I was sure they were there.

He shrugged off my arm with an irritated jerk. "Just five minutes. Meet me at the main entrance."

It passed like five hours. By the time I rounded the building from the street side, Hunter was already on patrol, dressed in a Valhalla security uniform and scanning the area intently. His back was to me, so I exhaled to let him know I was there. He whirled immediately, heading straight for me.

He was fearsome, even clothed as a mortal. His blue-black hair was no longer loose, slicked instead, and banded at the base of his neck. He had his warrior's face on, and though I knew who the game face was really for, the murderous look in his eyes still sent a chill down my spine. His whip was nowhere to be seen, but his mortal weapons were secured at his sides.

"Two guns?" I said, eyeing a holster on each side and a baton at his back.

"The Tulpa's paranoid."

The Tulpa wasn't the only one. I glanced behind me, staring down a senior citizen about half my height. I didn't like how exposed I felt on the street. And I could smell Hunter, his adrenaline and nerves as acute as smelling salts in my nose. "Let's go."

He shifted, and stepped in front of me.

"What are you doing? Move." I skirted around him. He stepped in front of me again.

"Act like we're arguing," he said.

Exasperated, I scowled at him. "We *are* arguing."

"I mean act crazy." I tilted my head, looking at him. He spoke again, through clenched teeth. "Give me an observable reason to detain you."

"I feel stupid," I muttered, but halfheartedly threw my arms up in the air. "Whoo-hoo!"

His large palm smacked my head so hard my teeth clattered.

"Ow! Bastard!" I pushed away, but Hunter angled his body, giving me some slack and pulling me back, three times in quick succession. I finally realized he was making it appear I was struggling with him, and that it had worked. Our progression through the porte cochere was marked by several wary, if curious, sidelong glances. At the entrance, politely attended by a blank-faced doorman, I spotted a smoky half globe on the ceiling and knew that not everyone eyeing us was on the casino floor.

"I said take off the mask," Hunter said suddenly, loudly. He hadn't, of course, but I was up to speed now.

"Fuck you," I said, placing one hand on my head as though to prevent its removal, pushing him away with the other. He twisted my arms behind my back and slapped cuffs on them.

"Hey!" The panic in my voice was real. I didn't like being cuffed, my conduit out of reach, but there was a warning in Hunter's eye and I stopped struggling so much. I knew there was no way a masked woman could get through Valhalla without being apprehended by hotel security. The outfit was one thing—it was Vegas, after all—but a mask was another.

I also knew that once detained, a suspected robber would be escorted to a holding room for interrogation, either by hotel security alone or in tandem with Metro. That's where I was headed now, though in this case the place Hunter was dragging me was precisely where I wanted to go.

Which got me to thinking. If hotel surveillance had caught me entering with my mask on, hadn't it also caught Hunter coming in off-shift, changing into a uniform, and escorting me to the back of the house? Wouldn't he be questioned about it later by those who worked for the Tulpa? And wouldn't the answers, ultimately, reveal his true identity?

His entire life would be compromised, I thought, and the Zodiac troop would have no one on the inside of the Tulpa's organization. Again.

Of course, I knew Hunter had already thought of this. He was giving it all up, I realized, everything he'd worked for. His identity. His life. The job that would help him infiltrate the Tulpa's organization.

For now, though, he was dragging me across the main casino floor, around slot banks and carousels, between bleary-eyed tourists who'd been at the tables all night and garishly flashing neon that seemed to me to say "Go back! Go back! Certain death lies ahead!"

We reached a pair of towering double doors and Hunter punched the handicapped access button. They swung open automatically like a cavernous mouth opening to reveal Valhalla's bowels. Where the real work, both natural and supernatural, was done.

"Stay close. It's easy to get lost," Hunter said, his grip easing, his pace increasing. "There are no cameras back here, bad for morale, but there are eyes everywhere."

He turned left, then right, then a series of quick lefts. After the first two passageways we saw no one, which was strange for a casino. Hunter gestured down a long corridor. "Loading docks are that way. Might be a possible escape route later, but I think the freight elevators are a better bet. Less traffic."

I looked at him. His face was drawn tight, as if strings were winging his features downward. "I can smell you," I said.

"I know," he said, and his voice was tight too. He wasn't sweating, but his scent reeked from his pores.

"You'll be a target."

He looked at me, still for the first time. "That's why I'm telling you where the loading docks are." I swallowed hard. "Now pay attention."

We entered a seemingly unending hallway, steel-plated from the floor to about four feet up, a barrier against carts and trolleys and other equipment that bumped along on the hotel's daily business. "The Tulpa is headquartered down the longest corridor in Valhalla. Ever see those horror movies where someone's running down a hallway that just keeps getting longer and longer?" I looked behind me. We were a hundred yards in. I looked ahead. At least a hundred more to go. Hunter glanced over at me. "Now imagine running it with a dozen Shadow warriors at your back."

I swallowed hard. "I'd rather not." But I looked above

for possible escape routes, at the walls and floor for possible weapons. There was nothing. Just smooth, shiny walls and a disturbing fluorescent trail of elongated wall lamps.

"They call it the Gauntlet," he said, watching me.

"Of course they do," I said. That earned me a chuckle.

The hallway dead-ended, which I hoped wasn't symbolic, and we shifted right, stopping abruptly. An elevator bank stood right in front of us, the numbers above winging from one to twenty-four. Hunter and I faced the doors, neither of us talking nor looking at one another as he unlocked my hands and placed the cuffs in his back pocket. Then he pushed the button. It began its downward descent with a loud *ding*.

I turned to him suddenly. "Hunter, I have to apologize."

"For what?" He was only half listening. The elevator was on the top floor. We were in the basement.

"For all this." His eyes flicked to me, then back. *Ding*. Floor twenty. "I know what you're risking today. I know you're going to lose everything."

I knew also what it was to lose everything.

"Let's not talk about it." He glanced up at the lighted numbering above the doors, but the way his jaw clenched gave him away. *Ding*. Ten floors away. "Are you ready?"

"Yes," I said, tentatively, "but just one more thing."

"What?"

Half turned, I didn't look at him as I rubbed my wrists where they'd been shackled. "I'm sorry."

"You said that already."

"Not for that." *Ding*. Eight now. "For this."

And I stepped into him, unwinding with my shoulders so my elbow struck him just below his temple. He went down like a tree trunk. I had to lunge to keep his head from whacking the concrete floor, and as I lowered him he somehow managed a belated attempt for my throat.

"Ungrateful bastard," I muttered as his hands fell away. *Strong* ungrateful bastard.

I pulled the cuffs from his back pocket, secured them

around his wrists, and kept the keys. I hated to cuff him but it would be less believable that he'd been overcome if I didn't. I told myself it was for his safety, then removed his guns—stuck one in my boot, the other at my waist—his baton, and the telltale mark of an agent of Light, his conduit.

"You'll kill me when you wake up," I said to him. "But at least you'll wake up."

Which led me to the last thing that needed doing.

Leaning over Hunter, who cut a fierce figure even in an unconscious state, I thought of what I'd learned about him. Not a lot. But there was that way he watched people, the quiet scrutiny belying his casual manner. I admired that. I thought of the way he created things with his hands— weapons, sure, but artistry was a skill I'd always coveted. Then I thought of the way he'd intended to sacrifice himself today, and hadn't said a thing about it, knowing nobody would realize his intentions until it was too late.

Ding. Until now.

Allowing this paltry information to coalesce in the forefront of my mind, I bent and very gently covered his mouth with my own. The spread of flesh upon flesh was intimate, but nothing compared to the even more private opening of minds and souls. I exhaled, breathing a soft stream of essence into his mouth.

My mother had been right. You could taste the Light in another person, like bubbles on the tongue, and you could smell a person's soul on their breath. I glimpsed Hunter's strength, the sweet ardor of his physical essence and the surprising gentleness of his inner spirit. I continued to breathe, allowing our breaths to mingle so that I drew him up, in, and knew that somewhere in his unconscious state he was doing the same with me. In doing so, he was experiencing far more of me than any man ever had.

I allowed it, seeking the connection that would allow me to pass not only my knowledge and memory and experience to him, but my power as well. My kiss became a prayer, my breath a shield. I cupped his cheek with one hand—my touch now a weapon, shared—and closed my eyes to pour myself into him.

And the filmstrip began.

Some memories take only a moment to burn into the gray matter, but their images are imprinted forever. The horrific death of his parents came to me in dull and numbing flashes, viewed from the eyes of a boy watching helplessly from the corner. Shadows were spinning around him, but he was too small and helpless to do anything but watch. I heard his vow, buried beneath hot tears and his parents' broken limbs, that he'd never be weak again.

The equally sad but still sharp death of my sister was my painful contribution. It came in the one image of that night I recalled above all others; her pinwheeling through the night, calling out my name in bald desperation.

Other memories passed in such blinding flashes they set my skin to prickling. Hunter making love to a slim dark woman, a lone tear sliding over his cheek.

My final night with Ben, a storm cloud breaking like a shot overhead.

The birth of a daughter, and a heart awash in more love than it had ever known or expected.

The birth of another, unwanted, unnamed, and untouched before being whisked away.

Had I not known what memories I'd lived and what I had not, I wouldn't have been able to tell which belonged to me. As it was, we alternated our lives' greatest hits in bright flashes, trading knowledge, secret desires, longing and regrets, along with our greatest loves and our most poignant sorrows.

Then a turn into such sudden blackness it was like being pitched down a roller coaster and careening off its tracks. A shiver went through my body and quaked into his. I showed him a hypodermic needle flashing, and Greta's death powering through my limbs. Breathing the memory outward, I gave the aureole up like a gift, and Hunter took it, his subconscious greedy in a way I knew he'd never allow when fully awake. He sucked the power away, and it pulsed through our mouths, our lips moving, our tongues intertwined, the memory a lead line weighted to our hearts, loins, and heads. He grew hard beneath me. I opened my eyes to find him watching me with his soul—wondrously, thankfully, lovingly—and my body responded. My heart did too.

You'll be safe now. I've shielded you as you shielded me.

But the Shadows will scent you.

So I'll have to kill me another.

His hips rose beneath mine, and I pressed into him, forgetting myself in the strong mingling of power and limbs and dreams. The raw sexuality pulsing between us surprised me—what had started out as a chaste kiss now burned torridly between us—but it wasn't as surprising as what I sensed him thinking next.

Brave, brave Joanna . . .

Shocked, I pulled away. Breathing hard, I watched his eyes flutter, heard him groan in protest and satisfaction. Then he fell still.

He knew my name. A bell chime, like a warning, sounded behind me as the elevator hit home. I closed my eyes and inhaled deeply, but sensed nothing of Hunter. There was only me now. Alone.

He knew my name, I thought again as the doors slid open.

And that comforted me. I rose, knowing I might die, but that somebody would remain behind to remember me. Someone who really knew me. After Olivia's death, and the loss of Ben, I hadn't believed anyone else ever could.

Placing a final chaste kiss on Hunter's lips, I left him lying spent and sprawled in the corner against the wall, and didn't have a bit of guilt. I had given him enough.

I entered the elevator, pushed the button, and lifted my head as the doors whisked shut. The cart began its ascent. Toward Warren, I thought. And toward my next, and possibly last, kill spot.

28

    I wondered if this elevator would have opened to me only a month ago. There was no doubt I was operating in an alternate reality. Ions and electrodes bumped along my skin like blind bees, and a metallic taste rose to fill the back of my mouth. There was enough supernatural energy up here, I thought, to fuel a nuclear power plant.

I'm coming Warren, I thought, touching my breastbone. There was no answer, and I began to wonder if it were all in vain. Then, suddenly, there was no time left to wonder.

The elevator chime sounded like the report from Notre Dame's bell tower. The doors sliding open were the hiss of a snake. My conduit was pointed at a mirrored image of myself, and my trigger finger pulsed. The doors began to close and I stepped into the foyer at the last moment. And they whisked shut, trapping me.

The Tulpa's anteroom was immediately visible, just beyond a great marble staircase leading into a sunken chamber flanked by four Roman pillars. An identical staircase rose directly across from me to disappear beneath a pair of oak doors carved with mythic symbols, none of which I understood. That, I immediately decided, was where I needed to be. I simply had to cross over this innocuous-looking sunken chamber that lay in between. A chamber, I noted, with a vast mirrored ceiling.

"Only in Vegas," I muttered, and took a step forward.

An invisible door slammed open and hard-soled foot-steps pounded on the marble. I braced, conduit in front of me, and two men rounded the corner and stopped cold, apparently surprised to see me. Everything on them matched; their suits, their earpieces, their expressions, all the way down to the guns held at their right sides.

I breathed a sigh of relief. Mortals. I tucked away my conduit.

"Hit her!" the second one said, drawing his short club.

"Don't hit me," I said, and thrust out my lower lip.

"Hit her!" he repeated, stepping forward.

The first guard regarded him like he was crazy. "I'm not going to hit a girl."

He was looking at his partner as he said this, so he never saw my arm swing across his cheek. The slap of my open palm reverberated in the air, and his head ricocheted back-ward, but he rebounded quickly and snapped it back to level me with a look of pure hatred. "Bitch!"

He still didn't touch me, though.

"I'm a bitch?" I asked innocently.

"Fucking bitch," he snarled.

I smiled sweetly. "Then why are you the one who just got bitch-slapped?"

Even gentlemen had their limits. He lunged, as I knew he would, and I used Hunter's baton to strike his wrist, sending the gun clattering uselessly across the foyer. The second man was already aiming at me, his gun chest level, point-blank. Superhuman or not, that was going to hurt. But his hands were shaking. I ducked below his sight line, darted in, and came up under those hands. My left knee came up with me.

Two quick strikes; groin, which had him doubling over,

and chest, which sent him pitching down the steps. His
trigger finger convulsed, sending an errant shot to rico-
chet off marble, but I'd already followed him into the
sunken room, leaping the last three steps to send a final
knee flying into his face. I let him fall, and whirled with
his gun in my hands. The barrel sank between the eyes of
the first man, who'd followed me down the steps. I withdrew my conduit and pointed at his chest. "Shoulda hit
me," I told him.

His mouth worked, wordless as a guppie's, his broken
wrist forgotten at his side.

"Step aside, Thomas. And I'd do it slowly." The voice
rolled over us, and my stomach clenched.

"But, Mr. Sand—"

"God, that's really your name?" I pivoted into an open
stance, arms crossed; gun on Thomas, conduit on Ajax.

He was poised at the top of the opposite staircase, coiled
like a watchful rattler, his transparent eyes shining with
anticipation. He was wearing black, which only served to
lengthen his bony frame, and I knew his barbed poker was
secured like a second spine at his back. I could smell it.

"Step aside, Thomas," Ajax repeated, sauntering down
the marble stairs to join us in the sunken room. "Unless
you want to die."

I waved the gun at him. "Most horrifically, I might add."

Thomas stepped aside.

"I was wondering how long it'd take you to find us, Archer," Ajax said, halting at the bottom of the staircase. "I
take it you met some of my colleagues in the boneyard?
How'd you like them?"

"I wasn't particularly impressed."

"But you killed only two."

And I tried not to let it impress me that he already knew
about the battle in the boneyard. "Does that bother you?
Their deaths, I mean?"

He shrugged. "Everyone dies. And everyone's too concerned with their own demise to worry much about another's.

It's a small thing, really, when you think about it. Now, if you hope to see Warren again, drop your weapons. And don't make me repeat myself."

I didn't want to, but Hunter's whip still gave me options. I dropped my bow, safety on, to my feet. The gun followed.

"Where is he?" I asked as Thomas lifted my conduit, examining it. The guard on the floor groaned and rose halfway to his feet.

Ajax shook his head, a grown-up amused by the antics of a small child. "Why don't you give me the gun in your left boot, and then I'll tell you."

He was lying and we both knew it. Unfortunately there was nothing I could do about it. His guards were crowding in again, so I leaned down, eyes on his, and dislodged Hunter's second gun. Guard number two moved to take it from me. I shot him through the chest.

As the body hit the floor, even Ajax looked surprised. "Well, well. An agent of Light who likes to kill innocents. How . . . invigorating."

"Nobody who works for the Tulpa is an innocent." And I shot Thomas twice. He cried out, and my conduit clattered uselessly to the floor. There. I liked those odds better.

"Done now?" Ajax asked, crossing his arms, looking bored. "I mean, there's really no one left for you to kill."

"Except you." I leveled the gun at his chest. It wouldn't kill him, but it'd sure leave a mark.

Ajax simply held up a finger, as if just remembering something. "Wait, we're both wrong!" He pointed across the room. "Look behind you."

I pivoted slowly, keeping one eye on Ajax while I faced whatever new threat lay behind me. But I gasped when I saw Warren there. His body was bound to a chair with casters, head hanging forward, hair loose, black blood pasting a third of it to his skull. But then even Warren was forgotten in a split moment. My eyes were all for the man holding him.

"You." And I released the breath I'd been holding for a decade.

He was the same as before. I hadn't imagined him. Of course, now the moonscape wasn't stamping hollows beneath his cheeks, and the gentle breeze off the desert floor wasn't rustling his hair into spikes, but the cruel, thin lips were the same. They were the ones I'd searched for in the face of every stranger for the last decade—walking miles and miles past syringes and feces, and alleys that never saw light, seeking them—and now here he was. Standing there. Watching me. Wearing fucking Armani.

"An old friend of yours, I believe," Ajax said, a smile in his voice.

"Hello, Joanna," he said, in the voice of my nightmares.

"Hello, asshole," I replied.

"Now, now. I don't think you're in a position to be calling anyone names." He leaned forward, lifted Warren's head from where it lolled against his chest and looked into his face. "Do you, Warren?"

Warren's neck swayed side to side beneath his grip, a motion that made my stomach roll over on itself. Carelessly, he let it drop again.

"Wow, Joaquin," Ajax said. "Look at her chest."

I didn't have to look to know it was glowing. Heat fired through my body, pumped madly in my temples and veins.

Joaquin, however, did look. Then leered. And touched himself. "Pretty."

I let my right hand drop to my side, a distraction as my left hovered over the pocket where Hunter's whip was hidden. I was certain they couldn't smell it—its master, after all, possessed the aureole—and both believed I was no longer armed. When Ajax took a step forward, I noted it, but made no move for the whip. I was biding my time. Drawing the tiger in closer. I inhaled deeply, but only smelled the two of them in the room. And the two dead guards.

And Warren's agony.

"Wondering where everyone else is?" Ajax said, circling me to start the game of cat-and-mouse.

I shifted, keeping him in my sights. "It had crossed my mind."

"Joaquin and I have thoughtfully planned this intimate little party just for you. Cozy, isn't it?" He took another step forward. Joaquin tightened Warren's body restraints, settling him at the top of the stairs like a king fastened to his throne. "We decided we want to get to know you a little better, Joanna. And Warren here gets to watch."

"In other words," Joaquin said, turning to me with a wink, "we want you for ourselves."

He tossed one of Warren's arms into the air in celebration. It fell limply back to his side. Warren, it seemed, wasn't going to be watching anything.

I shook my head slowly, astounded at the magnitude of evil in the room. Of course, I'd destroy them both if I could—I'd discovered that I too could do my fair share of killing—but a part of me thought, What for? There would always be more sick fucks to follow in these two's footsteps, and more after them. It was like treading water in the middle of the ocean, with no land, no ship, no help in sight. Eventually you'd have to stop, and let yourself sink.

"You didn't think we were just going to kill you without having a bit of fun, did you?" Joaquin asked, his fingers drumming carelessly atop Warren's slumped head. "You first, Ajax."

"Oh, I couldn't."

"Really, I insist." Joaquin waved the protest aside like he was swatting a fly. "I've had her before."

"You are too kind."

I had gone as cold and still as the marble blanketing the room. My mouth suddenly felt like I'd swallowed a quart of sand. "I'll kill myself before I ever allow you inside me again."

Joaquin shrugged. "Whatever. Suicide is of the Shadow too. Isn't that right, Warren?" He took a knife from behind his back and placed its hilt in Warren's open palm. Holding the lax fingers around it, he made a cutting motion across Warren's throat, miming suicide. Blood bloomed, and Warren's eyes fluttered open long enough to roll back into his head, but he fell limp on a faint groan.

I had jumped, expecting to feel a sympathetic score of the blade across my own neck, but didn't. Our connection was severed, probably because he was too far gone to be saved. And, I thought, for any of this to matter now.

An eye popped open from beneath the matting of Warren's hair. And blinked.

No, I thought, inhaling sharply. It *winked*.

I glanced over at Ajax, but he was watching me with an almost rapturous expression. Joaquin wore a similar one as he continued to thrum Warren's skull. I saw the bright red ribbons of newly healed scars winding across every inch of his bared skin, and had to clench my jaw against the anger rising inside me again.

"There's something I've been wondering forever now. Something I just have to ask." Joaquin stopped drumming. "Did you think of me often? I mean, of that night? Of the moment I penetrated you?"

I managed a mean smile. "Every time I sharpened a pencil."

Ajax laughed. Joaquin's eyes knifed into slits.

"Well, I thought of you," he said, licking his lips. "The way you screamed for mercy. Did you know the taste of your skin altered on my tongue as I pumped and pumped and pumped away? It was like innocence . . . gone sour and ruined."

My jaw clenched, but I didn't blink. "Well, I'm all grown up now. Not a shred of innocence to be found."

He shrugged. "That's all right. I prefer the powerful ones even more. Like your mother. She was tasty."

My heart jumped in my chest despite myself. "You lie."

Ajax laughed again. "Joaquin's toying with you. After all, your mother went into the arms of the Shadows willingly. She wasn't like you. She didn't distinguish between good and evil. And you know why? Because she *knew*. There is no light and shadow. There's only a gray rainbow, and a choice as to where you pin yourself on the spectrum."

"You mean like *your* mother?" I said, and smiled when he froze. Both pair of eyes were fixed on me. I was the only one who saw Warren's grip curl around the knife still in his hand.

"Don't you talk about my mother."

"Your mother, who was so bad she was good," I continued, watching his already pale face drain of color.

"You think you're better than me? Morally superior, because you're a so-called agent of Light?" And I suddenly knew that's what he thought.

"Half Light," I corrected, careful to keep my eyes off the sawing motion behind Joaquin's back.

"I told you before. There's no such thing as better or worse in this world, or any world. You think you're less evil than I, but all you really are is weaker. It's only a matter of degree, you see? And of knowing at what point you're going to break."

I jerked my head once. "I told you before. I don't believe that."

A slim grin snaked up his cheeks. "And I told you I'd *make* you a believer."

"You really want to know what I believe?" I said, taking a step forward, and I wasn't just buying Warren time to do whatever it was he was trying to do. I really wanted to tell him. I wanted Ajax to know there was at least one solid core difference between him and me. "I think it kills you to see what you'll never be. What your mother tried to be and couldn't. You destroy things because you think it'll erase her betrayal, fill you up, make you whole. Instead, with each death you grow emptier and emptier. The darkness inside of Ajax Sand casts its longest shadow over himself."

"Spare me your false righteousness," he bellowed, spittle flying from the side of his mouth. "You're no better than I am!" He motioned back to the foyer. "You killed those guards like they were junkyard dogs. Don't try and tell me you didn't enjoy the power that gave you!"

"Those guards," I said, through clenched teeth, "were initiates, not innocents, and killing them before they metamorphosed just saved me the chore of having to do it later."

"How does she know that?" Joaquin asked, but Ajax didn't answer. He was watching me. "We masked them. She couldn't have known."

"Because they stank," I said to them both. "Like you. And especially like you." I stared Ajax down, and found his blue eyes so empty they were like glass. But he was breathing hard.

I took another step toward him. "You do stink," I said, lowering my voice like I was confiding in him. I inhaled deeply, and wrinkled my nose. "When I'm near you, it's like being buried neck-deep in a Dumpster. And that goddamned cologne you're wearing isn't any better."

Joaquin was silent now, straining to hear us, watching Ajax's face, Warren all but forgotten behind him. Power had begun to swirl like a riptide in the air; I felt it. I was taking it from Ajax, and I began to smile. Even though I could see the outline of his conduit tucked inside his jacket, just one short thrust from my chest, I had the confidence he'd rather use his hands on me. Or, at least, he would by the time I was finished.

I dipped my own hands in my pockets, casually and cocky, and felt the hilt of the whip against my palm. I closed my fist around it. Meanwhile, I used words.

"I know why you like to kill star signs." I lowered my voice to a whisper. "And I know why you kill innocents. It's for their Light. You want it for yourself. You want to *be* Light."

"Shut up."

"You think their blood will cleanse you and you won't have to live in the stink and squalor of your own putrid flesh—"

"I said shut up!" Ajax thundered. It was amazing how a man could shake and remain so rigidly still. I could tell he was afraid to let it break, that he thought his control might shatter into a thousand pieces . . . and he'd never be able to piece it together again.

"But you're the one who's got it all wrong. It's not your flesh that reeks. No, no." I leaned forward and pressed on the hairline fracture that had snaked across his restraint. "It's your soul. It's fucking maggot-ridden. And nothing can mask that stench."

He hit me so fast I never saw him move. And so hard I flew across the room, my torso slamming into a marble pillar six feet above its base. He was bolting toward me even as I fell, and there was no time to reach for Hunter's whip. I gained my feet just as another cry sounded and there was a flurry of motion behind Ajax. He paused, hearing it, and I leapt.

My shoulder caught him in the diaphragm and the scent of fungus and rot spilled out over me as he grunted, losing his breath. Ajax was a seasoned fighter, though. He didn't need breath to perform; the madness of the martial dance was ingrained in him, and he kneed me as he backpedaled, pulling me tight so I couldn't draw away. He struck breast, ribs, and belly. My turn to gasp for air, and then he did release me . . . enough to send a fourth knee plowing into my face. My head snapped back, my mouth instantly filling with blood, and I glimpsed a silvery sheen passing over his head as he slipped his conduit from behind his back.

I tried to dodge, but his other hand darted out, lifting me from the ground by my neck, and he puckered up, blowing me a kiss before sending me rocketing back across the room and into one of the marble pillars.

It didn't jar or hurt as much as it would've if I were mortal, but I still crumpled to the floor and had to figure out if anything was broken before I rose to hands and knees. Of course, Ajax knew this, and was already heading my way with poker in hand, but confidence was fueling his ego, and it didn't allow his pace to quicken to more than a swift saunter. I remained where I was, head bowed in defeat while I reached into my pocket. Ajax laughed, grasping his poker in front of him with both hands. I still waited. The poker lifted. And three seconds later the whip lashed out like an unraveling tongue, barbed tip coiling tightly around his neck.

The pain contorting his face would've been satisfying enough. The underlying surprise, however, was icing. Not that I was into petty gratification. His mouth moved soundlessly and his free hand went to his throat where his Adam's apple had been punctured, seeking relief. There was no slack in the leather, though, and the more he fought, the more the barbed tip twisted, tearing him up inside.

He made a gurgling sound, and I jerked him forward, the steel points digging in deep. Over his shoulder I saw Warren kick at Joaquin. He was still half tied to the chair, and I had a brief moment to wonder where, and what, Joaquin's conduit was . . . until it dawned on me that his body was his weapon. This was his job. To use his body to steal innocence.

I yanked on the whip, infuriated. Ajax stumbled and fell.

"How are you doing that?" he choked from beneath me. "You look like him! You look like *him*!"

I glanced up and saw my face reflected in the mirrored ceiling. Then back down again, offering Ajax a wide skeletal smile. "Well, I am the Archer."

"No, no! My master is the Shadow Archer!" His feet found purchase and he began backing away, one hand pulling to slacken the whip.

"Call me mistress, if you like," I said, reeling him back in. I placed one hand on his chest, wrapped another coil around his throat, then secured it around my wrist and pulled. He clawed at his throat. "Now, look into my eyes, Ajax. Because I want you to know who I am, deep down, when I kill you."

A voice finally penetrated through the haze of my

fury—I realized it'd been crying out all along—and I had to blink several times to focus.

"Olivia! Damn it! Give me the fucking keys!" Hunter was across the room, supporting Warren within the circle of his strong arms, while holding his cuffed wrists out to me in supplication. His glyph was fiery and white-hot, but it had to be in reaction to Ajax. Joaquin was nowhere to be seen.

Ajax's eyes widened. Bulged even more upon hearing who I really was behind the mask. "Olivia . . . ?"

"Nice to meet you," I said, "but I have to make this quick." I yanked, and there was a bone-splitting crack. Ajax's neck broke with my sister's name still caught in his throat. Before the last of life could drain from his body, I ripped his conduit from the sheath at his back and slammed the poker through the core of his chest. Rancid decay hit me immediately, just as it had when I'd killed Butch, but this time I recognized it as a good sign, a death scent. The scent of Shadows. But stronger still was the power that flowed over me like buckets of rain, slamming into me, drenching my insides, coating my organs, and making my blood hum like a live wire. Ajax had been right about one thing. It felt fucking great.

Yanking the handcuff keys from my back pocket, I tossed them to Hunter, and unwound his whip. I dropped it at his feet as I lunged for my conduit, and without stopping, ran for the door that had been left half open.

"Olivia! Stop! I need you to help me get him out of here."

"But—" But Joaquin. But revenge was so close. The air was still infused with the scent of charred candy, so thick and cloying it was almost visible as it trailed after him. I could still run him down like he'd once done to me . . . but I had to act now.

Hunter saw my struggle and shook his head. "He's too weak."

I growled in frustration, looking from the door, then back at him, and finally said, "I have an idea."

We bent to Warren's mouth, alternately pumping life into him with our breath—the aureoles leaving our bodies through our mouths in bright beams—one of us watching his chest rise and fall, his breath steadying, while the other exhaled power and images and pieces of ourselves into his body and mind. It seemed to take forever, but after a few minutes Warren's eyes flickered open, focused, and he smiled. "Told you . . . one of the good guys. Like me."

Gently, I put a finger to his bruised lips, shushing him. "That's right, Warren. Just like you."

Standing, I cut my eyes to Hunter. "He's strong enough now. Get him out of here."

I didn't wait to hear his protest. I wasn't going to choose between saving Warren and having my vengeance. I wanted them both. I wanted it all.

29

I hurtled through the door where Joaquin had fled, following a rapidly disappearing trail of blood, only to find myself back in the Gauntlet. "What . . . ?" I swiveled back around, confused, but the door was gone. I slammed my palm against a solid length of wall, smooth at the seams, an impenetrable barrier to all that lay behind me.

A snicker echoed down the hall.

I whirled, bow and arrow braced in front of me, but saw no one. There was just the Gauntlet, smooth and narrow, stretching before me in silent challenge.

The sound raced up the other side of the wall, slipped along the floor behind me before wheedling up the back of my legs and spine. There was a probing at the base of my skull, like a centipede trying to burrow beneath my skin, into my brain, but I shook my head and the feeling receded, though whatever had caused it was still there. This sterile hallway, I knew, contained something that could reach out and touch me at any moment, and it wasn't Joaquin.

"Finally. Another Archer."

The voice was curious, friendly even, and each word

possessed the deep thrumming echo of a cello string, low, musical, and filled with vitality. I glanced up at the ceiling, looking for vents, shafts, cameras . . . anything I could be viewed easily with or through, but saw nothing. The walls and ceiling were unusually smooth, and if I didn't know any better I'd have said it was less of a hallway than a living organ, like an intestine unraveled from within a large beast, and me devoured, lost inside. I quickly pushed the thought aside.

"I was wondering who was punching holes in my energy field. I knew Warren was no longer capable, though he certainly served his purpose. Welcome." His chuckle came from nowhere and everywhere at once, and I didn't need to see a face to recognize the cool arrogance haloing his words. I was on his turf, and even though I didn't know what game we were playing—never mind the rules—I kind of doubted he was going to clue me in.

"You're the Tulpa." I said, and tentatively began to back up. I searched again for a door to escape by, but when my palm hit the wall, needles sprung up to stab at my flesh and I jolted away. Glancing down, I found dozens of bloody tears studding my hand, though they dried up and disappeared as I watched. Surface wounds. Not that that wasn't worrying too. Because now I was sure I had to run the Gauntlet, and I had a feeling there were more sharp little surprises awaiting me.

"Expecting someone else? An ally, perhaps?"

"Not really," I answered, taking a testing step forward, then another. "You just don't look anything like I pictured you."

Okay, so the false bravado probably wasn't going to get me very far, but my allies were busy escaping Valhalla, and if the Tulpa was here with me, he couldn't stop Hunter and Warren. He couldn't, as far as I knew, be two places at once. So that was the upside. The downside? The Tulpa was here with me.

"Then you haven't pictured me fully. You have to use

your imagination, you see. What's the worst thing you could face in an enemy? What's the most horrifying thing I could possibly be?"

Me, I thought, before I could stop the idea from forming. The worst thing I could face was someone who looked or felt or acted anything like me. Because that would mean he'd gotten inside, delivered more than just chromosomes at my conception . . . and that I was somehow like him as well.

"Elvis," I said, picking up my pace a bit, careful to stay centered in the narrow hallway. Was it me, or was it getting narrower? "If I see one more aging Elvis impersonator I'm totally going to scream."

"Sweetie. You're going to scream anyway."

The walls shook again, but with increased intensity, quaking so the floor swayed beneath my feet. I braced like I was riding a wave, struggling for balance even with my center of gravity low over the ground. He was fucking with me now, I thought, as the shaking slowly died down. I'd seen Luna bat around insects with the same patient and deadly fascination.

"I guess I don't have to tell you this town isn't big enough for the two of us."

"I'll just be moving on, then." And I continued the long walk down the Gauntlet, one foot in front of the other. The Tulpa, wherever he was, seemed inclined to let me. For now.

"Joaquin's long gone," he said after a bit. "You put a devil of a fright into him. What did you do, I wonder?"

"Revealed myself," I answered truthfully. A conversation was good. Conversations generally didn't include bloodshed.

"How about doing the same for me?" he said softly, and a breeze entered the room, like a fan had been switched on and directed at my face. Invisible fingers toyed with my mask, and I clamped a hand down over my head.

"You first," I said, though I wasn't sure I wanted to see

this being, this entity—certainly not a man—who was my father.

"Forgive me if I decline," the overly polite voice said. "I'm not accustomed to someone issuing me orders. But you go ahead." And that *was* an order. I ignored it, and kept walking.

"Come on, I've never seen a Tulpa before," I taunted, continuing forward. I'd gone about ten feet, but it felt like an inch in the elongated hallway. "Oh, I get it. It's the side-burns, isn't it?"

No answer. Maybe he'd gone away. Maybe, I thought, he'd stay gone.

I picked up my pace because the unnatural stillness was almost as bad as the hovering presence, but after about five feet the fluorescent lights along the walls flickered, steadied, then went out.

Or maybe not.

I kept inching forward in the darkness. I had to, though I was certain I'd hit something, *someone*, with each step. I consciously tempered my rising fear, not wanting to give him anything to feed off of, which was obviously what he wanted.

"Silly little agent of Light. Do you think you're standing there, speaking to me with that insolent tone by anything but my grace?"

Fuck. I still couldn't see the son of a bitch, but the soft steel in his voice had me biting my lip until it bled. I took another step, heel-toeing it at a faster pace as my pulse sped up as well. I needed to focus on something else, and my mind alighted on the memory of Marcus and his fierce intensity as he flew through the boneyard, a little light darting fearlessly among Shadows. If I centered my energy on that, and on the end of the hallway, I could keep my mind off the fear building in my chest. And if I could do that, maybe my conduit would stop shaking in my hands.

Then my glyph began to glow. Oh, goody. Nice to know I was suddenly in real danger. Though at least now, able to see a few feet in front of me, I could see death coming before I ran smack into it.

"Oh, look. A little night light." The Tulpa sounded amused. My glyph burned hotter. "Which reminds me . . . how've you been sleeping lately, little Archer? Having nice dreams? Pleasant memories?"

My jaw clenched convulsively. "I was wondering how much of that was my imagination and how much of that was you. I suppose you think you're clever, using Greta to open our minds to your energy." Heel-toe, heel-toe.

"It *was* one of my better ideas," he said, and I could picture him polishing his knuckles. "As for the rest, I just played on what was already there. Your fears, your conceits, your neuroses. They all let me know exactly what buttons to push."

"But Greta's gone now. There's no way for you to see inside of me any longer."

He laughed, and the walls shook with it. "There's always a way inside."

Again that pricking and burrowing at the back of my neck, and suddenly I knew he was right. A being made of energy, who could be nowhere and everywhere at once, wasn't going to settle for a bit of physical torture. Oh, shit.

"I know everything about you," he was saying, but now his voice was within, bouncing off my eardrums from the inside. My brain pulsed once, and my skull felt like it was going to crack as a fissure grew from the bridge of my nose up into my hairline. I pressed a hand to my head, surprised to find it smooth and whole instead of bloody and split . . . and moaned aloud, scared, because that meant whatever was cracking was on the inside. Still, I stumbled forward. "I knew the night your first life cycle ended. I sent Butch after you for the second—"

"Did you know the moment I killed him, then?" I asked, trying to keep him talking. The pain seemed to decrease when he was talking.

"Of course. I felt the power shift."

No decrease in pain this time. A white-hot line seeped over my skull, and raced back down my spine to tunnel viciously into my limbs. I could feel him inside me now, his unstable energy wriggling like electric worms and breeding like fiery maggots, and I had to fight not to stand there and scratch the very skin from my body. I had to be halfway down the hall by now. I forced myself to keep going.

"Impressive," the voice said, lifting from my own throat. He was right. He'd found another way inside. I panicked and lurched sideways. The wall studded my arm with microscopic needles, and the scent of my own blood lifted again in the air. "Oops. Careful."

"Get out!" My voice lifted from a whimper into a scream, and I whirled around myself blindly, losing track of which way I'd come and which way I had to go. "Get out! Get out!"

"Hmm . . ." the Tulpa said, considering. The pain abated. "No."

And with a flick of a wrist, *my* wrist, he sent me wheeling from my feet, slamming into the ground where needles not only sprung up to rupture my skin, they grew barbs and stuck there. I cried out and jerked up almost as soon as I hit the ground, but yelped when my neck was only inches from the ground. I let it fall again, choosing instead not to move. I was pinned in place from my neck to my calves, in the dark but for the steady burning of my glyph, and in a sterile hallway that was slowly filling with my blood.

"I've been waiting for you for a long time, Archer. And now my patience has been rewarded with another adversary, such that you are." He actually sounded regretful at that. "But I knew, deep down, that there was another. I could feel you out there, like a season yet to arrive. I could sense you growing in the world—my world—ripening just for this moment."

I'd caught my breath by now, realizing that if I didn't move at all, the needles didn't sting so much. The Tulpa was no longer speaking through me either. His voice came at me as if from speakers; above, below, to the sides as well as from the top of my head . . . as if he were standing just there. I guess he was fonder of physical torture than I originally gave him credit for, but at least I could *think* without him inside my mind. I could breathe again. And while I saw no way out of the situation, I easily saw the fault in his words. With not much else to lose, I called him on it.

"You didn't know."

The maggots began wriggling again. The soft tissue in my head began to swell. "I knew the moment you entered this building! This city, even! This fucking world!"

"No." I actually laughed, though barbs pulled at the muscles in my neck. "You didn't."

He must have sensed the honesty in my derision, because the floor began to shake and the dead lights rattled in their sockets. I realized then that he couldn't be two places at once. He was either planted inside me or manipulating the environment, but he couldn't do both. So, I thought, even imagined beings had their limits. Good to know. "I know exactly who you are! You smell like sweet desert sage and cactus juice, burning roses and freshly ground allspice."

I winced as each barb pinning me in place loosed more of my blood free. "It's my perfume," I said, gritting my teeth. "Available at Macy's."

"A tart tongue as well. Only one other person possessed all of that."

Don't ask me why I was doing it. Perhaps because the sarcasm Xavier had always chastised me for was, once again, my only defense. It seemed to piss off this cool, controlled being who feared nothing. So I went ahead and struck him with a low-voiced barb of my own. I figured I was dead anyway.

"Oh, and you knew *her* well too, didn't you?"

The needles suddenly disappeared, ripping from my flesh. I cried out as the floor tilted, and I was slammed into the wall again. I was able to free myself this time, and I rose to my knees and palms quickly. I grabbed my conduit, its outline visible in the glow of my glyph, but pushed myself to my feet too soon and stumbled, falling against the wall again. I righted myself dizzily and kept going. "You knew her so well she infiltrated your organization *twice* without you ever suspecting it."

Light casings began to burst up and down the hallway. I felt shards of glass stab and then settle atop my skull. I ducked, and concentrated on moving forward. I was free, and no matter what, I had to keep moving forward.

"I fucked your mother!"

"You men," I said, shaking my head when silence fell again. "I don't know why you always think that lends you some sort of power. I mean, let's be honest, okay? Just between you and me. My mother? *She* fucked *you*."

A vortex of wind whipped around me, so violent it sucked the air from my mouth and throat and lungs. My eyes were glued to my lids, even beneath my shield, and I actually felt my heart jump in my chest like a startled sparrow. Then it faltered. My liver and lungs ached from the hot, vapid suction, like a vacuum had been affixed to my mouth, and a strangled sound was lifted from my throat and ripped away like shredded paper. Like a baby in the womb, I forgot how to breathe.

Then the center of the spiraling wind shifted, amassed, and, limb over limb, I was catapulted down the Gauntlet. I slammed into the wall head first, and slumped to the ground as hollow pops fired down my spine. Fresh pain bloomed with each snapped vertebrae, and a buzzing sounded. It could've been the handful of remaining lights flickering on, but I didn't think so. It had come, again, from within my own skull, but this time there was no one else there. Maybe, I thought dully, that was just the sound soft tissue made when it seeped through newly rent crevices. I choked as blood welled in my throat and my tongue lolled on the floor, spilling it all forward.

The wind died down, as if a switch had been flicked.

The Gauntlet looked like a cave in the meager light. The silence was deafening.

There's usually a grace period before injuries are felt. Adrenaline, and the shock of being alive temporarily numbing the senses. Not this time, though. My limbs shook, my organs felt battered inside me, and I was sure my right shoulder had dislocated when I'd punched into the wall. I coughed, and more blood fountained from my mouth, like one of those ancient marble statues in the middle of some picturesque European marketplace. For some reason, that thought made me giggle. Blood bubbled from my nose, and I laughed some more.

"Who are you?" The words were evenly spaced, but so jagged they sounded a bit off. I realized, with some shock, that the Tulpa's voice was trembling. Lifting my head, I thought about that . . . and realized on another jolt that he believed I should be dead. That had been his parting shot, and it'd been a damned good show . . . except that I was still alive.

I opened my mouth, but I couldn't stop laughing. The laughter and blood mingled to bubble in wet gasps from my throat, hot iron gurgling to temporarily render me speechless.

"Now that . . . that is something you should know," I finally managed, wiping the tears from my eyes, the sticky warmth of blood spreading everywhere. I hacked a big glob on the pristine floor, and looked up at the ceiling. It was probably only blood loss making me loopy, but I figured I might as well get in the last word. What the hell? If this event was going to be recorded in the manuals of Shadow and Light, I wanted to go out in spectacular, if bloody, style. "After all, you created me."

Dead silence.

And that was it, I realized. He had created me, and once again that had saved my life. So intent on destroying his opposite, his enemy, he never even realized that I was of his blood.

So, maybe I wasn't dying after all.

"Interesting, huh?" I threw one hand halfheartedly into the air, the other creeping along the wall to lift me into a standing position. I ignored the red prints I left decorating the wall in a macabre geometric design because I was definitely feeling better. Stronger. More powerful. "What happens, I wonder, when the Created becomes the Creator, huh? When you're no longer just a Tulpa, but a *father*? What's next?"

It was so silent, I could almost believe he'd left. Almost.

"What's the matter, *Daddy*?" I whispered as I stood, knowing he could hear me as clearly as if I were shouting from the top of Valhalla. I was bent, wobbling, but I was standing. "Cat got your tongue?"

"The Kairos! The first sign of the Zodiac . . . but it can't be!"

"Can't it? You say I smell like her, but who else do I smell like?" I paused. "But that's right. An agent can't smell themselves. Even, it seems, a Tulpa."

I began making my way to the far door again, and as I stumbled forward, I felt his confusion grow.

"You sent a Shadow after your own daughter," I said, helping him out. "You ordered me raped and beaten and killed at only fifteen years old. Fifteen! And I would have died. Would have, except I was yours."

I straightened. You'd have never known that mere moments before I'd been a broken heap of bones and blood on the floor. My voice grew stronger. He couldn't kill me, I realized, until he was willing to kill pieces of himself . . . but I wasn't going to let him in on that little secret just yet. "You claim to be all-knowing. You set yourself up, godlike, in this tower, to mete out destruction and judgment as you see fit. You stalk the agents of Light, set on destroying them and this city. But you aren't all-knowing. You aren't omnipotent, or even omnipresent."

By this time I was within ten feet of the door, and my stride was almost normal. My hand was on the door when the voice sounded again.

"Wait!" Power flowed into me with the words; massaging my organs, all my wounds instantly healed. My shoulder popped effortlessly back into place, my bruises disappeared. I could see how a person, or a nonperson, could get used to this sort of power. "At least show me your face."

I didn't remove my mask. "Look in the mirror."

He tried again. "But see how easily I can heal you?"

I smiled at that. "I'd heal anyway."

"But I can do more. In fact, join me and I can *give* you more."

I hesitated. "More what? Power, money, status?"

"I can do anything. Give anything. But in return—"

"My soul, right?" I said, amusement lining my words. "You want me to join with the Shadows, leave the Light?"

"It is prophesied," he said solemnly.

"That is just so *Star Wars*."

"Then we talk," he said hurriedly. Not only did the man not have a face, I thought, he didn't have a poker face. But he still had his wits. "Bargain. Tell me your greatest desire, and I'll prove it's within my reach."

"All right," I said, and the hallway went still. It was as if he was holding his breath. "I want my mother and my sister and my innocence returned to me. I want my life back."

Wind whistled against my face on a heavy sigh. We both knew it was the one thing he couldn't give. "I can give you a new life, a better one. You will be exalted in my organization."

I blew a sticky strand of hair from my cheek and shook my head. "No, *Daddy*. I liked my old life, so you know what I'm going to do? I'm going to take it all back for myself."

I reached for the door. It gave, opening easily in my hand. Half turning, I studied the Gauntlet, the strip of bloodied and battered linoleum I had somehow navigated alive. "Next time—and we both know there *will* be a next time—I'm going to kill Joaquin."

"You may try." His voice was low and composed again, but it wavered with need—something I don't think he'd felt in years—and I lifted my chin, glad, knowing I was the one who put it there.

"But I'm not going to stop there." I paused for a reaction, but there was none. He was waiting for me, indulging me now that he knew I was his daughter. Both Light and Shadow. The Kairos. "I'm going to train and fight and study our mythology until I find a way to annihilate the entire Shadow Zodiac. I'm going to take my city and my life back. And then . . ."

There was a hesitation, an indrawn breath. "Then?"

"Then I'm coming after yours."

I yanked the door wide, and the blast that came, slamming it shut, was not a killing blow, but one meant only to shock, to stun. It didn't even do that.

He'd pulled his punch, I thought, and smiled to myself. And that was all the power I needed for now.

"Later, Pops," I said, and walked right out of the Gauntlet, and Valhalla. Into a new day. Into the morning. Into the light.

Hunter stood on the Boulevard, waiting as I cleaned myself up at the bottom of the long, ornate fountain leading up to the casino's entrance. Vanessa had followed us to the hotel despite Hunter's warnings, and he'd given Warren over to her care. They were now, presumably, someplace safe and undetectable until dusk and the time of crossing came again.

I sensed no one around us, neither Shadow nor Light, and after Hunter assured me again that the security cameras didn't reach this far, I pulled the shield from my head and handed it to him. I ran my other fingers through my damp hair.

"Joaquin got away," he said. "I'm sorry."

I lifted my face to the sky, breathing deeply of the morning air. "It's all right. I'll find him again. I have his scent locked in my brain now."

"And vice versa," he reminded me as we turned away from the hotel.

I shrugged, feeling a residual ache echo through my right shoulder. "Either way. Next time I'll be ready."

"Yes." His voice sounded almost tender. "I believe you will."

I glanced over at the man who was so dutiful he'd been willing to sacrifice himself for us all. His appearance hadn't altered, but now that we'd shared the aureole, and tasted of one another's souls, I was seeing him differently. For one, I knew his single-mindedness was a fear-induced response, as was his frightening composure. And while I didn't know what a man as capable as Hunter had to fear, at least now I knew he felt something beneath that calculating facade. Maybe I'd learn more in time.

"Sorry about your head," I said, after a moment.

"You apologized before you hit me, remember?" He rubbed at his skull. The swelling was already gone, however, so I didn't feel that bad. "I guess you were expecting someone from the hotel to find me knocked out at the bottom of that elevator before I ever came around, right?"

"That was the plan."

"Lousy plan."

How was I supposed to know he'd already taken care of the security tapes? "Well, I couldn't let you give up your entire life for me. Besides, we need someone on the inside." I paused. "My mother would have wanted it."

He didn't answer for a moment. We both knew I hadn't done it for my mother.

"Well," he finally said, shuffling his feet. For the first time since I'd known him, he looked uncomfortable. Not quite at ease in his gorgeous skin. "Thank you."

I looked down the street, smiled to myself, and asked softly, "Your daughter. What's her name?"

"Lola," he said, just as quietly. I had a feeling he rarely spoke of her at all.

"Ah, that's Lola," I said. For some reason, I'd assumed the woman he'd first spoken of in the dojo—the one no one else knew about—was his lover.

"Yours?"

I looked at him. The light from the morning sun set his dark hair to glow from behind, and he almost looked haloed. "I don't have a daughter."

"You do."

I shook my head. "I don't. I—"

He cut off my protest with one simple, jarring thought. "Our lineage is matriarchal."

My blood pooled in my feet, and my thoughts drained from me on an escaped breath. "Oh, shit . . ."

I'd had a girl child. She was now in her first life cycle. "Oh, shit," I said again.

"Don't worry about it now. We'll figure it out—"

I panicked at that, shaking my head hard, then harder. "No one can know. No one does know! And you can't—"

"Shh," Hunter put a steadying hand on my shoulder, and I fell silent. "I said we'll figure it out."

I swallowed hard, then nodded as I stared at my feet. He was right. There was time yet. I'd figure out what to do— Hunter would help—and I'd find a way to keep my secret as well. I looked back up at him, gave another small nod, and when he smiled back it was almost as if I were seeing him for the first time. A tendril of hair had come loose from his back knot, and after a moment I reached up to tuck it behind his ear. My fingertips skimmed his warm cheek, the delicate folds of his left ear, trailing down his neck. I remembered the softness of his lips, the way they'd yielded beneath mine; and I recalled the memories that were a part of this fierce, complicated man. And, I thought, were now a part of me as well.

"Thank you again," he said, covering my hand with his own.

"You're still welcome," I said softly.

"And don't ever do it again."

I peered up at him. "Can we go back to the thank-you part?"

We both smiled at that, momentarily at peace with the hand life had dealt. We were like cats bathing in the morning light, reveling in the freshness of the day as we took inventory of our body and limbs, each of us genuinely surprised, and nearly giddy, at being alive.

That was how Ben Traina found us. Stretching, smiling, happy. I sobered quickly when I saw him. "What are you doing here?"

"Whatever happened to 'Hello'?" Ben said, looking amused. He looked better than when I'd last seen him. Still too thin, but not reeking of desperation, and no longer quite as wild-eyed. I tried to read his aura, but I was too spent from my time in the Gauntlet, and all I saw was Ben.

"Hello," I said. "What are you doing here?"

My voice was too sharp, the query inappropriate, but he was too close to Valhalla and its still-fresh horrors for my liking. Certainly too close to me. I shuttered my expression and emotions before anything telling could leak out.

"You must be Ben," Hunter said, covering for me in the ensuing silence. Ben looked down at the hand stretched before him.

"That's right," he said after a moment. "Traina."

"Hunter. Lorenzo." They shook, civilized-like, sizing each other up. Hunter inhaled deeply. I cleared my throat in warning, which merely amused him.

"In answer to your question," Ben said, turning back to me, "I heard reports of something strange happening here this morning. Some sort of power outage or explosion or something. Thought I'd come down and check it out."

"Back on the force, then?"

He shook his head, one quick jerk. "One of the guys called me in. They know I've been . . . interested in this place for the last few months."

So he was still looking into my death. Looking for answers he didn't even have the right questions to. I didn't know whether to be alarmed or gratified.

"Anyway, I don't want to keep you guys. You've obviously been up all night. Just come from a concert or something?"

"Or something," Hunter said with a smile.

Ben nodded absently, then leaned in to politely kiss my cheek. "Olivia."

The air sparked, crackling between us. We both jerked back.

I shook my head. "Whew. Lots of static electricity. Must have been some explosion in there."

"Yeah." Ben rubbed at his mouth before backing away, frowning. "Well. See you later."

I bit my lip and watched him walk away.

"Static electricity?" Hunter said after a moment. I smiled, as he meant me to. "More like chemistry, I'd say."

"It's merely sensory-evoked nostalgia," I told him, turning away. "Micah explained it to me. Ben's scent is connected to pleasant memories, and my brain's limbic system is reacting to those memories. That's all."

"Uh-huh."

"It is," I said, but glanced up to hold his eyes with my own. "The only chemistry Ben Traina ever felt was with and for my sister. Joanna."

Hunter trailed his eyes over my face, his eyes hooded again, his expression unreadable. "Well," he finally said. "She must have been quite a woman too."

I acknowledged the compliment, and his silent agreement to keep my identity secret, with a tilt of my head. "She was."

We started walking again, and Hunter draped a comforting arm around my shoulder, surprising me by pulling me close. "Come on, Olivia Archer. It looks like we get to live to fight crime another day."

"Whoopee."

Still I leaned my head on his shoulder and let him wheel me away from the Hall of the Gods, following him into the crisp air of dawn while the city sparkled around us with the same hope it held for every new day. We walked down the Strip, kept walking, beyond Tropicana and Flamingo, Spring Mountain and Sands, Sahara and Charleston, to where the bones of the old city lay. I welcomed the light rising in that sky, bathed in the touch of the cool air against a whole and healthy body, and welcomed Hunter's warm and reassuring presence beside me. I was happy to be here. To be alive. To be Olivia.

Happy, even though I could still feel Ben's hot stare burning a hole through my back.

30

"Did you really call the Tulpa 'Pops'?" Warren asked, holding up the latest manual from Master Comics. I glanced at the title. It arched across the cover in bold silver letters. *The Archer*, it said. *Agent of Light*.

I'd picked it up for Warren the previous day, thinking he'd enjoy reading it while he recuperated. My experience in the comics store was markedly different than the first time. Carl had nearly flown to my side, taking liberties by grabbing my chin with one fuzzy palm, twisting my head from side to side, ostensibly to get his drawings right. I finally had to tell him I'd shoot an arrow up his nose to get him to stop. The twins peppered me with questions about the sanctuary and my eye shields, and even Sebastian had asked, shyly, to see my bow and arrow. Zane, however, merely nodded my way and said my trading cards would be in soon.

"Your twisted sense of humor must be rubbing off on me," I told Warren, inwardly pleased as he chuckled and continued to leaf through the comic. He'd been in the sick ward for over a week, and his color was only now coming back. Still, Micah said he'd been lucky. Ajax had skewered his insides with a mortal weapon, not his conduit. The latter, he'd said, would have killed Warren too quickly for Ajax's liking.

Instead I had arrived, Ajax had died, and Warren would now heal. Meanwhile, the latest comics, both Shadow and Light, showed our enemies backing off, licking their wounds, forced to rethink their strategy against us now that Greta was no longer marking us for destruction.

And now that there was a new Archer among the agents of Light.

"Lunch," Chandra announced, entering the room with a loaded tray. She was careful not to look my way—as she'd been for the past week. Goaded by Greta, it was Chandra who had slipped the newspapers under my barracks door that night, and she'd since apologized unflinchingly, like a recalcitrant inmate waiting for her sentencing. I'd acknowledged her apology gracefully, if stiffly, but if anything, it made her more antagonistic toward me.

This was further inflamed by my swift, unanimous acceptance into the troop the day before. She hadn't opposed the vote when given the opportunity to do so, and there'd been no further jabs about my resemblance to a rogue agent, but she'd been sure to wonder loudly about my true identity in front of the others. It was a little obvious, even for Chandra, not to mention totally unnecessary. Ever since Greta had revealed that I was not really Olivia Archer, they'd all been watching me curiously. Though that, I thought, was certainly better than suspiciously.

"Wonderful!" Warren set the comic aside. "Lasagna, chocolate cake, and a nice pinot, I hope."

"Try oatmeal, water, and a few sliced greens."

"Damn."

That drew a smile from Chandra, but after running a quick hand over his forehead, she only nodded her satisfaction and left the room without another word.

"She's still not talking to me."

"Give her time. She's a good person deep down." He dug

into his oatmeal, while I wondered exactly how deep that was. "Meanwhile, the first sign of the Zodiac has been fulfilled, and the legacy of the Archer grows. You've become rather well known in the paranormal world. How does it feel?"

I shrugged, recalling that I'd once told him I didn't want to be a part of this world. A superhero, I'd scoffed. A freak among freaks. "It's easy to idolize someone from afar. Most of the people reading those," I said, pointing to the comic, "don't know me at all."

"Rena knows you. She thinks the sun rises and sets on your shoulders."

I quirked a brow. "I don't know if you've noticed, but Rena is a bit impaired when it comes to matters such as, oh, say, the sun."

"But she's a damned good judge of character."

And I had to agree with that. She'd been willing to trust me when no one else had. I'd have never been able to prove Greta's culpability without her. For that, I, and Warren, owed her much.

He turned back to his comic, and I watched him for a bit. Greta had told me that something in Warren's past had made ruthlessness a virtue, and knowing what it was—that the man lying before me had killed his own father—I also wondered what he'd do from now on to make sure it'd been worth it. He'd already proven himself willing to give up everything for the troop. The group was worth more to him than the individual. I liked Warren . . . but I was going to be careful to keep that in mind.

"Tell me something, Warren," I said at last.

"If I can."

"Did you know there was a traitor in the sanctuary?"

After a long pause, he shook his head. "No. I didn't believe it. I *wouldn't* believe it."

"Then why was it so important to you that my true identity be kept a secret from the rest of the troop?" I asked him, shaking my head. That had thrown me. It'd even made me wonder, for a time, if he wasn't the real mole. "Why didn't you want that revealed if you trusted these people so much?"

"Because your arrival was the last prediction Tekla made before Stryker died. She knew . . . something." Warren dropped his head back on his pillow, his expression glossed over in one of pain, but it wasn't for himself. Guilt popped up in him, washing over his outline in a wave of mustard yellow the thickness of tar, its scent as sharp as tear gas. "I don't know if she foresaw his death or her own imprisonment, but she made me swear never to reveal your true identity once you were found. I didn't want to break my last promise to her."

That made sense, I thought, nodding slowly. If Greta had discovered who I really was, it wouldn't have been long before the Tulpa did as well.

"Okay, but there's one other thing I don't understand." I pointed to my chest, where his second heartbeat had once resided. "Why did I stop feeling you in here? Did the mark Micah gave us wear off?"

He shook his head. "Once I knew you were coming for me, there was no need for you to feel that kind of pain. It would have hampered your ability to perform. You needed all your concentration for the task at hand."

"So you took it all upon yourself," I murmured.

"I knew you wouldn't keep me waiting long." He shrugged, but there was a world of pain in the movement. It made me want to kill Ajax all over again. Seeing it, Warren changed the subject.

"What do you think of Tekla?"

I couldn't help but smile. He knew what I thought of her. I'd been spending nearly every waking hour with her since my return, listening to her rant about the "quacks" who read palms or tea leaves instead of looking to the skies. I tried to follow her astrological lectures on planets and houses, elements and polarities, meridians and angularity, but it wasn't easy. She spoke in code more often than not, had a tendency to begin mumbling to herself in the middle of a conversation, and—most disturbing—mourned Stryker's passing at the beginning of every hour. I also caught her studying me in the odd moment, worried eyes roving my face like she was reading something interesting and possibly disturbing there. Still, I found her fascinating. "She's been telling me stories about my mother."

Warren's face took on a faraway cast, and one side of his mouth lifted in a bittersweet smile. "There's a lot to tell."

"Do you . . ." I had to stop, and try again. "Do you think I'll ever find her?"

"In time. If it's safe. And if Zoe wants to be found." I caught his hesitation and lifted a brow. "For now, don't you think it's enough that you've found yourself?"

I nodded slowly. There were still things I didn't know, still places I couldn't go—like Olivia's computer, her true mind—but there were other doors open to me now.

"Thank you," I told him. "For that. And for . . . well, all of it."

His reply was cut off by Gregor's arrival. He appeared in the doorway and waved his lucky rabbit's foot at me. "Anyone who wants to cross with me had better come now. My shift starts in an hour."

Gregor had recovered more quickly than Warren, and was already back to driving cabs, fighting the evil in Sin City in his own superstitious way.

"I have to go," I told Warren, and stood.

He waved me away, flicking his hand in the air like it was nothing to him. Like there hadn't been tears in his eyes a moment before. "Good-bye, Olivia. Be careful."

"Aren't I always?" I said. I ignored his sudden coughing attack, and smiled as I looked back from the doorway. "See you on the other side."

Las Vegas, my Vegas, has two faces. There's the frenetic carnivalesque face of the Strip; pliable, garish, and bright, catering to forty million visitors a year, and striving to make each of their dreams come true . . . for a price. Then there's the small-town desert face; dusty, lined with age, and artless, with no pretense or need for it . . . the one I grew up in. One is all glitz, while the other is barren, but I see both faces—the light side and the dark—as one big, blank slate, like the great baby blue swath of sky arching over the valley itself. You can scribble your own fate across that relentless skyline, and I love that about this city. I also understand why others come here, taking refuge among the glitz and gild, the noise and lights, the talking and screaming and singing and laughter, the smoke and the drink . . . and forgetting there's anything at all beyond the garish casino walls.

Being a local, I'd always taken my refuge in my home. Being a loner by circumstance and profession, I also found it in my darkroom. But now my home was no longer mine, and my darkroom—where I spent as many hours lost in the smell of developers and toners as those tourists do in front of the green felt tables—was just a sad reminder of the person I could no longer be. So after I left Warren and the sanctuary, I decided to do what people had been doing in this valley for over a hundred years. I had to create a new refuge for myself. After all, anything's possible in Vegas, right?

But first I had to say a proper good-bye to Olivia.

"Are you sure you want to do this, darlin'?" Cher looked at me over the top of her shades, blue eyes filled with concern above the mirrored rims. She was driving again, and I jerked my head at the road, swallowing hard, though that wasn't the entire reason I was feeling shaky.

"I've already stayed away too long."

We turned into the long gravel lane of the cemetery's back entrance, bumping along in silence until we were dumped into the graveside lot. I looked out the window at the yawning stretch of lawn and let my eyes blur so the headstones didn't hump out quite so much, and the flowers left by those still living weren't as garish against the dying winter sky. I grasped my own bouquet tightly in my lap and wondered if my mother had been by yet to visit.

"Olivia?"

I jolted in my seat. Cher had been saying my name.

"Yeah," I said, shaking my head to clear it. "I'm coming."

I could do this, I told myself. I *would* do this. I would stand outside this car with my sister's best friend, then I'd walk across the lawn in my sister's shoes and bend over and place these flowers on my sister's grave.

Which bore my name.

"Who's that?" Cher asked when I'd finally found my legs.

I shielded my eyes, looked where she pointed, and sighed. I knew just who it was, even from that distance. "That's Ben Traina."

He was sitting cross-legged at the foot of a headstone, and he could have been a statue himself if the wind hadn't betrayed him, rustling the dark curls that kissed the nape of his neck.

"Poor boy looks lonely," Cher said, and he did. But he also looked self-contained, straight-spined, and resolute.

"You said before that he looked mentally unstable."

She bit her lip, studying him, before shooting me a wavering smile. "Stability is overrated. Come on. Let's go keep him company."

He heard us coming and half turned, standing once he saw who it was. I made introductions, Cher and he shook hands, and then there was a long silence as we all stood, facing the grave.

"Back on the force yet?" I asked, just for something to say.

"You keep asking me that." He sounded amused, at least, which was a step up from annoyed.

I shrugged. "You were a good cop."

"Well, now I'm going to be a good P.I."

I felt my brows winging up. "Really?"

He nodded. "I decided to go out on my own. Take only

the cases I want, and concentrate on those until they're solved."

I clenched my jaw, determined not to speak. If I did I'd probably start a fight over my sister's grave. But I was worried. I knew he'd loathed certain constraints as a cop, though he hadn't crossed any moral lines yet, not even with my death. I knew this because I'd turned our fates around, and I'd been trailing him. He was still looking for Ajax, but it was with a sort of despondent hope, and not the fiery anger that had frightened me so much in those early weeks of my death.

But what kind of man would he be without his badge? What would he become without his "second pair of eyes" to filter the evils he saw? Sought? How would he keep his world bearable?

"Oh, a private investigator?" Cher said, breaking into my thoughts, just catching on. "Like Magnum, right? I loved that guy. Really hot. You're a teeny bit shorter, sugar, but I guess there's no height requirement. Do you have to pee in a cup on really long stakeouts? I wonder how I'd manage that?"

She went on and I would have been annoyed if I didn't know her better now. Plus I could sense her nervousness. Her cell phone finally cut her off in mid-explanation of how great she thought it'd be to have a purse with a secret hidden camera, and did we think Gucci made one like that? Ben and I smiled at one another over her head as she turned to answer the call. She listened for a moment, nodded, then said to me, "Mama wants you to come for supper next week. Or lunch. She says she's met a perfect man for you, so when'd be good for you?"

God, I thought. Never? "Uh . . . maybe Thursday?"

"I'll set it up," she said, and strolled away through the plots to arranging my dating life. I sighed before thinking of Ajax and reconsidering my reluctance. It wasn't like Cher and her mother could do any worse than I already had.

"Want to sit?" Ben asked as Cher's voice died away.

"Okay."

I realized I was clenching the bouquet, and forced myself to relax. My palms were green with marks from the stems, sticky with the juice of the newly cut flowers. I placed them next to the bunch already lying on the grave, my store-bought buds looking almost plastic next to the wide, spicy blooms I knew Ben had grown himself. I don't know how long we sat in front of the grave that day, in front of the headstone bearing my name, letting the wind caress our cheeks, the cold from the ground seeping up into our bodies and bones.

"How's your father?" Ben finally asked. It took me a moment to realize who he was talking about. I'd already stopped thinking of Xavier as my father.

"He's fine," I said, mentally adding: ignorant, arrogant, despicable, and blind to the fate I had in mind for him. "He's just fine."

We were silent again.

"I was just thinking," Ben finally said, "of the time when Joanna chased that boy from the school bus. Do you remember that?"

I nodded. It wasn't as if I could forget. He had pulled my sister's hair and made her cry. He had called Olivia a tease and a slut. She had only been ten.

"I got mad at Jo for that. I told her I was the one who was supposed to fight the guys. I was the one who was supposed to protect my girlfriends. I told her I would keep you both safe."

And the boy who'd felt that responsibility was now the man who carried that guilt solely on his shoulders. I lowered my head, and as I did, glanced at his hand on the ground next to me. I remembered how that hand felt caressing my body, and desperately wanted to take it in my own, not caring if we crushed the stems of still-living things between us, if we could only reestablish that link. I wanted to give him comfort, and peace, and take a measure more of it for myself.

Instead, I sniffed. Scented brimstone on the air—faint, but briny with heat and ill will—and left my hand where it was. Then I spotted the token Ben had brought along with him. Not flowers.

"That's Joanna's, isn't it?" I pointed at the silver chain glinting in the sunlight as it hung from one side of the tombstone.

He nodded, swallowing hard.

"I . . . haven't seen that in a long time." How did he get it? The last time I'd seen it, it'd been in this graveyard, circling Ajax's neck as he tortured the man beside me.

"Well, it was lost for a while."

Oh, come on. I needed more than that. "So you found it?"

"It was mailed to me. Last week."

Last week. But Ajax couldn't have mailed it then. I'd already killed him days before. "Odd," I commented, hoping my suspicion came out sounding airy. *Very odd.*

Ben didn't answer, and I decided it wouldn't hurt to play up to Olivia's airheaded reputation a little bit more.

"Oh, hey," I said, as if I'd only just remembered. "You ever find that guy you were looking for? That one in the jailhouse photo?"

"Mug shot," he corrected with a sigh. "No. I think he's . . . disappeared."

"I'm sorry," I said, glancing over at him.

"That's okay," he said, too reasonably. "There are others."

Something flashed behind his eyes, and I had to look away. It wasn't exactly the look Ajax had pulled on me in the restaurant . . . for one, his skull didn't leap out at me. And it wasn't the glint of pure sadistic glee that Butch had worn in the moments before Olivia's death. But I couldn't kid myself. It was close enough to being the look of a killer that it made my belly flip-flop within me. And it looked all wrong on Ben Traina's face.

And you're partly responsible for putting it there.

I was. And I had no idea how to fix that.

Ben finally stood. "Well, I've been here for a while. I'm going to go."

"Okay." I nodded, afraid if I looked up he'd see how desperately I wanted him to stay.

"You wouldn't want . . . to go get a bit to eat or anything, would you?"

I steeled myself to the vulnerability in his voice and shook my head. I also frowned at the question. "I can't. I came with Cher." And then, so there'd be no mistake, added, "And I have a date later."

"Of course you do," he said, but there was no bitterness in his words.

"Maybe another time?" I said, knowing it'd never happen.

"Maybe," he said, knowing the same.

He left, and after a moment, when I was sure he wouldn't see me, I turned to watch him walk away. I wasn't going to give up on him. My second death had wrought changes in him that'd been lying dormant since my first. But as uncomfortable as his sudden fierceness and vigilance made me, I wouldn't give up. Because God, I thought, watching him, could that man love.

"'There is always some madness in love,'" I quoted as he paused to say a few words to Cher, the two of them huddled close in the late winter wind. They were braced like they'd survived the worst of the season and were now merely waiting for it to end. My mortals, I thought, protectively. I'd defend them both to my death.

I turned back to the grave.

The headstone was made of rose marble, black veins running through the surface in defiant streaks. It wasn't what I'd have chosen, but it fit Olivia perfectly. "I'm sorry it took so long for me to visit," I told her. "I've been . . . busy."

It was three months to the day since she'd died. Three months since I'd assumed her identity. And this really was the first chance I'd had to catch my breath. It made me wonder what I'd be doing if none of this had happened, and Olivia was still alive, and I was still Joanna Archer.

Probably still lingering in the shadows. Snapping pictures of every man who looked my way.

I sighed, not sure I'd want that back. I'd want Olivia alive again, of course, but walking around in her skin had forced me to do two things: put down my camera, which I *had* been using as a shield, and take off the mask of the woman I once thought I was. Underneath I'd been surprised to find I wasn't so unlike Olivia. She wasn't the opposite of me in every way that counted. She wasn't as weak and vulnerable as I'd once believed. By accepting that, I discovered myself in her. Still me, I thought, but more so.

I told her. "I'm more like you than I ever would have believed."

And what a strange world it was when a woman had to lose herself in order to find herself. But these last months had taught me that I was more than the culmination of past experiences, and much more than could be evidenced in my physical body and strength alone.

And so who was I now?

It seemed to be the question everybody wanted answered. But, as I'd told Greta, it really did depend on who was looking. And if someone were looking now, they'd see a beautiful young woman bent over the grave of her sister, her feelings evident in the way her hands shook as she released her battered floral offering, the way her shoulders hunched against the constant press of the wind. She looked, I knew, like a woman with no dreams.

But.

If they sucked in a deep breath of the same wind, fresh from her flesh, they might—if they used their sixth sense—perceive another emotion. One belied by that delicate body. A sentiment as strong as any elemental fury. And one that cast all shadows into light.

I do dream, the scent would tell them. *I dream in fierce color. And the hue is always red.*